ONE NIGHT
IN SIXES

'This author can really write. If you loved
Stephen King's *Dark Tower* series – or even if you're
a hardened Cormac McCarthy fan – you will find
this book right inside your wheelhouse. Living, witty
dialogue, and a familiar-yet-strange world inhabited
by vivid characters. I loved it. And I don't say that
about a book very often.'

Paul Kearney, author of *The Ten Thousand*

First published 2014 by Solaris
an imprint of Rebellion Publishing Ltd,
Riverside House, Osney Mead,
Oxford, OX2 0ES, UK

www.solarisbooks.com

ISBN: 978 1 78108 238 6

10 9 8 7 6 5 4 3 2 1

A CIP catalogue record for this book is available
from the British Library.

Designed & typeset by Rebellion Publishing

Printed in the US

CHILDREN
OF THE
DROUGHT
BOOK ONE

ONE NIGHT IN SIXES

ARIANNE 'TEX' THOMPSON

SOLARIS

For Nana
As time passed, Vincent grew older.

CONTENTS

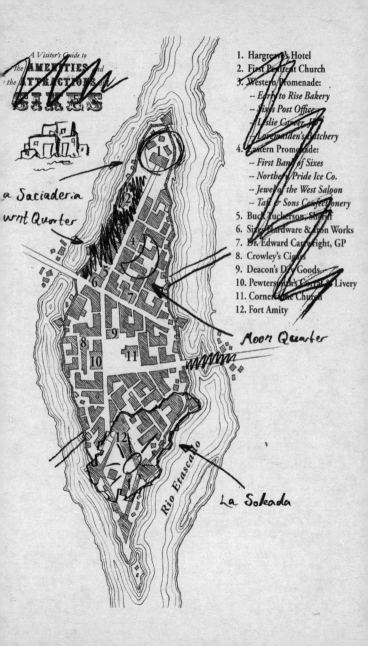

A Visitor's Guide to
the **AMENITIES** and
the **ATTRACTIONS** of
SIXES

a Saciaderia
wrnt Quarter

Moon Quarter

La Sokada

Rio Etascado

1. Hargreave's Hotel
2. First Penitent Church
3. Western Promenade:
   -- Early to Rise Bakery
   -- Sixes Post Office
   -- Leslie Corvey, J.P.
   -- Lovemaiden's Butchery
4. Eastern Promenade:
   -- First Bank of Sixes
   -- Northern Pride Ice Co.
   -- Jewel of the West Saloon
   -- Taft & Sons Confectionery
5. Buck Tuckerson, Sheriff
6. Sixes Hardware & Iron Works
7. Dr. Edward Cartwright, GP
8. Crowley's Cigars
9. Deacon's Dry Goods
10. Pewtersmith's Corral & Livery
11. Cornerstone Church
12. Fort Amity

PROLOGUE

ON THE THIRD day, God said: *now you just stay there and think about what you did.*

So Elim stood there where they'd tied his hands to the two posts of the main street promenade, leaning into the dwindling shade as the sun climbed higher. The rest of the dust-choked street was long since deserted.

Which left just Elim, standing spread-armed between the beams, struggling to keep his aching head shaded and his sluggish thoughts pious as his bare back and shoulders roasted in the sun.

That was a tall order.

It was powerfully difficult to let his gaze rest on the walkway without thinking of the people it had been built for. The raised wooden walk had kept their genteel boots out of the mud; the open sloping roof had guarded their reverend heads from the rude heat of the day.

They would have been fine, decent folks. They wouldn't have left even a bastard like Elim strung up like this. But they had long since passed on to their reward, and left him at the mercy of their brutal heirs.

He was close, though – so close his sweat dripped onto the weathered gray planks. If he could just get past the pain in his arms and the tightness in his chest and lean in far enough to get his head into that heavenly shaded space – just for even a minute – he would surely breathe in some of their deathless grace, and understand how to account for himself.

That kept him busy enough that the slow, rhythmic thud of hooves took him by surprise. Startled, Elim glanced back over one shoulder –

– just as an enormous brown face hung itself over the other. There beside him was Molly Boone: unbridled, unsaddled, and apparently having liberated herself from the corral. Elim's mouth cracked in a smile.

"Miz Boone," he declared in a parched whisper, "you are a brazen hussy. Is this you flauntin' yourself around town without your bonnet on?" Elim closed his eyes as her lips anointed his face with a streak of sweet green slobbers. "And dolin' out your affections to any man in the street, I see. Ain't you 'shamed?"

No, not hardly. Shame was for people – for creatures who could sort right things from wrong ones, and hold themselves accountable for the difference.

By that reckoning, Elim was shamed enough for both of them. He breathed in the smell of her sun-warmed coat, and steadied his resolve. "Don't listen to any of what they said about me, now. You know I ain't like that."

He had to get himself sure on that point as well. Back home, he could have said it as a certifiable fact: he did not and never had hurt anyone.

Here, though...

Elim glanced down the empty street, past the adobe walls shimmering in the midday heat and the burnt-out ruins of the church, to the black-iron manor at the end of the road.

He was just a boy.

Maybe this place had changed him into a murderer. Elim couldn't have said whether it had that power. But it certainly was fixing to change him into a dead man.

CHAPTER ONE
A BAD BUSINESS

Soap.

Glue.

Hide. Shaving-brushes, fishing line, fertilizer, bait, belts, boots – no, for sheer reliable marketability, you really couldn't beat a dead horse.

Unfortunately, the horses in the pen fairly radiated health and fine conditioning, which left Sil Halfwick to swelter, smile, and present himself as a livestock dealer with a special affinity for live stock.

"Only the very best," he said, and wiped his brow as he glanced over his shoulder at the merchandise in question. "What catches your fancy?"

"Horses, *eho*," the customer replied, impatience sharpening his tone. "I want to buy horses. Do you want to sell them, or are you just resting your *culo* on the gate?"

Eho. Boy. Sil swallowed on a throat worn raw from the habit, and though the searing afternoon promised to broil the very stench from the air, he strove to keep his voice as cool and pleasant as fine cellar wine. "Sure I do," he said. "As a matter of fact, I want to sell you eleven quarter-mile stock horses: two saddle-broke three-year-olds and nine long yearlings of the best breeding. Which ones would you like to see?"

The customer's gaze flicked from Sil's face back to the horses, and he might as well have asked it aloud: *what's wrong with them?*

It was a fair question. The honeycomb of stockyard fencing and the sea of hoof-churned earth and dung stretched on for nearly a quarter-mile, but the salesmen who had so assiduously flanked their gates on Friday had almost all trickled away to the white-tented spectacles in the distance, their business happily concluded.

Which left just Sil, conspicuously unsuccessful, and the customer, who fixed him with a suspicious coal-eyed stare. "How much for all?"

Sil did not move, nor take his gaze from the customer's sun-beaten face. But in his mind's eye, he conjured Father's old chess board and mentally swapped out the king and the rook, castling to put himself two healthy steps back from this present moment, and letting his imaginary older self come forward.

He was – would be – a splendid fellow: ten years older, and an ambitious four inches taller, with a close-trimmed golden beard and a bespoke suit and silk shirt and *confidence*, that was what – such confidence and fearless, friendly ease that he could conjure a price and make people see its worth as clearly as if he'd branded it onto the merchandise with a smoking iron.

"Twelve hundred," Master Halfwick said. "Papers included."

The customer's eyes went wide: he spat, the result missing Sil's boots by a pennywidth. "*¡Te-chinga! ¿Kién keyengañas creyes? ¡Wevoso timando eho de puta!*"

16

Sil couldn't help but flinch, and it was only ironclad mindfulness that stifled his urge to cough. With most customers, that wouldn't matter, but this one was a Sundowner, and an older one at that: all grit and suspicion, years of sand and sun worn into his dark skin and dusty black hair. And as the old joke went, the surest way to scatter the natives was to send a white man out to sneeze at them.

Needless to say, Master Halfwick would do nothing of the sort. He would do something marvelous, sophisticated, something no-one would ever expect.

Sil swallowed the rising itch in his throat. "*Sólo Dios'abe,*" he said, a phrase he understood to mean *That's as it may be*. "*But I think you know that these are the best horses here. Therefore, the real question is...*" He paused, fighting through a slow-roasted headache to twist the customer's words into a question. "*... am I the kind of brass-balled swindling son of a bitch you want to do business with?*"

Sil's fluency in Marín was his only trump card, but it was a good one: every miserable hour he'd spent diagramming and conjugating and learning how to twist the accents just-so was repaid each time a Sundowner blinked in open amazement as he, the sickly milk-faced Eadan boy, returned their salty parlance as casually as if a rabbit had opened its mouth and barked.

And it was working. Even now, the momentary surprise on the customer's face was souring into suspicion, and when it fermented into doubt, he'd ask whether they were started for saddle, or demand to inspect their feet, and then Sil would have him. Master Halfwick would be born from this moment exactly, his reputation kindled by one single, fantastic, almost-impossible sale.

Say yes, Sil willed his customer, loud enough to drown out the man's own doubts, and the cajoling calls of the few other salesmen still on the lot. *I respect you more than they do. I deserve this more than they do.*

The trudge of new footsteps on old straw halted his thoughts.

God dammit, not NOW.

The dull rattle of tin buckets and the slosh of water disturbed the heavy afternoon air in the pen behind him. Before Sil could even begin to choose his words, the customer hooked his thumbs into the waistband of his denim trousers and gave an agreeable nod.

"*Well,*" he said. "*I will buy your horses for twelve hundred... if you throw in the mule.*"

Sil let out a slow breath. "*I'm sorry,*" he said. "*He is not for sale. Not for any price.*"

Too late, Sil heard his own poor phrasing: this was a dead-end statement, a deal-killer. The customer's expression withered.

"*But it allows – I allow*" – the itch became unbearable; he aborted the cough with a violent clearing of his throat – "let me show you our prize filly; you'll want to see how she handles on the lead."

No. Sil saw the answer before he heard it.

The customer swatted a fly from his neck. "I have seen enough." He half-raised a hand and turned to go on. "Try again when you have some hairs around that mouth, *eho.*"

Sil kept his place at the gate, watching in dull-eyed stillness as his last chance of a sale walked away. His future self evaporated, banished to never-existence by the failure of the present.

A great shadow fell over him from the right, announced

by the telltale stink of horse and ripe sweat. "No dice, huh?" Punctuated by an empty pail being dropped onto the gatepost with a dumb *thunk*.

Sil continued to stare at no particular point on the horizon, not trusting himself to answer.

His name as it appeared on the Washburn County register was Appaloosa Elim. Yet Sil was seized by a sudden urge to shorten it to Ass Elim, Dolt Elim, Towering Idiot Elim, Barn-Born Ignorant Lumbering Ham-Fisted Ox Elim...

Sil glanced up, his outrage thickening along with the contents of his lungs. It wasn't Elim's ridiculous features that irritated him: not his improbably ugly long face, not the stupid wet cow-licks in his hair, not even the vast brown blotch over his left eye that seemed to commemorate the day on which God, irate with the genesis of yet another half-bred bastard, had muddied the palm of His hand and smacked Elim across the face. He couldn't help any of that. No, what Sil couldn't stand was that attentively clueless look in his creased brown eyes: half white, half Sundowner, and all country-bred blundering clod.

"Oh no, it was a smashing success, textbook really, just brilliant," Sil hissed up at him, "until YOU stuck your bloody big nose into it! God damn you Elim, what hellborn foolish idiot notion possessed you –"

The mutiny in his lungs finally overwhelmed him, but that hardly mattered now: bereft of any chance of a sale, he was free to cough to his heart's content, choking on snot, dust, and failure.

"Well," Elim said, "they don't advertise so good as horses if you parch 'em 'til they're jerky." And then, as Sil got on towards the last of his vile swallows and straightened, a big hand patted his shoulder. "And that goes double for you, Slim. C'mon have you a drink and some lie-down, and nevermind that trifling old flea-rustler anyhow. Been a beater of a day."

Appaloosa Elim, who'd had no more thought than fetching water for dry horses.

By now they were alone, and Sil was at liberty to pull off his hat and run his fingers through his sweat-streaked blond hair. He squinted out at the stockyards in the deepening red afternoon light. Yes, he could probably stagger back to the bunkhouse, and he could certainly carry on raging at Elim, but the overpowering wrung-out weariness in his limbs was fast reducing it to an either-or proposition. He sniffed, swallowed, and sighed.

"Right," he said with an asthmatic wheeze as he replaced his hat and waited for Elim to close the gate. "Lay on, then."

No, he decided as they retreated from the heat of the day, he didn't mind the horses so much – but the mixed-race 'mule' called Elim was going to be the death of him.

IT WAS A hell of a thing, really.

Elim sat hunkered over on the lower bunk of the old bedframe, half-packed supplies spread out over the worn quilt before him.

It was really just a hell of a thing.

The fall fair was a fixed part of his calendar, as regular and natural as spring foals and summer hay. Granted, anything could happen any time of the year: this was the far side of the Bravery, after all, and the only surer guarantee than storms and drought and wild-minded murdering Sundowners was that you'd be dead long before the government bothered itself to notice.

But you always figured you'd be all right, once you got to the fair, because it was such a small and human event: you just fixed up your herd and kept an eye out for thieves and stray nails while you waited for the sale, and that was that.

Except that this year, somehow, it wasn't. Something had gone wrong, not all at once but slowly, like milk that wouldn't churn to butter. And as hard as Elim tried to keep from thinking it, the problem most likely started when Boss Calvert had left Will Halfwick back home, and promoted Sil in his place.

Elim could not have said what essential quality had been lost in the swap. Sure, Sil was younger and frailer and powerfully more irritable than his siblings, but he had a solid knack for salesmanship, and Elim could look after him discreetly enough. Plus, Easy-Hey had taught him to speak that heathen Marín, which meant that he should have been even better than Will in spite of his greenness, that he should have been able to pitch to the new brown buyers and the regular white ones alike – that he should have had their business done in record time.

It was really just a hell of a thing.

Elim's piebald hands put their rations to readiness as the early evening light faded behind the dirty sackcloth curtains. They took five meals a day between them – Sil breakfasting exclusively from a coffee-pot – and it was two days on the road back to Hell's Acre, and Elim meant to see that they at least made it home without any further expense. So the hardtack went with the cheese, because they needed no fixing, the dried peas with the flour, because the water from soaking the one would make hoecakes with the other, and the beans with the bacon, because that was how you made beans and bacon.

It was important to be orderly with anything that could be ordered – that was what Boss always said – because the list of things that couldn't was just too long to keep track of.

And it included Sundowners, too. Sil could boil over about that all he wanted, and Elim was content to let him.

It hadn't cost Elim anything to make-pretend with a couple of water buckets, or to take a hollering for it after the fact. But Sil didn't understand what might have happened if he'd let that pistol-packing old sandsucker go on thinking there wasn't anyone else around to remark on him. Probably he hadn't even noticed the gun. And treaty or no treaty, you just couldn't trust those damned –

"Well," the voice said from above, "I expect you'll still be wanting your supper, regardless."

Elim looked up to see Sil peering down at him from the upper bunk. He was seventeen now, almost a man grown, but those deep, hollowed dark rings under his eyes always gave him a boyish look to Elim's mind, like a child sucked dry by dysentery. Their fading meant that the lie-down had done him good.

And it was high time to eat. "I expect I will, sure," Elim replied. "Does your lordship expect he'll suffer his-self to join me?"

Sil inspected him at leisure, taking in the sight of Elim's brushed hair and fresh clothes and clean-washed spotted face. "He might. Remind me why I should bother."

That was how you knew for sure-positive that he was a Northman: it wasn't the white of his face or the blue of his eyes or even the corn-silk gold of his hair that gave him away, but that almighty *attitude* that seeped out of him like so much cold sugared sweat. Elim sometimes felt sorry for Sil's having to hat his hair and smother his accent out here among strangers, but he never had wondered about it.

Instead, he reminded himself about how hard it was to be cheerful when you didn't feel well, and how lonesome it must be to live a thousand miles removed from your own natural home, and how tempting it could be to lighten the load of your inward miscontents by doling them out on everyone around you.

"Cuz it don't get any cheaper than free," Elim replied.

But also because Elim wasn't the right color – wasn't enough of the right color – to presume to go by himself. He was a mule, a half-bred bastard who wasn't enough of white or brown for anyone's liking, just like Sil was a Northman, a pure-bred pedigree who was far too white for everyone's liking. And at the end of the day, Elim's advantages – seven years, ten inches, and the better part of a hundred pounds – didn't amount to a hill of beans next to Sil's ability to button himself up and blend in with the ordinary folks around them.

The real shame about that was that Sil knew it.

A weary sigh drifted down from the top bunk, followed by one of those noxious gulping swallows. "That's a provocative thesis you've got there, professor." And then, sparing Elim having to ask what that meant, the creaking of the bed above assured him that Sil really was getting up.

Which was more than ordinarily reassuring, because the Verne County Fair fry-up was more than an ordinary tuck-in. In fact, it was nothing short of the biggest and greatest all-you-could-eat free meal of the year. For his part, Elim intended to stuff his guts enough to last him all the way through until next year... presuming of course that there was still going to BE a next year, which was another item on that whole long list of things that Elim had no ability to order, and sometimes even to understand.

In view of which, it became all the more critically important to keep a two-handed hold on your plate, and full faith in the immediate comfort and solace of pie.

HONESTLY THOUGH, SIL would still have taken Calvert's mule out for his supper. Even if it weren't a golden opportunity to fill Elim's bottomless gullet at no cost to either of them, even if it weren't the closest thing to a good time that either of them was going to have, even if he weren't all but assured that Elim would find a way to sabotage tomorrow's coffee if he didn't – he would still have gone with him, regardless.

Well, maybe.

At any rate, he did the nobler thing, fished out his cup and plate and cutlery, donned his tiresome old black hat, and submitted himself once more to the sensory assault of the crowds, the heat, the noise, the smells, and the bugs... even when all he wanted was another spoonful of paregoric and a night's sleep on something less wretched than that disgusting straw-stuffed sack of a mattress. Privately commending himself for his sacrifice, he followed Elim's relentless bulling towards the buffet.

The two of them dished up their plates in the queue and then wove through the crowded wooden trestle tables under the pavilion. Elim used his impolitely tall frame to spot and claim two empty seats, and Sil quietly seated himself between him and the two Sundowners on the other side.

He needn't have bothered: the two natives stood and left as soon as Elim set his big square baking-pan at the table.

One could almost believe Elim hadn't noticed, as busily as he laid into his fried chicken and cornbread. "Good, ain't it?"

"Magical," Sil replied, and halved a string bean with his fork. Though really, this wasn't quite fair: the earth was cooling with the approach of night, the carnival lights lit up again, and the rhythm of people clapping along to a fiddle tune enlivened a merciful evening breeze. Even Sil might have found this all rather satisfying, in different circumstances.

And it should have been different. It should have been – not easy, he'd known that going into the job, but *possible*.

For over a year now, Sil had spent his money and his afternoons at Wilford Watt's tannery. He'd perched up on that fence for hundreds of hours, copy-book and pencil in hand, braving the heat and the flies and that eye-watering stench so that Watt's hired help, Izi'hei – or 'Easy-Hey', as the locals called him – would sell him his second language, twenty cents at a time.

Hanging around the tannery had taught Sil more than Marín. And he'd long since decided that the best thing about a dead horse was its simplicity: there was no back-and-forthing about its conformation or the state of its teeth, no need for any negotiation beyond who would do the hauling and for what fee. If only those eleven leftovers in the pen would do the decent thing and die,

Sil could sell them in a snap – five dollars a head and done – and go home with his fledgling reputation intact. No, he wouldn't be able to style himself a dazzling young entrepreneur, but at least he wouldn't be an embarrassing blot on the family record. One box of rat poison was all it would take to wipe the slate clean.

Not that he would, of course. For the Calverts, those horses were the whole year's crop, and their loss would be devastating.

Still, maybe what the Calverts needed was a hard lesson in the importance of diversifying their investments.

"Well, look," Elim said an indefinite time later. "Boss won't blame you – I mean, he knows it's your first time in the saddle and all, and now you'll know all of what you want to do different on the next –"

"What *I* want to do differently?" Sil set down his fork and stared at him in festering amazement. "This isn't MY fault, Elim! I've said it ten times if I've said it once: you can't sell a nickel for a dime, you CAN'T, and nothing I do is going to change that! They aren't worth a hundred and twenty a head anymore – they haven't been for years! – and I'm sorry that's how it is, but we're not breeding them for the cavalry anymore, we're not... there's no wars left to want horses for, and no small-time shit-kicking farmer is going to buy our overpriced green-apple yearlings when the ones we sold him three years ago are only just now filling into form, and the fact that Calvert still thinks we can use his eight-year-old figures from the last time HE bothered himself to trudge down here and..."

He stopped then for his own self-preservation, as the blazing of Elim's brown eyes and the aura stiffening his overbuilt body reminded Sil of his impropriety. You could say what you wanted to or about Elim, but that privilege did not extend to his Boss.

"... doesn't mean I don't sincerely appreciate him trying me for the job, but really, Elim, there isn't anything I could have done differently: if I can't fix the prices, I can't sell the stock, and that's the end of it."

Sil waited then for that inevitable rejoinder, that petty little *well how come you took the job if you knew you couldn't do it?* or *well you sold one of 'em readily enough, why not the rest?* or that most hateful obnoxious inescapable *well Will always got along just fine – why can't you?* that sooner or later was going to provoke Sil to violence. He could actually see that thought in Elim's eyes, groping for words with which to pick-lock his brain and escape from his mouth to freedom –

– and then it apparently just died incarcerated.

"Well," Elim said, "in the meantime, I'm going to fix me up another plate. You quit your moping and eat that, hear?" *And don't stop 'til you find some manners in them greens* was graciously left unspoken.

In view of which, Sil smothered the first sharp remark that sprang to mind, and let Elim go find his seconds in peace.

For the record, though, it was only cheap novelty that had gotten him the asking price for that medicine-hat filly. And even Will had only managed to get a hundred a head last year, half of which he'd had to take in country-pay. And as for taking the job after having failed to get Calvert's figures down past the hundred-mark, well...

... arrogant as it sounded now, he really had thought he could do it. He really had thought he was good enough to win even on the long odds.

In fact, Sil had never considered losing at all.

But loser he was, with nothing to do but sit there and swirl the bitter lukewarm water in his cup. Then, because nobody was watching, and because his throat hurt and because he could, he folded one finger over the lip of the tin cup.

With a moment's focus, Sil applied his talent – the pedigreed birthright of any true-bred Northman – and leeched the heat from the water until ice crystals began to spread from the rim of the cup inwards over the surface.

Then he withdrew his single digit to a more seemly posture to drink, to numb his raw gorge with the blissful chill of cold water, and to feel at least nominally superior to the untalented common masses as the festivities promenaded on, and conversation of all flavors swirled around him.

"... wife'll kill me, but what could I do? These days, you can't afford not to..."

"... replace my awful old blue calico thing, but you know what mama said when she..."

"... said to him, I said, look son, I wouldn't pay three dollars if it was made of my granny's own gold teeth, so you can take your warranty and..."

"... eat my hat if they haven't already smuggled the whole herd across the border, but so what? It's not my business what they want to do with..."

No, it wasn't, was it? Sil paused, listening to find that particular thread again.

"...not like we left them any stock worth a damn, and as dry as it's been out there, you can hardly expect them to –"

The rest was obliterated by a sudden burst of feminine tittering from his left, but nevermind: his arsenic-laced fantasies already forgotten, Sil started up to go find the speaker and ask him directly what he meant.

A familiar shadow spilled over his plate again. "Thanks for saving my seat."

Sil glanced up at Elim, belatedly registered the sight of a tipsy old woman where he'd been sitting before, and shifted over on the bench to make room.

No, it wasn't their business what the Sundowners on the other side might trade for good stock... but maybe it ought to be.

He felt the creak of the wood as Elim sat down next to him, heard the flat *thap* of tin meeting table, registered the sour smell of horse and old sweat, and opened his mouth for some idle word of apology –

"Here, go dish you up some of that pie. They got apple raisin with calf slobbers on it, and it's going quick."

– but of course Elim had already forgotten about it. Sil glanced at the delicacy in question, slowly bleeding fruit and meringue there in Jane Calvert's second-best biscuit pan, and then up at Elim's cow-spotted profile.

"Elim, let's take them across the border."

Sil watched as Elim finished his bite without any special hurry. Chewed, swallowed, his attention fixed on nothing particularly as his over-prominent jaw did its favorite work, and finally looked down his steep nose at Sil. "Say what, now?"

"I'm serious," Sil said. "Let's take them out west and sell them there. Think about it: we destroyed most of the wild herds when we had the chance, and the drought will have done for a lot of the rest. So even if they've been breeding the best of whatever's left, there'll still be plenty of nations across the border that haven't" – how did one explain market saturation to a horseman?

– "that haven't got their fill of horses yet, and in any case they'll still want fresh bloodlines, right? And the geldings won't be worth as much, but we've still got six good mares, right?" Elim's face wasn't moving. "So you see? Even if half the dealers here had the same idea, we could still get half again our asking price, just by moving them across the river!"

Sil's voice hurried on in quick, hushed eddies until it finally broke into a sleeve-stifled cough, but that was fine: he'd said enough.

By the look on Elim's face, he'd said plenty. "No."

"Why?" It emerged as the instant, belligerent challenge of a six-year-old, but nevermind: no matter what reason Elim gave –

"Cuz we're going home."

"You're only saying that because you haven't got any good reason not to," Sil retorted.

But Elim's muddy brown eyes and the set of his mouth held firm. "I'm saying that cuz we're going home."

Like most of his fellow back-country homesteaders, Elim spoke with a Brave accent: a mash of drawled, warbling syllables traditionally ventured while squinting up at the sun and working a mouthful of chew. In the first years he'd been subjected to it, Sil had feared for his mind.

Now, however, he could charitably imagine that Elim's obstinacy reflected a simple failure to communicate. So perhaps he just needed to hear some simpler, more familiar words... several of which came rather promptly to mind.

"Or because you're too dumb to argue the point, too yellow to leave the beaten track, and too lazy to go an extra mile doing the job he raised you for."

Sil had him two for three then. But that third, that last, was an astonishingly ill-considered barb, a mistake he recognized even before he'd finished making it.

Yes, you could say what you wanted to or about Elim, and he had no right to answer you for it... but to suggest that he wouldn't lie down and die for his boss was a meanness that diminished you far more than him.

And that was assuming he didn't up and diminish the teeth right out of your stupid mouth. For a long, tenuous moment, Sil held himself perfectly still, staring at the huge fist on the table.

Presently, it picked up the fork – easily, casually, uncommitted to either bread or beans. "Say what, now?"

Sil let out his breath. No, on second thought, he really didn't care to invest in this particular venture after all. "I, ah..." Sniff, swallow, wince. "... I said, actually, I was just saying, I think I will have some of that pie."

Elim nodded and turned his attention back to his supper. "You should. It's real fine."

His head was nothing more than a worn gray hat and a few wisps of dirty brown hair; the rest hunkered down over his plate, oblivious and impervious beyond the vast blue-cotton wall of his back and shoulders.

When it seemed sufficiently futile to sit there any longer, Sil picked up his dish and left the table.

BUT SIL'S IDEA, that stroke of genius and his *passion* for it, didn't dwindle with dessert, or the night walk back to the bunkhouse, or his reunion with that poor excuse for a bed. It stayed all through the night, and ate at him.

Sil stared up at the dusty knots in the ceiling, and willed himself not to swallow again.

It *wasn't* his fault, but he was going to be the one to pay for it. After failing to accomplish this impossible task, there would be no more market trips for him, no more pretense for escaping Hell's Acre, and nothing to say when he was asked when he meant to start being a help to his brother, and wasn't it about time he finished with his schoolbooks, and what about that nice Rowena Timson who kept making eyes at him during sermons?

Sil turned over, closing his eyes to stave off a claustrophobia that had nothing to do with the cramped quarters, and listened to the deep, regular rhythm of Elim's breathing below.

Easy enough for him to snuff the light and pass out. Easy enough for the whole lot of them to spend their lives picking paddocks and pulling weeds and pounding fence-posts, hoarding their pennies and steeping their offspring in bootless piety and backbreaking labor in anticipation of the day when they themselves would be planted with the turnips.

That was all these rustics wanted – that was everything they understood – and any free-thinking soul who lived too long amidst their squalid contentment was going to drown in it like a fish in stagnant water.

Not Sil. Not like this. He belonged back east, back home, where beef came in a tin and fish didn't, where *y'all* was unheard-of and *your grace* wasn't, where people bleached their hair and powdered their faces and only hid their talents to avoid embarrassing those poor low-bred souls who hadn't any of their own. It had been twelve long years, but if Sil pressed one ear to the musty pillow and covered the other, just so, he could almost make Elim's faint snoring into the sound of cold salt waves crashing against vast stone walls, and hear sea-birds in the rasping of the crickets.

That world had a place ready and waiting for him – all he had to do was get there.

For that he needed money, enough to pay Calvert's stupid asking-prices and buy a one-way stage ticket with the remainder.

And at the end of the day, it didn't really matter where he got it.

Elim squatted on the ground in front of the gate, the morning sun already warm on his back, and chewed oats while he waited.

He liked waiting, though. There was a holiness to it. Waiting was admitting that yes, you had done everything in your humble power – ate, dressed, packed, fed, raked, tied, bridled, and saddled – and entrusting the rest to God.

The dull thump of hooves in the dirt behind him ended with a wet blast of heat down the back of his neck. Elim looked up into the moist and cavernous nostrils of one Molly Boone.

"I know," he said, "but it ain't going to hurry him along any faster, is it?"

Even so, Elim pulled his hat off before it could tempt any nibbles and leaned his head back against the gate planks, at peace amidst the smell of old leather and new manure.

It was the horses that did it to him. It was altogether difficult to get worked up about anything when you had the sun warm on your face, a pair of hairy lips browsing your forehead for salt, and a herd at your back whose greatest concern was the flicking of an occasional blow-fly.

Even if you hadn't sold them like you were supposed to.

Even if your partner was a willful wild-minded yearling with a dirty mouth and a head full of arrant balderdash.

Boy, Elim reminded himself. He was just a boy.

Molly left off her affections and lifted her head, ears pricked forward. Elim sat up likewise, and they watched as the flapping canvas walls of the exchange pavilion yielded up Sil, recognizable even at a distance by the contrast of his pale gray shirt against his black hat and trousers, and the yellow handkerchief with which he tarped his coughing.

Molly snorted and mouthed her bit.

"'Bout time, ain't it? And here we was thinking we'd got you all gussied up for nothing."

Presently, Elim rocked forward and up to his feet, not bothering with any more courtesy than a pull on the gate's far post. "That us, then?"

"Just about," Sil said, likewise not bothering with Elim, but going right on in and reaching up for Actor's reins.

Then he stopped. His hands hesitated there in midair, his face hidden from Elim's view, before he pulled something from his charcoal vest: a packet of papers, folded in sharp thirds. "Right. Take this to Calvert," he said, setting it on a fencepost, "and here's his money from the one sale."

Molly's ears swiveled forward as the leather purse with Hattie's asking-price weighted the papers with a distinctive *clink*. Elim hooked his thumbs into his pockets, smelling treachery. "Any reason specially why you ain't fit to deliver them yourself?"

Sil took Actor under the chin and led the sun-bleached black gelding out of the pen. Elim was sorely tempted to shut the gate in his path, but that was a rudeness still unwarranted. The boy had some funny ideas, and yes, he could be a handful, but this was Will's little brother. He wouldn't do anything *really* stupid.

Sil looked up at Elim. A sleepless night had deepened the shadows under his eyes. "Well, I was just thinking," he said. "I'm sorry I couldn't sell the rest of the horses for you-all, but really it isn't reasonable to take them across the border."

Well, thank God he'd cured himself of that notion. Elim led Molly out behind him. "Right..."

"So," Sil paused to slip the toe of his left boot through the stirrup, "I think the best thing will be to take them back to Boss Calvert and let him decide how to handle it." He hefted himself up and over the saddle. "And as for me personally – I don't think I've had my fill of traveling quite yet. In fact, I rather think a change of climate might do me good."

Elim stared up at Sil. "What."

Sil gave Actor a quarter turn, the reins light and loose in his hand. "I'm going on west."

Elim stiffened. "The hell you are."

But today the warning in his eyes and voice had no effect. Sil leaned forward over the saddle horn, so exactly-despicably like himself. "Well, Elim, the thing is... you can't stop me."

Elim suddenly blazed with a burning desire to do exactly that... except that he couldn't make a sudden grab for Sil without spooking the horse, and Sil knew it, and was even now nudging Actor on towards the main gate, and by the time Elim realized that he ought to take his chances on the spook, Sil was out of his reach.

Elim tightened his hold on Molly's rope, realization dawning brighter with every non-starter that occurred to him. Couldn't leave the herd to go tearing after him: there was no guaranteeing they'd still be here when he got back. Couldn't go tearing after him *with* the herd; it was as good as inviting a wreck. Couldn't just whip out his rifle and nail the little runt at fifty yards, tempting as that was.

Couldn't show up home again without him.

"Well, shit." Elim's grip slackened along with his outrage. Sil no doubt figured it was a clever plan, and Elim would be the first to admit as much – just as soon as Sil felt he'd made his point well enough to come back and settle down to business.

But Elim and Molly watched in vain as Sil dwindled to a black spot in the distance, and then disappeared.

He's not exactly sunshine and sugar, but try to bring him back in one piece, can you?

Presently, Molly stamped her hoof.

Sure, Will – I'll see him looked after. I'll do you right.

Elim was slow to acknowledge it, his hand absent at her bridle.

I know you will, old boy. You always do.

Surely Sil didn't mean to do it. He knew it was dangerous, and selfish, and idiotic. He knew that the Etascado Territory didn't belong to them anymore. He knew – he had to know – what had happened to it, to Harne and Brayton and Sixes and all the other frontier towns they'd abandoned to the Sundowners. What had happened to the people who lived there. What could very well happen to anyone who crossed over now.

Elim glanced back at the weighted papers. Then again, maybe the boy really had just up and beefed his own common sense. Elim sighed. "Well, Miz Boone, I expect we'll have to fetch him before he mislays himself."

Molly mouthed her bit, and raised no objections.

So Elim obligingly collected the purse and the papers, assembled his troops, and then set himself astride his big bay mistress to start her out at a sensible jog.

It was an orderly, sustainable gait to use for leading their little posse out of town, a natural choice for any reasoning fellow.

Now, what you'd use to catch up a snotty, arrogant, spoiled son-of-a-bitch, clock him clean off his horse, turn him over your knee, and then heat his frail hide one lick for every mile he'd ridden you out along his damn fool way – that would be a whole different gait.

And Elim felt mightily keen on trying it out before Sil made it to the border.

CHAPTER TWO
STRANGE LADIES

ALL THE SAME, Elim knew better than to think he could catch Sil up with a simple hell-for-leather gallop, even after they'd ventured back into open country. That was no fault of Molly's: she could have ridden down a greenhorn boy on a sedentary drygrocer's horse even if Elim had been passed out in the saddle. Here, though, he literally had his hands full – leading one string of baby-faced yearlings with his left, another with his right, and leaving the meekest of the bunch to herd along behind – and he and Molly were about as quick and agile as a sow nursing a pile of week-old piglets.

So Elim, unable to reckon any alternative, played along all that day: Sil rode ahead, and Elim followed after. Sil stopped briefly, Elim gained on him, and Sil likewise hurried on until he was once again a black blot on the horizon.

It didn't take long to see the pattern in that. Sil never intended Elim to turn back home: it was the horses he was after, and that damn sale, and he apparently knew better than to let himself within reach of Elim's rope until he got what – where – he wanted.

Well, let it be. Elim would do just the same without him: find a stream, settle his stock, make his camp, and lose not one wink of sleep over any of it. Here at the end of the day, the coppery-green grass still darkened to a soft black blanket of earth-fur, the warblers and the crickets still sang their evening songs as jack-rabbits ventured out of their burrows, the twilight breeze still smelled of horse and sage, and for all his trying and scheming, that Sil Halfwick still hadn't power enough to hold back even a single emerging star.

But as Elim set his dishes aside and rolled himself into his blankets for the night, the question still pestered him: how would you go about catching up a particularly contrary colt, assuming you'd been dumb enough to let him slip the lead in the first place?

THE RICHEST IRONY in all of it was that Sil, having finally escaped the constant sinus-ravaging assault of hay and dust and every horse save one, was exactly as well-set to finally get a proper night's sleep as he was ill-advised to take it. Elim would undoubtedly realize that night represented his best chance of getting the advantage, but Sil could not decide what that might lead him to do.

In fact, prior to this fair-going project, he'd largely been spared acquaintance with the Calverts' mule. He came into town on Sundays, of course, and very-occasionally stopped by the store on his boss's behalf, but apart from his whopping great size and the patch over his eye, there'd been nothing to him: just the same dry-rotted mind and prideful ignorance of any Brave, painted in mule-colors and made to sit out back during sermons.

Since then, Sil had learned that this Elim fellow could boast exactly three proper skills.

In the first place, he was a dab hand with anything that could be haltered and shod. No doubt an empathy born of intellectual kinship.

Secondly, he was a deadly shot with a rifle – not that Sil need worry about that.

And finally, the point of legitimate concern: he could spin and throw a rope at least well enough to catch up those pastured peers of his, and Sil didn't need specifics to understand that he'd better not get anywhere near it.

So he tried to cover all possible contingencies: he fed his fire, kept the horse close to him, and dozed only in five-minute intervals. As keyed-up as he was with this whole project, it was not difficult: part of him was still struck absolutely gutless by what he'd already done, and silenced only by the thought of what he had still to do. At least Actor's constant, anxious neighing was still answered in kind from the rest of the herd – a handy compass here in the dark, and a temporary guarantee that Elim hadn't started after him... yet.

Sil hadn't planned for any of this, that was the thing: he'd not done any research, nor garnered even secondhand specifics about where and how to go. There was no shortage of Sundowners on the other side, but where would they congregate for business – or rather, where would they consider trading with foreigners more readily than killing them? He'd heard that some of the surrendered towns still harbored their share of *sobrachoş*, or 'left-over' white settlers, but there was no guarantee that they'd be open for business even if Sil could find them. For one thing, the 187th had poisoned Flatiron Lake to keep the natives from marshalling their forces there, but that had meant evacuating Hereward and Flatiron City and every other downriver hamlet too, and there was no telling whether anyone had returned in the ten years since. Brayton was nearer, but its population had been faltering even before infected coyotes came swarming out of the ruins of Merin-Ka and started leaving half-eaten corpses on the road.

In fact, the closest and surest bet was probably Sixes. A goodly portion of it had burned under siege, with no more than twenty of its original thousand-odd citizens escaping to tell the tale, but it would be easy to find – west to the river, then south to the island in the stream – and likely saw all manner of trade from both sides of the border. If you were dead set on trespassing, that was probably the safest place to do it.

So Sil minded his horse and his fire and sketched half-remembered geography lessons in the dirt while he waited for Elim to make his move ...

... until the sky began to gray in the east and still nothing had happened.

Elim was there all right – already up and at the same dull routine of catching, tying, saddling – but there was nothing special about it. They might as well have been on the road home for all the urgency Elim had mustered; he might as well have forgotten Sil's whole enterprise for all it affected his mindless menial chores

Well, fine – maybe the ride had given Elim time to decide to come along sensibly. Or maybe he was just mulishly plodding along, just to keep Sil from enjoying his conquest.

Or maybe he really was just that sodding stupid.

Regardless, Elim was in for a surprise if he thought *he* was going to set the pace today. Sil extinguished his fire, mounted up, and without further allowance for Elim's recalcitrant dithering, kicked his horse into a rough and foul-tempered gallop.

ELIM LOST THE trail a couple of hours before noon, when the grass turned sparse and scrubby and the land began rumpling up into broad, shallow hills and dips. The day was blindingly bright, the sun warm at his back, and apart from some distant, mountainous irregularities far in the north and west, the brown grass and blue sky went on just about forever.

Until he got to the river.

It was a toad-colored thing, slow and withered by drought, and went sidewinding through a streambed as wide and dry as a sloughed-off second skin. Elim approached its crusty banks with full respect as he organized his posse for a drink: this here was the end of home – the end of Eaden itself – and that over there was wild country. Elim couldn't have said how far across its thirty-yard girth his right to live ended, and would not be caught leaving so much as a wet boot-print in the sand.

But the land beyond was so exactly like the land before, both stretches of wild autumn savannah as matched and identical as two halves of a ham sandwich, that Elim could understand perfectly how the first white men here had reckoned they had as much right to the one as the other, and helped themselves right to it.

Unfortunately, their most devil-minded descendant seemed to have inherited their slippery ambition. There was no sign of Sil anywhere.

* * *

"WHY?"

Sil stood cool and composed in the horse's shadow, the reins slack in his right hand, and spoke easily in spite of the blistering sun overhead. "*Because I know someone who will pay five. Or ten, or even twenty.*"

The old Sundowner appeared to consider the logic, although the cloth over his nose and mouth made him difficult to read. "*Why?*"

Sil had an answer for this as well. "*Because he has twelve horses, and does not swim.*"

This time, he could see his success in the narrowing of the old man's eyes. "*Three,*" he insisted.

Ridiculous – the raft itself wasn't worth three dollars.

Still, if there was going to be a three-dollar minimum on this transaction, Sil could at least try to get more than ferry passage out of it.

"*Well,*" he said, "*I have heard that Sixes has a very great want of horses right now. The bribe might cost less than that, if my friend and I decide to enter here on the eastern side.*"

This was the kind of thing Sil generally researched well beforehand: there might well be corrupt Federate rangers watching this side of the island, or native guards at the town gates who could be paid to look the other way. But as this was an extraordinarily recent addition to the itinerary, he was left to build his premise on recollection and guesswork, and lacquer it over with calculated ambiguity.

The Sundowner snorted, prompting Actor to look up from grazing, and dropped back to a high-kneed squat. His thin limbs all but disappeared in the shadow of his hat. "*Try it, then.*"

It was hard to know how to take that.

You couldn't tell much by looking at him – well, Sil couldn't, anyway. The ferryman didn't leave much of his face visible, and any ornament in his hair was swallowed up by his broad-brimmed straw hat. Still, some more experienced trader surely could have read the intricate triangle-patterns and fringes of his blanket, or perhaps the weaving of his battered yucca sandals, and said with respectable confidence which tribe or god would claim him.

Sil sleeve-scrubbed the sweat from his brow, and whittled his ignorance to a finer point. "*Perhaps I will – but I would rather give my money to you, and be confident in what I am buying. Sell me a good reason for your price, and I will be glad to pay it.*" He pulled the coins from his pocket as deposit on the bargain.

This was enough to prompt a nod to the south. "*To open the sun-bridge requires the approval of the town's master, and he is a long time gone. When you have finished bribing the walls and water, I will take you across the way and teach you how to present yourself as a left-over, and the moon-bridge will be open for you.*"

And having thus learned three useful things – a bridge on each side of the island, an absent mayor, and the continued admission of certain pre-qualified foreigners in the meantime – Sil would be more than pleased to include their value in the cost of his passage. He smiled and dipped his head in deference to the little joke. "*If it is all right with you, I will avoid the bribes, and buy your service instead. Here is the money.*"

The Sundowner did not move. "*Four.*"

Sil dropped his arm, dumbstruck. Even if he had four dollars to burn on this conniving blood-sucker...

... no, no, that wasn't right at all. It was useful, was and would be exceptionally useful. Elim could go watch a raised bridge if he didn't agree, but Sil meant to get this right on the first try, and that included learning how to pass for one of those rare Braves who had refused to leave when the army pulled back, and who for one tenuous reason or another hadn't been slaughtered at the natives' first fresh opportunity. That surely required one hell of a knack, and Sil wouldn't bet on having lessons offered to him ever again.

"*Well,*" he said, "*I have no doubt that what you say will be worth every cent, but I don't have four dollars.*"

Sil waited for the inevitable rejoinder, for a repeat of his last attempted sale that would see him flounder under some impossible demand for his horse, or his clothes, or an obscene quantity of his blood, and so herald another silly failure. Only this time, he wouldn't do the floundering bit: he would just steel his gut and take his lumps and let that be the end of it.

And that, perhaps, made all the difference.

The Sundowner tipped his head, the crows-feet at the corners of his eyes creasing. "*Then what do you have?*"

The space of five minutes saw the price fixed at three crowned Federate dollars, two spare horseshoes and twenty-five feet of plain-laid cotton rope, traded for a horse-and-rider's passage across the Eiascado River, five minutes' explicit instruction, and positive assurance that Sil's horse-leading friend would likewise be afforded good ferry service at a dollar a head.

Sil did not bother to mention his friend's sharply-contrasting features. The ferryman was going to gouge Elim regardless, and what did color matter when there was money to be made? Instead, he coaxed Actor onto the raft, and drank in the first of his four-dollar instructions as the ferryman lanced the water. It was all, finally, perfect.

ELIM SAW SIL first: a black horse with a black-clad rider coming at a canter along the other side of the river. His dark chimerical shape registered as a punch in the gut: by the grace of God, he was still alive, but by the luck of the Sibyl, he'd already crossed over.

Sil waved, a great big come-hithering gesture, circled around and dug his heels into Actor's sides to ride back downstream again. By all wrath, why did he insist on kicking that horse so?

More importantly, how had he gotten himself over there? And more importantly still... good God, what if Elim just actually couldn't catch him?

It was an awful thought, and so occupied him that it was only the turn of Molly's ears that brought his attention to the stranger ahead.

Elim mistook him for an animal at first, crouched there under the speckling shade of a mesquite bush, and maybe he was: he had wrapped himself in a heathenish red-and-yellow blanket fit for a coral-snake shaman, wore a broad-brimmed straw hat to hide the shape of his ears and a neck-cloth to do likewise for his nose and mouth, and showed his hands not at all. Only his dirty brown sandaled feet marked him for at least a part-time human, and that was not nearly surety enough to warrant Elim's further approach.

Any of them could keep a man's shape in daylight.

He glanced from the beached raft to the further shore, just on a slim hope that this was not his stop after all.

Unfortunately, Sil was stopping there, where the raft would meet the far bank, waiting for him.

So Elim brought Molly to a halt, his string-tied yearlings attempting a more muddled version of the same, and steeled his gut in the name of mannerly conduct.

"*Luho,*" he said, with a touch of his hat. "How much to cross?"

The Sundowner squinted at him, his creased brown eyes reminding Elim so discouragingly of his own... and then going wide in recognition and sudden fear. He stiffened, shifting something under that blanket of his, and answered with the complex *click* of a pistol hammer.

"Believe I take your meaning," Elim heard himself say, though it surely had to be Molly who took the liberty of excusing them: his knees were as slack as a dead man's grip, and the leads in his hands all slick with cold sweat.

But her sense substituted for his, and they went on along their way as slow and naturally as they'd come. Still, it was the better part of five minutes before Elim had recollected how to breathe again, expecting at every intervening moment to feel the crack of the gunshot between his shoulders, and on towards ten before he had worked up the gumption to look back behind him.

As it worked out, he did still have one short dozen of horses in tow, their ears and white-touched brown faces still bobbing along. Even so, Easy Daisy's cinch was slipping, and Prudence was flattening her ears every time Pete ventured too close behind her, and Elim, for his part, still felt sick at his stomach from that deadly-sudden whiff of lead.

So maybe it was time to stop and re-think this fancy-deluxe ear-boxing deputation altogether.

* * *

A TALENT, OF course, was a mark of pedigree – an ability exclusive to pure-bred people of one kind or another.

A knack, on the other hand, just meant that you had a certain kind of aptitude for something. And nobody with an eye in their head would accuse Elim of having a talent for anything, but back home, people who meant to make him a compliment generally said that he had a powerful knack with horses.

That might possibly be true. Certainly it would account for his present success in ponying his most boss-minded yearlings in a string without anyone up and kicking the daylights out of his neighbor, and getting the rest to herd along without anyone gallivanting off on his own. Personally, Elim had never credited himself with anything but a double ration of patience and a careful under-reliance on his mouth.

And if all his patience and practice and sensibility could not catch him one sickly little stray on a half-burned horse, now was the time to learn it.

It was this thinking that ultimately found Elim and Molly standing up to her fore-cannons in that fetid-smelling water, minnows and little silvery pupfish darting about her knobby ankles as he tried mightily hard not to think about what kind of furry trout or fishmen might be living down there.

Because the alternative was to give up and go home, to look Will Halfwick straight in the eye and say *Well, he was free, white, and seventeen, and I reckoned he could do what he wanted.*

Elim turned in the saddle, squeezing an easy creak from the leather. His freshly-unstrung posse had lost no time planting their noses in thick clumps of bluegrass, leaving their tails to fend off gnats and stoneflies. "You-all wait here," he said, fixing a stare at Two-Pie in particular. "Don't make me come catch you when we get back."

Then there was nothing to do but get on with it. "Well, Miz Boone," Elim said at last, "let's go fancy-dancing."

With that, Elim nudged Molly forward, and the two of them moseyed in to make the water's proper acquaintance.

SIL HAD LONG since given up wondering why Elim hadn't taken the ferry. Shadowing him like this was maddeningly slow, but Sil had come to it by his own fault: if Elim wanted to take his sweet winter-molasses time finding another crossing, Sil hadn't left himself much recourse but to sit and swear and swelter in the meantime.

Sil rationed another lukewarm swallow from his canteen, and poured a miserly amount of the remainder onto his crumpled yellow handkerchief. His hands absently kneaded the cloth, chilling it until it was cold enough to crackle with newborn frost, before he gave his face a quick swipe and then tied it back at his neck. The ice melted almost instantly.

It was a zero-sum exercise, of course – you were only leeching the heat into yourself when you did that – but it felt good all the same, as pointless and refreshing as quenching a powerful thirst with a cold beer.

And speaking of pointless...

Sil sighed as Elim stopped there at no point in particular

on the far bank, and all but swore aloud as he began yet another one of his endless tack-fiddling excursions.

Drowsiness soon sapped him, though, and Sil must have been slumping too far forward over the saddle horn, because Actor nearly popped him in the forehead when he put his head sharply up from grazing.

Over on the other side, Elim had unstrung the yearlings. Sil's disinterest sharpened into doubt as he realized what Elim meant to do, standing there mounted in the water like that, and then to panic as he actually began to do it.

The man did not swim. It was a point of pride with these field mules, one of those pious *I'll take to swimming when fishmen learn to ride* chestnuts they traded enviously between themselves whenever their town-dwelling cousins were caught water-holing on a summer afternoon.

Shit.

Sil did swear then, for lack of a more immediate plan. "Go back!" he hollered, casting his arm vehemently out. "Go back! Elim, you whoreson pig-headed ass, go BACK!"

But Sil was left to stare in dumbstruck amazement as Elim and his horse ploughed their way across in a cloud of churning water.

Behind them, the yearlings began to lift their heads. A few meandered through the brush in ones and twos, followed their leaders into the murky deep like so many 800-pound brown ducklings, and started drifting downstream just as surely.

All right, all right, so that wasn't a disaster of itself – Elim wasn't panicking, and the merchandise still had their heads above water – but Sil's great cleverness now served only to remind him that there was nothing he could do to help them if something went wrong.

No, no – he'd go get the raft, that was what. With a sharp pull and a hard kick, Sil spun his horse and tore back upstream at a gallop, and –

– what was he thinking? Elim would be soggy flotsam before the ferryman heaved the raft this far downstream, and here was Sil without a penny for the service.

No, to hell with it: any idiot could see that Elim and Molly would be coming ashore at a long angle, and Sil was just the idiot for the job. Another hard turn and he was beating tracks back down the bush-dotted banks, calculating and recalculating where Elim would most likely put aground.

In fact, he was so fixated on this geometry of fools that the sudden, sharp squeal of his horse took him completely by surprise. Sil grabbed for the saddle horn as Actor reared violently back, slammed his forefeet down to earth and bolted in a hot panic. Struggling to keep his wits and his seat, Sil pulled the reins for a hard right, running the horse in dizzy circles until he slowed.

They came to a gradual stop, Actor prancing and shying, Sil coughing in a dusty cloud.

As it turned out, it didn't need Elim to discover what had spooked the horse.

She was crouched at the foot of a low rise, the dust still settling over her natty black robe and ropy black hair and muddy black skin, and if Sil had been paying the slightest bit of attention before, he would not have missed the glint of her knife. She held it fast in an icepick grip just above her opposite shoulder, having made a shield of her forearm to ward her face and neck. Sil understood by her uncut hair and the wide, white rims of her eyes that this one was wild, probably free-born, and would not hesitate to prove it to him.

They were properly called Afriti, but back home, the older people still knew them as *skault*.

One wouldn't use the word in polite conversation now-a-days, of course – and Sil had every reason to be polite. "Pardon me, miss," he said in his most pleasant voice, "I didn't even see you there. Not hurt, are we?"

It was reasonably clear that she wasn't, but this was civility enough for her to lower her weapon. She was lamentably ugly – all swollen lips and broad nose and square chin – but that was the least of her problems. Sil understood by the glazing of her dark eyes that she was addled, saturated by the sun, and any brains she might have had baked right out of her head. That was the trouble, Father had always said: no matter how carefully you managed them, a certain few would just go barking mad in the heat – and judging by that parasol lying in the dust behind her, this poor thing here already knew she'd inherited the curse.

"That depends largely on the scope of the question," she said, her voice deep and smooth. "Who is 'we'?"

Sil could not have been more surprised if a doe had opened its mouth and roared. "Er – well, I'm Halfwick," he said, straightening the tied hat that had worked its way back behind his head. "And the man drowning himself out there just now is Appaloosa..."

Now where had he gotten to? Sil sniffed, swallowed, and nudged Actor back towards the shoreline.

The mare was there all right, browsing at scrub about fifty yards downstream as other horses accumulated around her. But the man was nowhere in sight. "... Elim..."

Sil felt suddenly ill. He squinted, but could not see anything adrift in the river, and clutched the reins, but could not decide what command to give. "I don't... by any chance, you hadn't just seen..."

Silence. Sil glanced back at the girl. Her eyes had gone wide, her gaze distracted. By the time the quick, muffled thumping of hooves finally reached his ears, she had already sprung into action.

Elim came tearing over the rise, soaked to his skin and bareback on the apron-faced sorrel horse, holding fast to its mane with one hand and spinning a loop with the other as he rode hell-for-leather at Sil.

He hadn't seen the girl, though, and this time Sil had a spectator's seat for the show. She tucked and deftly rolled out of the horse's path – but not out of its vision. Startled by the flashing silver edge and the whipping black tendrils of her hair, it snorted and reared, dumping Elim straight off its wet back to hit the ground, backside-first.

Which left the horse, bolting off in a ten-second terror; the girl, now poised to gouge out Elim's eye exactly as she had been Sil's before; and Elim, who just sat there in his sodden clothes and tangled rope and stared like a stunned ox.

And Sil, who laughed until he choked. "Made a pig's breakfast out of that, didn't you?" he said at last.

Still, Elim was coming to his senses, and Sil did not intend him to have the last laugh. He nodded at the girl. "Well, pleasant day, miss – and Elim, do try to keep up."

With that, Sil touched the brim of his hat and spurred Actor on his way. Good enough exercise, this little farce, but the real prize lay further ahead.

* * *

IT HAD BEEN such a good plan.

Especially for not having been a plan at all. It hadn't occurred to Elim to swap horses until Cannon Dan came up beside Molly in the shallows, but it was a hell of a notion anyway. Dan and Daisy were the last of the previous year's leftovers, and old enough now to have been started for riding. Even if Sil had seen Elim coming and bolted, he'd been busting leather on Actor all day long. Poor Ax wouldn't have a chance against a fresh competitor, especially not a bangtail like Dan.

Or at least he wouldn't have, if Elim hadn't gone trampling strange ladies while he was at it.

And she was a lady. Just like any gun was to be considered loaded, any woman was likewise a lady until proven otherwise – and God help any man without due and fearful respect for either.

So Elim sat there for a minute, sitting and dripping and thinking, but mostly figuring out how to look without staring, as he had never in his born days seen a lady like her.

He did know some about them, of course. The Afriti were what the Northmen had used before there was any such thing as mules. But they were purebred people, dangerous, with talents of their own – and they had given their old masters a fierce walloping.

This lady here was full-blooded without question, her features strong and strange, with corded locks of hair of two-finger thickness snaking down her back. Her bare feet said plainly that she was not afraid of bad blood or old ghosts, and the heavy blue umbrella lying in the dirt nearby suggested that she had no special love for the sun. As she crouched there and watched him, Elim thought it prudent to do his apologizing on the quick side.

"I'm awful sorry about that, miss. I promise it ain't usually my custom to go catawamping about like a stuck pig." He favored his right hand naturally, but his left was the white and cleaner of the two, and he used it to remove his hat as he glanced back at Sil's diminishing figure. "That there is pretty much standard yield from him, though. 'm sorry about that too."

He felt more shame about Sil than anything. The little weanling shouldn't have made it far enough to bother her, and that was Elim's blame as much as anyone's.

She still had her knife out, though, and glazed eyes that seemed to look more through him than at him, and Elim was put in mind of everything else he'd heard about her kind: that they went mad in the sun, that they weakened and died if you cut off their hair, that their men could melt iron just by staring at it, and their women call curses in heathen words they'd brought from the scorched flats of the old world. Elim flattened his hands in the dirt, just in case he might have to get up in more than his usual hurry.

"You have the sun and the moon in your face," she said then, "but a man may not serve two masters. Which one do you honor?"

Elim wasn't sure what to do with that. "I got no master but Him that made me," he assured her, "but I do my business in daylight, if that's what you mean." Because despite what Sil was hell-bent on conjuring here, Elim was neither a rustler nor a thief.

She sheathed her knife, and as she stood to retrieve her umbrella, he noticed the fresh plant cuttings she'd been guarding in her lap. "Then you shouldn't let it leave you here."

Boy, wasn't that the truth. "I don't mean to, believe me," Elim said as he replaced his hat. "I just got to catch him up, and then" – and then he noticed the droplets of blood spattering to the ground between her feet, and tracked down the inside of her ankle. "Why, you're hurt!" He followed the dark trickle of red with his eyes until it disappeared at her hemline, and with his mind thereafter. "Where'd…"

As soon as he said it, his imagination reached trail's end, and he dropped the thought with a bullet between the eyes. "… oh."

Well.

Elim faced forward again, and found other occupation for his thinking. He meant to apologize, but the gentlemanly thing was to let her give him hellfire for it first, and Elim was half a gentleman anyway. So he sat there with wet clothes clinging to his hide, watching Dan snack on scrub a little ways yonder while he waited to get his due.

But he got nothing at all, which meant that maybe he'd done worse than he thought and made her cry, or worse even than that and made her put curses on him, and when that fear prompted him to look back and see, she was gone.

He considered getting up to find her again – she must have taken herself down the curve of the river-bank to disappear as quickly as that – but soon thought better of it, and instead sat a little while longer, just to give her an extra lead.

Presently, Dan raised his head. Finding no other horses in sight, he seemed finally to realize that leaving his commanding officer in the dirt might have been a bad thing. He neighed once, and was answered in kind from a few dozen yards downstream.

Regardless, he was a safer target for Elim's attention than anything else here. "Well, come on!" Elim heaved himself up to his feet. "If you-all can't leave yourselves put where I tell you, you better light a shuck and keep up. Ain't got time to wait around on you, buster."

But he did wait, just long enough to gather his line and let the horse anticipate his leaving, before turning to trudge with squelching boots and an aching behind back to the rest of their motley regiment. "But we was goin' pretty good there for a minute, huh? Woulda had that little snotter in two hot licks, just about."

Still, as much as he appreciated her advice, Elim didn't need any strange ladies to tell him that he'd landed himself on the wrong side of the river.

As THE LAST disturbed eddies finally disappeared, a pale face emerged from the river. Its unblinking black eyes watched as the two-colored man first spoke to the horse, and then let it follow him as calm and surely as if he had ensorcelled it.

CHAPTER THREE
THE ISLAND IN THE RIVER

BUT ALTHOUGH DAN had performed admirably on the spur of the moment, especially considering he'd only been put under saddle a handful of times before, he couldn't seem to put himself back to rights afterward, and stuck coltishly close to Molly's side.

"Look," Elim said, "I understand. I do. But you're almost three now, buddy, and you got to start thinking about what kind of example you're setting for these greenhorns here. What are they s'posed to think when they see you spooking every time some nice lady drops her darning-needle, huh? Ain't we practiced about that?"

Elim kept up his soothing nonsense as long as he could, but not for the horse's benefit. Sil was still there up ahead, an unreachable black shape, and despair soon swallowed Elim's voice.

He hadn't caught him.

He wasn't going to catch him.

And he was running out of time.

Because already there were signs of what lay ahead: shorn grass peppered with goat dung, and strange clay mounds with empty black-mouthed doorways, and groves of gnarled mesquite trees, some of which bent and danced and shed their brittle bean-pods without a breath of wind to move them.

That scared Elim long after he had seen the first slightly-built Sundowner drop out of one to meet his basket-carrying fellow on the ground.

Otherwise, there was nobody else around, at least not within shouting distance, and Elim aimed to keep it that way. He followed Sil's lead in picking a quarter-circle around the vast heathen fields and fording a drought-strangled stream. By the time they reached the big sandstone marking-rock, whose long red hand-print designs reminded Elim of nothing so much as the scrabbling of bloody fingers, Sixes itself was well in sight.

It had used to be a fort, once, and it seemed parts of it still were. Here and there, you could still see the sharpened peaks of the wooden stockade that must have originally run the whole way around. There was proof of at least one rightly-made house too – a big white mansion-sized one – and what looked to be a church-steeple tilting to the east, reaching for the civilization that had abandoned it.

The rest was an adobe abomination, rising at least three stories tall in the southeastern corner like a town-sized termite mound. Its clay fingers snaked all around and through even the wooden walls, as if the logs had to be cemented in place to keep from escaping.

But it was what couldn't be seen that choked the last of Elim's dwindling resolve. As he led his string onto the broad dirt path, he looked in vain for any sign of the farms and barns, the fences or road-markers or even the graves of those Brave settlers who had planted their fields and trees and outbuildings here in the time before. It was as if the earth had plain forgotten them, or resented the inquiry of strangers.

That was only proof of what Elim already knew: the outside world was vast, full of wildness and witchery and things that carried off calves in the night, and God promised no safety to anyone who strayed from the good and orderly home He had provided them.

Elim hardly needed the reminder.

Something rustled in the fields to his left. Elim's gaze darted back to the endless honeycombed corn-hills, their yellowed barren stalks crawled over by some kind of viney bean-plant, their roots wormed around by a thicket of broad spaded leaves. It would be terrifically, tremendously easy for any gun-toting Sundowner to lie hidden in all that mess and finish what the ferryman had started.

Up ahead, Sil was slowing. His posture was poor, leaning too far forward, and Elim wondered if he hadn't fallen asleep in the saddle.

He could do it now.

It might be his only chance.

But before Elim could make his mind about getting the rope, Sil turned in the saddle, revealing coon-ringed dark eyes and a face the color of curd cheese. "Well," he said wearily, "if you were still thinking of hauling me off my horse for a whipping, I'd say this is the place to do it."

They were separated by about fifteen feet, and the dull thumping of four dozen hooves.

"I'm not," Elim replied.

Sil's eyes narrowed, as if he expected to find a lie pimpling up on Elim's face. "And why is that?"

Because at the end of the day, that wasn't what he was after. Elim's gaze flicked from point to point, scouring the fields for a set of words that would get them out of this backwards foreign place and leave him free to eat his dinner and dry his clothes on friendlier ground.

"Sil, I don't aim to hide you," Elim said in his most feather-fine voice. "I just want to go home."

"You think I don't?" Sil snapped, with a peculiar edge to his voice. That was surprising: to hear Will tell it, Sil never had learned a liking for Hell's Acre.

Still, sometimes even a peevish horse would stand for you, if you just came at him the right way. "Sure you do," Elim said. "We both do. Look, Sil, I tell you what –"

Sil brought Actor to a sharp halt. "No, I'll tell YOU what," he said, pointing at the looming hive of heathenism just ahead. "That's Sixes, all right. I got us here, and I'm going to take these horses and sell them here, and you aren't smart enough or quick enough or mean enough to stop me doing it."

So much for a reasonable parley. Elim steeled his posture and waited for Sil to finish emptying his chambers.

"In fact, what you are is solid and reliable and a horseman to the manner born, all of which would come in profoundly useful for getting us in and back out of there at a profit. But I'm not having any of it – not if it means looking over my shoulder at every turn and wondering whether this is the moment you decide to haul off and belt me. So now that we ARE here, you can either help me finish the job, or you can turn around and go home empty-handed. But if you do, it will be YOUR fault that we didn't sell, because I've got my part of the bargain right here waiting for us. What's it going to be?"

Bushwhacked, Elim let his string come to a jumbled halt beside him. "Chew that finer," he said from behind his most careful poker face. "That last part."

Sil seemed to relish being asked. "I know how to sell them here," he said. "I know who to see for stabling, and where buyers congregate, and how to offer terms. So as of right now, the only thing between your boss and his money is you."

That wasn't true, of course – that wasn't right at all – and yet, like a calf in a snare, Elim's efforts to extricate himself from Sil's logic only wound it tighter around him, twisting the truth until everything hung around *his* neck. As if Sil's failure to make their first shot counted for nothing now that he had handed the gun off to Elim to try for their second. As if Elim's sensible insistence on turning home again had become an act of treason.

Nevermind all the weaseling words, though: this was Elim's chance, and he ought not let it rot on the vine.

Elim looked ahead, across the bridge, to the motley mess of old store-fronts and adobe dens within. It was quiet there during the heat of the day, but there was no telling what would come out when the sun had quit the horizon, or what kind of devils would propose to buy his tame and trusting novices – if they allotted on paying at all. In fact, the only ground firm enough to stand on was that Sil didn't know nearly as much as he thought he did.

Which meant the only thing to do was to turn the herd around, leaving Sil no sound reason for staying, and go straight on home again.

To come back five days late, with eleven surplus

horses still needing boarded and mangered and kept all through the winter at least.

To suggest to Boss that they plant some of Hattie's hundred silver dollars in the garden and see wouldn't they maybe sprout money enough to live on next year.

To offer around Dan and Daisy and all the rest like so much day-old bread, cheaper and cheaper still, until finally they were bought for nag prices by some bootless drunk sod-buster who wouldn't spend a broken nickel for their keep, but grind their lives away in merciless hard labor.

Elim pulled his hat off and scrubbed at his forehead, still squinting unfixed at the patchwork town beyond the gates.

You could pretty much say what you wanted about these part-timers out here – rape and pillage and demon-worship and all the rest – and Elim was liable to believe it. But there wasn't any getting around the fact that they did love their horses, all painting their faces and braiding their manes just-so. And if his choice was down to the sod-buster or the Sundowner...

"Hell," Elim swore as he replaced his hat and nudged Molly back to a walk, "I was tired of living anyway."

... they'd get used to being mounted from the wrong side eventually.

Sil didn't make any answer to that, which suited both their interests perfectly, but picked up Actor's pace to lead the way on ahead.

Elim hadn't gotten more than a hundred yards along when another rustling-sound gave his heart a skip. Startled, his attention jerked instantly down and left –

– where a heathen child, not more than five or six, crouched amidst the corn and stared up at him. There was no telling whether it was a boy or a girl. But its wide dark eyes and half-open mouth made an expression of awestruck dread that matched his own feeling perfectly.

With this much agreement between them, Elim touched his hat with his native hand and rode on, mashing his anxieties down to the bottom of his stomach as the pagan gates loomed larger and closer and finally swallowed him up entirely.

IT WAS A *fascinating* place, though.

Hot and headachey as he was, even Sil had to appreciate that much.

As the horse's plodding steps brought Sil further inside the city, he couldn't avoid the grand hotel that dominated the northern end of the island. It was a striking, handsome thing, all elegant white columns and black wrought-iron cresting, clean and stark and somehow immaculately preserved.

The ferryman had called it La Saciadería, a strange word assembled from familiar pieces. The best Ardish would probably be 'the Satisfactory', with a mercantile emphasis on 'factory'. Given how many appetites the place apparently serviced, that sounded about right.

La Saciadería had her opposite much further down the road, in the ingenious native pueblo rooted in the far end of the island. A full four stories tall at its peak, it spread its free-flowing adobe arms in an organic embrace, a living wall for the southern parts of the island.

As the ferryman had said, this was La Soleada, the Sunny Lady, and it wasn't hard to understand the name. She was home and mother to almost half the local population, who had somehow contrived to make that beige clay sparkle like gold in the searing light. The other tiny details that caught Sil's eye – the paintings, the splashes of color, the dark wooden lines of ladders and the exposed ends of ceiling-beams – testified to the perfect expertise of her architects.

Between these two towering great matrons, the rest of Sixes scattered out in a jumbled compromise of clay and wood and sometimes clay-covered wood, as if the owners wanted to show off their houses' exotic bones for envious neighbors.

Who, for their part, seemed to have retreated inside to wait out the heat of the day, leaving just a few dogs and free-roaming birds to keep the peace. Aside from some turkey-gabbling and the distant cries of an infant, the heavy air hung undisturbed. Sil would be pleased to keep it that way.

Once you have welcomed yourself to Island Town, continue on the Western Way to the crossroads. Put your back to the white evening-house and make your distance from it until you see an old house in front of a barn of two-floors standing. You may ask for Fours, if at first you miss your object, but there will not be many who would speak with you.

Happily, the ferryman's directions proved simple enough to follow, and Sil wasted no more time with gawking.

He downed the last of his water and dismounted to grateful approbation from his aching seat, then tied Actor's reins to the post in front of the makeshift storefront. "Round them in here, and then meet me inside," he said once Elim had come within easy speaking distance, nodding at the corral. "We're to see the owner, Fours, for stabling and supplies."

Elim swung himself down from his horse, and answered with a sullen grunt.

Well, let him: now that they'd come to an understanding, he was free to go play with tack and saddles to his country heart's content. And that would make him feel appreciably more settled and agreeable about things, wouldn't it?

More importantly, it left Sil free to get out of the sun, on to more important matters, and – finally! – down to business.

OR MAYBE 'BUSINESS' wasn't the proper term.

"Yes, certainly," the little white-haired Sundowner said, though he didn't seem terribly enthusiastic. "I can offer you nine bits on the dollar, which at a half-bit per horse per day – night, rather – and two bits for hay will make it ninety-four cents, fairly rounded, per night for... how long did you expect to stay?"

'Brazen money-changing racket' was more the mark: it was twelve bits to the dollar and fee for service, and that was that.

And when he finally made it home again, Sil would be sure to write a strongly-worded letter to the Bureau of Finance, asking that if switching to the pearl standard absolutely couldn't be countenanced, would they at least consider adulterating the currency with something less worthless than speculated tin. In the meantime, however...

"That will be fine," Sil said: if he was going to be pick-pocketed, he'd damn well hold his purse open and show that it was happening by his explicit allowance. "Let's have it just for the night, and see where we stand in the morning."

Fours looked up from the figures on his ledger, the upturned trapezoid lenses of his spectacles reflecting a dull glimmer in the afternoon's dirty light. "Not long, then?" he said in his soft tenor. "If you were here to find a buyer, I'd be pleased to take them off your hands. I'm sure they're very fine animals, and I can pay you in the dollar, of course..."

He was a musty old fellow in a musty old shop, and except for his dark skin, white teeth, and refreshing powers of articulation, he would not have looked out of place manning the post-office counter back in Hell's Acre.

You will do well to quarter with Fours, but do not give him your sale: he knows there are no other day-merchants who would trade with a stranger who has not received the Azahi's blessing, and will offer fast and inferior prices to those would quickly rid themselves of such goods as may have come into their possession.

Surely there was a Marín word for *fence*, but Sil would get by without it. He smiled. "That's very good of you, but I was thinking I'd take tonight to enjoy myself, and leave business for tomorrow. I'll just get our purse from my associate there," and he gestured at the little window to Fours' left, behind his make-do counter-top. The soiled muslin curtain was drawn across, allowing nothing more than shifting light and shadows, and the muffled churning of human voice and horse-noises as Elim did his work in the corral beyond. "Oh, and speaking of which – could we take liberties to have a quick wash-up here, and make it a dollar even for your trouble? Whatever you have will be fine." Sil accounted this for thrift and cleverness, though his principal object had far more to do with getting quit of this chit-chat and out of his sweat-chafed clothes.

Fours' gaze drifted to the grimy curtain-cloth and the shadow-play behind it. "Yes," he said, his mouth seeming to operate quite separately from the fixed object of his eyes. "There's a pump outside, just through the side here," and his hand made some feeble indication at the door across the room to his right, "and buckets and soap in with the tack."

Fantastic. "Right, thanks very much," Sil said, and started for the side door. "I'll just go and get your fee." And then, just as freedom was within his grasp:

"Yes," the old Sundowner said again, still fixated on the window, "but about your... associate –"

Oh, to hell with this. "Elim," Sil supplied, as fast and cheerfully as possible. "Dab hand, very tidy in his work – he'll see that they're settled in and have your supplies put straight back to rights, no trouble."

"Yes," said the man who had assumed sole responsibility for every continuing minute Sil spent with his generatives stuck to his inside leg. "Only I did mean to ask –"

Sil stopped. "He's a mule. That won't be a problem, will it?"

Fours did look at him then, with a suddenness just short of a flinch. "No, of course not – not here, I mean, as long as he stays here, he's very welcome –"

Boot-heels rapped against wood on the steps outside, interrupting the sunlight that leaked in under the door. As it opened, Sil had just time enough to open his mouth to ask what the dickens had taken him so long –

– before a stranger strode inside, a peculiar Sundowner dressed in dark range-wear with a golden pendant, a bone-colored hat, and a hard-set face custom-designed to squelch any lingering notion of his being Elim.

Sil gladly touched the brim of his own hat in gratitude for service rendered. "Glad to hear it," he said to Fours. "At any rate, I see you've other business to attend to. Feel free to speak with him if you need anything particularly, and I'll see to it he understands the arrangement."

Any objections Fours might have had were quashed by the door's closing as Sil let himself out.

ELIM DISLIKED THE quiet. He especially disliked Sil's easy know-it-all attitude, as if it wasn't possible that he could have been steered deliberately wrong.

But the horses seemed to care not a lick, and took their confinement as license to set up a caucus of ear-flicks, nickers, and jockeying hooves, all casting a unanimous vote for supper.

It would have to wait. "Nope," he said, keeping his voice low as he unbuckled Actor's cinch. "You got to wait. It – God damn it Ax, didn't he ever unshuck you?" Swearing freely as he felt the first of the telltale mats, Elim pulled off Actor's saddle and blanket, liberating a humid stink from the salt-crusted black hair. He was thanked with one hearty groan and a profuse manuring.

That would have to wait too. Stepping around the pile, Elim hauled the saddle up over his own back, latched the gate, and set Sil's seat down with a gentleness he would not afford its owner. He marched straight over to the front path, cleared the porch steps in a single stride, raised his brown fist with a quickness –

– and froze as the door surrendered before the first knock. Elim halted in mid-lunge, one foot still rooted on the bottom step, and stared up at the Sundowner looming down at him from the threshold.

Except, unfortunately, that he wasn't a Sundowner at all.

He was about the right size, sure, and certainly the right colors, in spite of his eastern ranch-hand's clothing... but as soon as Elim dropped his gaze under the stranger's glowering stare, he had to look straight back up again. There, spattered over his nose and under his eyes, were freckles too big and stark for any full-blooded Sundowner to grow. And there, curving bigger and starker still below the golden pendant at his neck and under the gun holstered at his hip, was a round, soft, and still more peculiar truth.

For the second time that day, Elim found himself staring at a lady unlike any he'd seen before.

And crossing paths with her here in the outlands was a cursing shame. Elim backed down the stairs and away to one side, busying himself with wiping the edge of one manure-flecked boot on the ground. This was merely minding the milk-pail after the spill, though – a fact the stranger drove home with every hard, successive rap of her boots down the steps.

As a rule, the only person who hated bastards more than a Sundowner was a Sundowner's bastard.

So Elim waited until the speckled mule had gone before trying his approach again.

Inside, everything was dim and cool, with an added measure of quiet. The smell of musty cloth and peculiar herbs met him at the door, and as his eyes adjusted, he found it wasn't a house at all.

A few dusty sacks and barrels lined the walls, while rickety-looking shelves on the far side of the room collected second-hand pots and bottles, and third- and maybe fourth-hand fabric hung folded from a laundry-line stretched between the ceiling's opposite corners. Elim stooped cautiously under these as he entered, hat in hand, in search of Sil.

It was old and cramped and small, this corn-maze of found objects. As it turned out, so was the proprietor.

He stood behind the bleached gray skirting of his crate-and-board counter, guarding a floor-to-ceiling collection of bottled powders and medicines and plant-parts behind him, and wrote busily in his ledger. "*Dos'angres,*" he said, after Elim's shifting weight pressed a particularly sharp squeak from the floorboards. "*¿Algomás nese...* ah." Having maybe put his most pressing thought to paper, he left off writing long enough to look up and discover his error.

He was hardly bigger than a minute, this one, and old enough to make change for a century, if you went by his odd-cropped white hair and bent posture. But his skin was as smooth as Elim's, albeit a good deal more regular in its coloring, and his clothes were as plain and old-fashioned as any respectable granddad would wear. The high waist of his corduroy pants looked to be conspiring with the down-drawn hunch of his shoulders to swallow up what little bit of a trunk he had left between them, with only an overlarge shirt and an old buckskin vest to keep him upright. His eyes widened behind the bent wire frames of his glasses as he spied his accidental visitor, and adjusted his gaze upwards.

"Well, I expect you'll be Elim, then." This was said in perfect Ardish, spoken in an uncommonly pleasant voice, and addressed to the blotch over Elim's eye.

Elim had gotten this kind of inspection before. "I expect so, yes," he said, turning his head to the left, presenting just the cleaner side of his face for the old Sundowner's use. He would not call him *sir*.

"Fine, fine," the shopkeeper – Fours? – said, and resumed his writing. "Well, you're welcome to use anything in the barn, and I can sell you grain if you need it. Your master's just gone for water at the pump, if you were looking for him."

Elim followed Fours' vague gesture towards what had probably been a kitchen door. "Thank you kindly," he said, maneuvering his way across the little room.

Fours stared blankly at his book, letting the ink from his pen drip onto the page. "Certainly," he said to the pooling blot. "And then... that is... I imagine you must be tired. You weren't thinking of going out again, were you?"

Elim stood there, hand on the knob, as the words percolated in his mind. Cold comprehension trickled down into his stomach, making bad alchemy with all of what he already had churning in there, as it became apparent that Fours was not going to look at him again, nor muster any explanation for the warning holstered in his words.

"He ain't none of my master," Elim said, and let himself out.

SIL HAD BEEN long overdue for a good, cold wash. Still, he was growing tired of the conversation that accompanied it. "And you propose we do what, exactly?"

"Wait," Elim said, from around the windward corner of the barn. "Wait until their big-chief comes back and gives you permission. That's all."

Sil, his bare flesh seated gingerly on the old milking-stool in the barn's lengthening shadow, set down the coarse yellow soap and swallowed another sigh. "The Azahi," he corrected him. Strictly speaking, it was a nationality and not a title, like saying *the Eadan* or *the Brave*. All the more reason to afford proper respect to whatever bearer had singlehandedly appropriated the name of his whole nation. "And weren't you the one so keen to go home? You realize we could still get back before anyone starts worrying if we sell them tonight."

There was a pause then, which Sil used to squeeze another rag's worth of water into his hair, and comb out the dirt with his fingers.

"All the same, I expect Boss would rather you go slow and do it right," came the wounded reply.

Ugh. Shivering as a delectable breeze cut through the wooden slats behind him, Sil stood and emptied the rest of the bucket over his back. *God* it felt good. "Elim, be serious. We have no way of knowing when the Azahi is coming back. We have no way of getting guest-protection without him, and none of the day-traders will do business with us without it. We don't even have the means to stock up and wait him out, considering our money is practically worthless here, and how long do you think we can live on Fours' hospitality?" Sil set down the bucket and slicked water off his skin with brisk, hard sweeps.

This was perhaps not the fullest expression of the truth: nine bits on the dollar wasn't nothing, and neither was the present size of their purse. Still, they could not afford to sit around and politely wait, for two days or twenty, for someone who could just as easily decide to throw them out by the ear. Especially not when La Saciadería apparently conducted all manner of business without oversight from daylight authorities. That was four-dollar information, and something that every trader and outlaw and left-over entrepreneur apparently relied on for any commodity more valuable than fleece and beans. "We can sell them tonight and be home in time for Sunday dinner, but only if we move quickly. We HAVE to."

There was another pause while Sil stepped into his drawers, but this one was deliberate – mulish, even. Sil knew it before he heard the first word.

"... sure. Ready when you are, boss."

All right, then they'd play that way. "Excellent; glad to hear it. I'll be back by morning with a buyer."

There was a sudden creak from the wall – no doubt Elim pushing himself sharply out of a lean – before he appeared at the corner, all force and frustration. "Dammit Sil, you know fine well that ain't what I meant!"

Sil paused in doing up his trousers, and chilled his voice as easily as breathing. "Well, then what did you mean?"

He'd have him – he'd have him by his own inarticulate bullheadedness, see if he didn't.

"I mean you can't go without me, that's what, and I will knock you into a cocked hat but I'll be damned if you're leaving me here." Elim stood sharp and still at his fullest exceptional height, the sun on his right side adding extra shadow-spots to his left, and the cords in his neck strained to match the stiffness of his open, rigid hands.

That wasn't quite what Sil expected, that edge in his voice. It trickled into Sil's mind like mucus down his throat, thickening and pooling into doubt. He forebore his readied reply, sniffed, and swallowed. "Why?"

That left Calvert's groom groping for an answer. Elim's brows furrowed; he whipped off his hat and scratched his cowlicks with a vengeance. "... you said you wanted my help. So I'm here to help, but here you are still playing the lone hand –"

"– and YOU agreed to let me be, and here you are still threatening to frail the tar out of me the minute you start getting your back up about something," Sil snapped, turning away in disgust, "so I expect that makes liars of us both."

There was no answer to that, not in all the time it took him to pull on his blue silk shirt, tie up the collar, tuck in the tail, and pull his braces on over his shoulders. This was the trouble with these barn-raised rustics: they were all right in their element, but you couldn't conduct a conversation, nevermind an argument, except by lurching starts and stops.

But this particular rustic was the only advantage Sil had here, and he already accounted himself an idiot for mishandling him. He'd been so sure he had Elim well in order, and for him to start acting like a fretful child who refused to be left with the neighbors was as unexpected as it was irritating.

So he picked up his old charcoal waistcoat and shrugged it on along with a more even-handed air.

"Anyway, that's precisely why I need you here," he said in between button-holes. "I'm counting on you to get them presentable for sale, and who else can I trust to keep an eye on things while I'm gone?" Sil put his back to the wall, fished one ripe sock out of his boot, and pulled it on with the barest of grimaces. It was a wretched feeling, having to swaddle a clean body with dirty clothes.

When Sil had finished with its mate and still received no answer, he looked over. "Well?"

Elim had his back to him, as if he'd turned to leave and then thought better of it. He might have been staring at the hat in his hands. "Sil," he said at last, "I ain't supposed to be here. I ain't... it ain't right for me to be here."

Sil sighed. Of course – he should have thought as much, especially after Elim had avoided the ferry. The poor fool had spent his whole life keeping to his place, and here Sil had shoved him bodily out of it.

"I know the feeling," he said, not unkindly. "It isn't nice to be where you aren't wanted." He knew that better than Elim ever would. Even in Hell's Acre, even where he and his siblings lived and used their talents openly, they were never anything but well-tolerated others. Nevermind this odd handful of days here – let Elim spend years as an immigrant without parole, and he'd trample over anyone for the chance to get home again.

Still, Sil would do well to mind his own tread. "You see, though, you'll be all right here: Fours is friendly enough, and you don't have to..."

He was left to watch, dumbstruck, as Elim walked away.

Sil started immediately after him, a blistering oath on his lips as he jammed his stocking-foot halfway into the boot and hobbled inside. Elim had pitched himself into the straw next to their collected pile of gear, and was busily rooting through Sil's bag.

"Elim, what the deuce –"

"I lied," Elim grunted around something between his teeth. "I AN tellin' you wha' to do." He'd pulled out

77

Calvert's market papers and a sachet of powder, and clamped between his knees was Will's old flintlock pistol, which Sil had not been allowed to leave home without.

Sil's itching eyes widened on sight of the gun. He stared in plain amazement as Elim tore a corner from the paper packet, spat the musket-ball into his hand, and wrapped one over the other as deftly as if he were rolling a ball of dough.

He'd cracked. Sil backed up one nervous, half-shod step. "Now, Elim, wait a minute, will you..."

"Hell no I won't," Elim replied, leaning to the side as he dug something else out of his pocket – a hoof pick, maybe? – and used it to ram the bullet down the barrel with three sharp strikes from the heel of his hand.

By the Sibyl, he really might do it.

"Elim –" Sil said, angrily this time, but the sight of Elim heaving himself to his feet with the loaded gun in hand unnerved him into another backward step. Sil tripped over the heel of his odd boot to land gracelessly on his backside, coughing in the dust.

He stared up from an awkward sprawl as Elim cocked the hammer. Calvert's mule stepped forward, looming monstrously large.

Then he reached down to grab Sil's wrist and hauled him effortlessly up to his feet. "Now you take your old thumb-buster and keep it where folks can see," he said, "and don't give it up for nobody or nothing. I left it half-cocked, see, so you don't blow your own foot off, and – boy, are you listening?"

Sil, watched as the gun was shoved into the waistband of his trousers. He looked stupidly up, sniffed, and swallowed. "Yes?"

Elim grunted at that. "Be a first for you. And you get yourself back by moonrise, sale or no sale."

But this last was reminiscent of some infantile bedtime curfew, and that – as his heel finally found its way home with a soft, sucking *thuck* – was enough to shake Sil out of his harelike freeze. He narrowed his eyes and glowered right back up at Elim. "Or else what?"

Elim matched him, stare for stare. "Or else I won't never again have any truck with you, Sil Halfwick – not for all the gold in Galatene."

And that would be anything but a boon because...?

When it became apparent that Elim had nothing to add and no intention of backing down, Sil withdrew with an acid sneer. "I wouldn't pay a shaved nickel for the privilege," he snarled, turning to remove himself from Elim's fetid presence and the filthy afflicting air of the barn.

He hadn't gone but five paces when the reply caught up with him. "And see you're back timely, now." This in a nagging, almost nervous tone.

Sil kept right on walking, out of the barn and on towards town without a second's more pause than needed to grab his hat and jacket on the way. "And see you mind your own good god-damned business," he said, though probably not loudly enough. As if he cared whether Elim heard him or not.

As if there were anything Elim could do to him now.

ELIM STOOD STILL after Sil left, trying to shake the anger that clung to his back like a starving cougar on the kill.

When they got home, he was going right to Boss and telling him: never again with Sil, not with so much as a cracked bucket and a penny for the tinker. Nothing was worth the risk or the hassle.

Still, this was what was happening now, and Elim had handled it poorly. He hadn't meant to, but poorly all the same.

And the new now, in the sun-slatted dimness of someone else's barn, with the dust from Sil's exit still settling around him, left him with little remedy for any of the old now's misjudgments. There was no fixing his failure to catch Sil when he might still have been catchable, or his no-questions-asked submission to that bully-logic at the gate, or his neglect in assuming that Sil just meant for them to stay put and partnered, like at the fair. Those chances were all gone now: he had squandered every one.

Which left Elim with nothing but a painful mind and the same heap of chores that always needed doing, regardless of how he might currently feel about doing them. Presently, he roused himself to fetch the pail that Sil had left behind.

He shouldn't have let himself get left likewise.

He should have made a better answer, when Sil asked why.

But Sil hadn't been taken aim at today. He hadn't heard what the strange lady said about staying after dark, or heard Fours hinting at the same, or seen the way that speckled mule glared him down on the steps. He said he understood – he probably reckoned that he did – but he didn't have any feeling for how it might be possible for not just a horse or a dog but a whole entire *place* to flatten its ears and bare its teeth and give you a bristling full-body promise of what it intended if you didn't take the hint and remove yourself with a quickness.

And if Sil was genuinely ignorant of how dangerous it was for him to walk alone into a den of brown thieves, he certainly couldn't understand how Elim's life diminished in value when not visibly employed by a white man. There was an ugliness in the world, one that reached occasionally even to Hell's Acre, and it wasn't only calves that went missing in the night.

Elim could not now recollect what he'd been about to go do. But the oiled wood of his rifle comforted his hands as he squinted out to watch the street in the afternoon's last reddening light.

He wouldn't go missing. And if it came down to it, he wouldn't miss.

CHAPTER FOUR
MANNERS

NONE OF IT would matter by this time tomorrow. Sil cooled his temper by reminding himself of that. All they had to do was grit teeth and stand each other long enough to get this done, and then it would be home and business as usual for Elim, and something actually *new* for Sil.

No more holing up in his sweaty broom-closet of a room, no more peddling two-penny nails to squinting inbred imbeciles, no more asinine small-talk about whether it did or didn't look like sodding rain. After this, there would be plans to make, letters to write, and a ticket to buy.

The very thought of it tempted him to quicken his pace, but he measured his steps in accordance with the ferryman's prescription.

Don't arrive until after sunset. Speak first in Ardish; identify yourself as a guest. Appear pleasant, well-doing, and grateful for whatever enjoyments are offered to you.

The road to La Saciadería was – had been – flanked on either side by a pair of grand covered walkways.

These two promenades must have been fine in their day, fronting nearly a quarter mile's worth of shops and storefronts with raised wooden sidewalks and matching roofs, simultaneously keeping smart boot-heels out of the muck and genteel heads out of the sun. What little of the western promenade remained was falling to pieces.

Which made it a perfect place to conclude the business that Elim's mulery had so sharply interrupted. Sil sat down between two of the beams supporting what was left of the roof, and withdrew a repurposed tobacco tin from the lining of his jacket. A daub of masking-paste to correct the shadows under his eyes, first of all. Then a shaving of licorice-root to sweeten his breath, and the blade of his pocket-knife to neaten his fingernails. He put his fingers through his hair to quicken its drying, rose to pat his pockets for his drugs and handkerchief and a few silver dollars – and stopped as his first idle glance behind the promenade arrested his attention.

The northwestern quarter of Sixes lay in ruins. A garden of weed-sprouted rubble and twisting rust-sculptures overran the stumps of buildings rooted in the ground like so many broken teeth. In the center of it all, the church presided in stately grandeur over the graves of its neighbors. One wing had collapsed, leaving the tilting steeple to cast a shadow like the hand of a stopped clock. Here at sunset, it seemed to direct visitors back to the east.

Well, it was a shame about the fire, but Sil had no intention of taking the hint – not yet, anyway.

Instead, he returned to the main thoroughfare and rationed his steps until the earth had swallowed the sun's last red edge, leaving just its afterglow to warm the western horizon. Rustics referred to this time of day as 'candle-light', and it was at this time exactly that Sil removed his hat and tapped politely at the hotel's black painted door.

It was a beastly feeling, butterflies in the stomach.

A slot in the door slid back, just below Sil's eye level. "*Kién es?*" a pretty voice sang out.

"A guest," Sil amiably replied.

The door was opened, presumably by the winsome little thing hiding behind it. Her face and one bare shoulder peeped out, fawn-colored and fetching, and her scandalously loose hair shone like black silk in the lamplight. Sil's gaze was immediately drawn to the three tiny, shiny amethyst stones affixed in an arc over her right eye, and to the smile that welcomed him with impish delight.

"Good evening, our guest!" she proclaimed, her accent likewise melodic, and beckoned him inside. "Come in, come in, do come in – and how shall we call you?"

This was not what Sil expected, although it didn't disagree with him in the slightest. "Halfwick – at your service, miss," he replied as she closed the door behind him. Her dress had to be new for that watered-silk violet to shine as it did, but it was clearly patterned after something his mother might have worn in her maiden days. Middle-waisted and close-fitting, with little hint of any feminine cagery underneath, it offered free assessment of her upper arms and delicate collar-bones to any passer-by. The little spangles on her matching house-slippers winked merrily at him as she turned to secure his attentions.

"Oh, how handsome a name," she declared. "You will have come to us from a great far ways! May I take your traveling things before we go inside?"

"Yes, thank you," Sil said, and handed her his hat. That was a bit of a risk – there was no telling whether pedigrees were mistrusted here too, or how readily he'd be believed if he claimed to have gotten his blond locks from a bottle. Still, his hostess did not seem nearly so interested in his hair as she was in... well, what exactly?

There was an uncomfortable moment of silence. Then her gaze dropped briefly down to his side.

Ah.

"Terribly sorry," Sil muttered as he surrendered the pistol. "I forgot all about it." Leave it to Elim to make things awkward even in his absence.

But she only smiled, and produced a little set of keys from her side-pocket. "So will I," she promised, setting the useless rusty thing with great reverence inside the bootlocker near the door. Before Sil could decide what that was meant to assure him of, the old gun was happily out of reach and out of mind.

"Now come along," she enthused as her clammy fingers closed over his wrist, and drew him down the hall in a nose-itching cloud of perfume. "Brant!" she called to the man at the parlor door. "A drink for Master Halfwick!"

Sil's heart skipped, then fairly swelled with pride.

But if the lady was a mild surprise, the gentleman was nothing short of an astonishment. Here was a real prairie gentleman, young and amiable and masterfully built, with just a little too much brandy in his champagne-blond hair to suspect a perfect pedigree. Otherwise he was immaculate, with a fine silk shirt, an old-fashioned diamond waistcoat, and a million-dollar smile. "Of course," he said, walking Sil inside. "House special suit you?"

Sil shut his mouth and smiled. "Right down to the ground."

And the house *was* special. Sil was led through a positively splendid parlor, replete with plush jewel-tone rugs, overstuffed furniture, and cabinets laden with fine blue china and crystal glasses, the likes of which had never, ever been seen in Hell's Acre except in the pages of catalogs blithely appropriated for bogshed paper. They were older things, of course, some visibly patched and repaired, and all at least twenty years out of fashion. Yet this threadbare luxury reminded him of his own home, his *real* home, and Sil was perfectly, comfortably at ease.

When you are made welcome, look next for Way-Waiting. You will know him by his eastern clothing, and by the blue-green shawl at his shoulders, and by the abalone comb in his hair. He will be seen at billiards, or at one of the dice-throwing tables, and is known to everyone you will find there.

There was no sign of Way-Waiting, but Sil felt himself distinctly unbothered. He followed his host past the upright piano and the rich red billiards-table and the twin curving staircases to a grand polished cherrywood bar, where two well-heeled Sundowners were already at their drinks. He could not interpret their costumes any better than he had with the ferryman, but their bright colors and bejeweled features suggested that these were young men of high estate, and company worth his keeping.

Brant poured a dram of some dark liquor and set it before him. "See how that likes you," he said with a smile.

Sil accepted the shot and raised it at his genteel host.

His experience with liquid hospitality was limited, but one would have to be a tremendous idiot to refuse a drink out here. Sil was not that idiot. He tossed it back in one tepid swallow. "Thank –"

Then it kicked, searing his insides from throat to stomach and leaving him coughing hard enough to bring tears to his eyes.

"Want another one?" Brant said, his cheeks just slightly ruddier beneath the short trim of his beard.

"I haven't half done with my first, yet!" Sil finally choked out, and hoped that this bit of cleverness might excuse him from having a second. He wished he'd been clever enough to eat something beforehand.

"Brant!" the lady in violet sang out again. "*An-cuarto par Sansor Caracola!*"

Sil knew he was off the hook when Brant set down the decanter. "That's a regular, in for supper I expect," he said, his tone graciously insinuating disappointment at having been called away. "You'll excuse me, gentlemen."

Actually, what the lady had called for was *an-cuarto*, a room... but that was all right. "Of course – much obliged," Sil replied.

"Bye!" one of the two Sundowners chimed in, raising his glass over his shoulder in salute to Brant's diminishing back.

And that left just the three of them there together.

If Way-Waiting does not first appear, make it your object to drink, and to spend yourself freely at the games. Accept no invitations from the women – they have one purpose only – but be seen to have no great concern for your time or money. A true left-over goes to enjoy himself: make pleasure your first purpose, and business will surely follow.

They were a brightly-dressed young pair, as matched and distinctive as a pair of salt and pepper shakers. The drinker, plainly delighted with himself and his evening, turned from toasting their departing host to lean back, letting his slender frame rest by his elbows and the small of his back against the bar. His long black hair draped in lazy arcs over the wood. He had the high cheekbones and aquiline nose common to his race, and complemented his exceptionally dark skin with a bright yellow knee-length shirt, its green-beaded trimmings identical to the ones on his leather ankle-wraps. They made a sharp contrast as he crossed his otherwise-bare legs, one copper-belled sandal over the other, and leaned forward to smile at Sil from around his companion's back. "Hallo!"

This seemed to irritate his more sober associate. No drink was to be seen in front of him as he leaned over his thick folded arms, nor any hint of his friend's easy manner. Stronger in his features as well as his build, with deep-set dark eyes and a solid, tensing jaw, he wore a muddy red shirt, some manner of deerskin trousers or leggings, and fine silver ornaments at his neck and ear. The moccasin-boot he kept cocked on the bar's lustrous foot-rail revealed the wrapped handle of a knife, and the up-and-down glance he gave Sil seemed to assess the likelihood of his needing it.

Sil took prompt advantage of the warmer of his two welcomes. "Good evening," he said to the merrier man, with a more modest reflection of his smile. "I hope I'm not interrupting your conversation. May I join you?"

This was met with equal parts enthusiasm and incomprehension.

"Choin-yu," the drinker agreed, and elbowed his friend. "*Nankah! U ege, ke?*"

That was not Marín. The sober man shot his companion an irritated glance. "Could evening," he said, as if surrendering to an unpleasant necessity. "Vuchak," – this with a downward nod, and then with a jerk of his head – "Weisei."

"Hallo!" Weisei said again, just as cheerily as before.

"We are for the a'Krah," Vuchak continued. It was a short, harsh word, the first syllable a quickly-dispensed prelude to the second, whose rolled 'r' cut the air like a serrated knife through cold bread. "Ferry nice we me-chew."

By now Sil's mistake was abundantly clear to him; their nation was less so. "Halfwick," he said for simplicity's sake, "and the pleasure is mine. *¿Marín habla?*"

His ego swelled at Weisei's instant delight. "*Of course we do!*" he replied, as if this were the silliest thing to ask. "*Are you very good at it?*"

Sil smiled, and tipped his hand 'so-so'. "*I like to think so, but I hope you will tell me if I make a mistake.*" This was brazenly false modesty: in Marín, there was no surer way to separate the men from the boys than proper use of the subjunctive.

Vuchak's expression hovered between suspicion and boredom, but Weisei fairly beamed. "*No, that is very fine indeed! Who taught you?*"

"*I learned from a friend of mine, who belongs to the Ikwei. I –*"

Vuchak snorted. "*Of course he does. Did he 'make friends' with your mother too?*"

"*Vichi!*" Weisei scolded with a sharp poke of his elbow. Vuchak took no visible notice, but kept his gaze locked on Sil.

"*My mother is dead,*" Sil said with perfect aplomb.

"*But now that you say so...*" – and he used the pause to let growing incredulity bloom on his face – "*... great heavens, why was my sister always leaving his house?*"

This was met with about four seconds of blank staring, Weisei glancing apprehensively between them all the while.

Then Vuchak erupted in a sharp, barking laugh. "*Right. You we can drink with – but not this.*" He pushed himself back from the bar, jerking his head towards a nearby set of chairs. "*Sit there. Weisei, leave that. Our apologies, Halfwick of the Ikwei: I am sure your first taste reminded you pleasantly of mothers' milk, but we our cups así no llenamos.*"

Sil lost translation there at the end, as the first sight of Vuchak's wrists arrested his attention. Wrapped around them, mirror-bright and utterly unmissable, were a pair of thick silver cuffs – not loose, not hooped or dangling, but clasped as tightly to his flesh as would be expected from a native god's royal son, who relied on silver to keep his human shape after dark.

Suddenly, finding Way-Waiting didn't seem half so important.

So with a silent apology to Easy-Hey and Nillie, Sil picked up his glass and followed his new acquaintances to a low occasional table.

He took a seat in a magnificent oak chair with a plush wine-colored seat, as the two Sundowners – more specifically, a'Krah – paired themselves on a couch opposite. Weisei sank right in, arms and legs draping over the furniture with all the ease of a house regular. Vuchak sat perched on the edge, leaning forward with his forearms folded over his knees, as if he were orchestrating an interrogation or a conspiracy.

"*So,*" he said, "*who do you want?*"

Who... he had said *who* and not *what*, hadn't he? Sil crafted his answer to suit both purposes. "*Anybody who can show me a good time,*" he said, with only as much of a smile as would confirm this as a conscious bit of foolishness, and scratched absently at his wrist.

This time, it was Weisei who laughed right aloud. "*You're funny, Afvik! He means, are you bringing your business for the king or the queen? Or both?*" He twisted to flag down another one of the house ladies – a plumpish strawberry blonde frocked in pink.

That helped not at all. Sil's gaze flicked involuntarily to Vuchak's cuffs, which revealed no hints about whether his divinity came from his father or mother's side, much less whether a word like *king* would ever be used to describe one's own patron-deity. "I'm sorry," he admitted at last. "I don't – er, *I don't understand.*"

More people were trickling in, and Sil was glad to be seen already engaged in conversation. The pink lady approached, seeming happy enough to return Weisei's broad, flirtatious smile, and to understand the bottle-shape and the 'three' he mimed with his hands. Vuchak sighed. "*The owners of the house. You should start first with her, whom you must call 'Miss Addie'. She will provide you with a suitable one-night wife, and then –*"

Sil cut him short with a shake of his head, which also served as refusal for the girl's inquisitive glance. "*Thank you very much, but I am not here for her.*"

"*Mm.*" Vuchak did not rush to elaborate on the alternative, but glowered up at Sil from beneath his heavy brow, his stare openly challenging. "*Well, any idiot can see you don't know what you're doing, so do you have a reason for putting yourself here, or did you just come to make more 'friends'?"*

Weisei, seeming mildly shocked at his companions' failure to appreciate the lady's presence, recovered enough to smile at her and confirm 'just the drinks' with a thumbs-up gesture. She had hardly even turned to go before he checked and re-checked his gaze between her retreating back and Sil's indifferent front, apparently astonished that the two lovers had failed to hit it off in spite of their matching hair colors.

Sil was more concerned about the demise of his first tentative rapport with these strange gentlemen... and then caught himself scratching with unseemly vigor at his wrist. He glanced down in noxious surprise to find a rash of hives erupting where the door-woman had touched him.

Good God. Whatever blistering poxes she reserved for paying customers didn't bear thinking about.

Nevermind, though – he had customers of his own to consider, and pulled down the cuff of his sleeve. *"I'm sorry,"* he said again. *"I don't mean to be rude. The truth is –"* and he leaned forward, lowering his voice just enough to put an audible premium on his words *"– I have horses to sell. I heard that there was a gentleman here who would buy from me, but I don't know... what is the proper way to meet him."*

The eyes of the a'Krah lit up at the mention of horses. Vuchak tried to hide it, nodding in reserved contemplation, but Weisei clapped his hands to his knees in thunderstruck enthusiasm.

"Afvik," he said with a tipsy bright smile, *"do you like to play games?"*

* * *

SO ELIM, WHOSE new decisions had all come out wrong, went back to making some more usual ones instead.

He started by acquainting himself with the barn's native residents: a pair of mules, of the four-legged varietal, in the two stalls nearest the door. Then he set to work getting his regiment ready for their own quarters, hoof-picking and hide-currying and brushing them all over. This was basic sensible care, but also an exercise to see that everyone remembered their handling-manners, and would tolerate human fingers at their mouths and down their legs and under their tails with all the grace and comportment he expected of them.

Even if they ended up being browner hands than Elim had originally planned for.

One of the stalls was broken, and another was missing its latch, but Two-Pie was an inveterate escape artist anyhow. So Elim tied his door shut, put Shy Violet in the stall nearest the mules, and by the time he had situated everybody else and doled out their suppers, it was full dark. He avoided thinking too much about that by lighting the betty-lamps, fixing his supper, and then sitting down with a rag and neatsfoot oil to clean his saddle free of whatever residual mischief the river might have left in it. Doing likewise for his rifle ate up the rest of the hour, as it was a tricky job in dim light, and of course you didn't want to get any of your gun-parts too close to a fire.

But even after that, even after he had loaded his rifle and snuffed out the lamps and holed himself up in the hayloft to watch the moon rise, there was no getting to sleep. The moon climbed and little fire-lights burned more brightly, not only inside the adobe houses and the back of the eastern promenade, but on top of them as well. Brightest of all were the red and yellow lights of the boarding-house at the end of the road.

Sil would be there; Elim would have guessed it even if he hadn't been told. Whether Sil would come back, on the other hand...

He would, though. There were a dozen reasons why he hadn't yet, spite ranking chiefly among them. That alone was reason enough for Elim not to overly bother himself about it, and to trust that Sil would be back by morning.

Only you couldn't always trust about things like that. Or rather, you *could*, just like you could maybe trust that that fence had weathered the storm, even if you were too busy on that particular day to run the whole round checking it. And then when Sue-Fly didn't turn up with the rest of them... well, sure. *Then* you had plenty of time to ride out and discover that the fence had taken just enough of a knocking for that little filly to get her head caught between the broken planks, slip her footing in the mud, and strangle.

That was a misjudgment Elim meant not to make twice in his lifetime.

On the other hand, that was no friendly pasture out there. That was enemy ground, and it might be swarmed over by ordinary part-timers in daylight, but at night the world belonged to heathen gods, monstrous and terrible and so much older than the tiny walled-up spots of light that people called civilization. Without even one silver bullet to his name, Elim would be easy pickings for any of them. They *hated* trespassers, and bastards especially, and the surest way to see that he lived through the night was to stay holed up like a wintering field-mouse until morning.

Elim leaned forward and drew his knees up, threading his fingers through his hair, and immersed himself in the smell of wood and straw and his own dirty clothes.

He liked hay lofts, generally. They were high and safe and shut-in, and there was none better than the one at home. He'd been used to play in it with Merry and Clem on rainy days. It remained his favorite spot even later, when the girls had grown out of that and he'd played just with Yellow Kelly, the barn cat. At some point, he'd left off playing altogether.

But that was all right. He'd grown up, that was all, and although it hadn't left him much time for play, it meant that he could handle harder things. In his braver moments, he thought he could even face whatever native gods or animal-men or nameless night-striding demons might be waiting for him out there.

Couldn't face Will Halfwick.

That went double for Nillie.

Elim climbed down from the loft.

"*TAKE THAT!*" THE exultant cry rang through the room.

"*Idiot, will you sit down?*"

This Weisei did, but not without taking hold of Sil's sleeve, presumably to call his attention to the board. "*See, and now his is mine,*" he said, exchanging the two tokens with great ceremony.

"*I do see, yes,*" Sil agreed, gingerly extricating his arm with a nod to the gentlemen seated on the floor opposite.

The greater of the two, in both size and rank, was Huitsak, the masterfully obese 'king' of the house. Fairly dripping with bits of silver jewelry and a calculating kind of mirth, he swathed his great gravitas with a topaz-colored shirt and leggings, and a ruff of black feathers that put Sil in mind of a decidedly merry vulture.

But it was his companion who looked as if he were waiting for something to die. Middle-aged, muscular and grim, ornamented only by an intricately beaded bandolier, Aibak had temporarily surrendered his seat to Vuchak, and supervised the game in hawkish silence.

They were apparently regulars at the game, these a'Krah, and made a habit of playing here in the third-floor gaming-room. They did not seem to care much for trading outright for the horses, except for Vuchak, who did not seem to care much for inviting Sil to gamble with them instead.

Yet there he was, nestled soundly in a den full of Sundowners who evidently enjoyed his company – or perhaps just the prospect of fleecing him for his goods – enough to invite him up to the executive game.

"*Draw,*" Huitsak said to the blindfolded dealer at the end of the board. This nameless, unspeaking fellow performed his office with grave ceremony, pulling two cards from the deck as solemnly as a jury foreman reading a verdict. His undyed linen shirt and the plain leather thong used to tie his hair back suggested a lowly station in life.

"*Queen and five – but I will have you yet, Master Halfwick!*"

Sil returned Huitsak's dimpled smile and held out his hands – the right offering his token from the board, the left open in anticipation of return – to complete the exchange. Although Sil suspected that the name might be a corruption of 'baccarat', *vakat* could best be called a strange barter-economy version of faro, complete with ornate faro board and case counter. Here, though, the players each 'owned' three of the thirteen cards pasted to the board. Sil, in the 'southern' quarter, had been assigned the four, five, and six, and laid a token of value on each. At first he had expected these to be wagers, won or lost according to the turn of the cards. But the a'Krah seemed not to believe in getting something for nothing: they played their trading-game with all cards occupied but one, and let the cards dictate the exchange of valuables. In theory, then, one could never completely lose one's shirt.

In practice, however, Sil had just traded his shirt for six ounces of silver.

"*I am always very good with trifles,*" he demurred, "*but when the stakes are high, you will have me by the neck.*"

Huitsak tipped his head left and right with a gracious smile. "*Well, the truth is in the teeth.*"

It was a saying that had its Ardish equal in proofs and puddings, and wisdom which Sil acknowledged with a dip of his head as the next set was drawn.

"*Bastard!*"

"*Seven and nine – give it up, Weisei.*"

Sil hadn't worked out whether Weisei was some sort of companion-lackey or merely an idiot cousin. Regardless, his fortunes were swiftly sinking to match his social station: the dealer took Weisei's ring token and withdrew it to the unlucky, unoccupied seven at the end of the board.

A reminder, just in case Sil needed one, that he'd be well served to play with trifles here, and take his real business downstairs later.

Two more cards were drawn, and it was a 'dog-swap', prompting Vuchak to trade two of his own stakes. That left just the last three cards in the deck.

"*Last chance, friends,*" Huitsak said with a glance at the case counter. "*Two, seven and nine.*"

In faro, the player who bet on and successfully guessed the order of the last three cards would win four times his original stake. "*What is the prize?*" Sil whispered to Vuchak.

Vuchak pointed to the ring, which Weisei had lost to the dealer. "*It is your last chance to win it back from him.*"

Well, all right. Sil ventured his guess, and used the time afterwards to plan a polite exit. Under the circumstances, it shouldn't appear terribly rude to excuse himself from –

"*Ohei!*"

Sil looked up in time to see Weisei clap his hands contemptuously before the dealer's face.

"*Have that, you eyeless miser – he's finished you!*"

Vuchak reached over the board and presented Sil with the ring representing Weisei's high stake: the beautiful copper *concho* belt he wore at his waist. It was easily worth six dollars.

Still, Sil had a notion that the friendship of the a'Krah would be worth considerably more. "*Here,*" he said, handing the token back to Weisei with a half smile. "*I already have one at home.*"

Weisei dumbly accepted the token, his alcohol-soaked faculties struggling to process the gift in conjunction with the joke. Sil had just time enough to see the spark of comprehension before he was all but grappled to the floor by a sudden paroxysm of gratitude.

"*Thank you, Afvik! Blessings on your parents!*" Weisei hugged him sideways, his fine black hair spilling all down Sil's back. He smelled of cherry wine and an exotic natural odor that Sil hadn't known before. It made an oddly pleasant combination.

Across from him, Vuchak scowled. "*Idiot, will you let go of him? He will follow you to the end of the world now, Halfwick; there is nothing you can do about it.*"

"*I would be honored,*" Sil replied – because really, wasn't this a marvel? Here were people who an hour ago hadn't known him from a beggar, and now seemed inclined to regard him as a worthy guest and, in one case at least, a fast friend. And all of it was Sil's own doing.

When Weisei had disengaged himself, Sil gathered his tokens from the board, and handed them back to Huitsak. "*Thank you for my stakes,*" he said. "*I would like to keep my shirt, if I may.*"

Huitsak seemed taken aback at this, and the smile fell from his face. "*But they are yours – you won them fairly.*"

This was true, but he had not come to the table as an equal player: without laying the horses on the table, Sil had not been able to put up an equal wager. And, since he was about to excuse himself from the game altogether –

Then Huitsak smiled again. "*Ah. Now you are ready to try your own stakes: you will not have yourself indebted to mine. I do understand. Now, as for your horses –*"

He was interrupted by a knock at the door. "Welcome," Huitsak called.

The door opened, and at the threshold stood the

oddest young dandy Sil had ever seen. He was meant to be of good breeding – that much was evident from his smooth white skin and waxed golden fore-curls – and he looked not dramatically older than Sil. But Sil would not have been allowed at the dinner table, nevermind out of doors, in anything like that getup.

One could excuse the black frock-coat, as it had probably still been acceptable evening-wear when time stopped here. But he'd stuffed his black evening-trousers into his boots as if they were riding-breeches, tied a bottle-green ascot *on top of* the cascading white ruffles of his cravat, and arranged the provocative double-pointed cut of his emerald waistcoat to show off the golden buttons that secured his braces to his trousers, as if these custom-embellishments were not underwear but trophies to be exhibited before envious admirers. One would honestly wonder less at seeing a woman hike up her skirts to flaunt her crinoline, and Sil was helpless not to stare.

Yet this sort of attention seemed to be received as the greatest compliment. With a smile of perfect self-assurance, the dandy slipped his hands in his pockets and leaned his slight figure casually against the doorframe.

"Good evening, friends," he said, speaking exceptionally fine Ardish with an exceptionally fine voice. "How does luck find you tonight?"

"Very well, thank you," Huitsak replied in an equally correct, though somewhat less enchanted fashion. "And you?"

"*Fest*," Weisei muttered into his cup. "*Faro again*."

"*You play faro as well?*" Sil replied in the same undertone. Weisei flicked his hand out in a subtle "no" gesture. Across from Sil, Vuchak paid full outward attention to the visitor while almost absentmindedly tapping the jack of spades on the board.

"Delightful, as always – or delight*ed*, rather," he said, his dark eyes fixing on Sil. "How kind of you to entertain our new guest, friends – really splendid. Might I likewise impose myself upon you?"

Huitsak and Aibak exchanged glances, and though the former never lost his smile, it now belonged to a man who had just swallowed a fly.

"Certainly, yes," Huitsak replied, simultaneously inviting the dandy and evicting Weisei with one expansive sweep of his flesh-winged fat arm. "You see that we always have room for more. Have you brought any stakes?"

"Oh, something of the sort." The fellow produced an antique silver snap-case, such as one might employ to keep one's finer cigars. Sil half expected that to be his principal offering, but all expectation crumbled as the dandy opened the case to present a multicolored array of gleaming, lustrous fine pearls.

The mother Sil had so casually mentioned to Vuchak had lived in a house of eighteen rooms, supervised a staff of sixteen to twenty, and brought to her marriage a three-hundred-acre estate... and yet she owned just one genuine white-pearl necklace. They would have buried her with it, if it hadn't been auctioned to pay the debt.

And here, now, her last-born accident of a son might very well end the night owning more than she ever had. These were jewels of every size and color – large and small, round and irregular, black and pink and blue and cream – and therein lay all the beauty of that rarest saltwater currency. There was no shaving or counterfeiting that kind of money, no tiresome scratchings or weighings needed to assure the purity of that sort of wealth, and no inflation or devaluation when Nature Herself was the master of the mint.

It felt almost a sacrilege to leave off their admiration long enough to wonder how this over-dressed oddity had accumulated them.

"... yes, that will do," Huitsak said, making a peculiar sign with his hand.

"*I cannot play,*" Vuchak said, breaking the reverential air with a tone bordering on upset, and roughly indicated Weisei. "*Him either.*"

Huitsak blinked, scowled. "*Then get out, why don't you? Make room!*"

Then he turned back to the dandy at the door, all hospitality and conciliation. "Yes, that will be fine. We two can match your stakes, and our new guest has fine horses to wager. Come, sit – we will have four to play."

"Splendid – really first rate," the stranger said. He slipped gracefully inside, set the little case down next to the blindfolded dealer, and then stood apart in deference to the still-occupied places at the board. "I will be honored to join your game, Master Huitsak."

Vuchak stood. "*Come on, Weisei,*" he said, pulling him to his feet. "*Let's go eat.*"

Weisei lit up at the idea. "*Hey, Afvik! Come and...*" He paused, and belatedly counted four at the board. "*... oh. But –*"

"*Come on, idiot,*" Vuchak repeated, and left the room, pulling his bewildered fellow along behind him.

Sil had been about to say something – *do* something – important, he was sure. A great part of him longed to follow the two junior a'Krah down to supper, to eat and enjoy with his one-night friends, offload his business with Way-Waiting, and congratulate himself on having accomplished so much in an evening.

Then the dandy seated himself beside Sil with no end of pleasantness in his expression.

"Well-met, Master – Halfwick, is it? An absolute delight – Faro, if you like – and if I haven't said so already, it is so rare that we receive guests of both means and manners. Really, it will be a splendid evening, and I am so much looking forward to seeing these fine horses of yours…"

He smelled of pomade and lily-water and something else under all his beauty-regimen, something that had hardly sooner reached Sil's nose than it set it savagely itching, prickling down his throat and into his lungs, informing him with his first stifled reach for the handkerchief that he would be gambling on two fronts with this arrangement here…

… but there was no wiggling out of it without forfeiting his place, no begging off without advertising that he was nothing but a childish amateur out of his depth, and no doubt about whether to excuse himself or how.

Indeed, the only question remaining was what it would be worth to go back to Calvert, having turned his miserable fly-biting herd into so many perfect, shining pearls.

"Oh, but he DOES, Vichi; I am sure of it! See how he made a present of my belt to me! See how he smiled so kindly!"

It was by this fountain of embarrassment that Vuchak was accompanied downstairs, and he could not possibly plug it fast enough. "Would you keep your voice DOWN, idiot," he hissed, thanking all the still-living gods that the whore passing at their left would not understand what they said.

But although Weisei lowered his voice, he would not drop the subject nearly so easily. "And for what other reason would he do those things? For what other reason would he decline the attentions of well-shaped women of his own tribe?"

Of all Weisei's faults, his appetite for men was among the smallest. More vexing by far were his insistent fantasies about those exotic pretty foreigners he wished would share his tastes.

"Because he is here to make money, not to buy her diseases," Vuchak snapped as they crossed through the parlor. "And because your belt is nothing more than a useless tawdry novelty to him, and because he will speak and appear as whatever he thinks will more readily part you from your silver, and because he probably considered us all feather-waving fools even before you went and threw yourself on him to confirm it." The door-woman was watching them again, and Vuchak quickened his steps to avoid her. "Anyway, they don't have any such thing as *satlaka'a* where he comes from."

Because if they did, they wouldn't make nearly such a sport of raping native women.

"They do too!" Weisei protested behind him. "What do you think Brant is doing when he goes upstairs with –"

Vuchak stopped dead on the spot, and Weisei did not even have time to tread on his heel before he turned on him. "WEISEI." It was a whispered snarl. "NOT. HERE."

For a moment, Weisei's delicate features softened, wavered, and in that moment, Vuchak feared that he had cut too deeply.

But then, as if the incomprehensible chatter in the background confirmed for him that this was not the place to discuss such things – as if there ever was or would be one! – Weisei furrowed his brow, his wounded feelings retreating until they showed only in his eyes. "... well, he likes me better than YOU, anyway."

Which was as close to an agreement as they would get. "As well he should," Vuchak said as they went on their way. Because if it were left up to him, there would not be any Eaten here at all, nor any such thing as *satlaka'a* either.

And if either of those wishes were too much for the gods to grant him, then he would happily settle for having no smooth-talking Halfwick here to inflame his child-minded, woman-hearted *marka*'s regrettable affections.

ELIM NEVER HAD taken offense at being called a mule. Sure, you didn't always hear it from sugared lips, but it didn't mean that you were actually an animal.

That wasn't true for Sundowners. They were the brutish offspring of beastly gods, and Elim knew that for a fact because he had seen a dead one first-hand. They had her in the tent with the two-headed calf and the fish-baby, and she had been dried out almost to paper, but you could still see how the brown of her body-hairs turned to white under the upturned flap of her tail, and there wasn't any missing the leaf-shaped flowering of her doe's ears. They came in all sorts, and

Elim wondered sometimes what kind of beastliness he had living in his own blood.

So it was a powerfully strange reversal, now, to find himself hoping he had at least enough of it that whatever earthly gods had woken at sunset might mistake him for a local and let him be.

Elim made his tracks quickly, hat down and eyes forward in accordance with the errand-boy's creed: you were less likely to catch a hassling if you conducted yourself as if someone important was expecting you directly. He did not stop to look at the fire-lit festivities up on the roof of the eastern promenade, or listen to the shouting and laughing of the people up there, or smell the rich cedar-sweet aromas of their cooking.

But he couldn't avoid the boarding-house at the end of the road. Stately and sinister and old, the two front windows glowed luminous and alive with red light, its double set of sharp-curving porch steps dug like claws into the foundation, and high up above, lording over the upper story and even over the town itself, the twisted rails of the balcony exalted the house with a black-iron crown.

It was an evil thing, and not only because of its business hours. You could forgive people the need to do their sinning sociably – shoot, you could hardly expect them to make any less of a congregation in dirtying their souls than they did in cleaning them afterwards. No, what made Elim's hairs stand up was that the boarding-house was *still here*, unburnt and unbastardized, having apparently either out-fouled the conquering native powers, or else struck them one hell of a deal.

And now it had gotten hold of Sil.

That thought alone pushed Elim forward as he climbed the steps and knocked at the mouth of hell.

A slot in the door slid back, treating the viewer to a close inspection of Elim's dirty work-shirt and some loose-tied string.

That was apparently all right. "Saman!" an ecstatic feminine voice cried. The door was flung open, and Elim was briefly treated to the sight of a dazzlingly colorful little lady beaming up at him. She had light brown skin, long black hair, a sinfully-cut purple dress... and a swiftly-curdling expression.

"You're not Saman." She recoiled as if snakebit, her hand at her painted mouth, her gaze riveted to the spot over his eye, and her skin blanching to a sickly whitish-purple.

Elim blinked, astonished – but it must have been a trick of the red window-lights. When he looked again, she was an ordinary dun-colored Sundowner, squinting and staring at him with more-than-ordinary surprise. "Oh, *merde alors*... what are you doing here? What nerve do you have to come here now?" Her voice lifted with every word, her hands balling into fists at her sides, and Elim was instantly stricken at the sight. He could never in his life recall giving a lady such upset – and without one step left or right, without a word out of his mouth!

He took a step back, whipped off his hat, and turned his head to regard her with the friendlier side of his face. "I am awful sorry, miss," he assured her. "I don't mean to be here, only I came to look for my friend –"

"He isn't here and he never was!" she hissed, and then glanced over her shoulder at something further inside. "Are you stupid? Get out of here! Go away!" She took a menacing hold of the door's edge as if she would slam it shut, and Elim instinctively brought his arm up to ward his face –

"Shay!"

At least, that was what it sounded like. Elim looked up to see a white man, with sandy blond hair and close-clipped beard and nice respectable evening-clothes, step into view. "What's the matter here?"

The purple lady startled and spun to face him. "Nothing, nothing," she said, suddenly afflicting her voice with an accent. "Only a half-man, unimportant, uninvited – I am only just seeing him out."

The man came closer – sharp-eyed, clean-cut, responsible-looking – and Elim felt irrationally more secure.

"Is that so?" he said. "Because I could have sworn I heard you speaking unladylike to a visitor. I didn't, did I?"

"Oh no, Brant, no." Hands at the small of her back, she pressed herself against the old papered wall, and looked up at him with a frightened smile. "Only our visitor, he has come for his friend, who is not here, and I would not so rudely waste the – the visitor's time..."

The man, Brant, regarded Elim with an amiable nod. Elim stood straighter, and returned it.

"Well, hadn't we better make sure of that? Come on in, mister; we'll have a look in the drawing-room and see what's what."

The lady shut her mouth and bowed her head, her hands knotted in front of her skirts. Elim eased himself gingerly past her, mumbling apologies as the smell of perfumes and old wall-paper parched his nostrils. He could feel her glittering black eyes staring holes in his back.

Then the parlor door opened, and the bottom dropped out of his stomach. It was like looking into a barn-sized version of Mrs. Whitworth's living room on her mister's funeral day, all stuffed to the rafters with furniture and finery and people... so, so many people. A sea of faces swam before his eyes, brown and white as intermixed as on his own hide. Too late, Elim understood his mistake. "Shoulda come at the back..." he muttered, suddenly feeling sick, and took an automatic step backward. "He ain't here."

"Are you sure?" At his arm, Brant was all interest and sympathy. "Well, come have a drink and tell me about it; maybe someone will have seen him."

Brant moved forward, but Elim was blocking his way, and so Elim had no choice but to keep moving ahead, letting himself be herded past fancy tables and chairs, between strangely-dressed strangers, under delicate chandeliers and around ladies with swishing colorful dresses. Twelve different kinds of sounds wrestled at his ears, clinking glasses and cracking cue-balls and talking in at least three tongues, and despite the feeling that every eye in the room had to be leveled right on him, that constant tempest of conversation swirled through the hot sweetened air as if he didn't matter a lick in any of it. Elim kept his gaze fixed on the ground at his right, and his ears burned.

He ran out of room at the fanciest brass-railed bar he'd ever seen, and promptly occupied the least possible space beside it. This apparently suited Brant to the letter, as he busied himself with unseen somethings behind it, and went talking civilly on.

"Now what's this friend of yours look like, stranger? Is he white, or native, or...?"

Elim shook his head, and worked at gentling his stomach. "He's whiter'n rice and about half as big. Real young – between hay and grass – with cornsilk hair and a look on his face like you might come in useful sometime." He looked up from the rug as something *thunk*ed on the dark polished wood next to him – a shot glass, next to what looked to be a bottle of barrel-aged, double-rectified bust-head. "Oh – uh, no, but thank you kindly." He glanced out again, careful not to make eye contact, searching for any telltale blond spot in the crowd. "Range clothes, nice ones, mostly black. Thinks it makes him look older..."

"What did you say?"

The shift in Brant's tone was just slight enough that Elim didn't pick up on it. "He wears black – which is dumb as hell, as quick as he goes bad in the heat, but he don't seem to... oh." One belated look at his host, whose hand was still wrapped around the neck of the bottle, was enough to jog some recollection of fine-society etiquette. "I'm sorry – it ain't anything to do with yours; I don't drink, is all." Surprised as he was at the offer, Elim could only guess that there wasn't any mule law here. At home it was a whipping offense even to get caught holding. Of the two beltings he'd earned from Boss Calvert in his modest lifetime, one had been for getting at the brandy when he was twelve.

Brant's hand dropped to the bar with a ringing slap. "Boy, you have got a hell of a nerve."

Elim could not have been more surprised if Brant had struck him straight across the face. "What? No, it ain't – I don't aim to offend you –"

"Then I'd say you missed your mark, stranger. Would you believe," he said to the increasing number of turned heads around them, "that this boy here has the brass tacks to invite himself to Miss Addie's home in his hog-slopping shirts, knock on her door as bold as day and then refuse her house finest? Is that any way for a guest to act? Is that what you-all want to see here?"

By the time he'd finished, there was a conspicuously empty half-circle around them. Elim's face burned with a heat supplied by the sudden winter in his extremities, and a real, sudden fear for his life. Foul looks began to darken the white faces he saw, while some of the brown ones conferred, and others simply stared.

Brant leaned almost casually against the bar, and folded his hands. "Well stranger, it looks to me like you went and ruined a pretty good time. What do you think you ought to do about that?"

Elim shook his head and backed up, stumbling over an ornamental table. "I'm sorry, sir – I'm sorry, I'll go, I'll leave right now..." His attention flicked desperately between each door and exit, pinning his wild hopes on Sil's sudden appearance. Sil was clever and personable and had a knack for talking – he'd smooth it all over in just a minute, just as soon as he came back...

But there was only Brant, stepping out from behind the bar, advancing toward him. "Well, I guess you can't help it, if you weren't raised any better than that."

He pulled out a pistol, antique in design but gleaming as bright as new, and used it to wave Elim over to a seat before a low table. "And I guess it wouldn't be fair to expect you to know how we do things here."

Elim heard footsteps coming up softly behind him, felt the gun barrel tap down twice on his shoulder, and dropped forward to his knees. He stared straight ahead as a white hand set the bottle and glass before him. "So I guess it's high time we learned you some manners."

CHAPTER FIVE
ONE NIGHT IN SIXES

SIL'S EXHILARATION HAD long since burned down to a tense, grinding endurance as the wait dragged on.

Apparently, an exceptional match demanded exceptional preparations. A second dealer, plain and blindfolded as the first, had to be fetched to act as a recorder, and each player was expected to call a witness to the game. One of the painted ladies attended Faro, this one frocked in green, while Huitsak and Aibak summoned fellow a'Krah. Sil thought briefly of asking for Vuchak, but after the way he had left earlier, that seemed unlikely to please anyone. He courted favor instead by asking Huitsak to choose for him, and a third tribesman, Dulei, soon appeared on Sil's behalf.

To Sil's unpracticed eye, Dulei looked much like a younger copy of Vuchak, right down to those conspicuous silver cuffs. He affected no great interest in anything, but made passing flirtation with Faro's painted lady, and helped himself liberally to the drinks at the sideboard. Huitsak snapped at him whenever he perceived the boy to be insufficiently respectful. So maybe Sil had got it wrong after all: whatever else they did, those silver cuffs guaranteed their wearers neither rank nor respect.

And then there were the wagers. The pearls were divided into piles of one, five, and ten, and laid out on a tea-towel next to the playing board. Huitsak's silver and stones were similarly apportioned behind them. At the back, most dreadfully, were Aibak's stakes.

Rustics and laymen like Elim had been sold on the idea that Sundowners, being sired and governed by the demon offspring of the Sibyl, were strangers to virtue, and bought and sold their fellows like so much living meat. But certain historians – whose work had not been commissioned for a legislature or a pulpit – had respectably concluded that if certain tribes had recently expanded their human investments, it was because they'd learned the value of that sordid currency from other, decidedly paler trading partners.

It had been a thorough lesson. Aibak's lowest wager was an old woman, poorly dressed and allegedly deaf, who sat and stared at her updrawn knees. His middling stake was a white youth, with brown hair and native clothes, whose respectful silence was enforced by his conspicuously missing tongue. The last and most valuable prize was that second blindfolded fellow – though the winner would not own his person, but merely the right to commission a service from him.

Sil did not ask what that meant – there couldn't be any satisfying answer – but as the deck was finally shuffled, he swallowed his feelings and returned to his place beside that strange and strangely-afflicting Faro.

Master Halfwick was going to be a real businessman: not a two-penny dirt-merchant like Will, not a hand-wringing soft-hearted mark like Father, but a privileged and powerful fellow like these men here, who certainly hadn't got where they were by turning up their noses when they saw how the sausages were made. The world ran on blood and money, and here for the winning were ample quantities of both.

Still, he wouldn't tell Elim about the slaves. It would only upset him.

"NOW WHAT DO you say?"

Elim set the glass down with a trembling hand and bowed his head to the Sundowner across the table. "My obi-obligaddo 'stoy," he said, and then hurriedly repeated the correct version: "*Grese, sansor – muy obligado estoy...*"

He could see the man glance up over Elim's head, and understood then that it was no use: the mistake was made, and he'd have to do it again.

"*¿Ana-bebida le gustaría?*" the Sundowner asked.

"*Ai,*" Elim replied, trying for his life to remember what came after that. "*Ai –* uh, *ai, temaré.*"

The drink was poured, and he downed it in a swallow, not daring to cough. He was getting better at that part – he'd hardly tasted anything after the eighth or ninth. But the room was so much warmer than it had been when he started, and the rules, the hosts kept changing. One would ask him in Marín, and then Brant would replace him with a white man, who was to be spoken to in Ardish, and then the Sundowner woman would come back, which meant you switched back to Marín and said the same things, but had to change the ending on some of the words, and call her *sansora* and not *sansor*, after which there was another white man, and then the Sundowner fellow again, and by then drink and terror had ruined his memory, and it was getting harder to pronounce the words...

Elim looked up at a sudden shout. But no, there was no Sil anywhere here – just another blasted brown-faced stranger come to watch, albeit a merry-looking one with a fancy yellow shirt and long black hair.

"Well," Brant said behind him, "you see there's a new gentleman here. Why don't you do the polite thing and offer him a drink?"

"Sure – of course, sure..." Elim said, inwardly cringing. His partner was dismissed with a look Elim couldn't see. "Howdy," he said, gesturing to the empty place across the table in a stall for time: the Marín word for *hello* was so common even Elim knew it, and he knew he must've used it recently, but it hadn't come up here, and he couldn't recollect...

"Hallo!" the cheerful man said, dropping down into a cross-legged sit. Brant must have put the gun away, as this fellow here didn't seem to see anything but a fine old time.

Elim waited for the pour, and realized with galled surprise that the bottle was more than half empty. Had that all been him? Was it full when they started? And how much did you have to drink before you ended up like Mister Potter? He reckoned it depended on a number of things, and having any one of them wrong could make you sick or violent or blind – and that was doubly true if you already had moonshine cocktail in your veins, if you were already halfway to wildness before you ever took a swallow...

He felt a sharp nudge at his backside, and the chair-leather creaked as Brant leaned in close. "And what was it you were going to say to the gentleman?"

Oh – right – no, the first answer wasn't right; this one was different somehow, because the bottle wasn't where it was supposed to be, but his mind had wandered into a fog. "I was just, just going to – to say, I can't... hell, I don't know..." Elim's voice cracked; he put his hands to the back of his head and shuddered.

The Sundowner must have read it in his face: his smile fell and his fine brows furrowed. "*Oi, ¿ké pasa?*" he asked, his nonsense varnished with sympathy. "*Venga, mal non sientes. Si par un tiempo esperas, lo tuso gordo sube. Ah –*" he said, reaching forward as if struck by a sudden idea.

Elim watched stupidly as he picked up the bottle and indicated Elim's glass with a brilliant, guileless smile.

"*¿Ana-bebida le gustaría?*"

"*Three and eight.*"

The deck was almost half gone, but it couldn't go quickly enough. Every pair took ages, because it had to be recorded by the blindfolded fellow with the little string-loom, who braided threads to show the trading of the stakes, and bloody well took his time about it.

The room, filled to capacity with players and witnesses and slave-wagers and the rest, had turned stiflingly hot, and it was everything Sil could do to keep his eyes open. There was none of the rough play of before: except for Huitsak's solemn reading of the cards and Sil's own muted wheezing, everything was silent.

"*Ace and jack.*"

Faro and Huitsak exchanged tokens, and as a fresh wave of floral effrontery swept over Sil with the movement of Faro's overdressed arm, he closed his eyes and turned his attention inward, privately negotiating with his bronchial passages for their continued forbearance, for just a short while more...

"*King and four.*"

... because they had everything to gain by their tolerance. Because if this worked, he could tend to them at some more comfortable remove, some old and cold and far more agreeable place...

"*Master Halfwick?*"

The name registered only dimly; it was the recollection of the speaker that brought Sil's head up with a bolt of mortified energy.

"Ah – apologies, *sansor*, I didn't – er, *I just were thinking – WAS thinking, pardon me –*" Oh, bugger this for a game of soldiers. As Sil simultaneously worked at salvaging his grammar, smothering his cough, and completing the exchange of tokens between himself and Huitsak's open palm, he decided to take ownership of the situation, and gamble against his very-certain further embarrassment by risking no more than a tenth-portion of it now.

"*– would you like to smoke?*"

He fished in his pocket, retrieved the little tin case he kept there, and opened it to make an offering of blacktail cigarettes to the assembled company.

Aibak scowled at this presumptuous interruption, but Huitsak, after a moment's considered pause, opened his hand with a look of keen interest.

Which meant that the only real consequence for this hazard of etiquette was the disgust in Faro's voice. "Really, Master Halfwick, what a vile habit you entertain!"

Sil busied himself with emptying the case, and kept his gratification private. "I'll rely entirely on your forgiveness," he said, "if I feel the need to sedate my anxieties in the midst of so much illustrious company. *May I make the light?*"

"*If you can do it without burning the house down, certainly.*" The gleam in Huitsak's eye suggested satisfaction at Faro's discomfort.

So Sil turned aside, drew the match sharply through the folded sand-paper, and held his breath against its chemical reek long enough to light two cigarettes and hand one, set in the empty tin case by way of an ash-tray, across the board for Huitsak's use. Among the a'Krah, the etiquette of giving seemed to require that the lower-ranking person extend his reach to satisfy his superior, and Sil was nearly as pleased with his quick mastery of the idea as he was with his first peppery drag of the smoke.

It was fantastic stuff, blacktail: cleared the sinuses and the lungs, energized the mind, pepped you right up – a perfect prescription for the present moment. A shame it was so bloody expensive: by the time you imported it all the way in from the islands, you were smoking a week's wages with every one.

But as the dealer resumed his draw, and Faro shrank away with his handkerchief to his offended nose, Sil felt his passages mercifully unclenching with a second deep lungful of that hot herbal smoke, and decided that this apt handling of the situation should herald an equally artful recovery of his fortunes – that having mastered the social portion of the game, the chance of the cards should likewise fall perfectly into place.

"*Eight and six.*"

... or not.

Sil swallowed a sigh, picked up his set of three nails, and exchanged them with Aibak for a tied lock of brown hair.

"MUY, MUY OBIEGADDO, *es... es...*"

Elim was spared remembering the rest when a pair of white women in blue dresses passed by, and paused to scowl at something above his head.

"Brant, honestly. Take him outside before he's sick on the floor." They spoke with one voice, which was a hell of a trick, and flounced off without waiting for an answer. Elim struggled to keep his head up.

The voice in his ear was cotton-soft. "Well, stranger, I'd say you're about done here. Get up."

"'sir." Elim fixed his mind on obeying in spite of his body's sudden difficulties. Confused and ill-feeling, he was still sure about that much: you just did as you were asked, as best you possibly could, and everything would be all right, because...

He got up to a knee and one foot before the spinning room betrayed him. He collapsed back and bumped into someone – Brant – who caught him under the arms. Elim's back weighed briefly against the man's side, and he felt the press of something cool and iron-hard between his shoulders.

Gun. Brant still had the gun.

A stab of fear pierced the fog as Elim was hauled up to his feet, and he suddenly understood *done*. He'd done as he was asked, but it wasn't going to be all right: Brant had a hold of him, shouldering Elim's arm with a hard grip on his wrist, and he was leading him out a different way, not the way he'd come in with the door lady and people to see, but through the kitchen, out the back, where nobody would be liable to notice when Brant drew the gun and had done with him.

"Two and nine."

The burnt-out nub of the cigarette had long since cleared Sil's lungs, but his conscience remained damnably congested.

It was stupid, of course. The trade was legitimate, and regardless, it wasn't even final. The tied lock of hair sat on the six, and there were still two sixes left in the deck, which meant that even if one of them only served to move the slave to another of his own cards, there would still be one left in the deck to... no, wait, that wasn't right, because if he swapped it to one of his other spaces, then –

"*Five and six.*"

– that. Sil exchanged the pebble, which represented the one singular pearl, with the lock of hair. It was a trade between two of his own spaces, but there was still every opportunity to... well, hold on...

Sil glanced up at the case counter as the dealer pushed the last of the 'five' beads to the left.

That was it – that was the last five in the deck. Whatever else happened, the slave-token wouldn't move.

Sil risked a glance at his prize. Sitting straight and still, with pale fuzz above his lip and sleeves an inch too short for his wrists, the boy knew when he was being watched. His gaze crept over, made eye contact with Sil for just a second, and flicked back to the floor.

In minutes, Sil would officially own that, all of it – not

just the obedient rug-watching but that mirror's glimpse of a living, reasoning human soul.

"*Jack and nine.*"

But if you looked at it properly, on the board just there, that bit of tied hair was a commodity, just like horses or stones or pearls. Sil wasn't bound to keep his prize: he could sell it or trade it on at a whim, and the order of the universe would not be disturbed one bit. Sil hadn't stolen any children, after all – he could hardly be held accountable for the workings of the world – he was just using local currency, and it was all currency, of one sort or another...

"*Seven and seven – dealer's choice.*"

Sil glanced up, and found Huitsak giving him a significant look, as if the remark were made for his benefit. Sil had no idea what to expect – this minor rule hadn't come up before – but watched as the dealer put down the cards, pushed two of the 'seven' beads to the left, and reached out over the length of the board.

No – no, it was evil, it was wrong, and Sil would rather have nothing at all. He pushed the lock of hair straight at the dealer's groping hand.

There were murmurings from the onlookers, and visible surprise from the players. The dealer paused with his fingers closed over the token, as if waiting to hear an objection. Sil offered no explanation, made no eye contact, but stared at the hand in the middle of the playing field... and breathed a silent sigh of relief as it finally retreated with its prize.

"*Two and four.*"

Well, and so what if he'd offended by it? It was Sil's prize and his loss, and those three ought to be grateful he'd volunteered a piece before the dealer nicked one of theirs. And yes, he answered to the irritating thought of Father's disapproval, maybe he could have done something with the boy – what about it? What was he supposed to do, take him back across the border, put a dollar in his pocket and wish him well? Him, with the moccasin-shoes and the empty space behind his teeth?

"*Four and two.*"

Grand, excellent – terrific, really. That was the fours all gone, and him stuck with the horse again. Sil stared at the board and realized with growing despair that he was looking at the sum of his lot: one pearl, one horse, and an empty spot where he'd thrown out his common sense in a fit of pique. He felt wretched, hot and giddy and queasily ill, well ready to trade that one pearl for the chance to back out of everything.

"*Jack and seven.*"

Sil distantly registered the exchange of fates – Huitsak owned the white slave now, and the dealer had the service of his blindfolded colleague – and tried to remember what pearls had been listed at in last year's Consolidated Commodity Index. Something like $300 per scruple, if you went by weight, but it was a rare pearl that weighed in at a whole scruple, and Sil would scarcely venture a guess as to how much any single one might be worth. Probably enough for Calvert to see a magnificent profit on one horse. Certainly not enough for him to break even on ten.

"*Six and eight.*"

Good God, let it not be another slave. Sil numbly made the exchange with Aibak and was first relieved, then confused when he traded his pebble for... another pebble.

This one was considerably larger though, broad and flat, almost a miniature skipping-stone. A quick glance at the third, more modestly-sized one now sitting on Huitsak's queen confirmed it.

So this would be the ten-pearl piece, then.

Sil let it sit in his hand and watched the dealer slide the last of the 'six' beads to the right.

So this would be his, then.

Unless another pair of sevens – no, but there was only one left now. No more fives. The ten pearls belonged to him just as surely as the empty six, and he hurriedly replaced the stone on the board before anyone might contest its place there.

Sil was dimly aware of the last couple of hands, and the guessing-game to cap it all, but it was nothing to do with him now – no, the one horse and the ten pearls and the empty spot were all his. And all because of him: *his* ideas, *his* tenacity, *his* hard work and risk-taking and sleeplessness and damned dogged grit – his willingness to stare his own ruin in the face without flinching! – and if he'd listened to anyone but himself, they'd be going home pride-stuffed and penniless.

Huitsak made another peculiar handsign and declared the game ended, with muted congratulations made on various sides. Sil waited until his host began to rise before following suit, staggering up to his feet on a combination of pinprick-numbness, satisfaction, and exhausted euphoria. He'd still have to hoof it all the way back to the barn, present the merchandise and deal with Elim. It would be at least an hour before he got any sleep, two if they actually wanted to take the horses tonight.

It was worth it, though. Sil clenched the stone in his fist, and inched his way towards Huitsak. Absolutely worth it.

"Pardon me, Master Halfwick..."

Sil was halted in his tracks by that dreadfully pleasant voice.

"Yes, friend?" Sil made a game attempt to sound polite, patient, and not in the least like an ailing bellows, and put his moneyed hands behind his back.

Faro smiled. "Excellent game, really it was – I must congratulate you. I was wondering, though, if perhaps you'd still be willing to part with that one horse of yours... fairly compensated, of course."

Then the job was looking reserved, detached, and just lightly interested in the offer. "I'd be glad to consider your proposition," he replied. "What did you have in mind?"

For an answer, Faro held the smallest of the pebble-tokens between thumb and forefinger.

One horse for one pearl? Maybe it was too good to be true, but Master Halfwick wasn't going to hesitate long enough to find out. "Perfect – and very generous of you." He traded the nail for the pebble, observing an unpleasant dampness to Faro's hand as he did, and looked around for Huitsak. "I'll be happy to show you the horse – I'm actually just going to see about that now..."

"Oh, don't give it a second thought," Faro replied with a brilliant black-eyed smile. "I really must be retiring, or I'll despise myself for it tomorrow. Just leave it with my friend Fours and we'll take care of everything in the morning, all right? Excellent, really a splendid evening..."

And as the strange dandy finally – mercifully! – departed, Sil looked at the two stones in his hand, as complementary as the sun and moon, and privately agreed: splendid was the word for it. Now to cash in the checks and get out.

He maneuvered his way around the dealer packing away the board and the deck, stayed well clear of the corner where Aibak was issuing orders to his wagers, and finally found Huitsak in the middle of a knot of other a'Krah, talking at one of his cohorts while keeping his eyes trained on Faro's departing back.

Fortunately, Sil cut a distinctive figure, and was recognized with little delay. "Master Halfwick – well played. A generous god looks after you. We'll take care of your winnings, of course – here, here…"

Sil followed his lead, and knelt with him by the blanket. "Thank you very much for inviting me to play," he replied, and retrieved his handkerchief as Huitsak helped him fill the yellow cloth with so many tiny rainbow spheres. "I can take you to see the horses now, if you'd like. My groom is waiting there for me and has them ready for…"

Huitsak waved off the rest. "Will you insult my attention with trifles? Your judgment wallows in weariness, Halfwick. Go, sleep; stay here tonight, and we will finish business tomorrow."

Sleep in a proper bed? Why yes, he'd be delighted, but –

"Dulei! Boy, come here." Huitsak called to the finely-dressed youth sprawled out in front of the open balcony window. Sil had forgotten all about him – some witness! – but pocketed his pearls as the boy rolled up to his feet and wandered over, his long, plaited pigtails swaying saucily with every step.

"Now do something useful and go to Fours' barn, and when you see the half – what did you say was his name?"

"Elim," Sil replied, rising to meet Dulei's disinterested gaze. "He'll be suspicious, but tell him I sent you..."

"... yes, and that his master will be there tomorrow morning to send away the horses." Huitsak put his hands to his knees and began to heft himself up, but failed to achieve critical momentum on his first attempt. He stopped when he noticed the smirk on the boy's face. "Well, and what are you waiting for? Go, do it!"

"Yes, *maga*." Without bothering to wipe off his smile, Dulei turned and sauntered towards the door.

"And tell your uncle to watch the rocks!"

... or at least, that was what it sounded like, though Sil wouldn't put money on his translation.

Anyway, swapping an earful from Elim for a decent night's sleep was just the latest in a string of good bargains – and with no more thought than that, Sil extended a hand to the architect of his success.

He realized his mistake as Huitsak pulled himself up to his feet, swearing at the touch. "*Fest* – how do you have such cold hands when your women run so hot-blooded?"

Sil smiled, but it was pressed from curdled milk. Something quick and clever, something about women –

Huitsak waved him off. "No, I don't care to know. Well, see if one of them has a room, but don't tell them I sent you, or you'll be lucky to have a blanket on the doorstep. *And you, Tadai – come here, and bring with you the reason why you haven't returned my share from the dice...*"

By ignorance, indifference, or sheer grace of God, Sil found himself dismissed. As he withdrew, he scratched at the spattered rash emerging where Faro had touched him – what did these people put in their cosmetics? –

and contemplated his next move. He was reasonably sure that the bedrooms on the second floor belonged to the house ladies, and that the done thing was to solicit the latter before inviting oneself to the former. But he did not see any such ladies here in the hallway, and was not about to go knocking on closed doors.

Well, downstairs, then. Sil started down, finished one flight of stairs and had made it about a quarter of the way down the next when he caught a glance over the banister at the evening soirée. Three likely-looking bright gowns sashayed between the guests: the green one hanging on some punter at billiards, a yellow one near the kitchen, and a blue one right by that same occasional table, across from some whopping big fellow wearing a dirty linen shirt that looked passingly –

Sil startled at a sudden swishing sound from above, where the blonde woman in pink was just turning the corner.

"Oh, excuse me, miss," he said with an expression of pleasant surprise. "You're just the lady I was hoping to see…"

She stopped and leaned against the wall. Sil must have been a sickly sight by then, as warily as she looked him up and down, and he returned her unspoken contempt with plenty of his own: he'd seen sheep with better dye-jobs. "Is that right?" she replied, with a homespun accent that would have made Elim's heart flutter. "What can I do you for, mister?"

"Well, I've got a business proposition of a particular sort. Am I right in thinking that you have a room here?"

She smiled, promising delights that Sil would be happy to leave untried, and beckoned him up. "You are, 'cause I do. You reckon you might like to see it?"

"I reckon I would," Sil replied, following her up the stairs as he fingered the silver dollars in his pocket.

Five minutes later, he turned the key in the lock and leaned back against the door. On reflection, he quite liked harlots: they were just about the only women with proper business sense. Now she'd made money, and Calvert had made money, and Huitsak and Aibak and Faro would all have their horses, and as for Sil?

Why, he took out his pearls – the eleven stunning, perfect new jewels he had just now conjured out of six tons of superfluous horseflesh – and satisfied himself with a just a wheezy little chuckle.

Which ended in a croupy sort of gasp.

Which broke up like a wagon wheel splintering to pieces, until he was coughing himself hoarse, purging himself of mucus and frustration and suffering and injustice and a week's worth of stifled outrage, shuddering and coughing and *laughing*, riches clutched tight to his heaving chest, at himself and his infinitely-improbable new wealth and most especially at the soon-to-be stupefied look from every pig-eyed backwater idiot who'd ever cast aspersions on his health, his manners, or his ambitions.

And the reckoning would begin tomorrow with that insufferable bastard Elim.

ELIM DRAGGED HIS feet, trying for his life to think straight as he was hauled through the kitchen, but it was really just the one thought that kept repeating itself: he was going to be either dumped in the river or hung from a tree, and nobody was going to do anything about it, because nobody who knew cared, and nobody who cared knew.

Then Brant kicked open the back door with a *bang*, and the sharp night air hit Elim full in the face, and that was enough: he hurled himself to the left, slamming Brant into the pantry cupboards, and as soon as the white man's grip slackened, Elim rammed his elbow into Brant's neck and bolted out the open door.

He ran and fell, and ran and fell, and stumbled up to his feet and ran again, going left, back to the front of the house and the big street, back to someplace open and public and visible, and then –

Elim tripped, hit the ground on hands and knees, and felt his face brush up against something satiny-soft. He looked blearily up, past a waterfall of purple silk and into a pair of glittering black eyes.

"It IS you."

Elim had never been so close to an indecent woman before. He caught a whiff of flowery perfume drifting from her skirts, undercut by the fetid stench of fish and rotting algae. His stomach lurched, promising to be sick on the spot.

Then she reached into her bodice and pulled out a knife.

Elim threw himself at her legs to avoid her first downward slash. She toppled forward over his hunched back, and that was enough. Elim staggered up to his feet and bolted.

"*¡Oye! ¡Oye! ¡Un mestizo aqui esta!*"

Her shouts were enough to keep him running, fleeing from the fire-lights and the roof-walkers and into the dark warren of the northwest quarter until he'd lost himself in a maze of stumps and ruins, praying to God and the ghosts of whatever slain Braves still lingered here to deliver him somehow.

But their answer was already churning in his gut. Something was awfully wrong inside him: his vision sharpened and blurred and clashed with itself, whites and grays all overlaid with swimming dark colors as a horrible constriction wound tighter in his chest. He'd been poisoned, that was what, and it only worked slowly while he sat still but now it was climbing up to his heart and his senses were fraying, unwinding...

Something caught his foot. Elim tripped, crashing to the ground like a roped steer. He struggled to get his hands underneath him, to pull air back into his lungs. As soon as he did, the smell hit him like a ton of bricks, its source not two inches from his face.

Dog's droppings.

He *was* sick then, the sound of his own retching so loud that the Sundowners and their earthly gods surely couldn't help but find him there, heaving helplessly in the street.

But when he was done, he couldn't hear anybody anywhere. Above his own air-sucking gasps, every sound had been swallowed into silence.

Every sound but one.

"Uh, uh, uh..."

Elim looked groggily up from the mess between his hands.

The dog smiled at him. "Uh, uh, uh..."

She was just a plain ordinary Sundowner dog: browner at her top and sides, amber-eyed, prick-eared. She sat there and panted, almost cheerfully waiting.

She was sitting in front of Fours' house.

Elim lurched, slipped, staggered and ran for the side door – not the front, where the speckled mule might see him – and pounded it with his fist.

Nothing happened.

He tried the doorknob and then the window, calling for Fours all the while. But all that came from his mouth was a horrible bile-soaked rasp.

"Horrhh – horrhh…" Elim collapsed against the window-screen, his fingers hard and swollen against his throat. The porch-planks pitched and rolled under his feet, his flesh was alive with a hot running rash as if he were being savaged by ants, and he heard echoes of sounds – wood-gnawing, cricket-chirping, hoof-stamping, dog-panting – distorted as if he was listening with his head in the washbasin. He was dying.

But not out here. Not like this. Elim stumbled down the porch steps, clinging to the rail, and then bolted for the barn door. He had it open with a single hard yank of the bolt, and shut it again just as quickly from the inside. Then he hauled the huge storm plank up on his shoulder and hammered it down into the waiting iron slats so that nobody, not Brant or any of his brown devils, could get in after him.

But the world was all inside-out, and the barn was a dark hellhole reeking of mold and piss and raw animal fear. From every side came a thunderous din of squeals and whinnies and the gunshot-sharp banging of hooves on walls and doors, as urgent and deafening as if the barn were being eaten alive in a torrent of fire, and there was no retreat from it but up, up into the loft, and when he grabbed up his rifle and turned to peer back down into the stewing panic below, there was still no fire, no flood of rats, nothing to prompt their terror except —

– something was in the broken stall.

Elim stared, holding his attention apart from the

chaos, and let his eyes absorb the darkness until he could see. He registered shiftings, movements, and in them the figure of a man, huddled up behind the battered door, his hands laced over his head, his forearms clamped down at his ears, his every quick breath ending in a swing of the long, plaited pigtail draped over his nearer arm.

That was not Sil.

Elim did not need to check the rifle – he had loaded it long before.

He did not need to ask who was hiding there – he already knew what they'd come after.

And they wouldn't have it. He brought the gun stock up to his shoulder and sighted down the barrel, waiting without breathing for his swaying, shifting sickness to align for a clear shot. He was already dead, but he would not disappear. He would not go missing. He would not, he would not, he would not –

A GUNSHOT SOUNDED faintly on the warm breeze drifting through the window, but it disturbed the sleeper not at all. Sil rolled over, robed in cool silk sheets, and slept without incident through the night.

"ELIM! ELIM, ARE you there? Open the door!"

Elim was less conscious of the voice than the godawful pounding that abetted it, and he wanted no truck with either. He could just about ignore it, if he lay with his arm over his head just so. Still, there was no such fix for the hideous throbbing in his head or his bladder.

Ugh.

He sat up by painful inches, blearily rubbing the gum out of his eyes. Somebody had kicked him in the head, sure as Sunday, but then where was the lump?

"Elim, what the devil are you playing at? Open the damned door!"

Fine, fine – anything to quit that racket. Elim left off feeling his skull for goose-eggs and opened his eyes to a miserly thin squint. He negotiated the rungs of the ladder and the queasy turning of his gut as sickly-yellow tendrils of memory sprouted from his ploughed-up brains. Sixes. Bad bargain. Horses for heathens. Sil had gone to sell, and Elim had apparently entertained himself meanwhile with a concussion. No telling whose hind hoof had done him the favor.

But just as surely as if he'd heard the thought, there was Two-Pie come to greet him, having apparently untied his jury-rigged door.

How on God's earth had he contrived to do that? And come to looking at it, what in all wrath had prompted Shy Vi to kick the dickens out of her stall? And Prudie... and Sugarlips...

Elim stared in abysmal wonderment at the damage all around him, his palsied hands absently pushing away Two-Pie's investigation of his pants pocket. The rest of them didn't seem to know a thing about it. Even Molly and Ax just flicked and nickered and dipped their heads as anybody in reasonable want of breakfast would, as if they'd been nothing but steel-shod angels all through the night.

They'd have to be patient, at least until Elim had shut up his partner and had his morning ablutions in peace – which was fixing to be as awkward as it was urgent, given his uncommonly dire case of the old six-inch snakebite. "Got to wait," he croaked, and added a drink of water to his list of needful things.

"Oh, just *you* wait," Sil snapped, his voice not nearly muffled enough. "I've got a buyer waiting here – hurry up, damn you!"

Well, at least he'd left off the pounding. And what joker had barred the door? "Right," Elim grunted, stooping to catch the corner of the storm plank with his shoulder. It was far too heavy to lift, but he could slide it out of its fittings, just so.

When he'd stood the plank up out of the way, Elim gave the door a half-shove, and then retreated to the dimmer end of the barn to make his mark.

He never could figure out what mistake in a man's bodily calendar kept leaving him fixed to sow his oats right when he most needed to water his fields. But of course the whole thing was the Sibyl's blessing, and deaf to all reason, so you might as well consider it a good problem to have, and get on as best you could.

He finally managed to loose the buttons on his front-fall and get along with fumbling, shaky hands, but even that didn't make him feel much better. He'd never in his life felt so worm-eaten – even the door-shaped patch of sunlight on the ground hurt to look at. And on top of that, he'd have to see them off today, all going away to God only knew what fate. Sil had better have picked out a good one, but Elim wouldn't bet on it. He could hear them talking in Marín far back behind him – well, just Sil talking, really. Wasn't it always.

When he was done, Elim laboriously set his fore-flap back to rights and put his fingers through his hair. He could not fathom what he must have spilled to get a stain of that color on his shirt, or how he'd arranged to get horsehairs all on the inside for a change.

He turned to go take the measure of Sil's buyer, but stopped halfway there.

There was a man in the broken stall. A Sundowner fellow, dressed in heathen clothes and fancy silver cuffs. He was sprawled out on the hay-strewn floor, in the kind of posture that you would only credit from someone who was either soundly asleep or dead.

Elim approached warily. "Hello?"

He was not asleep.

CHAPTER SIX
SOMETHING IRREVERSIBLE

"WELL, AND THEN what happened?" Dayflower asked.

Step-Lightly snorted. "What do you think? When the thing was discovered, Aibak drew his pistol and brought the half-man down to his knees, and surely would have made an end of him right there in the barn... only the Eaten boy called for Fours, and Fours called for the law, and there my Yes-Yes found the four of them together. He had the weapon taken and the half-man tied before Twoblood arrived, you know. The Azahi will hear of it on his return."

Dayflower resisted the temptation to roll her eyes, and dandled the baby on her lap instead. Never since people had first climbed up from the World Below had there been a man so magnificent as Yes-Yes, if you believed his wife. "And the man who died?"

"A noble son of Grandfather Crow," Step-Lightly replied, her words as artificially respectful as her tone. Other Ikwei women were spreading out their blankets nearby, and speaking poorly of the dead invited evil on everyone. "I wailed to hear how the bullet pierced his reverend skull." But this with a click of her tongue, as if to say, *what more could he have hoped for?*

"Oh! Then what we heard last night –" Dayflower held the baby close, frightened all over again. How easily it could have been someone else! "But the half – what will Twoblood decide? Is it known?"

Step-Lightly squinted into the morning sun, past the heads of the men sitting in front of them to the empty circle at the crossing of the two great streets, and regarded it all with an air of smug indifference. "What does it matter? One of the a'Krah is slain, and the Azahi is not here." She glanced back over at Dayflower and favored her with a knowing look. "He will not see another sunrise."

SOMEHOW, SOMETIME JUST recently, something had gone horribly wrong. Elim could not account for it – not that he'd been asked to try. He did as he was asked and went where he was told; he did not speak and he especially did not look at Sil, but kept himself to himself and supervised the dirt between his boots.

The two of them were made to wait in the shadow of the smithy, at the big crossroads in the middle of town. They were guarded by two Sundowners: one caped and bare-chested with ear-cropped hair, the other shirted and ponytailed with white paint at his arms and scalp. Their only relation seemed to be the little gold discs they wore hanging at their necks, the holstered pistols at their hips, and their watchful, glowering stares. Sil talked to one of them, motioning at Elim's tied wrists, but nothing came of it.

It was a nice idea – more than Elim expected – but

what he really wanted was a long drink of water and a lie-down in some dark corner of the barn. Then he'd wake up again and be at home in the big bed, with Lady Jane dipping a washrag in the wooden bowl and saying that he'd only cracked his head on the doorframe again and was having bad dreams...

Busy as he was with wishing it true, Elim scarcely noticed his guards being called over towards the gathering assembly. Suddenly Sil reached up, grabbed a fistful of Elim's shirt-front, and yanked him down to eye level.

"WHAT DID YOU DO?" he hissed. His pupils were two ice-set black wells of outrage, his breath sour with curdled snot, and his face whiter than Elim had ever seen it.

"I didn't, nothing!" Elim protested, and shook his head before he remembered how fiercely that hurt. "I –"

Sil recoiled, nostrils flaring, and let go of Elim's shirt. "Ugh – and you're soaked in liquor! I leave you alone ONE BLOODY MINUTE and you're boozed up and on the shoot. Elim, what the devil possessed you?"

Elim's eyes widened. If he'd had the use of his arms, he would have cupped a hand to check his breath. "I didn't – I wouldn't! We had a cuss and you left, and I put them in for the night and waited up for you, and then..." He remembered loading the rifle, just in case. He could not remember falling asleep. His eyes filled, unprompted. "... I don't know..."

Sil looked momentarily dumbstruck at the sight. He turned sharply away. "For God's sake – what are you, six?"

Elim leaned against the wall and wiped his face with his shoulder, marshalling himself less by bravery than the sore sudden temptation to ask whether they couldn't maybe go back an hour and see how manful Sil felt with a pistol cocked to *his* head. "I asked you for one thing –"

"So did I," Sil instantly, furiously retaliated, "but I didn't realize that 'stay put' was mulespeak for 'get blind, pissing drunk!'" Sil knocked the back of his head to the wall behind them. "GOD I hate you!"

Well, slap that on paper and call it news. Elim sighed, and discarded this ripe chance to mention that he had likewise just about had his fill of Little Lord Halfwick. He swallowed on a dry throat, and watched a trail of ants mountaineering over the toe of his boot. "All the same," he said presently, "do you reckon I could have some water?"

He glanced over to see Sil ready some blistering retort – probably something about him having had plenty to drink already – but his ears were spared by one of the two Sundowners turning to motion him forward, to the empty space in the middle of the street.

The speckled mule was waiting for him in the middle.

IT WAS ONLY by heroic force of will that Sil swallowed his rage when the watchman beckoned Elim forward. The other one, the lady-sheriff of sorts, waited to receive him in the middle of the assembly. The watchmen called her *Dos'angres – Mixbreed*, or more literally, *Twoblood* – the curiously-titled Second Man of Island Town.

Well, man or woman, she was in for a surprise if she thought she was going to get anything useful out of Elim. Sil folded his arms to watch. Let Calvert's miserable lackey sweat it out there for awhile.

"*You are brought to answer the people of Island Town,*" Twoblood said, "*and you will speak only the truth. What are you called, and from where do you come?*"

Still, Sil was surprised that so many had turned out to watch the proceedings, and studied the crowd in search of an order to their gathering. The men had most of the nearest seats, elders up front. Women and children sat towards the back on blankets or yucca mats, while others perched on some of the nearer roofs. Sil felt sure that they must also have organized themselves by tribe somehow, and looked hard to see if he couldn't teach himself something about it.

"I, uh – I'm sorry, I don't know…"

He wasn't a quick study. Although some of the assembled had appreciably lighter skin or broader faces than others, their individual habits were of such vast and seemingly unpatterned variety, eastern and native styles intermingling not only between neighbors but sometimes even on a single body, that Sil could not have made clear distinction between the painted and the unpainted, or the shod and the barefoot, any more than he could have opened his cash drawer and said with authority which coins he'd earned by the sale of a hay rake.

"*Your name, half! Speak!*"

He'd have had no trouble in pointing out the buyer, though, busy as he was drowning in ignorance.

Elim backed up half a step, shook his head, winced, and turned to shield the spotted side of his face from Twoblood's ire. "No, I mean, uh, *non* – I don't understand…" He shot a panicked glance back at Sil's place in the shade.

Sil sniffed, swallowed, sighed. Fine – just to keep the overfed idiot from getting sick down his front. He pushed lightly out of his lean, affixed his hat, and stepped forward to the circle's edge, waiting to be recognized. Twoblood already knew from their encounter at the barn that Sil was fluent: her mistake was in assuming that the same was true of the silent, cowering mule she'd found at the end of Aibak's pistol.

Come to think of it, where was Aibak? Sil scanned the fringes of the assembly in vain. One of the watchmen had taken him aside when Twoblood arrived, and then...

"*You, Eadan – come here.*"

Sil walked forward into the attention of perhaps two hundred people, and sharpened his posture accordingly.

Twoblood was not impressed. "*Give me your names. Now.*"

Certainly. "*Silflec Halfwick, of the Baybride Halfwicks. He is Appaloosa Elim, and belongs to the Calvert family of Washburn County.*" He pitched his voice for the people around and behind him, but gave his attention exclusively to the woman in front.

She was peculiar, this Twoblood. Sil had mistaken her for a man at Fours' place yesterday, and when he realized his mistake this morning, he'd marveled at how badly she'd squandered herself. She couldn't help her spots – for her, God had thumbed the bristles of a wet paintbrush in her face – but if only she wouldn't wear clothes so ignorant of her shape, or – apparently – cut her kinky brown-tipped hair by introducing it by the fistful to a knife, or let that dandruff lie so starkly on the shoulders of her dark ranch-hand's shirt and rabbit-fur vest... truly, she would have been rather splendid.

Now, from this closer remove, Sil liked to think that he understood a little better. Her boots and belt and bone-colored hat, the pistol that slept at her side in its fringed and beaded holster, and most especially the golden sigil she wore tied around her neck – those were not the marks of a woman running away from her sex. They were the tools of someone whose job demanded unquestioning masculine respect.

Under the circumstances, Sil would be glad to give it to her.

Twoblood folded her arms. *"Then tell this Appaloosa Elim that a man is killed. If he is found responsible, it will require his life."*

Sil's composure was punctured by sudden understanding. *"His life? Do you..."* ... *have any idea what Calvert will do to me?* *"... do you not practice the giving of the man-price here?"* Surely they did – surely they had kept that much of the old ways. Surely that hadn't ended with Merin-Ka.

Twoblood's face softened just slightly. She came forward, and motioned Sil to do likewise. When she spoke again, it was for his ears only. *"The man-price is at the election of the family. This family will accept only blood."*

What, for Dulei? The insolent errand-boy? Sil was so sure he'd been wrong about those silver cuffs. Something was said about an uncle...

Sil replied with an absent nod. Twoblood would know that the a'Krah were a hard-edged lot – the way Aibak had instantly pulled the gun still elicited a shiver – but she wouldn't know that Sil had gotten in so well with Huitsak last night, and she couldn't know that he'd won enough money to buy the understanding of half a dozen weeping mothers, and perhaps she didn't realize that the one reliable human constant was greed.

Yes, one conversation would solve it all – but not if this mob got hold of Elim first. Sil nodded again, resolute this time, and backed up to reply in his public speaking voice. "*I understand and will respect your decision,*" he said. "*But it must...*" How to say it gracefully? "*... it must belong only to me. He cannot be responsible for his actions.*"

This was met with silence all around. Sil risked a glance at the seated men closest to him: quiet and attentive, their faces unreadable.

Twoblood looked suspicious. "*How not?*"

Sil was ready for that. "*I will show you,*" he said, "*but I must have his hands free.*" With a gesture, he invited their eyes to make the rest of the argument: there was Elim, filthy and awkward and frightened, standing unarmed and sober in front of two hundred people. What was he going to do, bite?

Twoblood seemed to come grudgingly to the same conclusion, and assented with a jerk of her head. The caped watchman came forward, and Elim thankfully submitted in silence.

That fellow belonged to the Ikwei – Sil was sure of it. He had Easy-Hey's same wide face and stocky build, and the back of his shaved head was shaped to that same perfect flatness. Sil couldn't have said whether that was the result of cradleboard custom among the Ikwei, or a mark bestowed by their earthly goddess, the Lady of the House. Nor was there any telling whether this fellow had the same extraordinary stamina that had made Easy-Hey a legend in Hell's Acre: as the saying went, you couldn't judge a man's talent by his handshake.

When it was done, Elim dipped his head in Twoblood's direction. "Thank you," he said, rubbing at his wrists.

"You're welcome," Sil replied. "Now take off your shirt."

Elim stiffened. "What? No!"

It was amazing, really, how he only needed two words to bring Sil to the brink of the abyss. "Elim," Sil said, holding his temper like a greased glass egg, "do you want to live or don't you?"

Elim seemed to consider that he did. But bewilderment and lingering distrust showed in his eyes as he pulled out the loose-tied strings of his placket, yanked his shirt up over his head, and spun it tightly between his forearms.

Then he just blanked out, staring at an abstract point six feet from his boots and waiting, apparently, for it to be over.

Just as well.

Elim made an eyeful all right, his colors clashing in a ragged arc across his back: Sundowner from left hip to right shoulder and all down his right arm and side, white in all the remainder. He was a draft horse of a man, with saddle-hauling shoulders and muscle packed into his upper arms. Under his hastily-swaddled shirtcloth was a soft white stomach, a ten-pound testament to a life well savored.

Sil was not interested in any of these things, but directed Twoblood's attention to the horseshoe-C branded into Elim's left arm. "*You will find this same mark on his horse,*" Sil explained, "*and on papers which we have brought with us. To us it shows that he cannot be considered a man under the law, because he is a slave.*"

This was clever strategy on Sil's part, especially for one so quickly improvised. Strange, then, this sudden desire to brush his teeth.

Twoblood snorted. *"A shame for you that there are no slaves in Island Town. And why should your niveles affect our decision?"*

Sil shook his head, having lost a crucial word in the middle. *"Our what?"*

"Your niveles, boy," Twoblood repeated irritably, her enunciation revealing an impressive set of canine fangs that Sil had missed before. *"The differences you people make among yourselves – why should we care?"*

Coming from a wolf-toothed she-mule in trousers, it was a fair question. *"You must decide as it seems best to you,"* Sil replied, reinforcing his total submission to her authority while stalling for time. *"However, if your desire is to do justice... then I am saying that killing him will not be just, because he does not understand his actions. I do."*

Too late, Sil realized that what he'd begun as a lie had led to the truth. He still pitched his voice to appeal to the assembly, but his eyes attended Elim's distant, unanswering expression. *"I ordered him to stay and to protect our horses, and told him that I would myself come back with someone to buy. I did not keep my promise, and I believe what he – I believe that he acted faithfully in shooting the man I sent to meet him. Therefore, what I am saying to you is"* – and it took a moment then for Master Halfwick to fully compose himself – *"the fault is not his for obeying the order, but mine for giving it irresponsibly."* Sil looked back at Twoblood, and through his eyes and face and voice tried to express how well they might understand each other in this moment: two poor-bodied souls striving to be seen and respected like men. "*I wish you to judge me in his place.*"

Twoblood narrowed her eyes at him, one hand to the small of her back. Sil dared to hope that she had grasped his sincerity. "*You are trying to have your way with me, Eadan, or else very brave. However...*" She scrutinized Elim's rigid, motionless posture. "*... it is difficult for me to believe that any unsleeping, well-reasoning man would shoot without giving a stranger the time to name himself... or that this stranger would have been careless enough to startle this man into shooting first.*" Twoblood tucked a thumb under her chin, and then gestured the Ikwei watchman back at Elim. "*Inspect his teeth.*"

Sil looked between them in surprise. "*What? Why –*"

Twoblood tipped her head left and right, an unsettling gleam in her eye. "*If he is a slave, he will not mind.*"

Sil opened his mouth to reply, but found no way to argue the point. He watched with a sinking feeling in his gut.

The watchman appeared equally unenthusiastic, but dutifully marched up to Elim. "*You,*" he said, pointing up at Elim's lips. "*Open your mouth.*"

Elim snapped back to the present, straightened to his full height, and glowered down at the hand in front of his face.

One didn't need stupendous powers of foresight to see where this was going. "Elim, don't –"

Sil was silenced by Twoblood's grip on his upper arm. "O-pen mout!" the watchman demanded, in Ardish this time.

"Like hell I will," Elim snarled.

But he did have to open his mouth to say that much, and the watchman seized the opportunity to reach up with his thumb and fingers in an open pincer, as if he would force apart a dog's jaws.

"Elim –" Sil began again, but it was clear that Calvert's mule had finished with listening to him. He drew his head and arm sharply back, his white-rimmed eyes staring angrily down at his accoster. Then he swung. With one brutal bone-cracking impact, his fist caught the watchman right under the jaw and sent him crashing into half a dozen seated men. Shouts of surprise rippled back into the crowd, punctuated by one horrified shriek from the back.

But Elim did not even have time to draw back his arm before Twoblood was right up behind him. With one sharp, fluid motion, she kicked out the back of Elim's knees, stepped aside, and struck him a terrific crack to the back of his head with the butt-end of her pistol.

Elim dropped like a stunned ox. Sil felt the impact through his boots as Elim's whole body hit the dirt like so much meat and lay there, wide-eyed and insensible with pain.

Sil had never even seen her draw the gun.

The watchman launched himself back up to his feet, as if he'd suffered nothing more than a hard shove, planted his foot on Elim's neck and aimed his pistol squarely between Elim's eyes. From somewhere farther away, a horse trumpeted a shrill whinny. All the rest was drowned out by the ferocity with which Twoblood took control. "*Barks, help me tie him to the posts. Yes-Yes, control your wife. You, fetch a lash. And someone get me that shrinking bastard Fours!*"

Sil, safely ignored, stood silent as people swarmed past him – still the unnecessary, unproven bystander he always had been.

Elim, on the other hand, was about to earn his stripes.

"COME ON, MISSUS – come have a look, see what I've brought for you..."

Fours held the cactus-fruits flat in his hand, but the big brown mare was having none of it. As soon as he got within five feet, she was off again to the other side of the corral.

So he stood still and waited, not so much irritated as marveling. He'd handled plenty of horses in his time, but this was the first one he'd met with a notion to own the eastern side of his pen.

"Having trouble with the round-up?" a voice said behind him.

"I don't understand it," Fours replied, watching as the horse vexed herself in her chosen corner – antsy, tail swishing, occasionally tossing her head. "Perhaps it's the blood. I raked it out and put down fresh straw, but they're very sensitive, you know..."

By and by, it occurred to him that he'd inadvertently struck up a conversation. Fours turned, and immediately recognized the slender, self-assured figure decked out in a charcoal frock-coat and matching flat-brimmed hat and leaning, hands in pockets, next to the weathered barn door.

Fours froze. "Faro – I didn't see you there..." He'd be angry that Fours hadn't managed to buy them yesterday.

But Faro only smiled his trademark smile, beatific, unperturbed, and strolled forward into the bright morning sun. "Do you know," he said, "that that half-breed horseman of yours is a slave? True indeed – I wish I could have stayed to hear more. Now what's this project here?"

"Oh. Well..." Fours glanced down at the fruit in one hand and the lead rope in the other, and imagined that he must look a bit foolish. "... this one isn't for sale, you see, and after – you know, this morning – the gentleman, Master Halfwick, did ask if I wouldn't mind putting her –"

One glance from Faro was sufficient to catch the error.

"– putting it, rather, aside with his own animal, before his buyers come to collect the rest. I've got the one penned up in the old sty already, but I can't seem to catch..."

Fours trailed off as Faro continued his slow, easy advance, stretching his arms wide and walking just near enough to the fence that the mare could not easily slip between the two. She flattened her ears and backed up, grinding her teeth.

"Oh, I think it will come along just fine. Now you stand there, see – don't give it room to run off again."

Fours did not like the idea of cornering a large animal.

Fours did as he was told.

"Thank you," he said, as it seemed Faro's plan was working.

Thankfully, Faro stopped just before her backside would have hit the fence. She halted there with a stamp of her hoof and threw her head high. "You're welcome," he said, his expression soured by either her attitude or the ambient smell. "But as fascinating as this is, I was hoping we could discuss some of your less pastoral undertakings."

Fours shuffled closer to Faro, so that the right angle they made between them effectively blocked her in. This did not seem add to her upset, so perhaps they could just wait like this for now, until she'd settled a bit... "Like what?"

Faro's smirk carried in his voice. "Like how you intend to explain yourself to the Azahi."

Fours glanced over at him, touched by dread. "Why? What have I done?" *He* hadn't gone and shot anyone, nor abetted anyone who had.

Faro raised his carefully-sculpted eyebrows in a look that Fours always found especially bothersome. "Well, you did offer to buy smuggled goods, quite illegally I think..."

"No!" Fours freely copied the mare's strident agitation. "You said, you SAID that I was to purchase any horse or mule of reasonable quality, no questions asked, and that you would –"

"That I would do what, exactly?" Faro replied in a very particular tone of voice. "Pick up the pieces for you after you CALLED IN THE WATCH? Was that part of our agreement? Do consider carefully – and rope this damned thing, will you?"

Fours hesitated on both counts, and finally opened his mouth to suggest finishing their discussion inside. His thought was cut off by a feminine scream from the gathering down the road.

The mare's ears swiveled at the sound; she turned her head to look. Fours quickly reached forward to slip the lead rope over her head.

Then she let out a piercing sharp whinny, rearing up as if she'd been struck. One hoof clipped Fours under the collar, sending him sprawling into the dirt. He froze, his skin blanching to camouflage with the pale, dry earth.

A vast shadow flashed in front of his terrified eyes, ending with a thunderous tattoo of hoofbeats on the ground.

A hand clamped down on Fours' wrist and yanked him back up to his feet.

"I said rope it, not frighten the daylights out of it!" Faro snapped. Still, he was shaken enough to let Fours off with a rough swat to the arm. "Master yourself, before someone sees you."

Fours looked down at his hands. They darkened to their customary shade of brown. Then he adjusted his wig and followed Faro's attention to the scene beyond the paddock gate, massaging the injury at his collar all the while.

Both watched the distant commotion with unblinking black-eyed stares.

But Fours also caught Faro considering the mare, now trotting off southwards in the aftermath of her fence-jumping panic, and fear slipped through his heart again. Fours' hands consoled each other; he prayed to the Artisan that Faro would not see anything more than an unreasoning animal, would not think anything more than unexceptional thoughts.

But perhaps he ought to do more than pray.

"Oh, I *am* sorry, sir." Conservative as he was with gender pronouns, Faro still liked to hear himself as a *sir*. "That was my fault for spooking her; I'll catch her up again directly..."

Faro crossed his arms over his chest. "You know, Fours, I think we might yet get you out of this little pickle of yours."

Of course. *His* pickle. But any escape [...]
questions was enough to command Fours' [...]

"Oh?"

Faro nodded, pleased now. "Yes, quite. I cannot [...]
of anything better for our Mother's fine new hors[...]
than an exceptionally competent horseman."

Fours' heart sank. Faro caught it instantly on his face.
"What?" he demanded. "That isn't good enough for
you?"

"Oh no, no," Fours raced to reassure him. "I am her
servant in everything, of course! Only..." he struggled
to think of a sufficiently convincing 'only.' "... only he
is charged with murder, I think, and I can't imagine that
Twoblood will let him free..."

A lone figure was running towards them out of the
assembly. Faro beamed, and clapped Fours on the
shoulder. "Oh, but I have every confidence in you,
Fours. Do think quickly – here's Twoblood's man
coming for you now – and I shall be sure to relate every
scintillating detail of your success to our very-grateful
Mother. Carry on!"

Fours dipped his head as Faro turned to see himself
out, and absently pressed at the damp pink-tinged stain
under his collar.

The reward for his success was vague and unpromised,
as it always was. The foreshadowing of his failure was
hurrying up to him now, wide-eyed and shouting.

'Pickle' wasn't the word for it.

LEFT ALONE, SIL had plenty of time to occupy a pocket of
isolation amidst the din, and to think.

He did not offer any comment as Elim was hauled down

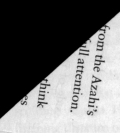

the wrists to two of the posts
overed sidewalk on the eastern
lid not make eye contact when
whose talent apparently included
tant face – was led away by a
id not even weasel himself within
e white-hot bollocking that Fours
received, althoug.... judge by his cowering submission
and Twoblood's explicit gestures, Sil wouldn't have been
able to keep up with the translation anyway.

But he did take notice of the whip as it was delivered
into Twoblood's waiting hands. Sil had long since
decided that no, if the slave defense was going to
work, then he'd have to let her do it – no protests, no
flinching. He tried with a queasy stomach to imagine
how many strokes Elim could take before it threatened
his life, and rounded down to find the number at which
he'd be forced to intervene. If he asked, though, for
an extra measure of caution, as this particular human
commodity was highly valued by Sil's employer...

... why yes, then everything would be just splendid,
and Sil could go to his death with a clear conscience
when Calvert saw the bloody gashes on Elim's back.

From up the street, Elim was already stirring. He did
not see Sil.

But Twoblood spotted him instantly, and Sil steeled
his nerve as the Second Man of Island Town approached
Elim and beckoned Sil over. Her expression promised
no niceties.

"*If he is a slave, then he is the most violently
disobedient slave I have seen. Here.*"

Sil looked down as the coiled whip was shoved into
his hands, and then back up at Twoblood. "*What?*"

"*Correct him, idiot!*" Twoblood fairly shouted with impatience. "*Is he yours or isn't he?*"

The verbal explosion elicited the barest flinch from Elim. Then his muscles gradually slackened again, his arms sagging all of three inches. One couldn't tell whether he didn't realize what was coming to him, or had simply given up.

Sil looked back down at the lash, its taut leathery coils alien to his hands. It was a smallish snake whip, meant to herd livestock mostly by noise and threat, but Sil had no doubt that it could score a man's flesh as quick and neatly as hot cross buns.

"*No.*" And again, with more conviction now. "*No – you can plainly see that he has never been handled in this way,*" Sil said, with a broad gesture towards Elim's pristine parti-colored back, "*and I will not begin to do so now. It is not our way.*"

Twoblood lifted her chin, as if this were the confession she'd been waiting to hear. "*Well then, 'Master' Halfwick, what is your way? He has killed one man and assaulted another – or must that also be your fault? Please tell us how you would handle such a man, so that we may better ourselves by your example.*"

Sil looked back at Elim, privately cursing him from the pit of his soul. He sculpted his demeanor to a cool, impervious surface. "*Leave him there,*" Sil said with a half-shrug, the idea gaining momentum in his mind. "*A whipping is over in a few minutes, and I would not let him off so lightly. Let us – let him stay there today and think about his crime*" – Sil emphasized this in the singular, indicating the one which had occurred just now – "*and let your people use him as they will. Let him be spit, cursed, fouled – I don't care, as long as he isn't damaged.*" Sil returned his attention to Twoblood. "*And let the time also serve to – to consider my earlier request, please. I would be very much in your debt.*"

"*You already are,*" Twoblood pledged with a glint in her eye. Still, her pause left room enough to entertain the idea. "*Go away. We will consider it.*"

Good enough. Sil walked aside, glad at least for an excuse to retreat into the shade, and forced himself not to pace. It wasn't as if worrying would avail him anything – hadn't he done everything he possibly could?

Well... there was perhaps one item of business remaining.

Sil put the whip down and stepped up onto the covered sidewalk. Its planks were elevated a good ways off the ground – a sensible precaution, if you'd taken it into your head to build on a river island – which meant that he could look Elim level in the eye.

Except that Elim seemed to prefer staring at Sil's boots. Or rather, didn't bother to change his field of vision when said boots entered into it.

"Well, look here, Elim..." Sil began with a cough and a glance up at the conference of Sundowners just beyond the soft brown-shanked crown of the horseman's head. "... I know that wasn't quite fair play, and I'm sorry, all right. I've got a plan to get you out: I think I've talked them out of a whipping, and I'll have everything straightened out just as soon as I speak to – well, it doesn't matter. The point is that I've got it sorted. You've just to hold tight here for awhile – a few hours, maybe – and I'll get us both out of here and we'll be home in time for church, all right?"

Elim's only answer was the rhythm of his breathing.

Sil waited until it was clear that this was too regular,

too perfectly non-responsive to be anything but a deliberate act of mulery. "Well?" he demanded. As if he wasn't worth bothering with – as if he'd done anything but work to save Elim's miserable spotted skin from a mess of his own making! "Damn you, don't you have anything to say?"

Elim looked up to regard Sil with dull, half-lidded eyes. "Golly, Master Halfwick sir," he drawled, "that sure is mighty white of y –"

Sil backhanded him hard across the face.

And although the force of the blow was enough to snap his head violently aside, it impeded him not at all. "You didn't have the right!" Elim screamed, hurling himself forward until the roof-posts creaked. "YOU DIDN'T HAVE THE RIGHT!"

Sil took a frightened step backwards. One couldn't tell whether anyone had noticed the blow, but nobody within a hundred feet could have missed what followed.

Elim let his head down again, the rest of him simply going slack. Twoblood beckoned Sil over with a sharp jerk of her head.

So he got down, hand stinging, stomach churning, and returned to the conference in the street, feeling worse than he ever had. All day he had carried the knowledge that a human being had died in violence. He'd inspected the body himself. And yet it was only here, with a man very much still living, that he suddenly turned ill, morbidly afflicted with the thought that something really, actually irreversible had just happened, something completely beyond his power to fix or undo.

Some of that must have showed in his face, or else Twoblood was waxing merciful. "*We see that he is dimeto*," she said, a word that Sil decided to interpret in context as 'psychotic'. She seemed to think that Sil was perhaps a bit *dimeto* himself. "*Let him stay there today. It will be for the family to decide.*"

Excellent. Marvelous. Sil thanked her profusely for her forbearance, and extended his gratitude to the senior men present as well. It wasn't long before the lingerers in the back got the idea that there wasn't going to be a flogging after all. By the time they finally began to disperse, Sil had gotten leave to go and make his personal apologies to the a'Krah... although Twoblood did not seem to regard this as an especially significant or useful thing to do.

Well, let her think so – Sil would do it anyway. One conversation would straighten it all out, and then after Sil had made his apologies and bought pardon and been reduced to penury all over again, he'd rescue Elim and then enjoy a good thorough vomit before they cut a straight path out of town.

Going home really wasn't sounding so bad after all.

CHAPTER SEVEN
VISITATIONS

ON THE OCCASION that he was stuck minding the store, Sil tried to avoid the mush-apple gossip of Hell's Acre. Still, it was common knowledge that Jane Calvert had come rather late to the table in marrying, and her subsequent difficulties were therefore strictly predictable.

She managed one living daughter, and a miscarriage, and another daughter, and a third, but not before the second had died in her cradle, and then two years and one bloody confinement later, a stillbirth. By that time, Calvert had got the idea that he wasn't going to have a son after all, at least not by natural means, and struck on the notion of buying one instead.

Which was perfectly sensible, except that the Calverts had then cultivated not only a child, but also a monstrous habit of treating their purchased addition to the family as if he weren't exactly that. Nestled amidst honesty and industry and all the rest of those carefully-inculcated redneck virtues, they'd fostered in him this insidious idea that he could comport himself everywhere in the same unchanging manner, like a dog always let on the furniture, with no regard to where he was or what behavior was expected of him.

That was foolish enough for any ordinary fellow, but for Elim, it promised to be a fatally irresponsible flaw in his upbringing.

Which Sil would not hesitate to correct with blistering vigor, just as soon as he finished getting that vast overloved idiot out of the snare he'd managed to make out of his own lifeline – just as soon as he found the right help.

But help was in short supply, and the house, damn it all, was empty.

It had seemed quiet that morning as well, when Aibak had come to roust Sil out of bed – demanding not the merchandise, fatefully enough, but the whereabouts of their truant errand-boy. Still, it was well on towards noon now, and he could not find a solitary soul.

Sil paused there in the stuffy parlor, leaning on the bar Brant had so cheerfully tended last night, and rubbed his face. It was no good tapping at closed doors upstairs – one indelicate encounter could ruin what little credit he had left. No, there had to be *some*one up and about somewhere, even if only a maid: as universal human constants went, greed was trumped only by laundry.

All right then: to the scullery. They'd call it a cellar here, perhaps more for use as a larder than a wash-up, and if you meant to keep anything cool in this wretched climate, you'd better dig deep. Sil retraced his steps, back downstairs and out into the kitchen yard, but this time circled around to the back of the house. There among the outbuildings, half sunk into the ground, was the root cellar's rear entrance.

And before it, as if set there exclusively in testament to Sil's cleverness, was one squatting Sundowner. Apparently idle and apparently a'Krah, if the dark skin and plaited pigtails were any indication, he chewed a root as Sil approached him with guarded relief: here at least was someone he could talk to.

Only this particular a'Krah wouldn't have met him yet. He glowered at Sil, making no move to rise, and greeted him with a short, upward jerk of his chin. "*Hihn?*"

That was not Marín, but nevermind. "*Your pardon, friend,*" Sil said with a deferential bow. "*Do you know where I can find Huitsak, our king?*"

The lackey was not impressed by Sil's facility. "*No. Fuck off.*"

That was less than promising, and carried a worrisomely heavy accent. Marín was the language of business – what border-dweller wouldn't know it?

"*Certainly,*" Sil replied, and did nothing of the sort. "*What about Vuchak, or Weisei – where may I see them?*" A man of Huitsak's prominence would be in the habit of qualifying his visitors; Sil only needed to seek a lower rung on the social ladder.

The a'Krah spit at their names, and declined to elaborate further.

Bloody useless menials. Sil's smile tightened. "*I see. Don't trouble yourself any more, friend; I will look with my own eyes.*" He reached for the door.

The a'Krah leapt to his feet, brandishing a knife. "*Ne tsika'kohai ene haga' weh'ne!*" he swore, lunging at Sil.

Sil flinched back, but it was lucky his opponent was only feinting: one clumsily-raised arm would have been no impediment to a stab in the gut. "*Why?*" Sil snapped from his safer remove, gesturing at the door beyond. "*What is there?*"

"*Dulei!*" The a'Krah retorted.

Oh.

Well, they would have had to put him somewhere, wouldn't they? Sil let his hand sink down to his side. There were things to do, particular items of business, when someone died – the washing and the dressing and all, usually a good bit of reading or praying or what-have-you. In the murky depths of Sil's personal recollection, it certainly had seemed to take up much of the day, and most of his relations besides.

And the row he was having with one of the bereaved wasn't a bit rude, was it? "*I am sorry,*" Sil said, and bowed again.

The a'Krah accepted Sil's apology with a contemptuous snort, a guardedly retaken squat, and an upward jerk of his knife at the eye painted above the door, which Sil had not noticed before.

He knew it, though. That was the sign of the Crow God. Which meant that *a'Krah* must be the self-given name of the Crow people – one of the three Great Nations, the empire of the west, who seemed to grow stronger with every tribe they swallowed into their ranks. If they had ever managed to secure an alliance with the wolf-riders of the vast northern grasslands, Eaden would have lost the Bravery altogether.

And now Elim had killed one of their sons.

Sil did not hear what he said to excuse himself. He retreated back to the house, through the kitchen and into the parlor, where, absent any practical notion, he sequestered his small and foolish person in an overstuffed chair and contrived to sit almost sideways, knees drawn halfway up... mindful not to put his feet on the furniture, of course.

Honestly, had there ever been so tremendous an idiot?

Yes, without a doubt – but Elim was already sunk up to his neck in a pit of his own making, and Sil's empty innards turned on realizing that he had no second strategy for pulling him out.

What if Twoblood was right? What if the a'Krah couldn't be bought?

Great God, what if Elim was about to die and there was literally nothing Sil could do about it?

That thought occupied him long enough for his eyes to sharpen their focus and observe, on the floor under the bar, a strikingly familiar weathered gray hat.

CHAMPAGNE, OF COURSE, was for special occasions, celebrations of one kind or another. And it had been a long time since there was anything to celebrate.

So Shea retained the plain mind of a common house-maid, and filled it with ordinary concerns as readily as she now filled her basket with wet clothes. She thought exclusively of the laundry, and of finishing it before the sweltering sun made it any more odious a job, and in her under-mind, of that foolish spotted boy and what needed to be done between now and sunset, when she would be expected to be all purple silk and painted smiles again.

And – out of loathsome present necessity – of Faro.

"You were supposed to be watching the river," he said.

Shea paused in scrubbing her tired half-onion over the

gravy stain on his second-best white shirt, and turned to look over her shoulder. He registered in her ruined vision as a blur in the shade of the staked timber wall, standing up there like a born overseer as she squatted ankle-deep in the stream.

Which afforded her feet a privilege that incensed the rest of her irritable frame all the further. "I was SUPPOSED to have changed the beds, swept the floor, and wiped down the bar, which I did, and to be ready at the door by eight, which I was. When do you think I sleep?"

This was not the same as saying she had actually *been* asleep.

Fortunately, Faro was as good at ignoring selective truths as he was at telling them. "Mind the buttons on that one."

"Sir." Shea dipped her hand into the stream and wet down her arms and face and the long-tailed kerchief tied around her head for what felt like the twentieth time in the past hour. The water was warm and bitter and stank of algae. "Anyway, I don't see what you have to be upset about. Didn't you get them all anyway?"

"At five times the trouble and expense!" he snapped. "If you'd been doing your job, I could have caught him as he went to Fours and had the whole herd for a song. As it is, I spent the better part of an hour playing childish games for the privilege of buying just one, and then had to wheedle the rest from Fatsack, which you know is money I won't see again."

That part was true enough: Faro had about as much chance of reclaiming a pearl from Huitsak's pocket as did the oyster. He was lucky enough to have closed the deal before they found out about Dulei.

"Shall I take it, then, that the money you spent beforehand WILL be seen again?"

Shea had suffered Faro long enough to know a smirk when she heard it. "Well, if Young Master Halfwit hasn't already figured out that he's playing with big boys now, it won't take him long. I may yet compensate myself for time and expenses. Which doesn't at all excuse your negligence."

Shea wrung out the shirt, ignoring the lewd attentions of the gnats hovering around the wet hem of her shift. "Of course. Do forgive me, sir – whatever can I do to make it up to you?"

That attitude was not one wisely taken with Miss Addie's *maître d'hôtel*. But if you were having a disagreeable conversation in a disagreeable place while doing disagreeable work, the only tone to take was a disagreeable one. Anything else would smell of dishonesty.

"Why, I'm glad you asked," he said, his voice unconscionably pleasant. "You can get me that half-man, alive of course, and all will be forgiven."

Shea stopped wringing as a cold pang seized her stomach. What under the sun did *Faro* want him for?

But she'd already betrayed herself by the pause, and now re-cast it, playing it off as a more vulgar astonishment. "Me?" Shea twisted to look back at him. "You want me to go and what, throw a wet petticoat over Twoblood's head as I saunter off with her prisoner? Go and make Fours do it – he's the one with daylight credentials!"

This was not the answer Faro wanted. "What makes you think he has any better idea for getting it done?"

She turned back to her laundry basket, conspicuously

unbothered. "What does he think we're going to do to
his daughter if he doesn't?"

His daughter. Nothing to do with Shea.

Faro's only answer was the sound of his approaching
bootsteps – soft in the dry soil, and then with more
suction as the heels met mud.

Shea did not freeze – she wouldn't give him the
satisfaction – but made a pretense of digging through
the basket. He sank down at her side in a better-dressed
copy of her leggy squat, keeping his coat-tails out of the
muck and his voice sugary sweet.

"'We'? Are we a 'we' now?"

Shea did not hesitate in meeting his gaze. "If it gets
us off this shit-heap island any faster, we certainly are."

Faro understood – *trusted* – nothing better than plain
self-interest. And if you made a consistent practice of
keeping your cards tipped just far enough forward, he
would spend far less time scrutinizing your sleeves.

He was disconcertingly close, his face so near to hers
that she could smell the sweet pomade he used in his
false golden curls and almost see the faint, vitreous
membranes of his closed inner eyelids. In that moment,
it was exceptionally difficult to avoid knowing things
that Shea the common house-maid wouldn't, about
what his thin lips concealed and how easily he could
turn violent before she had time to react.

But Faro smiled with ordinary human teeth, and
weighted his voice to tease. "And poor Fours? Will you
win your reprieve and leave him here?"

"I don't give a damn about Fours!" she snapped. "He
is no more kin to me than you are, and if he hasn't
learned that by now, he never will."

This was another one of those selective, technical

truths, and Shea would not give him time to dwell on it. "Look here," she said, surrendering to a request that Faro hadn't technically made, "I'll go find him, since what you're asking for is hardly going to be simple, and see if we can't manage it together. But after that, after you've got the – the half-man, Mother Opéra will hear that *I* was the one who made it happen, at your illustrious direction of course, and *I* will take the sum of her gratitude for whatever it may be worth. Promise me that, and I'll get it done."

Faro smiled at that, and Shea could only hope that her inward thinking was as invisible as his. "You know, Miss Shea, I have often thought it a shame that we aren't related. The project is yours, then, as will be all credit attending its completion. Let's have an eye for getting it done today, though, can we? You know he will be wasted on the a'Krah."

Good enough. "Fine, fine. Go away and let me get it done. Leave the key to the old pantry in the door, and we'll put him in there."

Faro stood. "Splendid – I'll look forward to meeting him." He turned and walked back up the bank.

Shea kept her hands busy, nominally still wringing the sodden mass in her lap. Fours wouldn't be pleased about it, but he was pathetically easy to coerce, and it wasn't as if she actually needed to *keep* the boy for anything. Once she'd –

"Oh, and Shea…"

Her heart skipped. She turned. "What?"

Faro tapped a muddy heel against the wall. "I'll just leave these by the door, shall I?"

"Certainly, sir; I'll have them shat in at once," she replied… but only within earshot of the laundry. After he had gone, she hefted the basket, spread her foreshortened toes, and hiked back up to the back of the house.

It was a miserable job, as most truly necessary ones were, and years of doing it and all Faro's sordid little side-projects had worn her into a miserable creature.

And if the two-colored boy was her ticket out of it, if there was any chance that his life could be used to restore hers, then Shea the common house-maid would bleed him at any cost.

SHE WASN'T REALLY Fours' mother, of course. It was Mother Melisant who had authored his life and would always claim his heart.

And Melisant would not have forced him to leave her – no, she had only to ask, because their Prince Joconde was going away to be married to Princess Opéra, and of course the prince couldn't go without family, without true and loyal siblings to care for him. Even though it meant leaving Mother forever, Fours did it willingly... because she loved him, and because she had only asked, and because it was very-probably his only chance to repay the care she had shown him throughout his small and unpromising life.

It should have been a good one, spent in the company of his kin.

But within the year, Prince Joconde was dead, and Fours and the rest of the royal retinue were as so many left-over wedding presents, to be used or discarded or forgotten at the bride-widow's sole discretion.

He could have lived well enough that way, a forgotten thing merchandising other forgotten things in a largely-forgotten place...

"Fours?"

... except unfortunately that it wasn't anymore, and neither was he.

Fours stopped there on the Street of the Brick-Makers, and belatedly turned to see one of the older Washchaw women, Ah-Shi-Shah in fact, watching him with serene interest from the pale clay arch of her doorway. Her large hands and plain smock were dusty with flour, her face framed by sweat-damp strands of hair, and although she was modestly-sized by Washchaw standards, her tall broad-shouldered frame marked her easily as a descendant of O-San, the Silver Bear. "Are you looking for something?" she said in Marín, the traditional greeting colored by her accent.

Fours glanced down at the rope in his hand, and remembered its purpose. "Yes, mother – a horse, a brown mare, which escaped me earlier. I hope she hasn't hurt anything."

Ah-Shi-Shah's age-softened features creased in amusement. "Ah. She gave her company to our goats, I think, or else I misunderstood the excitement this morning."

"I'm very sorry," Fours said, and moved forward until he was within her reach. This was how the Washchaw understood honesty: anything sincerely meant was not to be tossed off like garbage from a great distance, but put to the recipient's ear as closely as one would put a hand to his or her shoulder. "I'll look for her there, and make repayment for any trouble."

She flicked her fingers, the sign of something trivial. "There is no trouble, except that which I make by keeping you from your work. Please, go and fill your house again, and I will have Ki-Meh catch your horse and bring her. It will be our repayment to you, since he cannot work today."

She dropped her gaze there at the end. If Fours pressed her, it would surely emerge that Ki-Meh wasn't well, or had some pressing obligation, but his failure to appear for his usual chores in Fours' barn had just one gruesome cause. Death was abhorrent to the Washchaw in general, and to the Ant-Watching Clan in particular, and there was no death more dreadful than a violent one.

"I understand, and am grateful for your help," Fours said. "Please let Ki-Meh know that I wish him well, and will be glad to see him again when the time is right."

This small expression of kindness was a good one to make: Ah-Shi-Shah closed her big hand around the back of his neck as if he were a kitten to be lifted, and kissed her shoulder.

Fours did not register any new sensation as this little blessing presumably travelled down her sinewy arm and into his flesh, but felt himself warmed and gratified by the gesture. Ah-Shi-Shah's was a great family, with five children and three brothers and a sister and many more relations than even Fours knew about, and when she connected him with her touch, he felt as if he had been made a part of that great network, as much a child to her as Wi-Chuck or Ki-Meh.

So he took his leave with gladness in his heart, and that confidence that came from being a well-functioning and wanted part of a larger collective...

... and indeed he was almost five minutes down the road before he remembered that this issue with the horse was small, nearly meaningless in fact, while the matter of the horseman loomed large and unresolved, its solution invisible or nonexistent.

And there was no friendly soul who would help him with that one.

Fours stopped at the sight of his sorry-looking house, its bleached gray walls promising nothing, sheltering nobody, waiting for him like a bachelor's cold stove.

Ah-Shi-Shah had not forced him to leave her. He could, if he took leave of his senses, turn around and beg to be adopted into the Ant-Watching Clan. Even if that were not permitted, she would almost certainly give him a place in her home.

But Fours was not the one who would be made to suffer if he decided to abandon his loyalties. Faro had long since made sure of that.

So he returned home, exactly as she had asked. And having thus run out of achievable tasks and satisfiable task-givers, there was little left to do but attempt with more than his usual vigor to disappear into the dusty woodwork of the walls.

YES, THERE WAS something holy in the act of waiting... but every now and again holiness sure tasted like a scorching mess of miseries.

And right at the moment, it sounded like Elim had a considerable amount of waiting to do. Whether because the natives had been scattered by his mindless raging or simply because it was the time when all sensible creatures put themselves to shade, Elim had been left alone to bake in the sun and contemplate his sin.

He'd forgotten his own handling-manners, that was what.

Which you liked to think you could beat a horse in remembering, but it had been such a long time. Not since he was six years old and standing on the auction block had anyone had occasion for fingering his mouth, and the man who'd ultimately bought the right never had used it afterward.

Sil had probably not been born when Boss Calvert gave Elim his mark. He couldn't understand how easy it was back then for any colored body, and children especially, to be snatched right off the street, right out of the field, and never seen again. The brand wasn't about *owning* but *belonging*. It was a promise, a cauterized guarantee that Elim could not be lost or stolen, would never be sold or traded away – that he would wear on his hide what he couldn't hang on his name, and declare on his body what was already true in his soul. He was a part of the Calvert family, real and permanent, and Sil and the speckled mule and that whole bunch of ignorant gawking part-timers had no more power to change that than to alter his very spots.

Stupid, then, to behave as if they already had.

The blessing of horses, he had decided once, was that they didn't change according to how you called them. Molly was still Molly, no different whether he called her his sweet-heart sugar-loaf or a fly-biting fat tramp, and Shy Violet would not be made one jot more forward by calling her Brazen Bess, and Two-Pie would still be Two-Pie even if you hadn't given the world fair warning by calling him after his most notorious windowsill heist.

Probably that was because they didn't know their names as anything but a particular pattern of mouth-sounds. Which sure would make it easier not to be bothered about – not to be *changed by* any of the ideas stuffed inside them. That was all the trouble: the only thing more dreadful than how quick and easily those nasty heathens had changed him into somebody else – into the very thing Sil had named him! – was the thought that maybe they hadn't power to do any such thing.

There was a church-word for what you did to get clean of your wickedness, but Elim couldn't put it to mind just then. The homespun version was *sorry*, though, and he put his aching head to doing just that, to sowing and stockpiling nothing but sorry until Sil came back and gave him a market for it.

He would be all right with waiting, even, as long as he had that to look forward to at the end of it all.

So ELIM HADN'T stayed put after all.

Sil sat hunched forward as he interrogated the inside of the old gray hat. Surely it could not have got here any other way: Elim had had it last night and not this morning, and the only person known to have visited the barn in the interim had never returned.

So Elim had gone looking for him after all.

And then what, hunkered down to wait with a bottle of whiskey? It had to be – he must have done. They'd brought no alcohol with them and where the devil else could he have gotten soaked at such an hour? Brant alone, upstanding host that he was, would probably have offered hospitality even to a mule, and that didn't count the women or any pilfering servants that might have traded swigs with him on the back steps.

Sil's fingers curled to crush the hat-brim. One night, *one bloody night,* was all he'd asked for, but could this recalcitrant lumbering stooge afford him even that much? No, not Calvert's mule. The thought of Sil achieving his end, of proving that he'd been right all along, must have poisoned Elim through to his spotted soul: he lived in a rut between trough and toilet and could not stand the thought of anyone doing better.

Only the drinking did seem so very unlike him.

Sil looked up at the sound of the kitchen door opening, and was on his feet before it closed. *Finally* he could talk to someone, Huitsak or Vuchak or –

"Why, Master Halfwick," Faro said, folding his morning-coat over his arm with an expression of genuine concern, "whatever can be the matter?"

ELIM'S SHADOW SHRANK steadily, and he had nothing to do but watch it. The sun would be behind him soon, but there was still a sliver of shade under the roof. If he leaned forward just so and put his chin to his chest, he could just about keep his throbbing skull out of the light. He tried to fall asleep.

That was a taller order, and not only because of his bodily complaints. He hadn't shot anyone, and he was firm on that. If the rule was that he had to own everything within his recollection, like the fist he'd fed to that Sundowner earlier today, then anything he couldn't recall didn't belong to him.

The rafters creaked in the thick afternoon air.

Still... there had been a moment today, when Sil's vicious buyer had him down on his knees with a pistol to his head, that Elim had known for sure he was fixing to die. If death came back for him today, and his unbridled soul finally got to know the whole truth of things, what would he see that would somehow connect the blood-spattered stall with the dead boy inside it, and the barn door barred from the inside, and the aching hole in Elim's memory, and how would he be held accountable for it all?

The roof creaked again. Elim cracked one eye and glanced up. There was a great black *something* staring down at him from the rafters.

He plunged backwards, earning himself sharp pain in his head and both wrists, but not nearly enough distance from the shapeless horror.

His struggling provoked no reaction, though. When he looked again, it was only the strange black lady he and Dan had so nearly trampled yesterday. She was lying across the planks with her head resting on her forearms and her snaky rope-hair dangling down, watching him.

Elim hung slack between the posts, and let out a slow breath. "I wish like hell I'd listened to you," he said in a dry whisper.

"Hell is nothing to wish for," she replied.

It was good to see a familiar face, but her calm eyes unnerved him. Elim went back to watching his shadow. "I know," he said after a bit. "'m sorry."

There was a silence after that. One of the posts creaked as Elim leaned further into the shade, courting the pain in his arms in preference to the creeping warmth on the back of his neck. And then, because it didn't cost anything to ask: "I don't expect you could help get me down?"

"That depends largely on why you were put up," she replied.

The knot in that one plank looked like an eye. Elim studied it as he considered how to explain things in as few words as possible. "Seems I went and busted a man's face." And then, because it was probably pertinent even if it wasn't true: "Seems I might've killed one, too."

"Did you?" Her words were plain, unflavored by accusation or surprise.

"No," he said, which was short for *no, I wouldn't have, not for anything*. But that did not include the *except I can't figure how else it could have happened* part that kept wanting to get put at the end of it. "Only I think I must've done, only it don't... I don't even know." The act of confession failed him here: instead of lightening his soul, this dire admission only further leaded his gut.

"Why would you have done that?"

"I wouldn't!" Elim protested in spite of the rawness of his throat. "I didn't, I don't – I ain't like that, not ever." He didn't like Sundowners and that was fair, but he didn't like collard greens either, and he'd never yet felt compelled to draw on a vegetable.

And he never did anything without a reason, even a bad one. He let his eyes glaze over until the knotholes were so many blotches in a sea of gray. "I expect," he said as softly as would still carry in the dry space between them, "I might've put some lead in the wall, if I thought he was a rustler." He'd have to have been an awfully dumb one, though, to bar the door behind him. "But not in his head – not unless I thought he meant to fill mine first." It chilled him to think he would even be capable of that. Boss had taught him until he could nail a crabapple at three hundred yards, but Elim had never taken aim at so much as the chalked shadow of a man.

She apparently found that a weighty thought too. "I believe we have the right to guard our lives," she said at last. "I see that it is practiced by animals, who do not know sin."

Elim stared stupidly up at her lean, spotless features, unable to copy her reasoning. "I'm gonna die."

Her gaze returned his with supervisory assurance. "Yes," she agreed. "But we should hope not for a very long time yet."

Something must have troubled her then. Her dark brow wrinkled, and she snaked forward to let her upper body down from the rafters, hooking her ankles under one plank and her knees over the next and twisting at the waist until she hung down right in front of him, and studied his face. "Still," she said, "tomorrow is never promised to us. Have you prepared yourself?"

If she had come to comfort him, she was making a pig's ear of it. Elim half-shivered even in the heat. "No," he said, "not any. I ain't – I don't rightly know how." This was his worst, by far. He'd never in his life done anything so bad that confessing it hadn't gone some way towards fixing things, and he couldn't begin to right himself again.

She frowned, and by sheer abdominal fortitude leaned closer, thin cords of muscle pulling taut at her neck and shoulders as the tips of her thick locks traced little half-circles in the air. She brushed his damp hair from his brow with hot, careful fingers, and held her upside-down face three inches from his, smelling of smoke and wool and staring deep into Elim's eyes. "Would you like me to bare your feet?"

Elim felt a cold pang of fear. No. No, it was too dangerous. The earth was pregnant with the dead, watered with more blood than rain. Pressing your own living flesh to the ground gave every manner of spirit an easy channel up from their graves, as surely as leaving your front door open for the world to see – and for every kindly neighbor who might leave you a pan of warm corn-bread, there was a thief waiting to rob you blind. You might get haunted, possessed, afflicted with seizures or nightmares or any kind of madness. Even living people could hex you, if they bargained with the Sibyl for witch-powers, and here was Elim planted plumb in the middle of a whole festering hive of witchery. He'd be eaten alive.

And yet he couldn't break her gaze. "I'm scared to," he said. "I mean, if I did – if it is my fault..." What wouldn't the dead boy do to him?

With a sharp, sit-up thrust of her torso, she swung back up into the rafters and dropped between them to land feet-first on the floorboards, her robe swallowing the air into its heavy folds. Elim's back ached at the sight.

She straightened, hands clasped at her front. "If it is your fault," she said, "then you will have to answer for it. Your only choice is where and how to accomplish that."

Elim didn't miss her meaning. He could try to set things right now, while he was still living, or else...

She stepped a little closer, her voice and face going a little softer. "It's hard to put ourselves at the mercy of those we have wronged," she said. "But from our brief meeting yesterday..." Her gaze dropped to the ground. "... I thought you did that admirably."

Parched and sore-headed as he was, it took Elim a minute to remember what she meant. Dan. Gunning for Sil. The blood in the dirt.

Well, of course he had. Who wouldn't apologize after a thing like that?

Or maybe she meant what he'd done after, when he sat quiet and waited for her to curse him for it. And now here she was, a peculiar but welcome comfort in what might well be his last hours – and here he was, reaping the kindness he'd sown by sheer dumb-ass accident. Was that his warm-up lesson for this here? Was this his chance to make things right while he was still above-ground?

Well, if lying down and waiting to get his head kicked in was his ticket to grace, Elim would hit the dirt face-first. "All right," he said. "All right, sure – if you wouldn't mind."

So she climbed down to squat in the dirt by his feet, and he cocked his knee to give her a better angle for wrestling off his boot.

Still, it was a frightening thing to see her strip off his sock, and to feel the hot air teasing his soft naked foot, and to set that foot straight down into bare dirt for whatever spirits, witches, or hookworms wanted to have at it.

None of them did, though - at least not that he could feel. So maybe he hadn't shot that boy after all.

Or maybe it was just that she kept him protected somehow. She knew the Verses – he remembered that much – and she was as bravely barefoot today as she had been yesterday. Certainly he felt better when she sat up next to his leg like that.

Elim looked down as she finished with his second boot. He didn't reckon it was awfully pleasant down there – he'd been brewing a stockingfoot stew for days now – but she didn't seem to notice as she looked from the plain brownness of his left foot to the pristine whiteness of his right, and finally tilted her head back to meet his gaze. "How do you feel?"

Elim took a slow, steadying breath. He felt terrible, that was what - hog-tied and bust-headed and absolutely bone dry, not to mention half-naked in front of God and everybody. It took him a minute to whittle the list down to things she might could actually do something about. "Much obliged," he said. "And if – and it'd be right kind, if you could fix me with a drink."

She rolled out from between his feet and rose to stand at his side, hands clasped with clinical neatness as the dust drifted down from the corded knot-locks of her hair. "I'll need to get permission. In the meantime, I would advise you to pray, and to order your mind as best you can. Death is terrible for an unready soul."

If that was all the prescription she had for him, he'd take it two-handed. "Sure," he said, as much to convince the quailing of his gut as her personally. "Sure I will." Except she was picking up his boots and things as if she and they would go, with him still left here. Panic dug its claws in with a brutal quickness. "Only for that I got to see Sil – the, uh, the Eadan, my 'sociate, so if you might could ask him to come back, or if you could come back, irregardless of the water..." Or anyone, really, just anyone at all would do.

She made the sign of the sun wheel, which sometimes people used to say *God willing*. "I'll do everything the law will allow for you, and be back at the soonest possible moment."

That was as much of a guarantee as Elim got out of her before she turned and went – walking in perfectly ordinary fashion – and he was left again with just his own company, and he should have thought to ask her name, but hadn't.

Elim set his bare feet in the ground, freshly supplied with promises even as he ran clean out of shade. Back to quiet, then, and back to work as well, waiting harder than he ever had for someone – living or otherwise – to make up its mind about him.

TWOBLOOD'S CHAIR CREAKED with the force of her displeasure. Autumn always was an irritating time of the year.

There was the harvest, of course, and all the anxiety attending it. The longer the clouds cheated them of rain, the more exacting and peevish everyone became about doing this ritual or that sacrifice without the confounding influence of his neighbor's contrary practices.

Which only got worse once they set to work, and it was discovered that the So-and-So Clan had allowed their goats into the fields of the Thus-and-Such Clan before the last of the squash had been picked, or that Nose-In-The-Air of the Washchaw had made agreement with Irascible Idiot of the Ikwei to glean his fields, which the latter had not done to his satisfaction, and so on and so forth until Twoblood wondered whether it was really too late to sell the whole wretched island back to the Eaten.

But nevermind: the Azahi did an unceasing and ludicrous job all the rest of the year, and for the time of his annual home-going, Twoblood would shut the gate and separate the fools and steadfastly resist the urge to set fire to anyone who spoke to her... even if this year's crop of peddlers, thieves, and left-overs were making more than their usual effort to douse themselves in oil before demanding her attention.

She tipped back in her chair, boot-heels on the desk, gun and hat on her lap, and supervised the unluckiest of the lot from the barred window of her house. Apart from some passing investigation by a stray horse, the accused man was left alone.

Presently, just past noon, the cowbird came slinking down from the eaves to inspect him, relieved him of his boots, and then left again.

This was not a solution, of course. Twoblood glanced guiltily over at the two barred walls in the far corner of her little house. If either she or the half-man had been luckier in their parentage, she could have detained him in a far more civil fashion.

But the bars were forged for the keeping of men, not for their diseases. And although there was no law against two-bloods in Island Town, there was an unspoken law of prudence which urged her not to be seen with that other half.

The crow-shooting fool owed her that much.

After today, if nobody came to make a legal claim on his life, Twoblood could run him and the little white lordling out of town together, and shoot them on sight if they came back. That would be satisfactory for everyone.

If that became impossible, if she could not lawfully assign punishment or set the man free, Twoblood would have to do the humane thing and put him out of his misery.

That was why she had decided that it would not come to that.

That was why she was going to settle this today.

And so, when it had become clear that nobody was in any great rush to take the bait, Twoblood put her feet on the floor and her hat on her head, and went out walking.

The front door of La Saciadería was closed, the windows all drawn and shaded during the heat of the day. But Twoblood marched around to the back of the house, where the outbuildings were, until she caught sight of the man squatting there in front of the cellar.

This was how the a'Krah marked themselves as a worthless people.

The others, the daylight tribes, could just about be tolerated, because they occupied their lives with the work necessary to living – with all the goat-herding and cloth-weaving and corn-grinding which actually produced needful things.

But *these* people, the whores and foreigners and most especially the a'Krah, produced nothing and benefited no-one but themselves. Their sole service to Island Town was to attract crime and violence and disease. Words had been said about confining that, about keeping them here on the northern side of town and letting them do their sordid business only after dark. But garbage stank at any hour, and nowhere was the odor of indolence and greed more tellingly marked than here, at the sight of a perfectly able-bodied man whose only business was to squat in front of a door to ensure that the depravities inside would continue undisturbed.

He leapt to his feet and scowled at Twoblood's approach, though he did not quite dare to start shouting disgraces at her.

Twoblood rewarded this exceptional display of restraint with one of her own. "Bring me Huitsak," she said.

"Is not here," the a'Krah returned in his mangled Marín, lifting his chin as if to challenge her to leave a message.

All right. Twoblood glanced up at the sky from her periphery, inviting the a'Krah to agree that yes, the sun was high, its light glinting off the shaped gold of the Azahi's seal hanging around her neck. With this much understood, Twoblood drew her gun and took aim at the painted eye of Marhuk above the door.

The reaction was reassuringly prompt. "*Weh'ne!*" the a'Krah cried, lunging forward to block the way.

Twoblood stopped, and waited for him to make up his mind.

She was encouraged by the seething hatred on his face. "You wait," the a'Krah commanded at last, and slipped inside, pulling the door closed behind him.

All right.

Twoblood heard Huitsak's approach before she saw him. The door's shadow fell away to reveal the fullness of his fat bulk, as disgusting as ever if not as ostentatiously draped. Freed from its usual pigtails, Huitsak's long hair hung loose and half-kinked down his back and shoulders, its oily highlights accenting the sweat beading over his round face and double chin. He had swathed his prodigious girth in the dark, beaded garments that marked a high-ranking supplicant of Marhuk, the Crow God.

And he had the nerve to smile. "I am here for the a'Krah," he said in his honeyed voice, and opened his hands.

"I am here for the law," Twoblood replied, and kept hers clasped behind her.

Huitsak's dimpled cheeks creased further. He laced his thick fingers across his belly. "Well, and how may we do service for the law today?"

That tone never failed to set Twoblood's scalp itching; she gritted her teeth and swallowed her first reply. "I have determined the guilty man and am holding him for your judgment. If you will claim any right over him, you are to come and do it today, before dark. I will not keep him longer."

Huitsak nodded, so very agreeably. "We shall certainly keep that in our thoughts. Was there anything else?"

He might as well have patted her on the head. "Then keep this too," Twoblood snapped. "I know that Dulei was a son of Marhuk, or close enough for counting, and I know he wasn't the only one. You are keeping another, and I had better not find him or you or any of your men out on my streets tonight. If there is any blood or money to be had for this, you will have it lawfully or not at all." She would be damned if the Azahi would come back to so much as a purloined hat because of these pestering bastard a'Krah and their crow-feathered Marhuka Clan.

Huitsak never lost his unctuous smile, but something hard and knife-sharp showed behind it at the mention of the sacred name. "You do know many things, Second. So you will also know that the sire of the a'Krah achieves his own ends, and that I, lacking those gifts which apparently permit you to decipher the truth of events you had no part in, will humbly decline to decide the fate of your chosen guilty man, and stand aside as all-seeing Grandfather Marhuk makes his own determination for the death of his son. This will be obvious to an individual of your commanding insight."

Twoblood's jaw clenched; she envisioned the barrel of her gun pressed to the wattle of Huitsak's fleshy neck. He wanted to make her lose her temper. Nothing would please him more than to have it said that she was unfair in her treatment of the a'Krah – that she carried her Lovoka parentage as much in her heart as in her mouth, and had inherited a wolfish taste for crow blood.

He would have no such satisfaction. Twoblood kept her voice low and level, and her fangs hidden. "What is obvious to me is that I will shoot and kill any of you that I find within fifty paces of him after dark, and it will not matter whether you have taken the shapes of men or crows or gods."

But this was an over-reach of her authority, and they both knew it. By right, Twoblood's power extended only to the protection of the daylight citizens – the people of Island Town who had forfeited their own right of redress in exchange for the protection of law. Everyone who had not sought such protection, including the white boy and his half, were as much night-citizens as Huitsak and all his ilk: they were responsible for guarding their own lives, and Twoblood had no more right to interrupt their swindling and killing of each other than to adjudicate a lovers' quarrel.

But Huitsak seemed only charmed by her threats, and the sweat rolled down the cheek-flesh curtaining his smile. "Your vigilance in the matter of the half is reassuring, though I am not sure what you would have from me. I simply do business here according to the terms of our agreement. But the gods come out at night, and they do what they will. I wonder, how many of your men will you care to put between Marhuk and his purpose?"

This was pointless. "You had better not get close enough to count them," Twoblood swore, holstering her gun with a sharp downward thrust as she turned and stalked back up the hill. She resisted the urge to whip off her hat and scratch until she was sure Huitsak wouldn't be watching.

Because at its core, her job was about suppressing temptations – hers, and others'. That was what qualified her to be Second Man of Island Town, what set her apart from the petty fussing of the day-people and the vile debauchery of the night-people... and at the bottom of things, the only trait that distinguished her from that poor bastard tied between the posts.

Right now, the temptation was to knock the teeth out of Huitsak's condescending smile. To show that she was not a curiosity to be humored or pitied or casually ignored, that she could protect Island Town on her own, that she deferred to the Azahi but did not depend on him.

Twoblood returned home, sunk deep in the hope that Huitsak or Marhuk or whatever useless loitering gods still lived here wouldn't ask her to prove it.

To wash the newly dead was a solemn and honorable task. Still, Vuchak would excuse himself for having less than solemn and honorable thoughts as he did it.

There was rage, first and foremost. Dulei was useless, harmless, barely more than a boy – and his life had been taken by someone who didn't even want it, who could not have even the slightest idea of its worth. He had been ended as easily and thoughtlessly as a nest of quail eggs, crushed to yolk-dribbling mush by some ignorant traveler's foot.

And there was disgust, too – a peculiar mix of shame, outrage, and unexpressible resentment for Dulei himself. In fact, Vuchak would have been hard-pressed to say who was the more foolish of the two: the plague-spotted half without the sense to avoid Island

Town in the first place, or the sheep-witted a'Krah who apparently gave messages to strangers by hiding in straw like an oversized rat and then leaping out to surprise the hearer.

And then there was grief. In killing himself, Dulei had killed poor Echep too... wherever he was.

For now, there was nothing to do but observe the mourning. Dulei's debts would be paid: a seed-ball for the Ripening Woman, in gratitude for his final meal; a bundle of the best cedar kindling, to thank Breathing-Smoke for guarding him from sickness; his knife and bow for his mother, to apologize for having failed to outlive her. His feet would be tied, his garments burned, and when that was done, Dulei would be taken to the hidden place in the west to pay his last debt. Next year, probably in the summer, his nearest relations would gather his remaining bones and bear them back to Atali'Krah for Marhuk's keeping. Vuchak would look forward to that much at least: it had been a long time since he'd been home.

From his place in the cool recesses of the cellar, Vuchak registered a noise at the top of the stair, and an in-spilling of light from the open door. His hands and eyes still hastened to put the sacred cloth to all its necessary places before the growing rigor in Dulei's limbs made it impossible, but his ears were free to overhear Twoblood's rough voice.

So the dog of the Azahi had come to bark at them again.

Well, let her: she was a mongrel and a bully who thought the moon only moved because she howled at it, and she could strain at her rope until it strangled her and still make no difference at all.

It was important to remember that, to keep one's thoughts firmly fixed on the idea that Twoblood was powerless to stop what had already been put in motion, and presented no danger to any even half-sensible son of Marhuk who might presently have to leave off doing graces for his nephew's body in order to have another one put beside it.

Because otherwise one might not care to hazard one's life for this stiffening carcass after all.

The interview concluded above, and Vuchak moved to the head of the table. The hole at Dulei's forehead was easily cleaned, but to wash and plait his hair, when the back of his skull had been reduced to so many meaty broken pieces, would require more than ordinary diligence.

In moving, he caught Weisei's eye – who, since his mind could not house one thought without first evicting another, had let the bag of white corn meal go forgotten in his hand, leaving Dulei's lower parts only half-dusted with the fine flour. He looked across the table at Vuchak, his eyes red and wet with fresh grief. "This isn't going to end well, is it?"

Vuchak shook his head.

CHAPTER EIGHT
CHAMPAGNE AND PETITS-FOURS

"It's quite simple, really," Faro said in the midst of his alchemical preparations at the kitchen side-table. "Take your Ikwei friend for an example. You or I might think ourselves mighty indeed if we had his people's talent for days-long labor or going a week without sleep, but for him it's just the opposite. If he can work longer and harder than others, or shrug off a blow that would down another man, it's because he is more recently related to the Lady of the House – and therefore bears more responsibility for all she suffered in birthing and raising his ancestors. His night-marks constantly remind him of the debt he owes his divine parent: the greater his gift, the more potent his lifelong obligation to serve others with it."

Sil leaned against the pie safe and folded his arms, doing his utmost not to look as impatient as he felt. "Yes, all right," he said, and nevermind the indigenous ethics, "but how does that help me here?"

"Why, it shows you the enormity of what's been lost." Faro poured a careful stream of dark liquid from the crockery jug into the odd little tin apparatus next to it. "The a'Krah honor many currencies, but for Dulei Marhuk, a god-child whose lifetime of service was ended before it had begun... oh no, Master Halfwick, nothing will requite blood but blood. Milk and syrup?"

"Er... no, thank you," Sil replied, once he had managed to repunctuate *blood, milk, and syrup.* Faro put the lid on that peculiar tin mug and pressed the wooden knob until the metal straw disappeared into the can. He opened it again, and poured the result into a pair of pewter cups. "But I can't give them Elim's blood – that's the whole point. There has to be something else."

"Yes, someone else," Faro blithely agreed, returning his supplies to the pantry and the icebox. "Oh, I do hope you like this recipe; I am sure it will not be anything as fine as you are used to."

'Something' – he had said 'something,' hadn't he? "It will be splendid, I'm sure," Sil replied, "but you were saying..."

Faro turned his head, briefly meeting Sil's gaze with a few handsomely-coiffed golden forelocks hanging above the inkwell of his eye. "Did you know," he said in the tone of a school-master fascinated by his own subject, "that the divine children of the a'Krah are given bonded playmates? It's a most curious practice. Their companions share in all the best – they eat from the same bowl, sleep in the same bed – except that when the little godling should misbehave, it's his playmate that gets the smacking. Perhaps a good life for whatever poor common thing lands the job... but then, I suppose that depends on how much trouble your royal friend cares to make for you. Come along, we'll take tea in the dining room." He picked up the dishes and sashayed briskly forward, leaving Sil to trail along in his wake.

"A whipping-boy," he concluded, almost to himself. "You're saying that I should find a whipping-boy to take Elim's place." The term, and the idea, was repulsive on principle. Then again, hadn't Sil already volunteered himself as just that?

They sat down on opposite sides of the long table, Sil glad for this more respectable distance between them. Faro leaned forward, lacing his fingers together. "What I am saying," he said in conspiratorially low tones, "is that *I* will find your whipping-boy, and I will have him brought to justice before the whole town in Marhuk's name, and it will be so splendid and righteous a spectacle that no-one afterward will think anything about your companion."

Sil met his black-eyed stare out of politeness at first, but soon it was hard to look away. Faro's voice, exceptionally pleasant to begin with, seemed to become still more so as he went on. His words spilled gracefully over one another like water from a quick-flowing brook; he spoke clearly and quietly and with such perfectly-pitched conviction that when Sil finally said,

"That's murder,"

it was almost an afterthought.

This did not seem to perturb his host. "Well, old chap, I'm rather afraid it's to be murder regardless: unless you may somehow contrive to return the life of their slain prince, there can't be any question of that. The only question is, will you let the lot fall to your unfortunate menial, who as you've said can't possibly be guilty of anything worse than poor judgment, bad luck really, an accident, and one something of your own fault at that... or will you do right by him, and by yourself, and take advantage of the help available to you?"

"Yes," Sil began, "but I mean, that is... I have recourse in the law." He was so used to thinking ahead of everyone else, but here it was as if he could do nothing but listen so long as Faro held the floor.

Faro wiped his mouth, but could not quite keep the smile from his eyes. "The law? Twoblood? This law that commits to nothing and pleases no-one? She is the Azahi's dog, barking at anything in her master's absence – why, did you see how rudely she used my poor Fours only this morning? – and you will court her help only at peril of your servant's life. We don't want to risk that, do we?"

"Certainly not!" Sil replied at once, with a fervor that surprised him. But then he was struck by a colder, more cynical, and altogether more natural thought. His eyes narrowed. "Who is 'we'? And why are you so keen on helping me?" He was a smooth operator, this Faro: Sil knew his type because he *was* his type, and their type did not do anything without a sharp eye towards their own personal benefit.

"Oh, I have taken quite a shine to you, Master Halfwick," Faro replied from behind the arch of his laced fingers. "But I must confess that I am still more enamored with those wonderfully fine horses of yours. I have already bought all that you wagered last night, but I think I would like very much to own yours as well... provided, of course, that you don't find my solution too terribly unpalatable."

Sil's resolve towards suspicion, first weakened by Faro's admission of honest greed, buckled at the word *unpalatable*. It suggested snobbery on his part, and squeamishness, and bald-faced ingratitude at a time when helping hands were as desperately needed as they were short in supply. He rested his elbows on the table and his forehead in his hands, sniffed, and swallowed. "What you're telling me," he said with a bit more than the usual roughness in his throat, "is that someone will be killed tonight, regardless of what I do."

Sil did not care to look up, but Faro's tone was a smooth promise. "There is evil in the world that you cannot prevent, Master Halfwick. But you can choose whether to benefit by it."

Well, maybe so, but Sil would bet that this proposed evil of theirs would be news to Twoblood, and Sil would further bet that Twoblood wouldn't take it lightly. "But who would – why would anyone sell you his own life?"

"Oh, come now, old chap, surely you can answer that much," Faro replied. His voice was cloying, teasing.

Sil stared down, searching for clues in the cold black contents of his cup. "Desperation, I suppose. Poverty, unemployment, debts, obligations, shame..." Him, relate to that? Oh, not a bit.

"Well, and why not for charity?" Faro said. "Why can't it be some kindly grandmother at the end of her run, some poor sick soul weary of prolonging the inevitable, some consumptive youth plainly not long for the world? Why should they want to drag out their own suffering when, with a single generous act, they could relieve their pain and handsomely requite those who have so selflessly cared for them all this while?

"And why should you torment yourself with the particulars, Master Halfwick, when I am right here to assure you of the perfect humanity of my offer?"

Because it was wrong. Because it stank to high heaven, because no well-intentioned person should be so interested in two unexceptional horses, because nothing about Faro was right – not his eyes, not his name, not his smell or his touch – and because any cure-all nostrum offered at a bargain price, without any labeling of its contents or method of action, was absolutely a fraud.

For a moment, a ludicrous thought flitted through Sil's mind, and his gaze flicked involuntarily to Faro's fine mouth. But no, they were human teeth, flat and ordinary, and his boots weren't made for anything but common human feet, and Faro was every bit as human as Sil was overexposed to the superstitions of hell-dwelling hayseeds.

He glanced back up. "Not going to be snatching strangers off the street, are we?"

Faro positively beamed at him then. "You have my fullest confidence, Master Halfwick: my intended substitute will be a willing party to the contract, whose life will do more good in parting from him than it ever did in his possession – a perfect replacement for your unfortunate Elim, and one whom I shan't engage without his full and freely-given consent." He tilted his head. "What do you say? Shall we make it a deal?"

No, not at all – it was an ugly thing, a damning bargain no matter how nicely Faro phrased it, and Sil would bet anything that there was another way, a better way...

... but then, Elim wasn't his to gamble with. There was no telling about Faro's intended victim, but Elim certainly, positively didn't deserve to die here. There might well be less vile alternatives – Sil knew he hadn't thought of, much less exhausted all his options – but Twoblood and Fours and Huitsak and the rest had no reason to put themselves out for a pair of foreigners that had been far more trouble than they were worth, and Sil – Elim, rather – could not afford to find that out the hard way. Better to trust the avarice of a stranger than the charity of any friend.

Sil sniffed, doing his level best to ignore that unprompted itching in his nose and throat, and swallowed down his second thoughts. "What do I have to do?"

Faro leaned back and gestured airily with one hand. "Why, hardly a thing," he said. "You have only to return here later tonight to collect your fellow – around sunset, shall we say? In the meantime, perhaps you could visit Fours and ask that he keep your two horses there with the rest. I'm sure he'll give you a good price for your saddles."

Ugh. This was going to mean selling Molly, and if that was the idea, you had almost rather be merciful and let Elim take it in the neck after all.

Well, and Elim should have thought of that before he went on a drunken shoot. Sil sighed. "Of course. Of course, I'll take care of it." He still had all his winnings; maybe he could try buying her back after... well, after the fact.

Sil felt like he had swallowed a whopping huge fly, but Faro only flashed a smile and raised his cup. "Then we have an accord."

Sil matched the toast and drank to seal the deal, mentally committing himself as he did so: the price for Elim would be two horses and a suicide.

His first taste was shockingly cold and bitter and refreshing – in a word, damned fine hailstone coffee. "That's brilliant," he said, his brows arching in surprise as he gave it a second, proper look, and another long sip.

"How do you get it as clear as that?"

Faro seemed flattered at the compliment, and began waving it away with modest little motions of his hand. "Well, the grounds must be steeped, of course, but really the press is the trick. It's a marvelous new device, and I think – no, I've decided. I shall have to make you a present of mine; you simply must have one."

This overt friendliness nettled Sil to suspicion again, not because he found it offensive but simply because this Faro was just so damned strange: he dressed and behaved and spoke as if he were a cold-blooded gentleman from the high city streets, but he was not, *could* not be any kin of Sil's, and just where had he come from anyhow?

There did not seem to be a polite way to ask that, nor any answer that would lessen the need for his sordid services. Sil took another drink. The cold potency of the coffee soothed his throat, and he let out a breath deep enough to take at least an inch from his taut shoulders. "That's tremendous of you, honestly. I'd be honored." Only it came out sounding stiff and idiotic. Sil rubbed his forehead. "I'm sorry – I don't actually make a business of being awkward, only with all this just here, today, and having to" – oh, God, and having to do and say things he never, ever thought he would, and each one getting him in deeper and so much worse, and wasn't it high time some seasoned, responsible adult took a second look at him and stepped in?

Sil lost his voice. He took another drink and began again. "He's not like that, you know. Elim, I mean – you can't know how unthinkable it is." He looked up at Faro, just waiting for a patronizing nod or so, for one of those coy under-the-table expressions that polite society would use to suggest that the unfortunate fellow could no more help this staring defect in his character than the pitiable irregularity of his face.

But Faro only reflected Sil's own perfect gravity. "Of course!" he swore. "Why, after that little farce last night, a very saint would have been out of his head – I don't wonder at your poor chap, not at all."

Sil returned the cup to its saucer with a heavy *clink*; his brows furrowed. "What farce?"

THERE WAS EVERYTHING to do and no time to do it in, and all of it of the most critical, life-altering importance… but there was no surer way to raise suspicion than leaving a pile of wet clothes dumped in a basket.

Shea braved the heat of the upper floors long enough to hang it all in the attic and open both windows. On her way out, she snatched Brant's old buckskin vest from the mending-pile. Then it was back out into the sun and down the thoroughfare as fast as wouldn't draw attention to her hurry. She did not look to her right: he would only be a brown-and-white blur, and there was nothing she could do for him, regardless.

So Shea occupied her sunburnt eyes with the road ahead, and her hands with checking that her tied kerchief still excused her from any expectation of hair or ears, and finally, a handful of skin-desiccating minutes later, let herself in to the warm, dusty interior of Fours' little store.

"*Bon-día, okayei, welcome,*" he called, not yet looking up from his ledger.

In spite of everything, she still felt some sad little amusement at Fours' habit of paying attention with his mouth first.

"I need a button," she said in Marín. "Show me what you have."

His head lifted sharply at the sound of her voice. "You –" he began. Then he glanced over to the soft tapping sounds at the far end of the room – someone testing dishes, maybe – and his voice changed. "Come to me here, please."

Shea ventured through the maze of rickety shelves, and by the time she was close enough to lay the vest on the counter, there was no mistaking the upset in his eyes. "I thought we agreed," he said in low tones, "that you would not come here anymore."

"Nonsense," she replied. "I am as much a paying customer as any of those filthy any-colored vagrants you have crawling through here at all hours. You'll take some honest business and be glad to have it." She would trust that the browser in the back would mark him- or herself as a person of quality by remaining silent on this point.

Fours' jaw tightened at the word 'honest': he knew she wouldn't call on him for anything of the sort. "And what business am I to be glad for today?"

"Nothing more difficult than a button," she replied, and pointed at the gap in the row of whorled pearly discs down the garment's front. "Give me one to match these." As her mouth spoke, she let her hands do likewise: she pointed to her chest, drew her cupped hand in, and finally circled her right eye, which was as much as to say, *I need him.*

Fours sighed, and seemed to surrender to the inevitability of a transaction. "Well, I'll be surprised if we find one of precisely the same likeness," he said as he procured a wide wooden tray from behind his skirted table, "but you are free to search to your own satisfaction." A pained creak escaped from the old brass hinges as he lifted the lid and submitted the contents for her inspection. *It isn't him,* his hands replied. *His marks don't match.*

Which was the kind of lie she expected to hear from him, who would say anything to avoid bestirring himself for the cause, who'd never cared anything about it to begin with, and whose only interest now was in living as though none of it had ever happened.

It IS him, and he's mine! The boy was too far away to tell anything about it the first time, but she'd gotten a fine close-up look at his face when he came knocking last night – unwashed death-minded fool that he was! – and it WAS him, with the eye-spot to prove it, and she would be damned if Fours would shrug it off as if it were nothing. Shea looked down at the tray with naked contempt. "And what manner of service do you call that? You haven't even bothered yourself to look!"

"As it happens," he said, "I have already had one customer come to enquire about the very same thing, and I will tell you just the same" – *It isn't him, and even if it were I couldn't help* – "I don't have any such button, and if I did, I would certainly be obliged to furnish it for the first asker. So in the very-unlikely event that one of this type does come into my possession, it really isn't worth your time to wait for it, and I would encourage you to pursue your satisfaction elsewhere."

Then his natural timidity seemed to remember itself. Fours dropped his gaze to the garment between them, as if stricken by an overwhelming desire to have it for his only problem. "... anyway, you should have Hops-the-Stone sew in a new set. She does wonderful work."

A burst of frustration stiffened her posture. "What a thing to say!" she cried, quite loudly enough for the nobody in the back, and flung her fingers at the vest. *You CAN, whether or not you WILL.* "You'd have the whole thing torn half to shreds, at ten times the cost and trouble, rather than admit that you might already have the perfect thing sitting right here under your –"

"MADAM." *No.* Fours cut her off with rare temerity, and a sharp, flat-lining gesture. "If you will hear the sound of your voice just now, you will understand why I have asked you not to patronize my store." *You think only of yourself. You will use him and leave us here with Faro –*

Fours stopped at this sign, the drawing of the V-line point at his chest, as the two of them registered the close proximity of a human being. They froze. Fours stared down at his hands as if waiting to see how they would conclude that thought.

Shea stayed motionless and mannequin-perfect, save for a quick glance at the old woman setting a battered bread-pan on the counter.

"Ah – do you find your needs met, grandmother?" Fours said, his hands belatedly finding new occupation at the sides of the button tray.

She had a face like a rotting gourd, wrinkled brown flesh caving in at her eyes and mouth, and pale blue clouds in her eyes. She sized up Shea from the periphery of her vision. "Noisy slut."

With that, she shuffled obliviously on back to the housewares collection.

Fours' silent out-breath was confirmation that their exchange had gone unseen, and Shea knew better than to push it much further. *Please,* she said. "Forgive my temper — I intended no rudeness." *You know what he means to me. You know what he cost me,* and then she waved her hand to wipe the *me*-sign from the air, and replaced it with *us.* "You know I don't see well. If you tell me there is no matching button here, I'll believe it. Please, do me the great kindness of making one thorough inventory, just in case, and I will take your final word and no more of your time." *Do this with me for both our stolen children, and I promise you won't see me again.*

Fours, who had begun by opening his mouth, ended with his gaze fixed on Shea's hands, and seemed to resign himself to this unpleasantness of buttons.

"As you wish," he said to the box of notions between them. "Come back a bit later in the day, if you will. After I have checked my stock." *Sunset. Barn. Make a plan.*

Shea could have reached across the counter and bitten him in gratitude. "Thank you," she said, the plainest and dullest verbal substitute, and picked up the vest to go.

But the thought of leaving became suddenly intolerable. Easy enough to go months at a time without having to look at him, think about him – but now to be allowed only this much of his company, to have him only coldly and surreptitiously and with an unfeeling countertop between them, was beyond enduring.

"Do you know," she said, holding one corner of the buckskin up to his washed-out sleeve, "I think I will have to make you one of these. The colors go so well together, don't you think – like *champagne* and *petits-f –*"

They were foreign words, and sounded nothing like their neighbors, but she had not even got the second one out of her foolish mouth before a *bang* jolted the countertop from underneath, spilling a torrential rain of beads and buttons all across the floorboards.

"Oh, I AM sorry, miss," Fours said, declining to meet her gaze as he rounded his homemade bartering-table and bent smoothly down to begin picking bits of glass and bone from the crevices. "I've meant to fix that tilt for a crow's age now. Anyway, come back later, a little bit later, and we will see about your project."

She watched him for a bit, her arms folded to contain a sudden groundswell of emotion. It would be polite to say, *I am sorry to have inconvenienced you,* and *You've been so helpful already* and *Yes, I am sure it will work out splendidly,* but she wasn't and he hadn't and she already knew that it wouldn't – that regardless of whether the boy was or wasn't the right one after all, there was no boy in the world who could repair what was long since ruined between them.

Shea let herself out.

I DIDN'T MEAN *for it, Boss,* Elim had said at the time. He remembered that clearly, and how hard it had been to pull Sue-Fly's head from the broken fence-planks, and how long he'd spent getting her laid out right before he went back to tell about it. *I didn't mean for any of it.*

That had been seven or eight years ago, when Elim wasn't more than Sil's age, but he could remember it fresh as new: the smears of cooling saliva on his hands as he worked her head free, the feel of her soft, still ears as he settled her down, the earth-smell of the muddy furrows she'd ploughed up in her last panicked minutes. He could recall it as clear as yesterday, and he was sure-positive that whatever Boss had said after would lighten his soul again now, if he could just recollect what it was.

Elim hung still in the scorching light, sweat falling from his trembling muscles like sprinkles of rain in the dust. It had been a clear day, the air fresh with wet grass, but the clouds in his mind spread out thicker and darker, swallowing up Boss's silent shadow, until finally he recollected nothing at all.

"FOURS!" SIL BURST breathlessly into the store, wheezing as he clutched Elim's hat in his hand. "Fours, did you see –"

The shopkeeper and the Sundowner boy both looked up, startled, from opposite sides of the counter, and all the urgency of the last fifteen minutes was reined to a halt by a lifetime of social conditioning.

"Oh, I'm – *I'm sorry,*" Sil said, pulling off his hat, stupidly clutching one in each hand. "*Excuse me, please – I will wait.*"

He retreated to the porch, and busied himself with wiping his face, sedating his breathing, swallowing until he could appear at least halfway civilized again.

But Brant! No, it couldn't be right: Faro hadn't seen anything himself, but only heard some mismatched accounts from whores and tipsy guests, and none of it made any sense. Elim must have taken him wrongly, that was all: it was a silly parlor game that Elim in his infinite thickness had taken for a hold-up, and then, since he couldn't articulate his way out of a pile of blind puppies, there was nothing for it but to get violently drunk and smash Brant's head into the cupboard by way of excusing himself for the evening.

Sil was going to kill him. Pull his neck from the noose, and then kill him.

The door opened. Sil bowed from the neck and waited until the boy had let himself down the stairs before bolting back inside.

"Fours," he began again, both hats in the one hand now. "Please, did you hear anything last night? Anything at all?"

He was a slight fellow to begin with, and his thin, walnut-colored frame wound itself still smaller as he hunched over his ledger and kept writing. "I – I don't know why it would matter," he said without looking up. "Everyone knows he is guilty."

He was cowed – and after the roasting he'd gotten from Twoblood this morning, one could hardly blame him. Sil kept his temper in check, and replied to the part of Fours' disheveled white hair. "Yes, but did you?" He closed the door behind him. "There were two women talking about a terrific banging at your door, before the shot – I heard them on my way here. Didn't you hear anything at all?"

The pen, now barren of ink, continued making quick, dry scratches over the page. "I am not in the habit of answering my door after dark."

"Then you did hear him," Sil said, the sight of Fours' cramped, evasive posture lighting a fuse Sil didn't know he had. "You heard and you knew and you didn't do a thing about it. Bloody hell, you didn't even look in or pull the bell after the fact – you just holed up in here and waited for somebody else to find him!" Sil could perfectly picture Elim making an ass of himself in polite company, and drinking himself stupid if he felt compelled, and especially taking aim at shadows and bogeymen in the dark. But no Elim would pound and call at the door who was not absolutely frightened out of his head, and the fact that this sapless, shrinking son of a bitch here had just rolled over in bed and let it happen was suddenly intolerable. "Well? Damn you, don't you have anything to say for yourself?"

"Me?" It was almost a squeak. Fours did look up then, his black eyes wide behind his upturned trapezoid lenses, and he seemed to shrink in the face of Sil's outrage. "I don't – I don't know," he stammered, "I didn't mean anything – I TOLD him not to go out, I said, just like I told you, and you wouldn't – you didn't listen, you see, you didn't listen and you see what's happened, and now I've got Twoblood collaring me, and Faro, and Sh– and more than that, even, I'll have it from the Azahi too, and you know, I don't, I don't" – he shook his head at his book – "no, I don't believe I'll have it from you, Halfwick." His hands trembled, and some trick of the light made it seem as if his veins or wrinkles had turned darker, like the whorls on the wooden counter. Fours dropped the pen and held fiercely to the countertop, his white brows knitting together over eyes squeezed tightly shut. "Yes, that is what I have to say for myself: you are a bad guest and a bad tradesman and a bad master at that, and I think you had better get your horses and your things out of my barn."

Sil closed the distance in two steps and brought his hands down on the counter with a decisive *bang*. "FIRST of all, I'm not his master, because if I were, you can be damned sure I'd have taught him better than that. And secondly, our horses belong to your friend Faro now, so you and he are very welcome to saddle up and herd the lot of them down to hell together." Sil pushed away from the counter and stalked off for the door. "I'll have our things and be out in ten minutes."

"Yes, of course..." Fours' answer caught up with him at the doorway. "... only first you should know, there is just a slight problem with the mare..."

Sil halted on the spot, dread freezing out all his ire. "What?"

HALFWICK ALL BUT bolted from the room, taking Fours' last nerve with him.

That brazen young tyrant was everything Fours had called him and more besides, and *rude*, that was what: as if he were the only one with a troubled mind! As if this business with his foolish half-man was of no consequence to anyone but himself!

Fours pushed up his glasses and pressed the heels of his hands to his eyes, breathing slow and deeply. There was a bath and a jar of pickled eggs waiting for him tonight; he just had to get to them.

All the same, he probably should have mentioned Ki-Meh's intention to return the horse, especially as he'd just then come by to report losing her in the cursed grounds of the Burnt Quarter. Not for Halfwick's sake – not because he didn't deserve to go chase the consequences of his arrogance for awhile! – but because his time would have been better spent tending to his luckless manservant. Twice already Fours had heard astonishing tales of Halfwick's unconcern as he bid Twoblood tie the half up and simply leave him there, and Fours had to wonder at his logic. At what point did such a punishment become more monstrous than the flogging it was meant to forestall?

Well, it was a cruel thing to afflict a living creature, regardless of the method or the reason.

Crueler still to take no part in either the affliction or the remedy, to be at once able and idle.

Fours felt his guilt as so many eyes staring down the back of his neck. When he finally took his hands away and turned, it was as if all his medicines were bearing down on him: bottles of fennel seeds and rose-petals and hediondilla leaves looming down from the shelves, looped sprigs of camphor-weed and cows-tongue and globemallow hanging over him.

It was Doctor Cartwright who had taught him their uses. Back then, the town was still Sixes, and Fours was still Peter Fournier, no-one more interesting or exceptional than the doctor's apprentice.

He had enjoyed that work. There was a satisfaction to be had in good medicine, a connection forged between the healer and the afflicted that superseded all differences. For a few blessed years, he had shared a small part of that glorious connection, had been a wanted and welcomed visitor at every door.

He was still a person of good standing in Island Town, of course... but it was not really the same. The various tribes had their own healers and medicines. What they craved now was a middleman, some suitable in-betweener who would conduct business with the more suspicious and unclean visitors, filtering the goods from the goods-bringers as one would pan for gold in a muddy stream.

So he was given the Pewtersmiths' old house and barn, and dutifully learned the art of accounting, and of keeping a livery, and made no complaint as his new occupations gradually consumed his old one, until finally his plants and bottles were driven back to this last refuge behind the counter, and all the rest belonged to that insidious sea of useful things.

Fours had long since discovered that being useful was no substitute for being *wanted*.

It was just a shame that today, the one who wanted him most was the one to whom he could least afford to be useful.

And not out of spite – not anymore. The sun had damaged more than her eyes, and the remainder was ruined by years of thankless labor and constant, grinding, futile hope. She'd said at the time that it was for Fours' own safety, and their daughter's best interest – that it would be better if she put herself willingly at Faro's right hand to forestall his further reach. They both knew that that wasn't true. She wouldn't have sold herself so cheaply, if she had any better chance remaining... but after she had spent her sight and soundness in futile searching abroad, there was no better place than the hotel, with its constant influx of news-bringing foreigners, to wait for word of U'ru's missing boy.

The guilt had to be getting to her, though. Lately, they couldn't go more than a couple of years at a time without some report of an eye-spotted half igniting her hopes all over again. Last time it was the rumor of a runaway who'd made it across the border. By the time she'd tracked him down to Brayton, he'd been hanged, but recently enough for her to notice that his spot was on the wrong eye. And then there was the bounty hunter... but when she finally caught up to him, he was far too old.

And every time she ran away, it was Fours who had the knife put to his neck – not that that ever stopped her.

This one, this Elim, looked to be of the right age, and despite what Fours had said before, to have the right kind of mark: by her own account, it had been a great big patch, irregular in its shape and reaching nearly to the bridge of his nose. But it wasn't him, and Fours could say that without ever having laid eyes on the infant. For one thing, Halfwick's man was far too large: he might well have parentage from the Washchaw, for example, but the Ara-Naure were a slightly-built people, and U'ru's son had been remarkable only for the mixing of his colors.

There was no telling what had become of him, nor what might now happen to his unfortunate double.

Well, that wasn't quite true.

Fours' drifting gaze alighted on the right-hand side of the third shelf from the top, the winding thorny contents of the little basket peppered with the remains of dry white flowers. Thistle poppy was what you would want for a sunburn. Boiling it down made a salve for the skin, and the remainder could be drunk as a tea for relief of pain.

All the healing arts, of course, amounted to little more than a bunch of dandelions tied to a stick and waved menacingly at the titans of suffering and inevitable death.

That was merely the price of living, however. To have the remedy and not to use it, or rather, to *waste* the remedy on someone who should not have been made to need it...

Fours sighed, and by sheer force of will berated himself back outside. He tilted the white stick across the door and forced himself down the steps, out of his artificial habitat and into the bright world beyond.

He'd break open one of his sulfured quail eggs, that was what — a special treat for getting through the day with a few shreds of conscience still intact.

It was just viciously, wretchedly unfortunate that he couldn't get there without going through Twoblood.

THE DARKNESS OPENED her eyes, angry white tears tracked down her cheeks, and found him.

"MOLLY." NOT QUITE an hour later, Sil had tracked her down to a turkey run at the western edge of town, her huge brown behind instantly recognizable as she hung her head over the fence and browsed for tidbits. "Come on now, Molly..."

Sil scrubbed one wrist under the brim of his hat, and held out the wilted produce in Elim's hat by way of a peace offering. "Now come along, will you – you see what I've got here?" He did not actually know whether she was much for vegetables, but active interest or stationary indifference would equally suffice to get her within range of the lead rope behind his back.

She attended him with a scant flick of an ear and kept right on lipping at the missed bits of corn around the fencepost. Sil closed gradually in from her right, and kept talking on. "Yes, that's fine – nice day for it, isn't it?" He would have her in three feet more.

Then she brought her head up, compelling him to make a grab for it, but she was ready and far faster, and went trotting leisurely away.

Sil let his arms drop to his side, spilling carrots and cabbage over his boot with so many fatigued-sounding *plops.* Damn it all, this was an imbecile's errand, and Fours' fault to begin with, and furthermore...

... and furthermore, Sil was in fact the biggest and greatest imbecile of them all.

What the devil was he *doing* out here?

He quickened his steps in spite of the hot blood already pounding in his temples and crossed the street, sending a pair of young boys and a stray cat scattering out of his path. He cut a quick track along the road, further and deeper into town, until finally he came close enough to swallow up the raised edge of the promenade with one great knee-bending thrust of his heel, and began calling ahead.

"Elim! Elim, listen, I know you're out with me, but Molly's gotten loose and I need you to call her back, all right?"

The figure in profile hung slack from the wrists, head down, body leaning faintly forward – exactly the same sort of unresponsive obstinacy he'd taken to earlier.

Sil hurried on, absently scratching the wet stripes where his braces had pasted his shirt to his perspiring back. "See here, I've got the lead rope ready and I'll take her straight back, only we can't let her keep wandering about – there's no telling what she'll get into or who'll try to take her, and I don't... are you even listening?"

He was not used to standing on a level with Elim. With the way the sun was coming in from behind Calvert's mule and throwing his shadows forward, Sil was close enough to touch him before he even noticed his closed eyes. He was marinating in sweat.

Sil hesitantly gave his wet shoulder a prod. "Elim, wake up – I'm not fooling about with you."

There was no answer.

"Now look here..." He lifted Elim's chin to shake him to attention – and instantly dropped it again, shocked at the dead weight.

Sil took a horrified step backwards. It had been warm to the touch and heavy, like a hog's head from the butcher's.

He absently wiped his hand on his sleeve, his nausea having nothing to do with the heat. The awful idea spread out from there, crawling up his throat and snaking tendrils into his brain, and all the reasons Sil devised to explain why it wasn't and couldn't be true crumbled as quickly as he conjured them, undermined by the insidious thought that maybe it was anyway.

Well, if he was going to come completely unwrapped, it would not be for any 'maybe'. Sil stepped forward again and put his ear to Elim's nose and mouth. He would be happy to take a hideous fright as soon as the shamming idiot jerked to life.

That did not happen. But he did, presently, feel a wisp of a breath at his ear – thank God! – and stood there long enough to gain confidence in its quick, shallow rhythms. He was alive, all right – but only just.

Sil glanced up and down the promenade, perfectly ready to demand help from the first living soul he found. But the only person available was the same irredeemable idiot who'd left a thirsty drunk to roast here in the first place.

That would have to do.

So he steeled his nerve and put his hand to Elim's chest, more careful now than he ever had been, and began to leech the heat from Elim's flesh into his own – not in his usual fashion, not quick and impatiently, but with the slow, careful gentility that Nillie practiced so well.

Granted, his sister would slap him straight across the face if she knew he was using his talent on a living creature.

Or trying to, anyway. Sil's talent was weak and feeble – and of course it was. He'd scarcely turned seven when he was taken out west, torn away from the lives of his ancestors like a patch ripped out of a quilt. He'd long since lost what these Sundowners out here had fought so hard to keep... but God willing, he still had enough left to get the job done.

Sil closed his eyes. He concentrated on the smell of musty clothes and mothballs, boot-blacking and leather, until he was quite sure he was back at home, hiding in his father's wardrobe for a game of stowaways. At the first sound of approaching footsteps, he unfolded his small body and clambered down to make a mad dash for the stairs. He ran past heavy burgundy curtains and frost on diamond window-panes, bolted down the tightly-spiralling back stairs and through the kitchen, the air sharpened by Nanna's scolding voice and the smell of baking bread – bread, yes, with a smear of jam, and the little plate with the swirling blue-purple grapes painted on, and taking dinner with Mother at the table in the nursery – the nursery, with his books and paintbox and soldiers, and the slate he used to practice writing the old runes – the runes, church, starched shirt and painted glass and old voices – *Ealdor ure, ðū ðe eart on heofonum* –

With a great violent gasp, Elim jerked forward. Startled, Sil registered an instant of searing pain before he was staggering backwards to the wall, clutching his blistered hand and beating back a dizzying urge to vomit.

"... sees me," Elim mumbled, sagging against his restraints. "She she's me."

Sil straightened, elated in spite of the vicious throbbing in his temples. "Elim!" He shook him by the shoulders. "Elim, wake up – look at me, now!"

Elim muttered something unintelligible, and lapsed back into a stupor...

... and Sil's left hand came away coated with brown hair. He glanced back up, astonished, and stood on his toes to get a better view. But no, he wasn't imagining things: the sunburnt side of Elim's shoulder, his neck, his right arm – every exposed native part of him had been overrun by a short, smooth coat of fine russet fur.

Sil could scarcely fill a tea-cup with what he knew of marks. The Northmen had lost theirs long ago, casualties of the Ash Winter and the quest to forget the old gods. All that was left now was a ragpicker's bundle of half-remembered things – hoarded genealogies and copies of copies of fragmented manuscripts; a moribund language pickled in sermons and academia; old-world customs and rituals re-enacted with crude emigrant reverence.

Not so for the Sundowners – at least, not the ones out here. Steeped for hundreds or even thousands of years in their own living lands and languages, in the food and clothes and songs and manners that set each tribe apart from its neighbors, their connection to their gods and the life-patterns of their ancestors was strong enough to shape their bodies and change their faces...

But that couldn't have anything to do with Elim. It couldn't. He didn't belong to that world – he wouldn't want any part of it – and Sil didn't have to know which god or tribe had sired him to remember what was supposedly common to them all: any marks a native fellow had would appear at night, or in the presence of his god... or when he was pushed to the brink of death.

Sil gave Elim's shoulder another hesitant, experimental touch. The hair came right off, as clean and easily as fresh snow. He stared at it for a long, incredulous moment.

Then he attacked the rest in a frenzy, wiping and rubbing until his hands were covered in thick sweaty layers of it and he was coughing in a churned-up cloud of the remainder, irrationally desperate to get rid of the evidence. He hadn't meant to let it go this far. He hadn't meant for any of this.

Sil scrubbed a sleeve across his eyes, the pain in his throbbing skull and blistered hand not nearly penance enough as he dropped to his knees and set about angrily smothering the hair into the floorboard crevices, pushing the remainder into the dirt around Elim's...

... and where the dickens were his boots? He couldn't have got them off by himself – and his socks, too! – and no good God-fearing rustic would ever –

Bugger this for a lead penny.

Sil snatched up the hat and rope and ate up distance again, his heels rapping quick and sharp as they remembered how to run. If Faro was so keenly interested in having Molly for his collection, then he could bloody well get her former owner an advance on his own life.

CHAPTER NINE
INSUFFICIENCIES

THE A'KRAH HAD not come for the half: this was no surprise.

But Twoblood had been besieged with every other sort of visitor in the meantime. For the Ohoti Woru there was Feeds-the-Fire, making ingratiating insinuations about special recognition for his assumption of Yes-Yes's duties. Then Step-Lightly of the Ikwei, who insinuated nothing about what she thought of her husband's mistreatment at the half's brutish hands. And then mousy little So-Shy of the Set-Seti came by with a dish of turkey stew and all her usual hand-wringing compliments – and how glad Twoblood would be to have the one if it didn't always have to come with the other! Even the Fire Tribe had had itself counted at her doorstep today, as the bare-footed black cowbird came to ask the duration of the half-man's penance, and what comforts he might be allowed in the meantime.

So when the stick tapped at her door for what had to be the eighty-fifth time that day, Twoblood answered it with less than her usual pleasantness.

"Be here!" she barked as she whipped on her hat and swept the dandruff from her shoulders.

As the door opened, she realized that one of the races of Island Town hadn't yet inflicted itself upon her – and there to fill the missing place was Fours.

Twoblood could not have been more surprised if a mouse had skittered across the floor and commenced nibbling at her boots. "Are you coming to see me?"

Fours stood there in his rumpled old clothes and hunched posture, a dried-up bean-stalk preparing to apologize for its presence. "Second – I'd, I'm sorry to bother you; certainly I can return later, if the present moment finds you occupied."

Twoblood tipped back in her chair.

There was a satisfying amount of silence then: the sound of Fours working up the nerve to speak. "It is – that is, I wouldn't take much of your time; I only thought I should stop by to ask about the h– about the man, just there, and whether I can... whether there is anything I might do to help."

As a matter of course, Twoblood did her best to keep Fours' natural anxiety at its fullest flower. It cut through his dishonesty like soap through grease. So when she said,

"Help?"

it was in a tone as soft as a sack of dirty clothes.

Which Fours flinched from as quick and automatically as if Twoblood had hidden needles in the laundry. "Oh, not in that way – I do see that you have the present situation firmly in your grasp, of course. It is the future that concerns me."

Twoblood folded her hands across her stomach and waited.

And Fours, for whom silence was somehow an agony, knotted his own hands under the lowest button of his faded old vest and spurred himself on. "– What I mean to say is, your decisive command this morning was unquestionably correct – and I will repeat my apology for rendering it necessary in the first place – and there can't be anyone who disagrees that this, here," and he gestured vaguely at the window, "has been most effective in subduing him. But I wonder if perhaps I couldn't, that is to say, compensate you for my great indiscretion by drugging him to a stupor, so that you could safely keep him in here, without worrying about who might try to make mischief with him outside."

Twoblood's eyes narrowed, searching Fours' ageless face and bespectacled black eyes. "To whose benefit?"

Apparently, there was something of keen interest on the floor. "Oh – to yours, of course. It's just, you know that I hear things, when people come to visit me, and as shocking as last night's happenings have been, you can perhaps understand their concern about what might happen if the – if he were to die in captivity, to leave a vengeful presence which might further contaminate our town. Far-fetched, I realize, but of course you have no difficulty imagining what Yellow Bone and Voh'loh would tell their clans in such an event..."

Twoblood would shit in her hat before she lost any sleep over Yellow Bone *or* Voh'loh... but then, they would do likewise before they sent Fours to do their talking. Someone else had put him here. "So you are saying this not for any self-serving reason, but to earn my forgiveness by ensuring that the Azahi does not come home to any discontent."

Fours looked up far too quickly, with much too much

desperate gladness in his voice. "Yes, Second – you understand my intentions perfectly."

If only that were true. "Let me be sure that I do," Twoblood said, stifling the urge to scratch. "What you are telling me is that the people are concerned at having the half left tied in an open place, away from their homes, under my supervision, where all can see his condition and manner of treatment. That they would instead prefer that I keep him here, between walls, where nothing that is done by or to him will have any witnesses. And that I feed him and handle him and share a roof with him, one two-blood in close quarters with another, so that any contagion which takes root in our town can be blamed on my keeping of his diseases. This is what the people wish for me to do."

It would have been satisfying to watch Fours' expression crumble, if it weren't proof of a much greater problem. "... apologies, Second; I had not considered that." Then he glanced up again, and the palms of his hands pressed themselves flat against each other. "Perhaps I could keep him in my barn instead. He could be tied between stalls in much the same way, and if anything unfortunate does happen to him there, his spirit will not befoul any ground that was not already so polluted."

Twoblood ran her tongue over her teeth.

Someone wanted to get at the half, and they had realized that there was no chance of doing it so long as he was kept in the common eye. Certainly he was wanted by the a'Krah, who would contrive at any cost to give him a 'miraculous' death in Marhuk's name. Still, if they were using Fours to maneuver their victim into place, it would be an uncharacteristically inept low for them.

But anything was possible where Fours was concerned. He didn't really belong to the town, not the way that Twoblood did: he was old, with unknowable loyalties that pre-dated the Azahi – that pre-dated the retaking of Island Town altogether – and remained at least half an informant, if not a spy. Ordinarily that would be reason enough to get rid of him.

But it didn't take owl-eyes to see that this was no happy choice on his part, that whatever strings pulled Fours were beyond his power to break. More importantly, he was a poor enough puppet that his clumsy movements were more telling than threatening.

And he was useful, even if he was crooked.

So it was better, at least for the time being, to pry the little dagger out of his fumbling fingers and send him back outside with strict instructions not to try it again. "Well. I see that you are concerned for his well-being, so I will say to you exactly what I said when your cowbird –"

Fours looked sharply up. "My what?"

"– when the *ambassador* came by earlier today," and nevermind what passed for a relationship between those two. "She has my permission to bring him water, and to do for his spirit whatever pleases her judgment. She is not to give him any other comforts, nor do anything else beyond what is required to sustain his life – which, should it remain unclaimed at sunset, will be returned to him as he is escorted outside our walls. Is your understanding now equal to hers?"

For a moment, Fours looked as if he would give the proper answer. But then his bland features pinched, as if suppressing some hidden pain, and his thin shoulders hunched, as if they wanted to hide between his lungs, and with a voice that wobbled like a badly-made pot, he said,

"It is – certainly, I do understand – except that I would... I would earnestly beg you to allow me to remove him from the sun, or at least to return his clothing. Really, Second, you would be surprised to learn how quickly white flesh burns, and I am sure it would not be seen as –"

Twoblood's chair-legs hit the ground with a *thunk* not nearly equal to the force with which she stood, pressing her knuckles straight-armed to the desk. " – as what?" she snapped. "As favoritism, from one bastard to another? As weakness, a testament to our lack of stomach? As some tame currying of favor for the great white all-commanding master who bid us string him up in the first place? No? Are you sure?"

Fours had gone still in front of the oncoming stampede, his gaze frozen to the sight of her fangs. "No – Second, I would never –"

"You damned well would if you thought I wouldn't be on you like crows on a fresh corn shit!" But then she had to clap her hat down with one hand so that she could scratch that whoreish violent itch under the brim with the other, and that thrust an unwelcome stick through the spokes of her otherwise-perfect outrage.

Fours' wide-eyed stare was even then drifting up to watch this unwelcome spectacle. Twoblood tore away her hands and Fours' attention with equal force. "Look at me!" she snapped, gratified to be obeyed in an instant. "Half the town has been in here today to tell me what I should or should not do, so if you really want to help, you will leave off asking to do things and go tell the rest of them what IS being done. The half IS being held, exactly as he is, under exactly the terms that his master and I agreed to, until exactly one of the two events that I have named will happen. Anyone not satisfied by this arrangement may direct his complaints to his god or his elder or the horse who ploughed his mother, as long as he does it out of my hearing. Have we NOW reached an understanding?"

Fours nodded with a fierce and frightened alacrity. "Yes, Second."

Twoblood grunted, and dropped back into her chair. "Good. And while I think of it, where IS his milk-sop master?"

"He is out looking for his horse, Second." Fours reported this to an invisible point in the air between them, his voice ironed to perfect flatness.

Twoblood snorted. "Too bad for him; the sun is fierce today."

"Too bad, yes."

How the pasty boy had made an enemy of the least-offensible man in Island Town didn't even bear thinking about. "Well, when you see him, tell him that..." Twoblood paused. If Halfwick couldn't bother himself to come by, then he couldn't care much when his strange untouchable slave would be let down again. "... nevermind. Tell him nothing, and if he asks you about his man, have him come to me instead. Are we finished now?"

But here again Fours surprised her: he wadded up his hands, and answered them exclusively. "Yes – that is, yes, very nearly so. I was wondering if you could – if you would tell me, please, for my own perfect clarity... exactly what would happen, if I were to be found with him, for – for any purpose you might care to imagine. Even to give him some thistle poppy tea."

Twoblood could not have been more astonished to hear the bold mouse open its mouth and roar. Was this the sound of Fours admitting collusion to her very face? Was he trying to tell her that they meant to poison the half somehow?

And would she receive anything but frantically stammered falsehoods if she asked?

Twoblood did not sigh, but let her breath drain through her nose, and rubbed under her ear to quiet the lingering itch further up her scalp. She wished that she could be soft with him. She wished that he could be honest with her. Here in this place, where her name went unsaid in the counting-songs of Island Town's innumerable clans and families, and her ears thirsted in vain for the sound of her own language, it would have been a comfort to have Fours for a friend. They were two of a kind, if for no other reason than that they were each one of a kind.

Unfortunately, being one in a city of others also meant making sacrifices to earn a place not freely given. It meant giving up the luxury of belonging to one's own self.

So Fours would persist in his sad and feeble treachery, and Twoblood would persevere in wringing it out of him. Her chair creaked as she leaned forward. "I will ask you a different question. Who put those bars there?"

Fours' gaze followed Twoblood's gesture, and together they shared a view of the cell in the corner of the room. This had been a keeping-place for prisoners, in the time before, and Twoblood had made few alterations since taking up residence. The desk and the chair, the mantel, the small barred window and the door to the outside with the key that locked it, all were original to the house. The black iron bars that walled off the south-western quarter of this single room had once kept an eastern-style bed, which Twoblood had long since dispensed with, and now caged nothing but a few dust-balls and two empty buckets.

"Why, that was *Buk-Túkerzun*," – or some similar-sounding collection of Ardish syllables, – "not long after he became *sher*... Second Man. This was the *pos-dofis* before that, but after they set up the line to *calder-cídi*, we had to move that down to... to..."

Fours' face lost its habitual dread as he sank back into some other time and place, brows furrowed, finger pointing vaguely south-easterly, as if by indicating the direction of the place he would assist himself in remembering its name.

Then he caught sight of Twoblood again. "... to a recollection for another time. Er, why do you ask?"

Twoblood tipped her head left and right, noncommittal. "He did a good job." She leaned forward again to impart a serious, unblinking promise. "And if I catch you in even the suggestion of disobedience, I will take you by the neck and press your face between those bars until we have discovered the superior workmanship: his who made the bars, or hers who made your skull."

This was unquestionably the correct thing to say, because Fours acknowledged it with a sigh, a deflating of his back and shoulders that suggested a tied man at last relieved of the need to struggle any further, having finally proven his bonds unbreakable.

This was a comfort Twoblood was glad to afford him.

Fours made a ball of his hands at his stomach, and bowed over them from the waist. "Yes, Second. I understand, and thank you for the gift of your time." She never had figured out how he did that without his false hair falling off. And thinking of which,

"Wait," Twoblood said, as Fours turned to the door. She opened the bottom left drawer of her desk, fished through the clothes there, and tossed the empty bottle to Fours' nervous hands. "More of that. Greasy, but it works."

Fours nodded to it. "Yes, Second. Perhaps a yucca shampoo in-between-times, to reduce the oils. I will see to it."

And he let himself out.

There was a welcoming, all-soothing emptiness then, one which surely could not last. Twoblood pulled off her hat, put her feet back up on the desk, and went back to watching the half, the white flakes falling unbothered to her shoulders as she scratched.

There were to be no slaves in Island Town, and no torture either. Still, it was difficult to know which man better proved the limits of the law: the one out there, or the one who had just now been here.

Regardless, Twoblood would be content for sunset to find the half still alive, and for night to see him safely gone, taking the mystery of his unseen coveter with him.

HER LAWFUL NAME, as God had witnessed the giving of it, was Chrisaelte. It meant *marked* or *confirmed* in the language of the Northmen, and she would answer to it on the day when He finally called her away.

Her father had called her Serva Dei, which meant *servant of God* in the language of the first Verses, and she thought of her profession, her place in the world, in this manner exclusively.

But after he was gone, her *papá* amended that to Día, which meant nothing more than *day* in the language of common parlance. For the time that she had here in the world, she thought of her earthly person as Día, and did not bother much about whether and how other earth-persons addressed her.

Except that by the time she had consulted Twoblood and then her books, and fetched the water and boiled it and come back afterwards, the two-colored man did not address her at all. His body just hung there, glazed with drying sweat... and marked by a blistered red handprint, burned into the flesh over his heart.

Día frowned, and set her supplies down beside her. Had she been gone so long, and he been claimed so quickly?

Well, perhaps she was not too late yet. She spit on the fingertips of her right hand and with her index finger drew the sun sign on his forehead, being careful to link both the white of his brow and the dark edge of his eye-spot with the circle. They were worrying, these fractional people, and halves especially: although the numerators added soundly up to one individual, the denominators were fundamentally unlike, and could never be simplified. For this man here, God had written $1/2x + 1/2y$, and nothing he or she or any other earth-person did could make that 1. This unsolvable expression in his flesh had to tax his soul terribly, and she hoped that she had not come too late to assist it in performing the necessary operations.

Día blew gently on the mark until it dried, and then picked up one of his boots to commence testing her hypothesis.

* * *

ELIM COULDN'T HAVE said what had changed. He'd done such a good job of hiding in the dark place underneath that viscous tar-wallow of pain, where even his own mind couldn't find him. But then he felt as if he were drowning, unable to recollect whether he should hold his breath or swallow, and by the time he realized that his body was deciding without him, he was awake, gulping down warm fetid water, the sweetest and best he'd ever had, drinking and drinking –

– until his raw throat began clenching down on empty swallows. "More," he gasped. A bolt of pain shocked him as he brought his head up, the brightness and shadows before his eyes segregating themselves by degrees. Soon he could understand the strange lady before him, the water shiny and swirling inside the boot as she pulled it away, and rage followed panic. "More!" He threw himself at her, the pain in his wrists and arms miles distant, and would have strangled her for it if he'd had the reach.

"You are sick from the heat," she told him, "and will vomit if you drink too much. Remember how patience becomes us: 'God is my one Master; I will for nothing want.'"

Reason seeped into his fever-cracked brain by drops and trickles, but that tired old saw carried no weight with him today. Elim slumped back in his ties, dizzied by his own thundering, and stared at her with unfocused eyes. "... 's mine too, and I'm parching for a drink." And a bath, and a sleep – oh, God, he would lie down right there and sleep for days, if only she'd cut the ropes. He closed his eyes, and tried to find his way back to the place he'd been before.

"What is your name, as it was given to you before Him?"

No rest, then. He sighed. "Elim. Appaloosa Elim." As distinct before God from Elim Arkwright the postmaster, Blackeye Elim out in Clade's Corners, and Elim the goat, that had belonged to the Wheelbark family and died of the slough.

"That is what I thought he said. But why are you called 'Appaloosa' at all? You have the markings of a paint-horse, if anything."

Elim didn't purposely open his eyes then: the glower did it for him. "Shit, do I."

Which was a hell of a thing to say to a lady of any color, though you wouldn't know it by the ready poker face on this one. "You do... though perhaps it was rude of me to mention them. Please let me apologize. My name is Chrisaelte, a grave bride in the service of our Divine Master, and ambassador for the First Man of Island Town. You may like to call me Día."

He would, actually, as that first mess of syllables had blown right past him. "Día," he repeated, staring wistfully down at the folded blue umbrella and the dripping-full boots – *his* boots – by her feet.

Maybe he ought to start himself over again.

"That is real pretty," he said, "and you are real kind to come back so." A more silver-tongued fellow would have stopped there and let her soak up the compliment, but Elim had nothing in his mouth but the taste of ripe socks and leather, and could not seem to shut up. "You know, time was, I used to get pecans and bullseye oranges in my shoes every First Night. Be the first time I've drank out of 'em, though."

The strange lady – or Día, as she was – glanced down, as if she didn't exactly take his meaning. "Oh," she said. "Well, you will have lost both water and salts by sweating.

I believe that is a human constant. But I wasn't sure... it didn't seem advisable to test your tolerance with any foreign additives, especially without knowing their correct proportions. I thought the safest course would be to steep the water in your own garments, so that you would not be returned any substances but those of your own making." She picked up one of his boots again, and looked inside it. "I imagine the taste could stand improvement."

Elim wasn't exactly sure he took her meaning, either. But if he left off thinking with his ears and worked on understanding her like he would a more unspeaking fellow-creature, it seemed by her face and tone and posture that her aim was a kindly one, and this gesture as well-meant as any rat head or back half of a rabbit that Yellow Kelly had ever left on the front porch mat.

"Well, that sure is thoughtful of you," he said, as sincerely as he would to the cat, and with considerably more practical gratitude. "And I sure do appreciate it. And I'm sorry about all of that just now: I don't aim to be a cross-patch, really, and I know that this here is because I've done bad and Sil's doing his most to get me out. Only I got a head fixing to hatch, and I feel so awfully... would feel so awfully obliged, if you could fix me with another drink."

She stepped forward into his shadow again, and pinched the boot dip to let him drink without spilling.

"Wait, now," she said as he strained forward to keep from losing what she pulled away. "You will have it all before I go, only you must wait a little while between-times."

All right. Elim took it as a promise given, and felt the water eroding some of his desperate edge on its way down. "Sure," he said. "I can wait. I got a knack for it."

*   *   *

As it turned out, it was not the heat or his health that had been slowing Sil down all these years, but only his good sense and judgment: having tossed those aside, he found that he could cut quite a swift track after all.

At a certain price.

By the time he made it back to the house, his brisk trot had become a sprint, and his quick panting breaths had degenerated into labored gasps. Wheezing, coughing, he came in by the kitchen and checked the parlor after that, and then the back windows and the front hall and upstairs, where some of the rooms were now open and some half-familiar woman was turning over the beds. But the gaming room was still locked and she was no help at all – there was no sign of Faro anywhere – and he was heaving for breath, marinating in a sheen of sickly hot sweat, and the whole second floor was *stifling* in the heat.

By degrees, it occurred to Sil that he'd seriously overdone himself.

So he stopped there in the hallway, head spinning, shoulder at the wall, and reached with burnt, fumbling fingers for his little case of blacktails. He just about managed to keep the cigarette in his mouth as he folded the sand-paper just so.

But the match, god damn it all, wouldn't strike.

Another, then: Sil hurled the first away, beating off dizziness and swells of nausea to make a fresh go of it, every sharp ripping motion as forceful and futile as the last.

"Now what can be the matter, Master Halfwick?" the chamber-maid said from behind. "Aren't you –"

Whatever else the cow had to say was cut off by his abrupt cigarette-spitting cough, and a sudden, dire portent from his stomach.

She'd rob him, if he passed out here.

Sil waved her off as he dropped his useless tin, already stumbling full-force for the left door second from the end, and his every in-breath was a huge, hideous croaking-sound – he was sucking air through a pinhole – and his every out-breath another wracking, foreshortened cough, and his vision blurred as his balance failed and he caught his foot on the rug at the door and went crashing down to all fours and kept struggling on forward, blindly kicking the rug away, slamming the door shut with the heel of his boot as he did, crawling forward towards the head of the bed as the sight of the old ceramic thunder-jug underneath further incited the mutiny in his stomach...

... but he would not do it, would not even reach for it, would *not* be found choked to death on his own vile emesis, because he was not just smarter than the able-bodied idiots around him but harder too, and all of that tarry coffee-bile-slime trying to boil its way up from his gut was *his*, damn it, he had made it and owned it and would keep it where it belonged by sheer force of will, poisoning his reflexes with a tincture of grim determination and bloody-minded rage, beating back the swimming dark anaerobic shadows in his vision, holding white-knuckled to reason and consciousness as he grabbed up for the bottle at the bedside table, knocked it over, grasped for it again, his shuddering wild arm and half-prone posture sending the pearls all spilling and rolling out of his pocket and under the bed as he seized the bottle with one final straining reach, pulled it down and forced out the stopper and threw back a swallow in between back-arching constricted wheezes...

... and it was too much, twice easily too much, but nevermind...

... and having achieved that much, having proven to the universe at large that it had no power over him, he took the liberty of sprawling back against the bedframe, blotting the edge of his sweat-streaked brow against the bedsheet, and feeling absolutely *awful*.

Sometimes, when he was in an especially bad way, Sil longed for earlier days. He could still remember a time when weakness was not yet shameful, when someone else had all charge of him – not Mother, but Alfric, there was a good fellow – and his only task was to give his miserable body over for some diligent menial's safekeeping.

They were long gone, of course. Some of them had fled when sickness first seeped through the house. Some stayed, and had the good grace to wait until the master was dead before they indulged their own mortal proclivities. The rest saw themselves out once the state of Father's affairs came to light. They still had to earn their living, after all, and...

Sil's wandering mind all but tripped over the connection.

Servants.

Slaves.

'No slaves in Island Town.'

He'd seen them with his own eyes last night, all three of Aibak's living wagers. What would that be worth to Twoblood? One visit, one conversation, might be enough to get Elim off the hook, along with who-knew-how-many of his unfortunate fellow-properties. That poor tongueless white boy might just come out all right after all.

Sil stared at the old papered wall until its floral patterns softened in a blooming opiate haze.

The boy – the game. That was it. Sil had been going to lose – it was only when he'd refused the boy that his luck had changed – and if he'd kept him, if he'd done *all* of the right things instead of leaving the job half done, he'd have won the boy and personally brought him back to the barn, and Elim wouldn't have fired a shot, and this, none of this would have happened.

Great God, what had he let Faro sell him on?

No, no – he'd put it to rights, though. He'd get up, gather his spilled riches and chill a little water for himself, and a whole lot more for Elim – that was the principal thing. Then he'd see Twoblood, and make a deal – a sensible one this time, slaves included – and get the horse back, and call things off with Faro.

Then he'd get out of town with his money and his mule, and go back to Hell's Acre to make good on his commitments, and pack off back east, back where he belonged. He'd get a job and a wife, and presently he'd start a business and a family: he'd bring the Halfwick name back from the brink of extinction, back to greatness, and when his children asked how he'd done it, he'd be able to look them in their pale blue eyes and say that he'd made his fortune honestly, bloodlessly, with nothing but tenacity and shrewd hard work.

He'd get out of this the same way he'd gotten himself in, face-forward and without hesitation: one way or another, Sil would do it all.

All in just a minute.

*   *   *

As STORES WENT, Halfwick Wholesale was a fine one. You could buy all the usual dry goods and durables, send your mail, and look through the catalogs they kept at the counter. But the real gem, the hidden treasure of Hell's Acre, was in the back room, where Nillie — who had by far the strongest talent of the three — would freeze anything of yours as long as it was wet, and make ice that Will sold for three cents a bag.

Elim lusted to have her there with him now, to have her reach up and comb through his wet hair with her pale fingers until it turned cold and stiff and made ice water run over his scalp. And he wanted her to do as Lady Jane did the first Sunday of every month, after he'd had his bath and knelt down in front of her chair, and before she cut his hair she would put her fingers through it and massage his scalp until everything in his whole body went slack, and all his senses were swallowed up by the gentle kneading of her fingers and the clean linen smell of her dress.

But they were miles and days away, and the one lady left to Elim had nothing to comfort his headache.

"I did," he said wearily. He stared down at the handprint burned into his chest, feeling the dirt between his bare toes, and knew the Sibyl was closing in on him. "Everything I might've done wrong and how I'm sorry for it and everybody that might've done me wrong and how I don't blame them for it and everything I have and how I'm thankful for it. I done and said it all – there ain't anything left." Elim stared at the sprinkling of brown hairs in the dirt around his feet. Leave it to Molly to make him a rosary from her summer coat.

Día gave him another drink. "Then you have done all you can. Is that no comfort to you?"

No, it wasn't. Getting down would have been a comfort, and a mercy. Going home would have been a comfort and a mercy and a signed guarantee of his forgiveness. Hanging here heathen-marked and baking to death just proved that Elim's oldest fear was justified: that although by grace of God he had been picked up out of bastardy to enjoy a privileged life, had eaten at table and had presents at First Night and been groomed and tutored and doctored and loved, that this love was at last conditional, and that having failed Him once, he had now been stripped of all blessings, and left to the fate of a common mule.

Elim closed his eyes. "Please, I don't want to talk about it anymore."

If there was any such thing as a universally correct remedy, Día had yet to find it. Everything had to be done carefully and according to the individual.

In the matter of diet, for example, the coffee and fried biscuits that gratified the appetite of an eastern visitor would likely make any native dining-companion ill for hours afterwards. Just so, the licorice root that so happily soothed Dayflower's teething first-born had blistered the lips of her neighbor's child.

So it was important to assume nothing, to work as carefully as time and urgency allowed, and to rely as much as possible on precedent and observation.

Even so, Día was disappointed by her lack of result with this observable but unprecedented Elim. Yes, he was revived and seemed to be well-reasoning: if the alcohol on his breath was any indication, he'd been dehydrated even before he'd been left in the sun, and needed little more than water and salts to restore him. But his spirit seemed to suffer some deep malaise, and he had solicited no prayer or counsel.

Which she was ashamed to think might be for the best, as she had no explanation to offer for that damning handprint burned into his flesh. Día had never seen such a profound, inexplicable mark – and only hours after he'd consented to stand barefoot.

Reluctant as she was to believe it, perhaps he really had shot the a'Krah boy. Perhaps he was being claimed, and was even now fighting for his salvation. Perhaps further intervention would only distract him from his work.

Sometimes the best remedy was nothing at all.

So Día shelved her ego, rationed out the remainder of his water, and when it was gone, she took a cross-legged seat in his shadow and opened her formulary to make notes. Her duty to the Azahi prompted her to record what was done in his absence, but her duty to God compelled her to learn everything she could about this strange visitor, so that his suffering might someday help relieve the suffering of others.

She grew so engrossed in that, busying her pencil with his unusual proportions and the patterns of his flesh and that mysterious supernatural sign, that when she looked up to take better note of his blended facial features, it was nothing less than a surprise to see them contorted, as if by the weight of some exceptional strain.

Día sat up straighter, and put down her book. He still braced himself against pain and muscular exhaustion, but he showed no sign of stroke or seizure, nor even hysterical tremor. It might be unkind to inquire, as he'd earlier asked for nothing but her silence...

... but on second thought, no: if she truly wasn't wanted, he could ask her to leave, and if she was going to stay, it would not be at the cost of her own good sense.

"Tell me something," she said.

He did not make any answer.

Día belatedly reconsidered her choice of words: in Ardish they were most commonly used to preface some specific question, while here she had intended only to take the temperature of his thoughts. She was on the verge of trying a different phrase when at last he said,

"They had a jumping jack."

Here, as before, she'd glossed his words but missed their meaning. "Did they?" she asked.

"Ahuh," he replied, this time almost at once. "It was over by the corn-huskers, a tent with a special-made stair almost ten feet up and a big giant tub full with water and a sign outside that said the times, and a big jack donkey, that's what it said, that they'd taught to clamber up and jump right off the edge." His forehead furrowed, redistributing some of the perspiration beading over it. "I made real sure I was gonna go see that, as soon as we got our business done. Laid my nickel by and everything."

His voice rolled rough and thick, his words still sticking to each other like over-crowded dumplings in the pot. Even after she'd separated them, Día was left with great gaping holes in her understanding. "That sounds like quite a feat," she said. "I wish I could have seen that."

A fresh trickle of sweat tracked down the left side of

his long nose, and dropped into the dirt. He rubbed his face at his shoulder. "Me too."

And that was all.

Día watched him a little more, her mind thoroughly divided. Finally, she put aside her book, shifted forward on the boards until her feet met the earth, and lowered her backside down to follow them. With a pang of selfish guilt, she unfolded her parasol and cocooned herself in its shade. Twoblood had not given her permission to shade him likewise.

Her cassock brushed the side of his leg, and he cocked his knee again, presumably in case she might care to make a second inspection.

But Día, who was beginning to feel that she had grasped the essentials of this unlikely Appaloosa Elim, did not require much of her eyes just then. Her hand answered him instead, beginning at the sole of his foot and proceeding to idle claspings and soft kneadings of his calves and ankles.

I don't mean to be here. Día had not been herself yesterday, but she was fairly sure those had been his words.

Her gaze wandered over the familiar sights of the late-afternoon street, and watched the shimmering trails of smoke from the great pueblo beyond. It was called La Soleada, because *soleada* meant 'sunny' and the straw they mixed with the adobe make the whole thing sparkle beautifully in daylight. But to Día's ear, *soleada* was not so very far removed from *soledad* – solitude – and sometimes the pueblo was nothing but a sprawling four-story reminder that although her status as an ambassador earned her respect in Island Town, her duty as a grave bride guaranteed that she would never be welcome at any of those fires. This Appaloosa Elim seemed to grasp that feeling more acutely than most.

Me neither.

He slackened again, the posts creaking as his body eased itself down at gravity's behest. Nothing more was said after that. Having at last established satisfactory communication between them, they waited out the afternoon in silence thereafter.

BY THE TIME they had finished with Dulei and purified themselves, half the afternoon was gone, and Vuchak was sorely tempted to lie down right there and sleep. On any other day, he might have.

Today, however, the cool darkness of their underground bed-quarters was pre-occupied, and of course the living could not lie down with the dead – that was blasphemy reserved for the Azahi's grave-woman. So even the best of Huitsak's men were obliged to share sleeping-room with menials and slaves in one of the barren west-side rooms of La Saciadería, whose vulnerability to the afternoon sun had rendered them unfit for paying guests.

And unfit for Vuchak, who still had living company worth braving the sun to lie with.

So after seeing that Weisei was mired in sleep, Vuchak rose again, picked his way around his sleeping cohorts, and slipped silently down the slave-stairs and out the kitchen door.

With his hand at his face and eyes closed to miserly slits, he made a rough quarter-circle around the side of the house, out of sight from the main road and to the eastern side of the town.

It wasn't really cursed ground, of course. That was the Burnt Quarter, where fire had eaten all of the original buildings, and most of the people inside them. No-one could live there now. In the Moon Quarter it was not so bad: you would not become ill or deranged by living there, and it was rare that spirits would disturb your sleep. But the high-nosed hypocrisy of the Ikwei and the Set-Seti and the rest of the sun's preening slaves guaranteed that foreigners and night-people would always be made to live here, where their nearness to the old blood in the ground kept them at a safe disadvantage.

Vuchak was fine with that: he needed no kindnesses to prove himself superior to the clay-stained drudges to the south. But it was tainted ground, damn it all, not a garbage-heap, and he swore freely as his light-blinded eyes nearly let him step in a fresh mound of horse-droppings in the middle of the road. Barbarians.

There were newer houses here, clay ones mostly, built by the Ohoti Woru in the first years after the retaking of Island Town. They were nothing similar to the style of the a'Krah, but served the purpose well enough.

Still, Pipat had made hers a home worthy of Atali'Krah itself, and the gladness Vuchak felt on entering was only partially owed to the relief of his eyes. Everything inside welcomed him. The curtain hanging from the door bobbed and fluttered to recognize him, the hundred painted eyes of Marhuk on the walls awarded him their exclusive attention, and even the remains of the hearth-fire greeted him with the lingering smell of sage and a bowl of fresh white corn cakes nestled in the warmth of the ashes.

Which meant she knew about Dulei, and had known it long enough to grind good white flour, purify it over the

-fire, do her cooking, and have all sign of the work gone before he returned. Her pots and jars were arranged in their usual order under the window, her mortar-bowl and grinding-stone as clean and empty as if unused for a week, and any flour she might have spilled swept and gone as if it never was.

Vuchak would not profane her discretion with any lack of his own. He pulled off his moccasin-boots there at the threshold – facing north, left foot first – and removed his silver and jewelry in the correct manner. He untied his plaits and combed them out with his fingers, right one first, until he had emptied his mind of all the pettiness and unworthy thoughts that had accumulated in crevices of his hair. He poured water first in honor of the Mother of Rivers, then to wash his hands, and only afterward did he take one of the white corn cakes, spitting the first bite into the fire, and consuming the rest with no thought but the taste of the food.

The living ate the dead – that was the way of the world – but the worthy-of-living did it with attention and reverence.

Vuchak did not look at Pipat until he had swallowed the last bite, until it had purified his insides as thoroughly as he had already done for his outsides... but even then, even at his cleanest, he was hardly worth her keeping.

She was long since asleep, lying on her side on the mat furthest from the fire, her face turned to the wall. It was too warm for any blanket, which afforded him an all-desiring view of her bare little feet, their bottoms lightened by earth-stains; her generous curved shape, presently wrapped in a light cotton dress; and her long soft hair, a silver-streaked black wash falling in coiled pools before her neck and shoulders, and her only untidiness, even in sleep. She was old enough to be his mother, and as desirable as any girl.

She had left a space for him beside her, and he was glad to lie down and fill it – lying at her left, in the manner of an unmarried man – and to let his tired gaze rest elsewhere.

There was nothing of his here, of course. The knife and the bow on the wall did not belong to him, nor the moccasin-shoes in their reverend place by the door, nor even the woman at his back. Though it had been six years since any of them had received their master's touch, his presence still ordered them as surely as if he'd left at sunrise. She was called a widow, but in truth, in sleep, Pipat was a two-man woman yet.

So Vuchak left her to visit her husband in the dreamworld, and thought of the work that awaited him.

His task was to be the vessel through which Marhuk's will was poured out upon the world, as perfect and unseen as the spider-silk netting that carried the clouds. This was his life's great purpose: the sign of the *atodak* guaranteed it.

Vuchak's attention drifted from the tattooed mark on his wrist to the far side of the room. For all anyone could say, Marhuk himself had commanded the ashes to yield up that bowl of white corn cakes; just so, the half-man's death would have to be produced as if from nothing.

Certainly, it would have to be done out of Twoblood's sight, and by some method – some snakebite or trampling or other such accident – which would not suggest a human actor.

Ideally, it should be done tonight, so that no-one could say that Marhuk had allowed the murderer to see two sunrises.

Hopefully, it could be done without infection.

Vuchak's stomach tightened at the thought. Sired from rape and theft and slaughter, dropped from the loins of shackled women, the half-breeds were a second death: they brought foreign diseases as readily as their foreign fathers, but in them the knife was sheathed, hidden. The evil they inherited could not be seen in their faces, nor heard from their lungs, nor smelled on their breath, but it seeped out of them as surely as fluids from a corpse, contaminating all they touched.

And when the two-colored refugees first came streaming out of the east, they had found no shortage of welcoming arms to greet them.

Halfwick might well demand answers, if this went wrong and Vuchak's part became known. *How could you*, he would say. *I thought you were peaceful.*

No, Vuchak would reply then. *We are a'Krah. The peaceful ones are all dead now.*

And thus the task of healing the world fell to the survivors: to the a'Krah, to Marhuk, and by extension, to Vuchak.

The half-man's life would be ended, removing one source of contagion from the world, and preventing the generation of any more from his line.

The reclamation of stolen wealth would continue, gathered with infinite patience as it slipped from the careless pale fingers of the Eaten.

The time of restitution would come.

And Vuchak would sleep a little in the meantime, and strive to avoid dying for greater causes until he could be sure that Pipat would occasionally visit him too.

CHAPTER TEN
CONCERNING FISHMEN

IT WASN'T ANY dearth of gratitude that made Elim such bad company, in those hours. It was only that he felt so all-over awful. He'd have torn off his own arms, just so he didn't have to feel them anymore, and even that wouldn't have done anything for his back.

But almost worst of all was the fact that Sil hadn't come back.

Elim heard the sound of people out and about again, late in the afternoon, but they were far away and none of them had the right voice.

Could Sil have gotten stuck in something? Gotten his fool head blown off trying to cut a deal in some nameless back-end street? Or what if they'd decided to string him up somewhere too – out in this sun, with his white hide? For Elim it was an almost-unbearable trial; for Sil it would simply be a death.

And the last thing he'd done was to holler at him.

That thought sunk its fangs into him slowly, over the course of minutes, until Elim was so poisoned with it that he had to pull himself upright again, igniting fresh fiery needles in his hands, and crane his neck to see whether there wasn't some deathly-pale picture of himself hanging from the posts across the street.

His movement didn't escape Día's notice. Having long since moved back up to sit on the planks in the narrow avenue of his shadow, she looked up from a book he hadn't properly noticed before. "Are you all right?"

No, not any. "Have you seen Sil – my friend, the Eadan?"

Elim saw her answer before he heard it. "I haven't. Would you like me to look for him? I can ask at –"

"No," Elim said, because his worry about Sil didn't yet equal his worry at what might still happen if anybody found him here alone. "Only maybe you could tell him something for me, if you – if you was to find him later on."

She was no dull-edge, of course; her understanding showed plain in her face. "Elim, I should have told you before: you're only meant to wait here until sunset, and if anyone had intended to make a claim on your life, I truly believe they would have long since –"

– and that was good to know, but Elim hadn't spent the day making expectations about getting out of this alive. "Ahuh," he agreed, "only I'd feel a heap better for not having all my eggs in – for your having the same piece of my mind as I mean to give him."

She closed her book and scooted further back, where he could see her without putting a crick in his neck. "What would you like for him to know?"

There was no telling about Sil, but at least he could be sure about her. "Molly – uh, my horse, she got loose this morning, and I don't know where she's at. I was hoping he could see to that. But, uh…" … and it was somehow much harder to say than it was to just think… "… if the worst comes to it, I mean that he should forget about the horses and the money and see that he gets himself back home in one piece, so as – so that my folks will know about me." He watched her as he said it, anxious to see a return-understanding bloom in her expression. "I know he was short with you before, but you got to make him understand: one way or other, one of us has to get home. Can you get him sure on that for me?"

Día nodded, clear and slowly. "I'll make certain of it."

He sighed. "Thanks." And while they were putting things to rights... Elim stared down at the handprint. "You reckon they were right about me?"

There was no immediate answer. "Alcohol is a powerful force," she said at last. "It often inflames our emotions to extremes that our reason would not otherwise allow."

Elim closed his eyes, and let disappointment have its moment. "I kinda figured so. Wish I knew what made me do it."

It didn't matter much, anyway. Nobody had put a gun to his head and made him: whatever he'd done, *he'd* done, and if he was going to die, his job was to do it owning more than his share of the blame, not less. "Thanks for checking me, though. And I guess, not as any principal dickering-point, but just if it happens to come up... you might could tell him too that I'm sorry about all this. I didn't mean for it to go bad like this, and I know he didn't neither." He swallowed. "That's about the size of it."

She didn't hurry to an answer, which was a nice way for anybody to show that they had really heard you. And then: "Are you sure you don't want me to find him for you?"

No, no – she was calm and reasonable and kept him safe from the people above- and below-ground, and it was selfish to even think it, but none of his what-if-maybes about Sil scared him nearly as much as the might-well-could-bes if he were left alone again. Sil wouldn't have just absquatulated and left him here, but he was *exactly* the kind to go find some cool shady spot to rest himself until this supposed sundown roundup-time arrived.

If that was true, then Elim only had to stiffen his lip and abide a little while longer. If it wasn't and Sil was already hung up dead somewhere, there wasn't anything he could do about that. So the biggest favor he could do himself was not to whittle his mind down thinking about it, but to thrust his attention into something else as deep and fully as Two-Pie's face in the slop-bucket.

Elim lifted his chin at the book in her lap. "What's that?"

It was a hell of a thing, a big rough-bound brown slab of paper – too big even for the Verses, unless it was one that had pictures in.

Día joined him in studying it. "It is one of my formularies – a written collection of the things that I know to be true." She glanced up, gauging his face for interest. "Would you like to see it?"

"I would, sure," he replied, though he was not at all sure what to expect from its insides. She shifted around to sit with her back at his legs, and opened the book to rest on her black-draped knees.

"Well, let's see... here, if it takes your interest, are the elements as God has made them," she said, and flipped over to a page half-covered with little circles, each one filled in differently and labeled, almost like

Boss's branding-book back home. "The holiest of them is hydrogen," and she pointed to the large circle at the top with the cross drawn through it, which Elim had more commonly seen on church-steeples, "because it is the unifying substance. Once dissolved from earth-metals such as iron," and she pointed to the circle with the sideways-H shape a bit further down, "it becomes a flammable gas, which when burned produces water." She followed the cross with her finger as she spoke, from earth at the bottom up to air, and then across from fire to water. "We could not have any of our world without it, and I think it cannot be an accident that we also use this shape as the sign of our Divine Master."

As a rule, Elim was careful not to get overly educated. There were certain people, like Macready the schoolmaster and Mrs. Crackstone at church, who thought knowing more made you better and ignorance was a demon, but that just wasn't true. Sure, you had to know as much as you could about your work – and there was a lifetime's labor just in that – but after that, to hoard up learning just for the sake of having it... why, that only spoiled the brain as bad and surely as sugar rotted teeth. It led people to believe that they were too good for their place, too smart for their station in life; it ruined them for every useful occupation, and nobody proved it better than this very same Sil Halfwick.

But although Elim was careful not to learn anything that might accidentally discontent him, 'hydrogen' beat the hell out of hanging here. "That is a heck of a thing," he agreed, dizzied by all the little symbols added up on the facing page.

She turned a few pages, and stopped at two matching pictures of a man's body. "Now here," and she pointed at the one at the left, "are shown the organs by which we perform our living functions, and which are common to all the higher animals. But here," and she indicated the one at right, which instead of guts and innards was drawn over with tremendously fine bundles of lines, "are the nerves by which we have mastery of our bodies. Do you see what a great many of them have their endings in the face and hands and feet?"

"I do," Elim said, as she held it a bit higher for him in the dwindling light.

"I think that is a remarkable fact," she went on, "as I notice that these are the most sensitive parts of our bodies, and the ones through which we express what talents we may have, and the ones which animals lack. It seems to me that God has put all our discerning senses into these parts, and made us to put our labors out through the very same, so I think these nerves must be the most direct conduits to our souls, which is to say, to God Himself. Is it not a tremendous thought?"

Elim thought there was another part that fit her list, except that animals had it too, and it might be from God, but it seemed to do the Sibyl's work oftener than not. It was not drawn in on her diagram.

"You sure do seem to know a heap about it," he said, as much for a compliment as in hope of turning the subject to safer understandings. "I bet you know the Verses front to back, huh?"

Día looked up from her book to the wall ahead. "No," she said. "That is, I have the Genia and a few pieces of the Penteia, but our original copies were all burned, and the Azahi has asked us not to replace them. I understand they were used for evil purposes a long time ago."

Elim felt he had put his foot in it with that one. "Oh," he said, and tried to dredge a sensible reply out of the exhausted cramping of his muscles. "So the Azaz – the Azahi, he's your boss?"

Día let her knees back down again. "We are his ambassadors. Those of us who remained after – that is, those of us who remained, he asked to be his ambassadors, to stay and be a help to any guests that would visit. There were three of us: Fours the merchant and Miss du Chenne the schoolmistress, and me." Then her voice went flat and quieter. "Miss du Chenne is not with us anymore."

"Oh," Elim said again, and this time his part was clear to him. "I am awfully sorry to hear it." Though of course he knew better than to ask how she'd died.

He looked down at the woven-wool roots of her hair, and then back out at the reds and purples coloring the sky behind him. It was almost dark.

"Thank you for helping me today," he said. "You have been right kind, and I'd tell him as much, if it wouldn't make trouble for you later." Probably that was why she'd kept his company: not because she was partial to him, but only because it was her job to be here. He was glad for it, regardless.

"It wouldn't," she said, and made another little space of silence afterwards. "There is a better favor I would ask, though."

It was hard to picture anything he could do for her just then. "Be pleased to try," he said.

Día didn't look up at him, but her hands folded to rest on the crevice of the book's open pages. "Are there any others like me, where you come from?"

Elim's hope of returning her service faded then. Asking for pure-bred Afriti was as good as asking for hen's teeth, at least back home. "Not properly," he said. "My friend Clydie's Tom, his ma was half, but I don't believe he knows anything about the rest. Dirty Merl says his grandma was full-blooded, but she got sold to some kind of traveling whole-saler when their crop went bad, and he never did hear anything more about her." He pressed the edges of his hands to the posts and leaned into them, a poor effort at taking some of the weight from his stiffening knees. He wished she'd show him her face again. "I'm real sorry about that. I know there's plenty out on the islands, but that's a far ways from Hell's Acre. We're most of us just piebalds and skewbalds, now."

Which was a terrible way to end it, and when she didn't reply, he thought that maybe he wasn't finished after all. "Reckon it must get lonesome here, sometimes. You got anybody to keep your company?"

He knew he was venturing onto soft ground with that one: from the sound of things earlier, she must have run clean out of family when the town changed hands. If she didn't dig up the sad story itself, she'd probably assure him that she meant to keep it buried.

He didn't expect her to so suddenly take a hold of his pants-leg, though, and he was nothing short of amazed when she twisted around and looked up at him with such a harrowed face. "Elim, I am sorry – I meant for you not to come here – I did not at all intend to be rude yesterday, and I would have stayed to see you understood why, except that you – that is to say, I was surprised, and... prideful."

Elim understood all of the words, but it took a minute to untangle their meaning.

Horseshit. "I don't believe that's the word for it," he said politely. The word for what she was yesterday was embarrassed, as any modest soul would be when they caught a stranger contemplating their own personal particulars. Still, the emotion in her face, coupled with her grip on his nether-hem, both flattered and alarmed him.

Well, maybe he could even with her for his accidental understanding yesterday.

"Ever seen a appaloosa?" he asked.

"I have, yes," she said, plainly confused.

"Know what a 'blanket' mark is?"

"Oh, yes," she said, suddenly all collected again, and flipped to yet another page in her book, this one with three horsey shapes drawn from varying sides. With her finger on the one in profile, she traced a rough quarter-circle from the top of the horse's hip down to the back of its thigh. "It is a great white patch covering its –"

"Ahuh," Elim agreed.

Día looked up at him, and back down at the picture again, and finally – momentarily – to his approximate middle-section. Then she snapped the book closed and bolted up to her feet. "How extremely unkind!"

Elim shrank back from the sudden burst of motion, but afterwards his frayed nerves registered only a tired disappointment. He hadn't meant her to take it that way. He studied the blazing vexation on her face – so very like the one Clem had used to make whenever he made a show of ignoring her – and his dry lips quirked up at the corner. "Fixed your face though, didn't it?"

Her eyes widened, her expression darkened, and she backed away from him. "This is ludicrous," she said, with a vague, angry gesture at his face and body. "It is not right, it is not just, it is not – you are not an animal!"

Elim would have agreed with that, but his attention

was arrested by a red glow in his periphery. He looked to the left, to the northern end of town, where the left window of the boarding-house at the end of the road glowed with a vivid red light. Another flickered to life from the right. And although he could not recall how he had come by the thought before, he decided again, now, that it was an evil thing, and felt suddenly desperate to be out of its view.

"It's night," Día said, and again: "This is ludicrous. I'm calling Twoblood here, and – no, I'll do it myself." She dropped her book, reached up to the rope, and groped for the knot.

Her urgency was infectious, and it was all Elim could do not to fidget as her hot fingers brushed the raw flesh of his wrist. Nevermind her Twoblood – where was Sil?

The thought seeped through Elim's mind as he stared at the house, Sil's absence illuminated by twin red lights, hope sinking with the weight of a familiar dread.

"God bless this knot!" Día swore, jerking him back to the present with a painful yank of the rope-end.

"They tied it under again," Elim said, "after Sil said I was to be here awhile." And he had been hanging and pulling on it most of the day – if it wasn't wire-tight before, it would be now. He tried not to sound as fearful as he felt, powerfully tempted by the urge to just pull hell-for-leather until something gave. "Do you got any kind of a hair-pin or a nail you could slip und –"

"My knife," she said, and slapped her hands to her waist. "Bless me, I've left it. I'll get it, just wait – wait right here and I'll fetch it back –"

And before he could tell her not to, before he could even ask what had put her in such a hurry, she hit the dirt toes-first and was off at a breathtaking sprint. In a matter of moments, Elim was left with nothing to watch but the lights coming on in the upper floors of the house at the end of the road, illuminating distorted, moving shadows that couldn't be promised as human, and somewhere in there they had Sil.

Elim gave in to the urge.

It WAS ALMOST dark by the time Shea managed to slip away. Her violet evening-dress was not her ensemble of choice, but there was no helping that: anything but the usual would have raised eyebrows and dampened her chances of leaving unremarked. As it was, she simply walked out back as if to visit the ordinary, then took a right and kept going.

But the house and barn were deserted, with nothing but a puny little light illuminating an unremarkable sack of something next to the barn's back wall. She crouched down and felt over its rough canvas lumps: a traveling-sack, maybe, smelling of horse and human sweat, with a rifle propped up behind it.

They had to belong to the boy, and Fours had to have put them there, but then where was he?

Shea turned and turned, scrutinizing the ground as if she'd dropped a hair-pin in the dirt. Surely he wouldn't have just abandoned her to her own devices. Surely he still knew how to keep a promise.

And then, just before she would have cursed and sworn aloud, a soft tapping caught her attention. She followed the sound, squinting in the twilight. The weathered gray planks of the wall were watching her with baleful black eyes.

Her shoulders sank in relief.

Mereaux generally did not camouflage unless they were distressed or stalking something. With Fours, it was almost his natural state of being. *Thank you,* she signed, and again: *Thank you.*

He answered with a slow blink of his eyes.

Go outside the wall, she signed, *and make a disturbance to the south or west. Anything. I need the north gap to be unwatched.*

Another slow blink.

I will see you again, her hands promised.

If Fours made any answer, she couldn't see it. He left with quick, silent steps, the contours of his body invisible to her as he changed to match the shadows.

And that was all.

Shea stood still, struck by this appalling anticlimax. Didn't he know how important this was? Didn't he realize what was at stake?

Her resolve faltered. For a moment, she was nothing but a squandered body and a wasted life, a wretched, loveless shrew whose sole accomplishment was the accidental ruin of the Ara-Naure, and of her last remaining sibling's affection.

She hadn't intended anything of the kind.

She never would have stolen the child if she'd thought for a moment that its mother might suicide trying to find it again.

She'd been a *good* servant – not a miserable maid, not a tarted-up door-keeper, but the devoted right hand of U'ru, eternal mother of the Ara-Naure. And her devotion would be rewarded, now, tonight, when she spirited away the great lady's last son – again! – and poured his blood out on the ground to call his divine mother back from her living death. Mother U'ru would return for her child, would heal him and remember herself and then pardon her true and loyal servant for that one most well-intentioned error of judgment, and make everything right again – put things back in their proper place again! – and leave all these frustrating empty years in-between to melt away like sand washing out to sea.

Then Fours would see that everything she'd done was necessary and for good purpose, and all would be as good as forgiven.

Righted and resolved, Shea picked up the rifle and the lantern, slung the gunnysack over her shoulder, and doubled back on her careful, circuitous track between buildings and through darkening back avenues. After twenty-three years, it was time to live again.

ABOVE EVERYTHING, TWOBLOOD prided herself on consistency: she did what she said she would do, when she said she would do it.

And if tonight there was a reason why sunset had come and found the half still hanging, it was because Twoblood was busy standing at the window, listening to Barking-Deer tell her that the Eadan boy was nowhere to be found.

A terrible suspicion took root in her mind.

"How do you know?" she asked. "Who did you speak with?"

Barking-Deer could not have straightened his posture any further: in the gathering dusk, he carried his tall, wiry frame exactly as he had when standing watch over the foreigners at the crossroads that morning, and answered with even more careful precision than before.

"The door-woman at the House of Satisfactions. She said that he had quartered there last night, and had gone and come back again early in the afternoon, but that his room was now empty, and she could not tell what he might have intended." He tipped his head once to the left. "She was lying, at least in part."

Twoblood studied Barking-Deer's shadowed face. His gift was not a strong one, by Set-Seti standards, but he had long practiced the art of reading in strangers' faces what he could not always hear in their thoughts. "What did you do then?"

Barking-Deer dipped his head, a blotted silhouette. "I went next to Fours, in case he might have left town. One horse is still missing; both have been sold to the madam's clerk."

There was an irritating superstition among some of the daylight tribes, which held that a white man could overhear the use of his name from any distance. Something to do with the unholy naming-rites they performed on their infants – Twoblood had never bothered herself about the particulars.

But nevermind, as the meaning was clear enough. The madam was Addie, the clerk was Faro, and the boy, it seemed, was finished.

Fuck.

Twoblood turned to the mantle and set about lighting the lamp, cursing herself for a near-sighted fool. She'd been so occupied with watching the half...

Well. There was still a job to do, and little time and even fewer men to do it with.

Twoblood opened the teapot to the smell of cold grease, and threaded the wick through the spout. "Where are the other three?"

"Wi-Chuck is at home for dinner. Feeds-the-Fire is... the Burnt Path, I think?"

Twoblood spared a sideways glance to Barking-Deer. He had fixed his gaze to the corner of Twoblood's desk, as if emptying his own senses made others' easier to read. Maybe it did. "And Yes-Yes?"

That required no concentration: Barking-Deer looked up at his cousin's name. "He... apologizes, Second."

Twoblood snorted, and triggered the fire-pistol to light the wick. "I wouldn't have hired him, if I'd known he'd made a bride-gift of his balls." Nevermind, anyway: Yes-Yes was lucky enough to have a family to go home to and a wife to lie beside him, and if he got as much satisfaction from her in the dark as Twoblood did from his service in the daytime, then it was a deal well-struck.

Twoblood had others to rely on at night.

As she lit the lamp and set it on the mantle, its yellow light told the time in Barking-Deer's changing face. He was broadly-speaking still unaltered: still wearing the same white paint over his arms and the part of his hair, his long hair tied at the nape of his neck in the same sober style, the golden disc hanging from his neck still marking him for a servant of the Azahi. But here in the wake of day, his body grew just that little bit larger, more splendid in form, and his eyes flashed like golden mirrors in the flickering lamplight, and the brown of his skin parted into brilliant sunset-colored reds and grays, and then there was then no mistaking him: from his father he had inherited the hardiness of the Ikwei, but from his mother he had learned his place among the Set-Seti, and been blessed with all the gifts of the Twilight Twins.

Presently, it was the gift of night-seeing that most interested Twoblood. Whether dead or fled, the Eadan boy was a lost cause, and that meant someone else would have to see to it that the half was put back on his own side of the river without stepping on a crow-feathered knife.

"Find Feeds-the-Fire, and have him take your place at the western gate. Then put Wi-Chuck on watch for the north. The night-people can do as they like in the Moon Quarter, but I want them off the main road and away from the gate." This was less than ideal, as Wi-Chuck couldn't see any better than Twoblood in the dark, but the job needed a steady manner and a clear mind – and fists that could snap femurs never hurt either. "After that, make a bag with food and water enough for three days, and meet me at the eastern gate. I will wait for you there with the half, and we will close it as soon as we have put him across. Do I have your understanding?"

Barking-Deer dipped his head again. "Yes, Second. I will meet you there." He let himself out and was gone in a moment.

Which left just Twoblood, who had no gifts but those she had crafted in herself, to look again at a long angle through her barred window. The half pulled violently, struggling with something unseen, and the cowbird was nowhere in sight.

Twoblood bolted across the road, the lamplight extinguished by the slamming of the door.

FOURS SLIPPED ALONG back-streets and between houses as quickly as stealth allowed, cursing himself all the while. He'd made a bad job of it, all of it, and it was all beyond fixing now: nothing remained to chance but the size of the disaster.

There wouldn't be more than a sliver of a moon tonight, but he didn't need much to see by: he crept into the charred remains of the church through the collapsed wall of the nave, his foreshortened toes splaying out over the odd tuft of grass growing in the dirt, and in no time at all he had taken the steps down to the narthex.

Distant footsteps sounded behind him.

Fours paused with one hand on the broken stone rim of the well, the loose skin already stretching between his fingers, and listened. They were light, fleet-running bare feet, and Fours' delicate ear-membranes quivered as he recognized the pattern.

Día couldn't find out about any of this.

He dropped headlong into the well, and for a moment the rush of cool water elicited an amphibious euphoria, and he was happy. The whole sunlit world could go out in a blazing apocalypse and he would not have to know about it or care: he could simply curl up in the deep, silent womb of the earth and stay there until he died.

Only he had promised that he would help.

Fours registered the most gentle of impacts as his body finally sank to the bottom, and reluctantly unfolded himself for the swim. It was blind going down the narrow tunnel, guided only by a dim awareness of non-water barriers around him and his own memory of helping to bore this conduit through the shale so many years ago. But even if he were feeling his way through for the first time, he still would not have had time enough to devise a plan.

Somebody, most likely Barking-Deer, was going to be watching the western gate. Fours needed something dramatic enough, important enough to make him call for his fellows, long enough for Shea to get to the boy uncaught. He'd thought of arson, which was guaranteed to roust every able-bodied man in town, but there was no calling fire without people looking sideways at Día, and he couldn't have that. A call of invasion would get a crowd, especially with nerves taut after last night's shooting, but that was a difficult one to fake, and common thievery might not command enough attention. Of course he had been far too stupid to think of bringing a gun.

A faint light rippled in the water ahead, and Fours approached it with the reluctance of a tardy schoolboy. He had no plan, no tools, and no hope. He could not deliver Elim to Faro, who was therefore going to get in him in *such* trouble with Opéra. He was already in trouble with Twoblood, which meant that he would be in even steeper trouble with the Azahi whenever *he* finally came back. And Shea...

... there was not really any consequence for failing Shea, except that if he did his job well, she would escape and leave him here to deal with the mess, and if he failed, she would probably get shot and die.

Fours scowled as he swam up towards the surface of the river. He was cowardly, useless, and had no power over anything – why the devil did they all act as if he were the master of their affairs anyhow? – and was only going to get himself killed trying to please them. In fact –

Fours stopped dead, his spatial senses alerting him to something big in the water downstream, something much bigger than fishes. He glided up to the surface oh so slowly, making not one more movement than necessary to emerge just to his eyes, just enough to see...

The party on the farther bank must have come from the south, and had now nearly reached the western gate, but Fours' worm's-eye view still caught their dark silhouettes against the last lingering red glow of sunset. There were two horses, one mounted by someone wearing a helmet, both held at the reins by another someone on the ground, whose opposite hand carried a bright spot of yellow light. Fours suspected he already knew the two in the water: one crouched neck-deep at the shoreline, presumably addressing the earth-persons above, the other submerged deeper down, closer to its mistress.

It was much too dark to see details in the water or out of it, but Fours sensed her all the same: the great fish-tailed queen of the river, her enormous delicate hands making signs to whichever of her voices presently attended her – almost certainly Alto or Soprano. With one giant sweep of her tail, she straightened her long royal body and swam towards him.

And such was his fear that he scarcely even noticed when the man on horseback turned his head, and what looked like a helmet in portrait became a short, skirted headdress in profile. It took longer than that for Fours to understand the design, and most particularly its centerpiece, which glinted where the lantern-light caught it: a gleaming, golden disc.

Fours hid there in the water, watching, mentally assembling the pieces as he waited to be taken. Shea was about to get her panic after all.

SHEA FLATTENED HERSELF against the wall and listened. She heard wind, and crickets, and sharp, frantic creaking-sounds from the posts of the covered walk ahead, punctuated by peculiar gasps and grunts. A door slammed from somewhere across the street.

She risked a peek around the corner, but aside from a few scattered pinpricks of light, everything was dark to her. More telling was the sound of heavily-shod footsteps eating up ground between their origin – somewhere by Twoblood's lair – and this nearer side of the street.

And damn it all, where was her commotion?

"Stop that," Twoblood snapped. The thudding creaks of the building ended. "Now hold still, do you understand?"

"*Lemmedown, please lemmedown, I ain't sposedabehere, I –*"

Oh, this wouldn't do – what had gone wrong with Fours?

She'd have to take care of Twoblood herself, then. Shea picked up her skirts and opened her mouth for a bloodcurdling scream –

– and had hardly finished filling her lungs when a not-quite-masculine shout beat her to it.

"Second! Second!" Someone was running up fast from the right. "Second, sir –"

"May the gods take you off!" Twoblood swore. "You're supposed to be on watch!"

"The Azahi is here, sir – he's calling for you at the gate!"

Shea's heart leapt. Fours had delivered after all – what a splendid diversion!

"Feeds-the-Fire, I am going to set you ON fire if I find you've left your post for anything less. Now stay put and mind him." By the sound of her voice and her heavy steps, Twoblood was already off and running for the western gate.

Blessings on Fours, then!

And blessings on Feeds-the-Fire, too, who was living proof that the gifts of the gods did not pass uniformly among their descendants, not to mention the dumbest coyote that Shea had ever known.

She counted to fifteen, swallowed and swiftly re-tuned her artificial alto. When she spoke again, it was in a voice very much like Twoblood's. "Well, what are you waiting for? Get to it!"

It was a masterfully fine imitation, even for a mereau, and enough to make Feeds-the-Fire jump. "S-Second, sir, I thought you said -"

He'd figure it out, if she gave him even half a minute to think about it. "I said hoof it and find him – the Azahi, you witless lout, the Azahi!"

"Yes, sir!"

Shea held still as he dashed past her in the dark, and counted to one. "No, not THAT way – will you disgrace me in public? Go around the back and escort him in – now, idiot, now!"

"Sir!"

He doubled instantly back, and Shea could not imagine him sprinting more quickly if he really were on fire – but there was no time to wait for Twoblood to discover her errant man and test that for her.

There was just time enough for Shea to open her knife and finish the job.

ELIM COULDN'T HAVE said what drew off the speckled mule and her fellow, but it didn't hardly matter. He steadied himself, mentally walling up more sandbags between his right-thinking mind and the raging pain at the end of his left arm, and then threw his weight to the right, strangling his rope-scorched wrist. Again, and again, and –

"Oh, I SAY – is that any way to conduct yourself in public?"

That wasn't Día.

A petite woman-shape moved toward him in the dark, announced by rustling petticoats and soft-footed shoes.

"Please let me down," he begged, and didn't wait to see whether she would.

"Honestly, now," she sighed, and suddenly Elim's senses were all full of silk brushing up against his bare chest, smelling oddly familiar, of fruit and flowers and something else –

– and then the left rope snapped. He pitched forward and grabbed the post to catch himself, and looked up in time to see her finish the right one with one final flick of her knife, and when that one broke he didn't even try: after hours upon hours, Elim was at last done with waiting, and collapsed onto the boards in agonized relief.

Maybe that wasn't mannerly of him. "No, no, no – get up, boy! Get up, damn you, get up!"

Under any other circumstances, the sound of cuss-words from a woman's mouth would have been appalling. Now, though, Elim registered only a collection of familiar one-syllable ideas as he curled over to more fully experience the exquisite lightning-arcs of pain in his back, and pulled in his arms to blunt the distant prodding in his side. There was a groaning, long and low, and it might have been coming from him.

He had his eyes open, though, and when they finally noticed that he was being kicked in the ribs by the little lady's shoe, he began to suspect that he ought to do something about that.

"Elim," he said, laboriously pushing himself up to a sit. "My name's Elim." That was the first of several considerable courtesies he owed her. The second would start with 'Thank you.'

She didn't seem impressed by that either, but at least the kicking stopped. "Is that what they're calling you nowadays? Well, that is just delightful, really it is – now get UP! Move!"

His arms were shaking, palsied, but that was no excuse for the rest of him. Elim had just gotten his feet planted and his tingling hands braced when he took a sudden hit between the shoulders. The force of it wouldn't have woken him from a nap, but the heels of her hands rammed into his fried flesh with all the delicacy of a branding iron, and he instantly lurched up and forward.

He had not taken more than two steps before he felt a surge of dizziness. The night seemed to close even darker around him, and he suddenly felt like maybe he ought better sit down again.

"Don't you dare!" he heard, as if from a great distance away, and his unaccountable swaying was interrupted by a sharp nudge from the left. "Don't even think about it," and this one was more of a snarl, coming from six inches away and about two feet down. "Boy, if you pass out, I will cut you. I will pull out my knife and cut out your spots, d'you hear me?"

There was a second, counter-acting nudge, followed by a constriction around his ribs, as if a child was hugging him sideways. Elim put a hand out to steady himself and found a fistful of slick cloth with a sharp shoulder underneath. He stood there, leaning on her until he felt her straining under his weight.

But she bore up without another word, and he didn't need long before his head and eyes cleared some. That left him staring at the red-lit house, remembering it all afresh.

"Sil," he said, not much more than a whisper at first. "He went to go sell the horses and he ain't come back yet." Elim looked up at the blackening sky. Hadn't he made him promise to come back by moonrise?

"Yes, yes," the little lady agreed, pushing him forward and left, away from the house. "He's sent me to fetch you, and we're going to meet him – hurry up now, mustn't keep the master waiting!"

That didn't quite fit: Elim couldn't tell what master she was talking about, or why Sil wouldn't have come himself. Then he remembered how he'd shouted at him just this morning after Sil whacked him across the face. They'd had a fight, and he was supposed to be getting the horses ready to sell, but he couldn't even recollect feeding them their supper.

So maybe he'd better take her word on that.

"Sure," he said, and let her lead him around the corner of the promenade and then east-ish, towards the closed gate that went back to Federate land again. Only when they hit the wooden stockade wall, she didn't let him go south to the gate, but pulled him the other way, to the left and the north along the wall, and he would have objected about that, except that he couldn't afford to argue or get left, especially when he couldn't hardly even walk, nevermind see. So he kept his pace with her under his left arm and the rounding wall at his right....

... right up until his right hand ran clean out of fence.

There was a gap, like a missing tooth in the town's sharp wooden jaw, which she used to lead him out of the town proper and down the sloping island shore. Elim was plain amazed to find his gunnysack and rifle right there on the ground waiting for him, their shapes brightened by the light of a battered old barn-lantern.

So maybe she was right about that.

"There we are, you see?" she said, as if reading his thoughts, and slipped out from under his arm. She was dazzling in even just that little bit of light, all fine violet silks and glistering long black hair and shiny little bits and bangles, not just on her dress but at her neck, around her eye, even on her shoes. There was no telling what Elim might have done differently if he'd known at the get-go that she was a Sundowner, except that probably it wouldn't have been smart. "And he's already waiting for you on the other side. Now let's get your things, quickly now, and we'll just go nicely across the river and meet our –"

Elim, who had stooped for his bag, looked up at the sound of her gasp.

Two small, nearly identical people walked up out of the water: one light-skinned, one dark, both bald except for a pair of strange plumes, like backwards-facing dog-ears behind their heads, and tails like flatwise-turned tadpole tails draping down behind them. By their costumes they might have been meant to be female –short-skirted wet white dresses, matching their peculiar white-painted half-masks – but Elim knew better than that, even before he saw what rose up out of the water behind them.

Beside him, the little lady dropped into a curtsey. "– Mother Opéra," she said.

Fishmen, he thought.

"MASTER HALFWICK?"

The tapping at the door was too light to disturb him. That was left to the creak of the door and the footsteps on the floorboards.

"Master Halfwick, are you quite all right?"

Sil opened his eyes. The brown bottle lay on the floor in front of him, visible only by the light spilling in from the doorway behind, and he felt wonderfully refreshed...

Then the bottle and its contents and the darkness and the throbbing in his right hand all collided and burst into panic.

"Oh shit oh shit oh SHIT –" he swore, and staggered to his feet. "Water," he said, lurching for the ewer and basin on the bureau. "I need water – Elim's not well, I have to get him water – God help me, I'm such a bloody idiot –"

"Oh, there's no need for that," Faro said with perfectly pleasant aplomb. "It's already been taken care of. That's what I was coming to tell you."

Sil stopped, pitcher in hand. "It has?"

Faro smiled his neverending smile, and spoke to soothe. "Yes, of course – you don't think I would neglect a thing like that, surely? Come along; I'll take you to him."

Sil sniffed, swallowed. And then he remembered what he'd asked for – what he'd agreed to – and all the sleep evaporated from his mind.

No more great notions of seeing Twoblood or freeing slaves. No more chance of even belated heroism. Sil had commissioned a death to pay for Elim's life — gotten exactly what he'd bargained for – and now there was nothing left but to live with it.

Sil set down the pitcher, numb in spite of the pins-and-needles in his legs. He picked up the battered gray hat from where it lay at the foot of the bed. As he did, he noticed a gleaming little spot amidst the dust, reminding him of what he'd spilled under there, which had to be retrieved before the maid or the whore or anyone else could pocket them –

– but no, this was no time to go arsing about under the bed. Elim, that was the first thing: he'd bring him straight back here and then retrieve the pearls. Sil followed Faro's expansive gesture out to the gaily-lit hallway, though he took care to close the door after him. "And he's free to go? Just like that?"

"Oh, very nearly," Faro replied, all comfort and assurance as he led Sil to the stairs and up to the third floor. "There is just one last item of business, you'll recall, and then we can be said to have truly completed our bargain, and put all your worries to an end."

Sil paused in pinching the sleep from his eyes, his irritation at Faro's vagueness fading as he recalled that other part of the contract. "Oh – yes, of course. I'm sorry about that – we'll get the other horse for you straightaway. I was just rather hoping I could have Elim to help with that." They paused at the door to the gaming-room. "He's here, you said?"

Faro opened the door to the same opulent splendor, the room as elegant as it was empty. The only movement came from the burgundy curtain drawn across the balcony, its soft wine-red hems fluttering in the evening breeze. There was no sign of Elim – not so much as an oversized bootprint in the plush rug.

"Is he not?" Faro's smile ended at sight of the vacant space. "Why, I'm sure I told Shea to bring him here for you. Well, perhaps she's made accommodations elsewhere; let's just see."

The house was all alive again: as Faro crossed the room to the grand balcony, Sil could hear people down below, and at least two more coming up the stairs. He strained his ears in case Elim's voice might be somewhere among them. What then, if he wasn't here? What if somebody else had taken him? Really, what if –

"Ah!" The soft peak of Faro's delight cued Sil's every nerve as he paused, hand at the rail, and pointed down. "Yes, look, you see, that will be her at the door, and – say, isn't that your fellow there?"

This damnable shortfall of certainty moved Sil almost without his own direction. In a handful of steps, he crossed the room and pushed the curtain further aside. "I'll just have a look," he said, in some token effort to arrange for an unobstructed view before his impatience compelled him to shove the fop right out of his way.

"Certainly," Faro said, beckoning Sil out onto the balcony beside him. "I think that must be him, just there under the porch – oh, but perhaps the angle is better from over here."

Sil stepped forward over some odd coil of rope, Faro moving obligingly back behind him as he leaned out over the balcony-rail to see.

CHAPTER ELEVEN
A NECKTIE SOCIABLE

ELIM FROZE – GAPED – as the fish-queen rose from the water.

She was not a woman, not any earthly woman. She had no bust or navel – nothing for motherhood at all – nor even any rightly-made face. Hers was round and out-snouted like a hellbender or a mud-newt, with vast black eyes and a lipless wide mouth and a back-sloping forehead ending in a crown of fleshy bones, like fingers, like antlers, every one of them fringed with wet plumes of something more algae than hair. Her arms reached out, each one twice as long as Elim's and ending in spindling-thin webbed fingers. Her wet flesh was the whitish-green pallor of a drowned man. And all of this, right down to the swaying of her hips as her unseen fish-parts worked to hold her even that much upright, conjured a horribly twisted picture of all real womankind.

She was a lady who was not a woman: in other words, the Sibyl Herself.

Elim could not look away. In his periphery, the two handmaids had stopped to stand waist-deep in the river, turning in place to watch their mistress as She began to weave sharp, fluid gestures with her skeletal hands, and then they both spoke at once.

"*¿Champagne, ké con esto terríkolo ases?*"

"Champagne, what are you doing with this earth-person?"

Their girlish voices sounded no special interest as they stood facing inwards, and spoke with hands clasped neatly in front of their white smocks.

There was some meek stammering beside him, and foreign words stranger than Marín. "*Oh – oh, Mère, pourquoi –*"

The fish-queen's hands picked violently at the air, as if she was plucking an invisible instrument hard enough to rip the strings out of it.

"*Par-ke elo teyentienda nos-dí.*"

"Tell us so that it will understand you."

Her bleached green fingers paused to listen for an answer, and Elim dimly felt a hesitation from the little lady beside him.

"Why, of course, Mother – I was only helping him to leave."

The fingers began their weaving again, slow and more gracefully this time.

"*Petifor ke par la muerte de otro terríkolo buskado está nos dise.*"

"Petit-Four tells us that it is wanted for the death of another earth-person."

The edge of an enormous finned fish-tail flipped briefly out of the water, making a greenish backdrop for a bald figure, perfectly river-colored, who crouched at the shore's edge and stared back at Elim with a pair of sorrowing black eyes.

There was a faint in-suck of breath next to him. "Fours!" And then, at a more moderate volume: "Fours – why, Fours is quite right, of course," she said, "and the man is quite dead. But I must help this boy to leave, Mother, because he did not do any of the killing – I did."

Elim's fear snapped in a second; he tore his gaze from the Sibyl to her lady-painted offspring. "You did WHAT?"

But she didn't look up at him – all he had was a view of the shining black-silk top of her head – and the interview played on as if he was invisible.

"*Par-ke?*"

"Why?"

"Why, because – simply because our honored sibling Faro asked me to, Mother, and I am sure I don't know why. Perhaps I could bring him here to tell us about it..."

Elim's head spun, and not only from exhaustion and thirst. He *knew* he hadn't killed the Sundowner boy – they had almost got him believing he had, but now the truth came out and he wouldn't take the blame for it, not for a coven of fishmen!

"*¿Cómo se mató?*"

"How was it done?"

Elim glanced over at his rifle. Surely not. Even if she wasn't too small to aim four-feet-ten-pounds' worth of gun, the recoil would have busted her shoulder, and she couldn't have known about how you had to jimmy the setting-trigger just-so before you could fire...

There was a rustling of petticoats beside him; Elim looked over just in time to see her hike her skirt up to the thigh, exposing a black stocking and what he wasn't supposed to know was the beginning of a garter-belt. He couldn't look at that, but he sure as hell couldn't miss what she pulled out of it.

"I had it from the boy's master."

Elim could not fathom how the little lady, 'Champagne' as they pleased, would have gotten hold of Sil's flintlock pistol against his will. But he could all too easily imagine just how willing he'd been.

He watched, horror-struck at the implications, as Champagne handed it over to the brown-colored handmaiden, who turned it over and around for her mistress's inspection.

And then She turned her salamander face to the huddled figure at the shore's edge, and this time the motions of her hands went untranslated.

But when it began to reply in kind, its movements showed clearly even in the scarce lantern-light, and Elim began to understand. There really was a man there, small and naked and just about the right size to be Fours the shopkeeper, almost as invisible as if he had been painted to match the water. Even his flat wide feet blended with the mud.

Elim heard a distant shout, far away from inside the town, and a whisper of rustling silk beside him, and he was hot and turning queasy as a smell like fish and ripe algae seeped out from the pageant of horrors before him.

Then that spindling She turned back towards them, and Elim had just time to see her whiteless eyes narrow before her hands and voices began again.

"*Petifor ke anayarma vieha es, y ke sólo ana-vez disparar puede, nos dise.*"

"Petit-Four tells us that it is an old weapon, and can fire only once."

Except that that old lead ball probably would have left a bigger hole, not that Elim had any virtue of experience.

"Once was all I needed, Mother."

"Petifor ke antes de ke utilizada ser pueda en ana-manera sierta preparada ser nesesita nos dise."

"Petit-Four tells us that it must be prepared in this certain way before it can be used."

Except that it was half-cocked, just the way that Elim had given it to Sil. Even as he watched, the darker handmaiden pulled the hammer clumsily on back until it clicked.

"I used it easily enough, Mother."

Elim glanced down. Champagne was standing right beside him, and he still could not see her face. But she clutched fistfuls of her dress at her sides, and the edges of her hands had purpled to match the silk.

And then She gestured at the whiter handmaiden with a royal swirling of her hand, and when she began to sign again, it was translated in just one voice:

"Then, Champagne, if what you have said is true, you must be guilty in the death of an earth-person. But if we find that you have lied to us... it will be seen that you have done something infinitely worse."

The fish-queen took the pistol. It did not fit her huge hands, but She threaded her bony finger through the trigger-guard and cupped the barrel as delicately as if she was cradling a baby's head, and Elim had no doubt that she understood exactly what was required.

Champagne curtseyed again as the weapon was aimed squarely at her chest. "I am your servant in everything, Mother."

Elim felt a cold rush of fear, like that morning when he'd had a gun to the back of his head but different, because this time it was happening to someone else and it shouldn't ought to happen at all. He ought to do something, fast.

Then the Sibyl turned the gun on him instead. Elim registered the crack of the gunshot, and the shriek from beside him, and felt the impact just below his chest – maybe not all in that order – and staggered back a step.

Something cool and slippery began to slide down his stomach. He looked down, and caught Champagne under the arms.

She looked back up at him, her black eyes wide in astonishment and what maybe you could call expectation. But Elim was at a loss, marveling at her flowery smell and her weightlessness and the cool wetness spreading under her right arm, and could not fathom what she meant for him to do.

Her eyes half-closed; she sighed in bottomless disappointment. "You always were an ungrateful child."

Elim's brow creased in deepening confusion. He looked up for any kind of help, just in time to see the Sibyl's free hand slice through the lingering smoke in the air. Her two handmaidens turned their masked faces to him as they drew identical white-handled knives, and advanced out of the water on wide, webbed feet.

Elim didn't wait to see what came next. He grabbed up Champagne and bolted away from the water, through the gap in the wall and inside again and past the nearest little outbuildings towards the street, to the main road where people would be and he could get back to the barn, bolt the door and hole up in the loft. He would not disappear, he would not, he would not –

"*El eho agarra! El –*"

He collided with someone, hard enough to knock him back a step. The street was dark; he couldn't see who he'd run into or make out what they were hollering about, but he understood as soon as he saw the front of the red-lit house and the rope swinging from the black-iron balcony and the man kicking, twisting, strangling at the end of it, his pale white hands clawing at the noose, his face contorted in apoplexy but otherwise unmistakable as Elim stared, and Sil hanged.

"– CAN DISGRACE THE dead if you want, but I'm not having it from Huitsak, not tonight," Vuchak hissed. "Are you listening?"

No, of course not. Weisei never listened. He did what he pleased, and tonight, right now, it pleased him to wait until the last fathomable second to remember that he couldn't do honors for Dulei without his cloak, and of course nothing would do but that they racked the house like a pair of sun-touched imbeciles looking for it.

Vuchak glanced over his shoulder, delivering up a silent, selfish prayer that Grandfather Marhuk would at least shield them from the eyes of women and foreigners as they skulked about in their mourning-clothes, and all but clipped Weisei's heels as he shadowed him up the stairs.

"No, I'm LOOKING," Weisei replied, "for my cloak, which is..." He trailed off as they approached the top, his silence making room in Vuchak's ears for the sound of Ardish voices. One of them belonged to Faro, and the other...

"... hey, do you hear that?" Weisei didn't wait for an answer, but charged up into the hallway. "*Afvik? Afvik, hallo!*"

Vuchak lunged for him, too late, as his one-thought *marka* chased the sound as an infant dog would some bumbling fat insect, down the short hall and to the gaming-room door. "Weisei, don't –"

They barged in, one after the other, as Faro dropped a noose over Halfwick's unsuspecting head.

"– Afvik, NO!"

Weisei saw it first, but Vuchak was faster. He charged forward, eating up ground, and elbowed Faro hard in the face – but not before Faro's shove toppled Halfwick over the rail. Vuchak grabbed for the rope, yelping in pain as it first seared through the flesh of his palms, then yanked him bodily forward. He twisted before he could be pulled over the rail, winching the rope over his shoulder and doubling forward to hold his ground –

– even as the air was cut by a savage, wet snarl. Vuchak looked up, just in time to see Faro's delicate white features contort in an inhuman rage. He spit out his broken human veneers, his lips curling back over rows of his own vicious jagged teeth. The tip of his polished black shoe shone as it coiled back like a viper –

– and then Vuchak's eye burst in pain. He gasped, caught without air enough to cry out, as the force of the kick snapped his head sideways and knocked him to the ground. His grip broke in an instant – there was nothing he could do – and he felt a distant warm pain as the rope spun out of his hands. The coils under his left arm jerked away one-two-three, concluding with a crushing line of force across his chest that slammed him breathlessly back against the rails. The ominous wood-splintering *crack* did nothing to drown him out as Vuchak doubled over, pressing a hand to whatever was left of his eye, and screamed into his sacred shawl.

* * *

ELIM STARED, AGHAST, as a man's muffled cry carried over the night air, and Sil plunged another four feet. The drop would have snapped his neck if he'd taken it all at once: as it was, the break in the middle had condemned him to strangle instead.

No, not condemned – pardoned. Elim dropped Champagne and barreled back towards the gap in the wall, and he would have found it by the smell if not the Sibyl's children worming through it. He put out his right elbow, crooking his arm in front of his body as if he would offer his arm to a lady, except they weren't ladies and he wasn't offering anything but a quick and brutal hit –

– and then they broke neatly apart and kept right on walking. Elim quit his stride, spinning in case there might be a knife meant for his back, but no, they were going right on past and that was fine. He turned again, staggering as his eyes struggled to match with his body, snatched up his rifle and nevermind the Sibyl. Elim squeezed back through the wall and out to the street, giving the fish-daughters a wide berth as they closed in on the spot where he'd left Champagne. He halted in the middle of the road, set his feet apart and took aim –

– before being bodily accosted by someone trying to grab his gun.

"¡Alto! ¡Alto! Maldito pendeho!"

"Get off!" Elim swore, jerking the rifle away. "God damn you, get off me!" He yanked the gun back towards his body, then shoulder-rammed his attacker hard enough to break her grip and send her sprawling to the ground.

Elim didn't wait for the speckled mule to get up again. He cocked the gun and jimmied the setting-trigger with a flick of his finger, and then took aim at the knot where they'd tied the noose to one of the balcony-rails. He could see that there were people up there – a fight had broken out and one of them, maybe a Sundowner, had his back and one arm shoved up against the rail, but nevermind him: it wasn't more than a fifty-yard shot and Elim would make it easily. Even with the cramping shakiness in his arms, he'd do it for Sil, take aim and fire –

– and nothing happened.

Elim cracked the barrel in disbelief.

The rifle didn't fire because it wasn't loaded.

It wasn't loaded because he'd already fired it once before.

Elim barely felt the blow. He hit the dirt knees-first, just in time for the second kick to lodge right up under his ribs, knocking the wind from his lungs and the gun from his grip and doubling him onto all fours.

And from his dog's-eye view, he could see it all. There were people gathering in front of the house, their silhouettes lit from behind by the red lights in the windows. Above them, his struggles dwindling from a man's desperate throes to the kicking, fading jerks of a rabbit with its throat torn out, Sil was losing his hold on life.

"YOU STUPID FISHMAN – *look what you've done!*"

Vuchak was dimly aware of Weisei's outraged cry – of running footfalls and then the dish-rattling impact of two bodies hitting the floor. The tempest of pain savaging his face also clouded his thoughts, but he *knew*, just as surely as he knew that Weisei had dived in without a second thought, that Faro was about to pull out a knife and stab him in the neck. Vuchak thrashed against the rope that pinned him to the rail, struggling in vain against the weight of Halfwick's mortal agonies.

"*Jelpimé! Sómbodijelpe – dikróz av-kéltim!*"

Vuchak halted in mid-jerk. He did not understand much Ardish, but he picked out enough words to know that Faro was calling for help — and about to tar them with the filth of his own despicable act.

Vuchak forced his eyes open. He could just make out a blurring, doubled image of Weisei, straddling Faro on the ground, seizing the fishman's up-thrown arm and prompting an even more strident howl of pain as he bit down hard.

"Weisei, stop!" Vuchak cried, twisting around to brace his foot against a rail and pull for all he was worth. "Stop, stop – let him go!"

Another sharp *crack* split the air. Vuchak froze at the tiniest of jolts in his back. He looked down, to the rail's end beyond his feet, where the bars now jutted out beyond the end of the balcony at a dizzying angle, their tops tipping forward like spears thrust out to skewer the first of a cavalry charge.

Vuchak held still, breathing only shallowly. He winced at every jerk of the rope from the dying man on the other end, shuddered as the distant vibrations in the floorplanks grew closer, louder, until the people – not his people; he did not recognize one set of a'Krah moccasins amidst the colored harlot-shoes and heavy boots – came thundering into the room and saw them there: Weisei hauling Faro up by the collar and Vuchak tangled in the rope and the rail, displaying not only their mourning-clothes but also their apparent guilt, for all the world to see.

He closed his mangled hand over the rope across his chest, the commotion of discovery muted as he listened to the soft, gentle creak of old rivets about to give.

ELIM WAS FORCED down to the ground, his arms pinned to his back and then sat on amidst a clamor of heathen shouting. He lifted his gaze in despair.

It was not Champagne's gun that had been emptied last night but his, not her who had pulled the trigger but him. But she'd died for it and Sil was next: already the twisting arcs of the rope were winding down as each spastic jerk shuddered out weaker than the last, and Elim's time to act had all run out.

He didn't catch the quick dark shape at first, blending as it did among all the other obscene figures at the house's gabled porch. But it stood out by its speed, dashing up from the right, clearing the porch-steps in a single bound and launching itself at the left-hand column with a brilliant, fluid urgency. It was not until it had shimmied halfway up the white-painted pillar that Elim caught the glint of something bright at its side and recognized it – her, her – and surged up to resist the weight on his back and help her somehow.

A distant, echoing *crack* rang out. Elim dropped back down, and Día stopped too, and for a second he thought she'd been shot. Then she started climbing again. Now she'd made it level with Sil's knees – Elim winced as she narrowly missed a kick to the head – and now she'd inched up past his head and kept going, close enough to grab the rope as it passed near again. But she couldn't cut it too, not without two hands free, and that was one more than the smooth-sided column looked willing to grant.

She kept right on going, caterpillaring up with grasping hands and crossed ankles, her wild hair and black robe billowing as she crawled up nearer the knot where the arcs swung smaller. Then she pulled her knife and reached out for the rope –

– but no sooner had she latched onto it than another terrible *crack* echoed in the night. She suddenly grabbed up for the balcony, and he couldn't make out what she found to cling to up there, but he saw all too clearly the silvery flash of the knife. It tumbled from her hands and fell two stories in a heartbreaking instant.

Elim cried aloud and heaved himself up for another surge of resistance. He'd go and fetch it back and throw it to her, somehow he would! Then someone grabbed a fistful of his hair and shoved his face back into the dirt. He had just time to look up, straining his periphery to make out Día hanging by fingertips onto the balcony's edge, her feet crossed and smoking over the rope just inches above Sil's head - because of course, because she was Afriti and talented and as much fire as a Northman was ice, and could surely scorch through that line as readily as Sil would chill a glass of milk. Then she was suddenly swallowed by a blooming burst of smoke, one last *crack* split the air, and it all gave way.

THEY DIDN'T KNOW anything, not one blessed thing, but that never stopped the Eaten. They crowded into the room, grabbing Weisei's wrists from behind and forcing him to the ground – their sheer *audacity* provoking Vuchak to outrage in spite of his panic – and the pink harlot was helping Faro to his feet as he coughed and wilted and made a great show of injury, and not one of these snake-bellied fools had any idea that a man was hanging and another was about to be pulled to his death after him.

"*Make help!*" Vuchak shouted in his clearest Ardish, clutching at his face with one hand and making chopping motions at the rope with the other. "*Half the rope, half the rope* – you bitch-whelped pig's leavings, *half the rope!*"

They didn't understand. He could see by the expression on the fattest man's face that he thought Vuchak was raving violent, and if he came anywhere near him, it would only be to put *more* ropes on. And Faro wasn't going to tell: he feigned a coughing fit, hacking up trivial amounts of blood in an elaborate show designed to ensure that all would be too late by the time he finally 'recovered' enough to speak.

"Stop, let me up!" Weisei cried all the more pitifully as the black-mustached man drove his knee between his thin shoulders. "I didn't do anything – he's killing him, let me up!"

But he was telling the truth, a language that none of these savages understood – not that they could stop barking commands at each other long enough to listen anyway.

"*Bastert-kreisi króz! Juéirz Brant?*"

"*Goatil-Ádi! Shill tróedemout forgúd –*"

The weight on the other end of the rope abruptly doubled. Vuchak gasped as the breath was crushed from his lungs and another *crack* lacerated the air. With his good eye, he could see the sawdust sprinkling down from the jagged hole where an old rusted screw now jutted out at nothing. A split second later, a grasping pair of hands grabbed on to his shirt and shawl.

"*Get off!*" he cried in Marín, his voice half-strangled by the weight.

"*Be still!*" a strident female voice answered.

An acrid, burning smell singed the air, followed by more grasping and clawing behind. The unseen woman seemed be losing her grip. Vuchak felt the line across his chest suddenly relieved of Halfwick's weight, just as the woman grabbed onto the iron bars behind him, and then it was all too much. The last of the bolts ripped loose, the rope pinning him was abruptly sucked away as he rolled forward from the edge, and then the woman, the rail and Halfwick all went crashing down to the ground below.

THE ROPE BROKE and Sil fell, disappearing in a split second behind the gathering heathens. Then the house roared out one last great *CRACK* and bit down on him with its black-iron fangs. A terrible, ear-savaging crash of metal on stone brought everything to silence in its wake.

That didn't last long.

"Get off!" Elim cried, bucking upward with a fresh surge of desperation.

"*¡Alto, alto!*"

The enemy jammed a pistol to the back of Elim's head, but Elim only threw his head back against the barrel: Sil was lying somewhere up there, alive or dead, and Día with him, and Elim was done with fear. He'd go and get him, and they could shoot him for it but he'd go –

"... Elim..."

Elim froze. A voice very much like Sil's – no, Sil's, it was Sil's voice! – broke off into a wet, hacking cough.

"... Elim, just go with them, will you? I'll come for you tomorrow..."

"Sil? Sil!" For a moment Elim thought it was coming away from the left, but that was only his addled brains fooling him. He surged upward again, joyfully this time, and had his face smashed back into the dirt for his troubles, but that was fine: Sil was alive, that was the important thing, and Elim was perfectly content to lie there counting his blessings until he was hauled up to his feet and shoved forward. He stumbled down the road with the gun jammed into his back, and that was fine. Sil was alive, which meant that everything was going to be all right.

VUCHAK LAY STILL until the last echoes of the crash died away. There was a great quiet from the whole room – even Faro had stopped his pretending – and even after it was broken by exclamations of ignorance and amazement from the foreigners, the feeling in the air was nothing of what it had been before. Weisei was let up and went to Vuchak's side. Vuchak crawled forward to peer down over the edge.

The woman was nowhere to be seen, but Halfwick was all too easily found. He lay crumpled on his side under the rail: not gasping, not coughing, but only fidgeting a little, his purpled face animated only by the odd twitch of his lip and a few blind, flickering glances. Even these soon died away, leaving only a lingering, horrible stench to drift up into the night.

CHAPTER TWELVE
THE CROW PRINCE

WHEN DÍA RETURNED to herself, she was lying on her side, breathless with fading pain.

The first explorations of her fingers discovered a hard wooden floor, its seams packed level with the dirt of ages. The soles of her feet tingled with lingering warmth.

And on opening, her eyes were instantly assaulted by the gaze of a dying man.

He lay crumpled under the iron grate not three feet away, staring right at her. But although his clenched fingers still seemed to tug and tear at the noose, there was no human thought behind his bloodied eyes. He shivered uncontrollably, his boots drumming a faint staccato on the porch-planks, and his swollen features twitched and shuddered in nervous trauma.

Día flinched, but that was the base part, the animal part of her that did that. With her higher thoughts, she returned her gaze and looked in him for God, searching his face not for his consciousness but his divinity, his holy animating force without which not even one eyelid could flicker. *Must you?*

And it seemed that the answer was *Yes,* because even as her own animating force gathered her to get up and take hold of his, his limbs stilled and his body slackened and he went, with nothing but a deep-throated gurgle to mark the going.

The sight of an emptied human vessel was nothing new to Día. But in witnessing the act of emptying itself, she was disappointed to find the air distinguished not by any discernable passing of the man's spirit, but only by the surrendered contents of his bowels.

And presently, by the voices of the night-people gathering beyond the porch steps. They were of several kinds: dark-skinned a'Krah in ceremonial dress, androgynous Ohoti with bright shawls drawn over eastern clothes, a pair of Washchaw standing conspicuously tall among the rest, and –

A terrifically loud *BANG* sounded behind her. Día startled and rolled to one side, reaching for a knife that wasn't there.

"Wait!"

The voice called out in Marín, and could have belonged to a man or woman. Día glimpsed just a mass of flying black hair as the stranger came shrieking out the front door, halting with belled sandals just inches in front of the crumpled body on the floor.

"Afvik, don't go!"

He was a man, to judge by his knee-length white shirt and white-leather ankle-wraps, but not one that Día recognized. Fine-featured and slender, with exceptionally dark skin and tangled hair billowing to his waist, he stared at the body with wide, horrified eyes, and then bolted down the porch steps.

The night-people retreated at his advance until he had

carved a semi-circle out of their ranks, staring up at the black sky and turning in random quarter-circles.

"Afvik, come back!"

He was half lost in the night, the bright copper discs of his *concho* belt flashing at the edge of darkness as he waved his arms like a marooned islander. The watery whites of his eyes flicked from point to point, scouring the heavens in desperation and growing despair.

"Please come back..."

Then he accosted one of the Ohoti in shadow, taking him or her by the collar and shaking until the little bells at his feet rang out a tiny cacophony. "You! Why did you let him go?!"

Día could not imagine what importance this Halfwick might have had. She had met him just the once, and her conversations with Elim had done little to change her first impressions about the Eadan boy. Still, the upset taking hold of his native friend tugged at her sympathies.

She would not let it distract her. Halfwick's soul had spilled from his body like the yolk from a broken egg, and someone had to clean up the mess.

Día pulled herself back over to the body, stifling her aches and pains as she did, and pushed the rail aside.

"*Weisei, weh'ne!*" a man's voice called down from the balcony.

The delicate veins in Halfwick's left eye had burst from the pressure, staining the white a wet red. But that did not explain why his eyes felt so cold and swollen when she tried to close them, or why they slowly opened again afterwards, staring back at her with dilated pupils.

"*Dechendi, hagat vutla? Kui' hagat ne!*" the man above continued.

Well, she would try again after some of the congestion had drained from his face, and meanwhile work his curled fingers free from the noose. The former were cold, but the latter was frozen so stiff that she could not loose it from his neck.

So he was a pedigreed Northman after all.

Día could not have said whether the frozen rope was a testament to Halfwick's last-ditch efforts to save his life or merely a mortal spasm peculiar to his race. She would not forget to record it in her formulary.

"*Veh'ne eihei, vichi!*" the grief-stricken man cried with sizzling anger. "*Ne KE dechendi, tse ne KE kui' agat ene!*"

The knife – now where had her knife gone? Día rose gingerly to her feet, negotiating the lingering cricks in her back. From further out in the distance, she could hear the watch calling for order.

"Back! Move back – make way! The Azahi commands it!"

There was a silvery glint in the dry bushes, and Día's heart quickened as she helped herself down from the left side of the porch. Had he really come back, then, and was he really meant to arrive just ten minutes too late?

She picked the knife out of the dirt, having torn the sacristy apart looking for it just minutes before, and returned to kneel by the body. Had God really meant that all Halfwick's help should have come just a little too late?

That was not right, of course. It was not God who had killed Halfwick, but a fatal constriction of his airways and venous passages, not God that had dictated the Azahi's arrival, but the rate of his travel, a function of time and distance as fixed and fair as it had been since the genesis of the world.

This distinction occupied her so fully that she scarcely noticed the eclipse in her light.

"*Ohei!*" an accusing voice cried above her. "What are you doing?"

Día flinched back, blade close to her body. The grieving man stared down at her with wild, desperate eyes.

She gestured from the knife to the notch she had sawed in the frozen rope. "I am cleaning his body," she said. "It isn't nice to leave it this way."

He straightened, towering above her, and he was thin but he was a man, and an unstable one at that. His hands flexed and curled at his side.

Perhaps she could put them to better use. "Please, will you help me?" she asked. "I wouldn't like to carry him by myself."

He stared down at her, and for a moment she thought he was going to be violent after all.

Then he dropped to a crouch and moaned – a long, plaintive sound. "I don't want him to be gone," he said, lacing his hands behind his head and burying his face between his knees as if he never wanted to see daylight again.

It was an understandable feeling, and Día could already imagine how it would be expressed by mourners yet to come.

He'd called him 'Sil'.

She rested Halfwick's head on her lap and worked with the knife as she considered her reply. Finally, she cut the last of the frozen fibers and loosed the rope as delicately as if unclasping a fine golden locket from his bruised and swollen throat.

"Neither do I," she said at last.

* * *

THAT HADN'T GONE quite according to plan.

It was growing increasingly difficult to keep track of things, and also to breathe, but Shea gave it her best effort. Fours took her arm across his shoulder, hurrying them towards somewhere-or-other. Under her wig, her dry gills ached and tingled in a futile effort to pick up the work her punctured lung was leaving undone.

But underneath the pain and that disquieting exchange of blood and air was just the smallest little bit of satisfaction. At the end of it, he hadn't left her after all.

"You know," she said, with difficulty at first, and then continued in a softer, steadier and exceptionally confessional voice: "I wouldn't have seen him at all, if I hadn't gone to the river to keep an eye on her. She's grown so splendidly..." The thought ended with a wet cough.

"Be quiet," Fours said. He smelled of keen distress.

Shea obliged. It was dark and getting darker still, but nevermind: U'ru's boy was alive and safe for the night, and Fours knew what to do.

When you thought of it that way, things hadn't worked out so badly after all.

THE AZAHI'S DECISION was final. So Twoblood and Feeds-the-Fire dragged the half to Twoblood's house for the night, meeting Barking-Deer along the way.

The half had enough sense to go willingly now, but Twoblood kept the gun pressed to his flesh, just in case.

"– and I was sure you'd told me to stay with him, but then you said –"

The Ohoti Woru were renowned as a race of architects and crafters. To date, however, Feeds-the-Fire had never been observed to craft anything but excuses.

"I SAID, 'stop talking'."

Nothing more was said until they were close enough for Barking-Deer to open the door and see them inside.

Twoblood didn't let go of her gun or her fistful of the half's hair, but indicated the cell with a jerk of her head. "Open it, and put water in." She made the half wait in stillness while Barking-Deer pulled open the old barred door and Feeds-the-Fire hefted the tarnished copper drum from behind Twoblood's desk. He poured a third-portion of its contents into one of the two buckets in the cell.

The door had hardly even shut before the half was on his knees, gulping water as if he would drown himself in it.

Which left Twoblood at leisure to holster her pistol and fish the flask of turpentine out from her top-left drawer. A little on her hands, rubbed together, ensured her cleanliness. Its clean pine stink was a courtesy she was glad to extend to her inferiors –

– but obviously they couldn't be too concerned about it, busy as they were staring at a man debased by thirst.

Twoblood slammed the flask down on her desk, earning her the attention of three pairs of eyes, and slid it forward. "Clean yourselves, or explain to your wives why you didn't, and then go put yourselves at the Azahi's service. You will be dismissed at his word, and you will not return here again except at his request. Am I understood?"

Apparently she was, and with refreshing simultaneity. "Yes, Second!"

They hurried to it, but the half did not return to his drink. He just continued to stare, his gaze fixing less on Twoblood than on her deputies, who – to judge by the stranger's stricken face – might well have been slavering man-hungry *marrouak* from the wastes of Merin-Ka.

Nevermind, though: they finished their ablutions and were gone soon enough, leaving just a pair of two-bloods alone together.

Which was exactly what Twoblood had tried so hard to avoid.

Which was now, by the Azahi's order, how they would spend the remainder of the night.

Which perhaps was a compliment, as certainly Twoblood in his place would have been inclined to assign the job to the thought-hearing deputy, or the one with the best night-seeing, or at least the one with size and strength enough to break the prisoner or any would-be assassins cleanly in half.

But as she blew out the lamp and dropped into her chair, Twoblood felt less like a woman complimented, and considerably more like one assigned to the task for which she had demonstrated the least record of failure.

There was a shifting from inside the cell. The half stretched out to lie with his head in the crook of his arm, becoming still before Twoblood had finished putting her feet up on the table. That was fine.

So Twoblood, having been relieved of all present duties save one, tipped her chair back against the wall, leaving her gun and hat ready in her lap, and settled in to watch through the night.

* * *

THERE WAS A persistent superstition among certain earth-persons, which held that a mereau was as good as a doppelganger – that it could replicate anyone with little more than five minutes' watching and a rightly-made wig. Their child-frightening tales would have it believed that a 'fishman' would replace your very mother if you didn't eat your porridge, copy her face and voice so perfectly that you'd never even know, not until she dragged you from your bed in the middle of the night and drowned you in the river.

The reality required considerably more sacrifice.

In Fraichais, they were called *taillé*, the 'clipped' or 'trimmed', who had had their tails and toes amputated and the wounds burnt to prevent any future regeneration. The better word would have been *mutilé*.

But tonight Fours found himself actually grateful for his *cul brulée*, and more pertinently for his missing toes, as they afforded him an advantage not shared by Opéra's voices. Their fan-shaped feet were no good for running, their lungs had never been used for anything but crafting airborne speech, their shoreline experience afforded them no map of Island Town's interior, and all this together meant that Fours could haul Shea up from where she had been left bleeding on the ground, drag her along the northwestern wall to the church and to the long drop of the well, and still have time enough to hole up somewhere safe and unseen afterwards.

Almost.

"*Champagne ou est-lu?*"

The high, strident voice from behind didn't slow him: the hole at the back of the promenade was right ahead, and Fours went for it like a rabbit to its warren. He dropped to his hands and feet and emptied his lungs, flattening himself out for the quick dive under the kickboards, and then everything was black. He would have done well to stay still, but he couldn't trust that Soprano hadn't seen him slip under, and to be caught in the crawlspace, to be seized blind and dry and helpless and hacked to pieces under there and found only weeks later by the smell –

– and so he fought his way through the hellish nether-space full of loose dirt and ancient droppings and chattering disturbed things fleeing from his approach, ahead and left and left more, towards the faintly-lighter spot that had to be the back-side of the steps where the big black-striped queen had had her kittens just that spring. He flattened again and heaved himself out, gritting his teeth as the broken boards scraped a bloody gouge down his back, but nevermind, nevermind, he was out and up and going to run left, to Twoblood's, and once he got that far –

"Champagne ou est-lu?"

He spun to see Alto advancing around the corner, breathing heavily, knives still clenched in its hands. Hope for Twoblood died as it cut off his escape, and Fours vaulted up to the floor of the promenade and ran right instead, north again, where he might be able to lose himself in the firegrounds around the church –

"Champagne ou est-lu?"

– where already Soprano was climbing up the burnt northern end of the promenade to cut him off, its swishing tail and flapping flat feet unmistakable on the boards, its voice labored but still as pleasant as if it were offering him sugar for his tea.

Fours froze, hope dying. He could bolt right, though, hop down and run across the road...

... except that as he turned back again to gauge his chances, he saw that Alto had dropped down to a long-legged squat, its feet splayed wide under its meaty, sinuous thighs.

They couldn't run for much, the unclipped, but they could make a terrific leap.

"*Champagne ou est-lu?*"

"*J'ne sais pas,*" he replied, his voice a quavering whisper as his flesh faded to match the wall.

"*Champagne ou est-lu?*"

"*J'ne sais –*"

Hypnotized by the sight of Alto's tensing muscles, Fours had no chance against the assault from behind. With one solid *thap*, a hundred-pound weight hit the floorboards right behind him. Startled, Fours bolted forward, caught his toe-stumps on a gap, and pitched forward onto his hands and knees.

Alto rose up out of its crouch and advanced again at a leisurely stride.

"*Champagne ou est-lu?*"

A cool, wet hand clamped down on his leg.

"*Champagne ou est-lu?*"

Fours held perfectly still as Soprano climbed over him in some lethal parody of a mating toad, the dirt on his flesh dampening to mud as he perspired in distress. He wondered dimly whether it was Champagne or Petit-Four who would have the honor of being the last of Opéra's wedding-presents, and found it sadly appropriate that they should rediscover their kinship in the scant handful of minutes that would separate their deaths.

Then his instincts took over, that oldest part of a mereau's mind that compelled him to mimic mortal danger in the hopes that it would mistake him for one of its own. His flesh whitened to match their livery, and before his voice petered out against the feel of the knife at his neck, he heard himself copying that as well.

"*Champagne ou est-lu...*"

"Stop, please."

The voices froze in place, their masked faces tilting to regard someone at ground level behind him.

"I dread to cause any offense, gracious voices, but must kindly ask you not to damage my ambassador. I am still much in need of his service."

And by the time the fog of fear dissipated enough for Fours to recognize that rich, steady tenor, his flesh had already darkened to a deep, gold-tinged brown.

"TELL ME AGAIN – the last part."

"Certainly," Día replied in Marín. She crafted the Ardish words slowly and with more than her usual care.

"*We move as You have moved us,*
We love as You have loved us,
We live as You live in us,
And die in Your grace perfected."

The man, whom she now knew to call Weisei, looked back down at Halfwick's head in his lap, and repeated the sounds with studied diligence. "... *an-die iñor greis perféktet.*"

There was precious little light to speak of: except for the yellow glow of the lamp that sat beside them on the stone lip of the well, the church was all dark. But as they knelt there with rag and bowl and body between them, the moonlight streaming in from the collapsed nave wall caught in Weisei's copper ornaments and the whites of his eyes. "And it will not anger the Starving God to hear us using his words?"

One stray thought protested at that: he was not a 'Starving' God, she wanted to say – he was God, infinite and complete, as far beyond hunger as the oceans were thirst.

"I don't know," Día said. "But I have always preferred to risk offense by an excess of care and service, rather than any lack of it."

Weisei cupped his hand into the water bowl, and worked his palms together to make a lather of the yucca-soap shavings between them. "That is right. That is how it should be." And then, with a pause in his hands: "What will you do after he is clean?"

From her kneeling-place at Halfwick's right side, Día kept the cloth moving over the soft and unnaturally cold flesh of his stomach. "I will go to bed," she said, "and tomorrow I will wash his clothes and put them out to dry, and then I will go to Elim – his partner, of sorts – and find out what I can about Halfwick's wishes, or those of his family."

"*Ylem,*" Weisei repeated, with a disconcerting flatness. He worked his hands through Halfwick's wet golden hair, and did not look up.

Día chastised herself for mentioning him. Weisei belonged to the a'Krah, and Elim was wanted for the murder one of their number, and she could not begin to guess what relation Weisei might have had with the dead man, or what they might still intend for his killer.

So it was prudent to turn the conversation back to its original object. "You are very generous to do this work," Día said. "Had you known him long?"

"No," Weisei said. "Only an evening, half an evening,

not more." His black hair hung down as a curtain before his face, and his fingers went still at Halfwick's temples. "And it wasn't – it wasn't what they say of me. He was pleasant, and clean-smelling, that's all, and said clever funny things, and he was good to me – and for no reason except that it pleased him. And it pleased me also, to think that I would cause him to do and say all those splendid things, and I began to think that he liked me – that we should be friends."

Well, either this Halfwick was extraordinarily adept at changing his manners, or this Weisei was sorely lacking in company. At a different time, Día would have asked what they said of him.

Weisei glanced up. "Is it true that you lie down with them?"

Día conceded only the briefest faltering in the movement of the cloth. "Sometimes," she said. "When a body is given to me, and the wishes of its master aren't known, I work to the limits of my best estimation, and supply the remainder through the Penitent traditions, at which I have the most practice and skill. As we said before, it is likely better to perform a wrong or needless task well, than to let dread and uncertainty make misers of us."

And the traditions she held most in reverence, though they were surely written somewhere in the Verses, had been taught to her by her father, who had received them in the very same way – in a chain of unwritten understanding as real as anything printed in a book, and so much older.

"But I would have you understand," she added thereafter, "that we do not lie down with the dead as we would with a living partner. To the elders of the faith, it was understood that a man was not complete without a wife. If he should die without one, his deprived spirit would linger, and bring jealous misfortunes upon his living neighbors. For that reason, at least one woman in each community would keep herself apart, without taking any husband, so that a man who died too young could have a new bride to lie beside him on the first night following his death, and feel his body warmed by the love of the living while his spirit separated itself for the journey to the next world."

Día picked around the center of the idea, unable to bring herself to venture on the subject of virginity, or to say plainly what she meant: namely, that a corpse had no more need of sex than it did of food, and certainly had no part to play in the satisfaction of her own appetites. She was a grave *bride*, not a grave *wife*, and worked the cloth with perhaps more than necessary vigor over Halfwick's abdomen, between his thighs and under his generative organs, mystified by this continuing myth of their appeal.

"Our way is a different one," Weisei said after a little time, "but I think there is much kindness in yours. I will be sure that it is said only with the correct understanding in my presence – oh, but be gentle with him now, please do."

Día was as gratified by his pledge as she was ashamed by his entreaties, and amended her manner accordingly. "Oh – yes, forgive me; you are very right. And I am honored by your interest."

"Well, I am grateful that you would add to my understanding." He shivered in spite of the warmth of the night, and she imagined that the death-saturated ground must discomfort him considerably. He poured a careful curtain of water over Halfwick's lathered hair, the thumb and first finger of his opposite hand imposing a gentle boundary over Halfwick's white forehead, as if the dead boy might be pained by having soap in his eye. "Will you tell me a second thing, if the question does not displease you?"

There was only one answer to that. "I am always pleased to share any of what I know, with anyone having a well-intentioned wish to know it."

Weisei set down the empty bowl, his eyes finding something of interest at her shoulder. "Your hair – how was she made?"

"By my father," Día replied, "when I was five years old. He made sections of it, and combed each one so that it would cleave to itself as it grew. He said that our family should always keep their hair in this way, to hold our strength to us as it grows through our lives, and to remind us that we have no more power to separate ourselves from the rest of God's creation than to separate every strand from its neighbor." The memory of it tempted her to smile. "Do you know, I cried as he did it. I thought that once he had made it so, it would grow that way for the rest of my life, no matter how I tried to cut or change it, and that I would be called *fake-snakes* as long as I lived."

Día no longer pined for those far-distant days with her father. But she often wished that she had been older when they ended.

And then, as she was never quite comfortable leaving the conversation directed at herself: "I would have given anything for hair like yours when I was a girl — though I am surprised to see you keep it so freely. I had thought that the men of the a'Krah wore theirs plaited."

She meant it as something near a compliment, the first part anyway, but Weisei kept his gaze to Halfwick's unseeing expression. "The men of the a'Krah do exactly that. And I – and you must forgive me now, please, as my mouth doesn't wish to speak any more about it."

That was perplexing, but Día had no reason to force an unwanted topic. She stopped her washing and sat straighter. "Weisei, why did he die?"

He did look up at her then. "Afvik? Oh, no, we didn't – oh, you mustn't think anything of the kind! We didn't intend anything, not any necessary thing for him, and if it wasn't..." He trailed off in dawning horror. "... oh. No, no – what would become of you if he knew that I'd named him? And what of me, and of – oh, and Vichi!"

Día could not have been more surprised as Weisei heaved himself to his feet, disentangling himself from the corpse as if it might drag him to hell. "And he was wounded, oh, and I've LEFT him there, with, with him and all the rest and they won't know – he'll fill up their ears with all the wrong understandings and they won't be able to hear the truth at all, and Vichi – oh, you earnestly must forgive me, fire-child; I have to go to him!"

He didn't wait for her blessing, but bolted from the church, the jingling *thap-thap-thap* of his belled sandals receding from stone to dirt before finally vanishing altogether.

Which left just Día, alone with her astonishment.

Even that was fast melting into fatigue. Had she given him her name? Had he even asked?

Well, nevermind. She rubbed her face with tired fingers, and set them back to work. There was still the remainder of Halfwick's legs to wash, and then he had to be turned, left and right, so that she could see to all of his back-and-sides without prostrating him face-down on the ground.

Día was fairly sure that Halfwick's living sensibilities would regard what she did for him as an indignity of equal or greater magnitude, but certainly someone had taken such liberties a thousand times in his infancy. She doubted it would console him to know that this at least would be the last of all such affronts to his person.

So it hadn't been the a'Krah, then – at least, not collectively.

Día rarely considered ignorance a virtue, but she did not acquaint herself with the nuances of the hotel's nightly business. She was glad to keep the church open to the madam, Miss Addie, and to those house ladies and visitors who likewise came to make their devotions and keep the old holidays, but she did not inquire about their secular occupations.

It was rare, though, that any of the hotel's 'early departures' left behind a living partner to return home with his body and the story of his death. Could Halfwick's still-ungrieving relations have any satisfaction in knowing the particular reasons why their son had strangled in horrific public spectacle at the end of a rope? Would anyone tell her the truth, if she asked?

From somewhere to the south, a dog ventured a few tentative barks. Día stood and brought up a fresh bucket of water to wash Halfwick's face and hands and feet. When that was done, she would have only to carry him to the altar, and to cover him suitably with the shroud, and then she could finally retire to bed – her own bed, unshared with the living or the dead – and think of the rest in the morning.

But it was strange, as she resumed her washing, to find Halfwick's right hand blistered, as if by a very recent burn.

Día sat alone with him for a long time afterwards, her understanding of his body humbled by what it suggested about his character.

"*AIA!*" VUCHAK SWORE between clenched teeth. "Don't push!"

This changed nothing. Pipat still knelt with perfect serenity on the blanket, using her knee and shin to pin his forearm to the ground, and daubed piñon salve into the blistered red rips in his palm and fingers. "Be still," she said.

Vuchak voiced no more complaints, but pressed the warm cat-claw poultice more firmly to his eye. That was a trick, as his left hand was almost as rope-scorched as his right, and did not want to be touched anywhere but at the heel of the palm.

It was not enough to keep his thoughts from going elsewhere.

He was stupid, and this, here, was proof of it. The warm medicine smell in the air, the pain-and-sleep tea brewing in the pot over the fire, Pipat's knee on his arm and his back on the floor as if he were some witless child who had fallen out of a tree – all of this was time and effort wasted in cleaning up after a failure caused by a mistake caused by an incomprehensible lapse of reason.

It was Weisei's fault, that was all. If he hadn't shouted, if Vuchak hadn't jumped right in – if he'd taken just two seconds to stop and think about it! – then he could have simply grabbed Weisei instead, leaving Faro to do his murdering in peace. Halfwick would have died fast and instantly, as the rope-loop invention of his people intended for him.

Vuchak would have liked to extend him that courtesy. As the Eaten went, Halfwick wasn't a bad one: he was clean and unstinking, for one thing, and less ignorant than most, and shaded his profit-making intentions to a degree that any a'Krah would have considered respectable. And if he wasn't sensible enough to smell a fishman's greed, he deserved at least to go quickly, like an unsuspecting deer taken by a single clean shot.

Instead, he had died in gory and fruitless agony, Vuchak and Weisei had been soiled with the filth of the crime, and as for the half...

"*Shit.*"

The word came out in Marín, the ancient and noble ei'Krah language having little to offer in base profanity.

Pipat stopped her work. "Take your mouth outside, if he wants to dirty the air."

Vuchak would have waved off her scolding, if he'd had a free hand to do it with. "No, no, he's done – please, hurry and finish."

... and as for the half, Vuchak had rendered himself unfit for the task. Wherever he was, he would now live through the whole night and beyond, proof to anyone that Marhuk's children could be slaughtered at will – that even a dirty mongrel two-blood could manage it! – without any trouble or consequence.

Vuchak stared up at the creosote stains on the ceiling, shining black above the glow of the fire, as Pipat's shapely leg warmed the silver cuff on his forearm. It had been difficult enough to escape from the press of foreigners at the house. Even if he'd been thinking clearly, he wouldn't have had the chance to ask after the half.

Still, it might be salvageable. The night was still new, and everyone was occupied with Halfwick's death. They wouldn't suspect another one.

Vuchak flinched as Pipat's finger spread more of the sticky warmth over his palm, and waited with barely-contained impatience as she reached for the linen wrap.

Five drops of *tlimit* in his water, if he was being kept somewhere: nobody else would be foolish enough to drink after a half, and there would be no thought given when he went to sleep afterwards. And if he'd already been made free –

For a moment, something blotted out the stars and lights in the window. Vuchak's gaze flicked automatically downwards, and his stomach resented it.

And then, from behind the door-curtain: "Pipat, where do I find you?"

Huitsak's soft and pleasantly-shaped voice stopped Vuchak's blood.

Pipat looked down at him, her graceful age-lined features hardening as she began to understand his refusal to speak about his wounds. "Inside," she called back as she wiped her hands and stood up, "awaiting the honor of your company."

Vuchak sat up – fast, too fast, making his stomach surge and the room spin – as Huitsak brushed aside the curtain and eased his massive frame inside. Like Vuchak, he still wore his mourning-clothes, unadorned except for the black-feather mantle draped over his plain white shirt and trousers.

Unlike Vuchak, he appeared in the best of health and

spirits, and addressed Pipat as if she were alone in the house. "And how does Grandfather see you tonight?"

Pipat clasped her hands her under ribs, and bowed to receive his courtesy. "Very well, *maga*, and just now going out for fresh water. May I trouble you to watch my fire?"

Huitsak smiled, and put himself further inside, as if he would defend the fire simply by imposing himself between the window and the flame. "I would be honored to be of so much service to your house. Go freely, *ima*; my time is yours."

Pipat did not keep her water in the water-pot, of course. It lived inside one of the red-painted flour-pots under the window. This allowed her to keep the little white water-pot always empty or nearly-so, so that she had a ready-made excuse for leaving whenever it served her interests. She took up the vessel by its mouth, set it to her shoulder, and left as if pleasing no-one but herself.

Which left Vuchak alone with the great spreading shadow in the room.

He said nothing – he hadn't been invited to speak – but tried to order his mind as he made a start at standing up. He'd wait until Huitsak had finished whatever terrible rage he had inside him, that was the best thing, and take responsibility and make his apologies and then, when he was asked and the time was right, he would tell him exactly the solution he had in mind, and find out what else...

Huitsak bent to pick up a stick from the fire – a little half-burnt juniper twig. He straightened, took four steps towards Vuchak, each one silent except for the swishing friction of the cloth between his thighs, and then he was there.

He loomed over him, a towering great presence with a face dark and absolutely inscrutable, and when he reached down and grabbed a fistful of his shirt, Vuchak knew better than to resist. He dropped the poultice, and let himself be hauled effortlessly up to his feet.

Outsiders dismissed Huitsak as a fat, pampered glutton. But any sensible person would kneel in awe to see how the master of the Island Town a'Krah concealed his monstrous strength.

Vuchak could not kneel just then: his feet still touched the floor, but Huitsak had taken up at least half his weight already, and could have the rest with a moment's thought. So he watched, unbreathing, as the ember-hot end of the twig came nearer to his face, so close that he could feel its heat on his cheek. He tracked it with his eyes, to the left and to the right, and then down and upwards. His upward gaze split the world into two separate visions, only one of which followed the burning stick as it threatened with the first voluntary twitch of Huitsak's hand to blind him. Vuchak felt his wrists turning by themselves. "*Maga-Kin*, please – your mercy –"

"Broken," Huitsak swore, and hurled the stick back into the fire.

Vuchak felt himself likewise dismissed, his weight abruptly returned to his own keeping, and hurried to re-cover the offending eye with the heel of his naked hand. "Yes, *maga*, but that doesn't change anything – Weisei will take my injuries, and then I can finish with the half in exactly the way that we had discussed –"

"And why should you bother with any of that," Huitsak replied, his voice as soft and bitter as an over-ripe squash, "when Marhuk has already made his judgment plain for the world to see?"

Vuchak felt ill, almost breathless, and it had nothing to do with his eye. "You aren't serious," he said.

"*Then I must have a very devil's sense of humor,*" Huitsak snapped in Marín, "*because you two are a pissing awful pair of clowns.*"

"But we didn't," Vuchak heard himself say, his mouth salivating foolishness. "That is, you can't believe –"

"Oh, but let me first tell you what I believe," Huitsak said, pacing to the fire. "Some of my thoughts would have me accept exactly what appears before me: one son of Marhuk has been slain, and another has somehow contrived not only to deny him justice, but to have himself publicly painted as a bungling stooge. These thoughts suggest that we may as well give our nation up for lost, as Marhuk has obviously long since discerned what is only now becoming evident to us: any stumbling drunk with a gun may pick off His children as readily as ticks from his own spotted hide, and sleep well afterwards, having done our impotent old grand-sire a favor in cleaning His failed spawn from the earth."

It was horrific, blasphemous, and sent any answering words deep into hiding in Vuchak's stomach.

"There are other thoughts, though," Huitsak said to the fire, "more faithful than the rest, which suggest to me that Marhuk still spreads His wings over the world – that His unsurpassed wisdom decided to have the boy's life instead, and His unparalleled greatness reached out and took it. These thoughts kneel in reverence to imagine how He seduced the covetous fishman with the song of greed, confounded the hand of the Eater's blackened servant as she attempted her vain defiance of His will, and assigned the deed to His still-living son, for reasons which my mind is not yet fit to understand. Perhaps

He foresaw that His offspring was too weak to act on his own." Huitsak glanced over his shoulder, sending long shadows spilling across the floor to swallow up Vuchak's feet. "A tremendous thought, is it not?"

What answer could there be to that?

"Yes, *maga*," Vuchak said, with as much voice and sense as he had remaining, and made the sign of an all-seeing god. "It must – it cannot be other than as you have said. Please give all your faith to these well-reasoned thoughts and, and tell me what they would have me do."

Huitsak returned his attention to the fire, and seemed to judge that it was growing hungry again. He picked up a wrist-thick piece of cedar, and when he spoke, his voice was as fine and pleasant as if he were making courtesies with Pipat. "Certainly I will. It's just unfortunate that Weisei isn't here to appreciate them as you do."

Vuchak began to hope that the storm had finally passed. "I'll bring him for you, *maga*. He was upset about Halfwick and shouted at me when I called him back, but he won't have gone far."

"Was that all?" This time, Huitsak's voice was *too* pleasant. The log crashed down on its half-eaten fellows in a burst of snapping pops and floating cinders. "I thought you had simply grown tired of your *marka* and wished to be rid of him."

A queasy, fearful suspicion bubbled up under Vuchak's heart at this casual suggestion of lunacy. "No, *maga*, never – how have I caused you to think so?"

Huitsak did not look back at him, but tipped his head from side to side. "Well, I couldn't think of any other reason why you would want to accept Twoblood's offer to shoot any of us she finds out on the streets tonight –"

If there was more, Vuchak did not hear it: even Marín did not have words to express his mind as he tore from the house in a wild streak of panic and freshly-fouled night air.

BUT WHERE WOULD the idiot have gone? Vuchak's last bloodied glimpse had shown him a top-down picture of Weisei with Halfwick's body and the charred woman – Sun or Dawn or something like that – and now there was no telling at all. The church, or Oyachen's, or in the depths of his stupidity even the whorehouse again... he could be anywhere.

The Moon Quarter had long since come alive, though, and Weisei was as subtle as a braying ass. If he'd been anywhere near here, someone would have seen him.

Vuchak ran north up the River Street, then ahead and right towards the Clay Way, and if his eyes belonged to any but the a'Krah, he would have slammed right into Teitak as the boy came tearing around the corner. Vuchak swore as he smothered his forward-motion; Teitak halted likewise, until the coyote-child giving chase crashed into him from behind, and sent him staggering forward an extra step.

"Boy –" Vuchak pressed the palm of his hand to his eye to force a civil tone. "– where is Weisei? Has anyone seen him?"

Teitak was at that middle part of childhood: old enough to wear a breechclout and leggings under his shirt, but too young to plait his hair. It was the Age of Insolence, and Vuchak saw it igniting in his eyes, fed and fanned by the presence of the child behind him, before he even spoke.

"*What's that?*" Teitak said in Marín, as if he hadn't heard. "*You miss your blanket-friend? You need me to find him for you?*"

Child-beating, of course, was a sign of barbarism, the mark of depraved savages. The a'Krah practiced a better way.

Vuchak's gaze fell to the coyote-child, a horrible little half-dressed thing in a dirty beaded skirt and a too-large eastern button-up shirt. He or she was claimed for the Ohoti Woru by a pottery shard pendant, and by the damned unguessable sex for which Grandfather Coyote's children were known. Vuchak returned this one's wide-mouthed stare with as much height and presence as he had in him.

"*Yes, I do,*" he said to Teitak then. "*My loins burn to have him, and if he isn't found, I will have to settle for second-best and gratify myself with your mother instead –*"

"You will not!" Teitak cried, in ei'Krah this time. But he'd started the conversation for everyone's hearing, and Vuchak would finish it in just the same way.

"*– and strip away her clothes, and have her take my fruits in her mouth, and when she has ripened them to my satisfaction, I will turn her over to make the mountain-cat and then –*"

"YOU WILL NOT!" Teitak shrieked, loud enough for the whole neighborhood to hear.

"Then GO AND FIND HIM!" Vuchak roared back, and had not lunged forward even half a step before the two of them bolted away like startled hares, down the Clay Way and out of sight behind Lavat's lime-kiln.

That was not satisfying, as it only proved that Teitak and the rest weren't being raised properly. It wasn't productive either. Vuchak ran on, left and then right to put himself on the Bright Path, where the parade of lantern-lights made foreigners and night-blind citizens welcome for business and entertainments. The street was alive with their collected body-warmth and the din of voices buying and selling in five languages at once, all carried over a night breeze saturated with the smell of dung and perfumes and fresh-fried squash blossoms.

Vuchak slowed his steps. Anyone could be here, and there was no telling whether he or Weisei were wanted, or by whom. He took his hand from his eye, folded his arms to hide his silver cuffs, and observed from a safe distance.

The great fire had spared this side of the town, and the Ohoti Woru had left the street-facing side of the promenade largely untouched. On top, however, and all along the inward-facing side, they had made it over with clay, building a great long row of wall-sharing adobe rooms, with half-moon windows to mark them as places for business. On the long roof above, the cooking-fires lit up all the right side of the street, brightening the blanket-laid spaces for those who would sit above the street-level clamor and take their meals in company with the moon.

Weisei wasn't there, and Vuchak squinted to make out the eaters near Oyachen's fire. It was first place in Island Town where an even half-sensible a'Krah would go to escape his wife's cooking and enjoy a drink, and a good start for Vuchak: Oyachen would have heard everything from everywhere by now, and if he'd already been spoken to –

"Hey, Vuchak – where do I find you?"

Vuchak stifled a flinch at the merry voice behind him. "Deidalei – with my nerves under your foot!"

Deidalei's pleasant round face fell, and he made the sign of a fickle god. "Oh... so it's true, then? Did you really –"

He was likable enough, forty and turning to fat, with his hair always poorly plaited and his shirt usually stained with the marks of his occupation. Cloth-dying was no profession for a respectable man of the a'Krah, but with Deidalei it was a passion, and one that reflected as beautifully in his fabrics as it did sloppily on his person.

In light of this artistic affliction, Vuchak would try to be gentle. He put his hand back to his eye, making a unified whole out of the world again, and tempered his voice. "I'll tell you the whole wretched story from first to last, but my feet won't let me stay just now. Have you seen Weisei?"

Deidalei's face lit up at the name. "How funny that you should ask! He came running by here not half an egg's hatching ago, in a horrible hurry to find you.

"I would have helped him, of course, except that Way-Waiting has caught a marvelously big brown mare, and he says I can have her for twelve drams of silver, and I'll feel so much better if I know my boy's got a fine horse between his knees when he leaves tomorrow, as the roads now are –"

It was mostly the state of Vuchak's hands that kept them from Deidalei's neck. "Yes, very good, but Weisei..."

"Oh, Weisei! Yes, he was going to find you – I saw him coming from the Burnt Quarter, if you can believe it – and he said it was terribly important –"

Vuchak could feel rage actually knitting his wounds. "And WHERE, Deidalei, WHERE did he go then?"

Deidalei's expression opened in surprise, as if he'd been asked which of his shoes had been the first on its foot that evening. "Oh... why, to the house of beds, of c –"

Vuchak dashed off down the road, using the last of his patience to avoid any ruinous collisions with the rest of the imbeciles on the street.

"– but be careful, do be careful! The watch is looking for you, and we've been told not to..."

Whatever they had been told would have to stay a mystery: Vuchak had no more time to waste in picking little kernels of information out of those vast piles of mouth-droppings.

It would still be all right, though. Twoblood's original shoot-and-kill directive would have been counter-ordered by the Azahi, who would be much more interested in having them alive and whole. It was always Feeds-the-Fire who kept watch here anyway, as he was the only one with both night-eyes and friends in the Moon Quarter, so even if Weisei had been caught, there was every chance that he could be un-caught by a well-made promise and a sufficiently large –

"... *don't understand, though – please, I'll explain Afvik and everything about it, if you'll just let go...*"

As Vuchak's running steps finally stopped him at the mouth of the main road, his eyes showed him twin copies of the same dreadful vision. There in the middle of the road, a yellow light swung tall from one brutish big fist. The other clenched Weisei's hair and force-marched him to the south, towards Vuchak, towards Twoblood's house and a humiliating end that would confirm Huitsak's blasphemous conclusions as surely as if Marhuk had dropped dead out of the sky.

Vuchak sighed, a death-rattle for hope. With no more need for hurry, he spared an expectant glance upward as he trudged out to put his task at an end.

When Elim woke again, up from a dream he didn't recollect, he opened his eyes to the blackest part of night.

"Uh, uh, uh..."

There was a noise, muffled but coming from someplace close-by, like heavy breathing or the panting of a dog.

"Uh, uh, uh..."

Elim lay still long enough to get sure on whether he was even awake. There was a little bit of quiet, almost enough to convince him that he had imagined it, and then the *sktch-sktch-sktch* of claws digging at the gap under the door.

It was constant and patient and finally interrupted by the sharp *squeak* of a wooden chair, and the heavy *thunk* of a boot hitting the door.

Elim lay awake and listened awhile more. The starlight from the barred window showed him the speckled mule's shape, still settled with head down and arms folded, and the sounds didn't come back.

After a time, Elim threw off the blanket, and finished listening in his sleep.

That wasn't Feeds-the-Fire.

And *that* was a terrible misfortune.

Because although Feeds-the-Fire would never consider that he could be *bribed*, it was often possible to help

323

him understand that whatever he had caught you in was much better rectified by the payment of a suitable fine than by any public shaming, which accomplished nothing and profited no-one.

With Wi-Chuck, however...

She was a considerable presence even in the daytime. At night, she was a relic from the Time of Giants. Vuchak's cleverness scattered like ash in the wind as he watched Twoblood's enormous bruiser change her long-striding paces to meet him there in the middle of the street. The swinging light vexed Vuchak's abused eyes, but he would have to go blind to miss the head-and-shoulders advantage in Wi-Chuck's height, or the claw-marks shaved into her hairline, or the swirling short yellow hair that grew in a smoke-trail pattern down her right arm, where she had been painted with the blood of a royal bear.

And then there was the little golden disc that hung from her neck, so much smaller on Wi-Chuck than the others, which gave her every word the force of law.

But whether her confidence came from the Azahi's mark or the pistol at her hip or the natural gifts of the Washchaw, Wi-Chuck conducted herself according to her reputation, and stopped six paces away to make her acknowledgements.

"*Well, prince, I am sorry to meet you this way. Have you come in search of your manservant here?*"

This kind of respect was a welcome change. Vuchak spared a glance for Weisei, who returned it in the sorry manner of a child caught digging up a buried melon. He didn't seem to have been hurt, though there was no telling what the charred woman might have done. "*I have. Did you come to bring us for Twoblood?*"

Wi-Chuck dipped her head. "*For the Azahi. May I trust you to walk peacefully with me?*"

Vuchak sighed, and surrendered with as many shredded pieces of his dignity as could still be found. "*Yes... though I would ask that you not hold him by his hair.*" He dropped his voice in respect as he said it, though: Wi-Chuck would not have known what an affront that was for any man of the a'Krah – even for Weisei.

She put the lantern's long handle between her teeth like a horse's bit, and with both hands freed, applied the right one to take over for its fellow as the left gathered the neck of Weisei's shirt. Then she took the lantern again in her free hand, and made her apologies to him. "*Forgive me that, brother.*" And then, to Vuchak: "*I would not have held him so freely, but I didn't want to hurt his clothes, and I wasn't sure what parts of his person might have touched the Eaten boy's body.*"

And there, just there in Wi-Chuck's voice, was the kindling spark of a good idea. Could it be made to catch?

Vuchak searched her for inspiration, his gaze flicking from her shirt to the wrap around her waist to the bracelet of dried corn kernels at her left wrist: yellow for health, blue to guard against evil. She favored her right hand, of course – that was the one she'd had blessed with the bear's blood – but it was the left that she used to hold Weisei.

"*A very good precaution,*" Vuchak said, beating back his headache to rub his thoughts together. What of Weisei could be used to affirm this fear? "*And you – were you honest with her? Did you tell her where you'd been?*"

Weisei, who had no notion about anything, widened

his eyes as if to make them better absorb Vuchak's intentions. "*Ah... yes? I didn't say anything that wasn't right, Vichi; I only helped the fire-child take Afvik's body to the church and then –*"

This was unquestionably the right way. Wi-Chuck said nothing, but her strong-boned features reflected uncomfortable thoughts.

Vuchak wouldn't let that go to waste. "*Yes, and then? You did do as I asked, didn't you?*"

The small part of Vuchak's mind not praying for Weisei's correct answer busied itself with searching for something on his person that could be used. His earrings were too plain for misunderstanding, and his rumpled white shirt had no promising little weights or bulges hanging over his copper belt, which –

"*... yes?*"

– still carried the little sack of flour that he had kept to use in doing honors for Dulei tonight.

"*And what was that?*" Wi-Chuck's voice was openly mistrustful as she put Weisei out at arm's length and scrutinized him, as if on second inspection she might discover a severed hand hanging from his neck.

Vuchak had his answer ready. "*I had him do the rituals with the Eaten boy's body, in the way that our ancestors require of us, and to bring back the... ah, my mouth fails me.*" He gestured to the bag at Weisei's side and made churning-motions under his chin, as if he would coax out the correct term. "*In our language, we say it as, 'throw me her weapon when she flinches.'*" This, not daring to make eye contact with Weisei, but instead with a prayer to Marhuk himself. "*In Marín, I think it is called 'corpse powder.'*"

He might as well have dropped a snake down Wi-

Chuck's back. With a strangled cry of shock and disgust, the great towering Washchaw dropped everything, the lantern-light shattering to extinction at her feet. Weisei wasn't as quick, but ducked low and whirled to make a grab for the gun – an effort that worked beautifully as Wi-Chuck jerked away from any second contact, and left her side open for Weisei's pilfering.

Vuchak caught the gun with his bandaged hand, smothering the pained grunt that surged up after it. Weisei didn't have to be told how to finish his part, but darted behind Vuchak to take shelter from Wi-Chuck's rage.

But she only stood there, fixated on her left hand as if it would now have to be cut off and burned.

Vuchak gave silent thanks to all the still-living gods, his insides awash on floodwaters of relief. "*Please don't be afraid, elder-sister. I see that you wear the blue corn, so there is no harm that can come to you from us. You're very wise to take such precautions.*"

Wi-Chuck looked up, her gaze unfocused in the newborn darkness, her face and voice alike in their confusion. "*I'm supposed to take you to the Azahi,*" she said, as if this were news to everyone.

Vuchak certainly could empathize with that feeling of useless, preventable, humiliating failure. "*Well, I don't think that would be wise right now. It would be a terrible injury if he were accidentally contaminated.*" Vuchak considered the pistol in his damaged hands, and whether it was worth remembering how to remove the bullets. "*But we wouldn't wish you to have any shame because of us, so let's think instead about the future. Let's all go away separately, and clean ourselves and order our thoughts, and tomorrow when we are restored*

*and the Azahi has finished his first homecoming rest,
our very-reverend master Huitsak will come with us
to visit him. We will be sure to make mention of your
great care and diligence in extracting this promise from
us.*" No, nevermind about the bullets; it wasn't as if Wi-
Chuck would touch it again anyway. "*And here to show
you our noble intention is your weapon.*" Vuchak set it
carefully down in the dirt, the barrel facing south.

Wi-Chuck looked down, though it was hard to tell
how much she could actually see. "*... I think I will come
for it later. Please, don't keep him waiting.*"

And that was a job as good as done. "*Certainly we
won't,*" Vuchak said. "*Be safe tonight, and we will see
you tomorrow.*"

Wi-Chuck did not make any answer, but that was fine.
Vuchak excused them with the sign of a kindly god and
retreated back down the Path of Cats, walking without
slowing until they were well inside the Moon Quarter
again.

His feet began to falter at the sight of Cloud-Drinking's
silent house. The old man had been dead for nineteen
days now, and the custom of the Ohoti Woru said that
his house could not be lived in again until the twenty-
seven days of mourning were finished. The noise of the
Bright Path could still be heard here, and the houses
around were alive with light and smoke and the sounds
of children playing, but this small corner of the street
had made a promising cocoon of darkness and quiet.

"Vichi, wait for me!" called the inevitable voice
behind him.

Vuchak slowed, though it wasn't in him to stop. More
inviting by far was Cloud-Drinking's house: if he were
reasonably careful about things, he might be able to

sleep undisturbed for eight days before anyone found him.

"Wait, please wait – my foot is undressing himself!"

But he was expected to attend to a great number of unpleasant things before he would be allowed to sleep again anywhere. And there as a living reminder was the originator of all unpleasant things, not content to stay behind as Vuchak finally stopped, but putting himself front and center, blocking Vuchak's view of the empty house with his worry-pinched features and cherry-water smell and hands already reaching up to take touching-notice of Vuchak's swollen eye.

"I'm sorry, Vichi. I shouldn't have shouted at you earlier. Here, let me –"

Vuchak jerked his head back. Everything was finished now; there was no point in any of that. Weisei withdrew his hand and waited in anxious silence for an answer.

Weisei, with great mysterious wet patches at the hem of his disheveled mourning-clothes, and the end of his white leather ankle-wrap trailing in the dirt, and his tangled mess of hair which couldn't be plaited, and his big fearful wide eyes – not knowing-eyes, not crow-eyes, but vast helpless hare-eyes which never admitted any canniness or understanding of anything until he was drunk enough to guarantee that whatever understanding he *had* found was the wrong one.

Weisei, without whom there was no wrong-headed affection for meaningless foreigners, no ridicule from badly-raised children, no shame or backwardness or spilled efforts of any kind.

Weisei, who would be with him for the rest of his life, and never be any different than he was in this very place and hour.

"You embarrass me," Vuchak said. "You embarrass everyone."

He was rewarded for saying so, as understanding did come to Weisei's eyes then, even if it was only an understanding of cruelty. They turned wet, and his mouth flattened to a hard line, and there was more than the usual space of silence in the air.

"Go away," Weisei said.

Which would suit both of them perfectly, except that someone had to see that this woman-hearted fool was kept out of trouble. "You already know –"

"No," Weisei said. There was no more wetness in his eyes. "If you don't like my behavior, then I'll act just the way I'm supposed to."

This time, Vuchak knew better than to resist as Weisei took him by the back of his head, and pressed his other hand palm-first to Vuchak's broken eye. He soon felt the familiar achy tingle in his palms, his ribs, the arch of his cheek-bone. Weisei's brow furrowed with the effort. There was a sickening, muffled crack as the flesh under his eye discolored, blooming with fresh blood under the skin. The palm he pressed to Vuchak's face flinched just once, its soft pads splitting open like a kernel of fire-roasted corn.

Vuchak's own hands were left to curl in frustrated, freshly-healed impotence as Weisei finally released him. "Now I'm going to go finish doing honors for my nephew, and YOU are going to excuse yourself from my presence. Go to your half-wife or whoever else will clean you up, and don't come back until you have made yourself fit for my seeing."

There could be only one answer.

"Yes, *marka*," Vuchak said, and made the *ashet* with his upturned wrists. And as there was no softening and no reply and therefore no excuse to delay, he followed his orders and went.

He turned after about twenty paces, just in case. But Weisei was already kneeling in the empty street, a flash of silver briefly visible at his ankle as he re-wrapped the white leather over it, and did not glance in Vuchak's direction.

So Vuchak walked back towards Pipat's house, for lack of any better idea.

For a moment, he thought of going to Oyachen's, to see if he couldn't find Echep there. He was always game to swallow their joint miseries with a little wine, and a flicker of enthusiasm lightened Vuchak's heart at the thought...

... except that Echep was weeks gone, had let Dulei die in his absence and was now as good as dead himself.

And their ongoing backwards-competition to decide which of them had the worst from the mark of the *atodak* seemed as unlikely to be settled now as it ever had: Echep, who would be slain on sight if he hadn't already died on his errand, or Vuchak, who continued to live in public mastery and private servitude for this wrongly-made, poorly-suited, and wholly unacknowledgeable Weisei Marhuk.

CHAPTER THIRTEEN
THE WORST OF ALL THINGS

As it worked out, Elim didn't get to finish his sleep after all: the slow, hang-fired scorch in his skin finally did it for him.

He'd had sunburns before, but this one was easily the blue-ribbon winner. He felt fevered, queasy, the white parts of his back and arms reduced to a deep-fried segregated screaming, the handprint on his chest seared like a steak in the pan.

But what made it tolerable, what stayed his craving for the shady mud-wallow where the creek dried up in the summers, was the daylight creeping in through the window, withering away the last of the night's horrors and leaving just its blessed conclusion. Sil was alive, because they'd gotten to him just in time, and he'd called for Elim and was coming for him today. He'd work things all out with the Sundowners, and then they'd go home and there *would* be a good soak in the mud after that, and a bath and some cold buttermilk compresses before bed...

Which meant that Elim's only mission was not to make a mess of anything, not to say or do anything that could ruin his reprieve. So he rolled over to rest on his browner side and lay still, for what felt like hours and hours, waiting and breathing and thinking of what he could do to earn his reprieve.

He never had seen what had become of Día after she fell. The pigtailed boy and the fish-wife Champagne had to be accounted for as well, and they were past any earthly reckoning. Fresh horror curled around him as Elim recalled fishmen and heathens and hanging, and how somehow the three had compounded on each other to prove that he had, apparently while out of his head with alcohol, picked up his gun and killed a man.

Boy, Elim reminded himself. He was just a boy.

And a stranger had taken a bullet for him, apparently to try and prove he hadn't.

And before that she'd made funny remarks like she'd known him before, and maybe she had and then maybe she hadn't, and in any case she was dead now, and Elim couldn't think of any personal particular of his that would better him for knowing it.

All the same, though, it had been an awful thing to feel the blood seeping through her silks and look into her strange black eyes and find no clue about who she was or what she'd intended, and he couldn't pretend it didn't matter. She had bought his life with hers, and there was only one thing to be said about that.

Good Master, Elim thought at the dust-caked crevices of the wall, *I have woke to a day not promised to me, and praise You for it. Please you to forgive me the sins of all my days previous, and know that I will do with this one every good work you put within my power, for as long as my life may astain me. Amen.*

That was probably not quite right – it had been a sorry long while since he'd recollected exactly all of the words.

But what it lacked in ink-pen propriety was made up in weight by unsifted gratitude. By sheer grace of God, he had survived another night, and now had only to make amends according to what it had shown him... and try like the dickens not to be here for the next one.

THERE WAS A skill, as Fours had discovered, something of an art to sleeping in a trough.

In execution, it was not terribly different from his own flooded basement at home. Just smaller, and requiring somewhat more folding to stay submerged, exposing just enough of his face as would allow him to breathe. The gill-plumes behind his head flowered and bobbed, relishing the water, but there was not nearly enough of it for them to relieve his lungs.

No, the real art of sleeping in a trough was finding sleep at all. It was right and generous for the Azahi to require Alto and Soprano to take the horses promised to their Mother with no further violence, and to order that Halfwick's horse should stay until a decision had been reached about its late owner. It was especially kind of him to offer Fours the luxury of this hidden resting-place. And if Fours couldn't have slept even in the clearest and sweetest free-flowing stream in the world... well, that was no fault of the Azahi's.

She wasn't really his sister, of course. She had been a gift, a payment from the House of Marsanne to make amends for the lesser-born attendant that their princess had killed in a fit of unthinking rage.

And so the House of Melisant received Champagne... and a sorry reception it was, too. Fours had found her hiding between sacks of rice, seeping her distress from every pore until it pooled at her feet. Then there was nothing to do but to match her colors and sit with her until the worst of her sorrow subsided. He kept her company long afterwards, until they were as close as if they had been born from the same roe.

In hindsight, he probably should not have wondered at how readily, years later, she had volunteered to join Fours in being gifted to the House of Opéra. Perhaps she'd used up all her grief in being parted from her first Mother, and had little left when the time came to leave her second and be made property of her third.

And now, just now, to suicide for the sake of her fourth.

She might still be alive, if she'd managed to get through the night unfound. Her wound would close quickly enough in the water, and it would take days, weeks perhaps, before the lead in that bullet finally provoked her body into convulsions strong enough to kill her. Fours ought to be rending his mind with guilt at the thought, wishing and worrying and offering up prayers to the Artisan that she might still be alive, that he might still have a chance to find her and at least try to save her life.

But in the place in his heart where love and fear should have been so violently combusting, there was only that sad, gray little thought, that maybe it would be better if she were dead.

They were five, when they accompanied Prince Joconde to what would become the House of Opéra.

Four, when they were altered and sent to live with the earthbound.

Just three were assigned to Sixes.

That became two, after Mille-Feuille excused herself from service with a double dram of laudanum.

And now, today...

Fours would see Día, when this was done. It had been too long, and their visits always made him feel better.

In the meantime, he had to find whatever was left of his last sibling. Tonight, maybe, when he could be sure he wouldn't be followed. Faro's service to Miss Addie began well before dawn, and he usually retired as soon as Brant had opened the doors for the evening. Fours would be safe by midnight.

But for now, the faintly-rippling sky lightened with the promise of a new day, and Fours began to wonder what he ought to do with it.

There was the Azahi, of course, and what remained of that hapless fool Halfwick. Would it have been any different if Fours hadn't made him go and chase his horse?

And there was that Elim, too. The Azahi would decide about him today – he never let anyone linger in Twoblood's dog-house – and Fours suddenly felt desperate to know whether Champagne – whether Shea had been mistaken in recognizing him.

She wasn't his sister, not truly, and perhaps that was why their fraternal façade had come to this sad and absurd ending. Perhaps it was as false and nonfunctional as the human sexes they'd assigned themselves. But her life had *meant* something, and she had all but killed herself trying to prove it.

Which now left just Fours to finish the job.

But how to do that? Her idea couldn't work: it would take an injury that threatened his life to force him to change, and there was no telling whether he even had it in him, or whether Mother U'ru still lived and had enough sensibility remaining to call her back to her child. In fact, the only absolute certainty was that Fours wouldn't be caught even *thinking* about putting a knife in him.

No, he'd just...

Well, he'd...

In the end, it wasn't any epiphany that finally spurred Fours out of his water-bed, but only the uncomfortable intensity of the rising sun. When he finally climbed out from the trough, he still had little idea of what he would do with the day, except that *this* time, *this* day, the answer would not be 'nothing'.

And it would start, in deference to rank and gratitude and naked amphibious necessity, with the First Man of Island Town.

THE TAPPING OF Twoblood's door-stick dredged her mind out of a much deeper place.

She brought her head up and belatedly realized that time, that petty larcener, had absconded not only with dawn but half the morning as well.

The half was still asleep, or at any rate lying with his face to the wall. The sun had caught up with him during the night, inflaming his white parts to a blistered, angry red. Even his native flesh had darkened to the color of burnt leather.

That was unfortunate, and not only for him.

Twoblood did not hurry to answer her visitor, but watched until she had satisfied herself that the half was still breathing. She could at least avoid adding that to the list of irregularities for which the Azahi would require an explanation.

When she finally heaved herself out of her chair, put on her hat, and unbolted the door, it was thankfully only Barking-Deer, holding a half-full linen sack and looking as if he had spent the night running laps around the town wall.

But even with his hair half out from its tie and full pockets under his eyes, he still knew better than to wait for an invitation to speak. "Second, sir, the Azahi sent me to – that is, he is waiting for you at home, sir."

Twoblood eyed the bag. "And what are you waiting for?"

Barking-Deer dipped his head. "To feed the half, sir. The Azahi is... concerned for his health." He kept his gaze strictly to Twoblood's face.

Twoblood folded her arms. "And what does the Azahi know about his health?"

Barking-Deer did let his attention drift then, to a predictable place behind Twoblood's shoulder. "Not more than what Fours has already told him."

"Shit." In a moment of weakness, Twoblood likewise glanced back at the half, whose back presently resembled a burnt tortilla.

This would not go over well.

Better to jump to it, then. Better to go when she was called, before the Azahi decided to conduct a personal inspection.

She'd done it for his own good, though. She'd done it to keep him safe, and the fact that he had avoided his master's misfortune was proof that Twoblood had done the right thing. It was important to be firm on that, not just to say it but to *believe* it, and to have it believed in turn.

Because if Twoblood didn't manage to put that across, if the Azahi and by extension the citizens didn't share her understanding, then it would be seen that she had allowed a half-man into Island Town unquestioned, had essentially left him at liberty to shoot the crow-prince in the first place, and then subjected him to a slow-roasting torment that had failed not only to prevent the a'Krah from having their vengeance, but also to forestall this very same disease-courting intimacy, which Twoblood had so adamantly meant to avoid, and whose suspicion she would not soon escape.

"Sir?"

Twoblood returned to the present to find Barking-Deer watching her, and her fingers scratching shamelessly behind her ear.

"What?" she demanded, jerking both ends of her hat-brim down with startled irritation. "Stay here, feed him, see if you can get him to clean himself, and don't open his door for anyone – is any part of that unclear to you?"

Barking-Deer straightened, as sharp and attentive as he had been at this time yesterday. "No, sir. I'll see it done."

There – just like that. Four words, problem solved. What did the rest of them find so difficult?

Twoblood grunted her appreciation as she stepped out into the bright morning sun. Her next task was to sharpen her thoughts before her feet brought her to the Azahi's door, but the only one that held any edge was the creeping notion that Barking-Deer might be Second Man of Island Town sooner than either of them would have wanted.

* * *

NOBODY HAD EVER found Sarvan Deacon's body. His wife, Tulia, and their daughter, Gracefully, were well accounted for: they had taken shelter in the church with most of the others during Sixes' last night, and were identifiable afterwards by the ring on the child's finger. But whether Sarv had died in the fighting or burned in the fire or somehow managed to escape alive, nothing was ever heard of him afterwards.

Still, he had left behind a fine business. And after all the pillaging and upheaval was done, it was Deacon's Dry Goods that the newly-appointed master of Island Town chose for his home.

To Fours' mind, it didn't bear much resemblance to the original: the false front had been sheared off, and the rest plastered over with adobe. The window-glass, for which Sarv had once paid so extravagantly, had long since been gifted to Miss Addie for replacing the broken panes of her boarding-house. And where the Deacons had once kept their marital bed upstairs, there was now a very-generous hole in the ceiling, with a ladder threaded up through it, so that the master of the house and his callers could sit up on the roof and visit amidst all the exotic flowering plants as could be coaxed to flourish so far from the Valley of the Sun.

Still, Fours always found it difficult to visit the current owner without thinking of the previous one, and the same part of his mind which divided the home-concept into *house* and *casa* and *maison* and *flat-hand-over-cupped-hand* likewise conceived of this one in both its past and present forms simultaneously.

So when he finally did step out from the trough, it was to sneak directly to both the delivery entrance and the back door, and to admit himself inside to the stock-room and the steam room, its pit of river-stones cold and dry and draped over with an odd set of clothes.

They smelled clean, so Fours erred on the side of modesty and helped himself. The long gray tie-string drawers were of the kind that eastern men wore under their trousers, and the blue pull-on shirt was one of the knee-length cuts especially favored by the Ikwei, and the single piece of linen did well for a cap, tied into tails at the base of his neck. The yucca sandals didn't fit so well – he'd never brought himself to cut that last bit of webbing between his first toes – but it would have been rude to bring the dirt of his bare feet into the house. So Fours slipped them on, curled his toe-stumps over the edge, and when he received no answer to his tentative tapping at the inner door, let himself in to the house proper.

It opened to show him what Sarv Deacon must have seen daily as he stood there behind the counter, except that all the shelves had been stocked afresh with gifts from the citizens of Island Town: carved antlers and brightly-painted pots and exquisite jewelry from the most gifted a'Krah silversmiths, all displayed in place of pride for any visitor to admire. The cast-iron box stove in the corner was original, but the sitting-table in front of it was a later addition, as were the flowering vine-curtained windows and the black-spotted jaguar skin draped across the front door.

The jaguar had a living cousin around here somewhere, but she was nowhere to be seen at present.

So it was all a very definite and deliberate kind of splendid, now. Even the upstairs, packed to the rafters with the decidedly more practical gifts of the people – with all the seeds and tools and cloth and staples which formed the town's ample treasury – was kept in immaculate order.

In fact, the only less-than-elegant part of the house, the only feature that marked it as a *home*, was the under-counter and a couple of the bottom-most back shelves, out of sight from visitors, where were kept the clothes and dishes and those personal articles which any earth-person would require. It wasn't in best order just now: the little pile of bags and shucked-off garments said plainly that their owner hadn't had even a minute to unpack, and the rumpled blankets beside them suggested something less than a whole night's sleep.

Still, there was no surer proof of the Azahi's fitness to govern. The necessities of this new age, which had forced together so many disparate and even hostile peoples, absolutely demanded the service of a great man, in equal parts foreign and impartial, who would divide his priorities exactly as he had his home: the far-greater share to the needs of the people, the lesser share to his image as seen by the people, and the least of all – the space of a stock-room and a half-dozen hidden shelves – to his own personal provision.

Fours would not be caught trespassing in this scant private space, and slipped around the end of the counter to the more public part of the room. In this little pocket of splendor and quiet, it was much easier to order his thoughts as he waited for the gift-master's arrival.

ELIM HEARD THE tapping and the door and the incomprehensible exchange between the speckled mule and her visitor, but squelched the temptation to roll over and look. He would get up when Sil came for him, and not before.

Then the door shut on the sound of footsteps receding outside, and everything was quiet.

Elim couldn't believe his luck at having been left alone, but he didn't think twice about it. He pulled himself up to sit, his arms protesting with a dull, spent promise of soreness yet to come –

– and froze at the sight of the Sundowner standing there with a tied cloth sack, knocked acock at how easily he'd just given himself away.

There was something familiar about this one, too. His green shirt and sand-colored leggings looked long in the wear, and he had smeared white paint at his forearms, which Elim had seen before.

Yesterday. He'd seen it yesterday, about five minutes before he'd given the other one a hard smash in the jaw. The golden disc confirmed it, and pressed a groan from Elim's throat. That little bit of heathen jewelry was a uniform, and this was a deputy, and he was in trouble.

But the stranger's mistrust seemed directed specifically at the handprint on Elim's chest. He stared at it for a long, uncomfortable moment, and Elim suddenly felt guiltier still.

Still, if the deputy had any evil in mind, it was hidden under a heap of tired. He crossed the little room in four strides and dropped the sack at the bars. "Eat," he said.

Elim couldn't have obliged if it had been stuffed full of fresh-baked biscuits and Lady Jane's honey-butter spread. "No thank you," he said.

The deputy folded his arms, glancing between Elim and the bag as his lean features creased into a frown. "Master say eat."

Elim couldn't have said whose master that was. "No thank you," he said again.

The deputy's brow furrowed. He pressed the palms of his hands together, indicating Elim first, then the bag. "Do pray, then eat?"

He was uncommon, this one. "*O-sento*," Elim said –he did at least remember how to say *I'm sorry* – and pressed his hands to the soft flesh of his gut. "I feel sick."

The deputy didn't seem to know what to do with that. He picked up the bag, and then leaned back to sneak a glance out the barred window.

Which was as good as a promise that he didn't want anyone to see what he was fixing to do next.

Then he turned, dropped the bag onto the desk, tore open the cloth, and began bolting down its contents as if it was the last meal of his life, or maybe the first.

That was fine. Only seeing him from the back, now – seeing his tied hair spilled between his shoulders like that – was a second and more recent kind of familiarity, one that came remembered in shadows and smelly yellow lamp-light.

That was the fox-man.

It wasn't the realization that made Elim gasp, but the searing sudden pain of scraping his back against the wall when he startled.

He'd seen him last night, with no silver to keep him human after dark. His red-and-gray skin had looked almost cloud-patterned for a minute, but then he'd turned around and his eyes had flashed yellow, like a wild animal at the edge of firelight, and there wasn't any mistaking him: he was cousin to the rabid wolf-men of the high plains, subordinate to their speckled bastard daughter, and brother to the pelt that hung behind Jack Timson's bar.

And when the fox-man turned, he was by some miracle still human, without any colored hide or wild eyes to announce his having been found out at last. He hucked something at Elim, who had to guard his face by catching it.

It was a little pink cactus-fruit, no bigger than a peach pit. Elim looked back up and found himself staring –not for the first time on this trip – at the business end of a pistol.

"Eat," the deputy said.

Elim ate.

The gun went away.

Elim sat still, ripe tart sweetness lingering in his mouth, and watched his keeper's back for the next sudden ultimatum.

But he went right on feeding himself, as hungry and human as you pleased. When he finished, he swept the remainders into the bag, returned to the bars – Elim sitting straight and readier as he did – and tossed the little sack inside with a significant look, tapping at the corner of his presently-peaceable eye before pointing first at Elim, and then at the bag of rinds and crusts beside him.

Elim nodded to confirm that yes, he sure had enjoyed all of those fine victuals.

That seemed to be the right thing, as the fox-man returned to his boss's desk and dropped heavily into the chair behind it. He ground the heels of his hands into his eyes, and then let his forearms fall to rest on the old finished wood. He glanced back at Elim, just once, and they agreed between them that yes, it had been a hell of a night.

Which returned Elim to thinking about his prayer of

thanks-giving, and his resolve to get out of here with no more trouble on any front, and by now it was probably safe enough to ask: "Please, when is Sil coming back?"

He got a blank stare from across the room.

Elim made vague come-hithering motions at the door. "My friend, the Eadan?"

The deputy followed his gesture, but it was hard to tell how much he understood. "Wait," he said at last. "Master do come."

"He ain't – ah, nevermind." If 'Master' was his biggest problem today, he would be in fine shape indeed.

OF ALL THE gifts the Artisan had granted to lesser-born mereaux, the one that Fours had absolutely no knack for was the *voix-douce*, the sweet voice. It wouldn't get you out of anything really dire, but where there was any quantity of doubt or indifference or hesitation to work with, it served very handily to sugar your speech, to induce the listener to swallow the pill of your reasoning all the more readily, and often without any awareness at all.

Small wonder that Faro should be such a master of the craft.

But Fours had long ago discovered that this was no talent unique to his kind: there was another creature so endowed, one whose powers of subtle, tranquilizing hypnosis dwarfed those of even the most accomplished mereau.

So he had to pet the cat, or rather, to squat there by the counter, baggily dressed in clothes and sandals meant for someone much larger than himself, as she walked back and forth under his flexing fingers, seducing his higher-order thinking into helpless contemplation of her natural warmth, her strange chesty vibrations, and the hundred million tiny nerve-thoughts under her soft, living fur.

If there was any proof that he was not a wholly unsalvageable individual, it had to be spelled out somewhere in the consenting ripples of her coat under his blue-white hands.

The feline effect probably accounted for his surprise when voices and footsteps suddenly barged into his awareness, coming from behind the front door as suddenly as if they had been belched up from the ground.

Fours froze, instantly blanching to match the counter behind him, as the cat leapt away. The Azahi was deep in conversation with someone else, and Fours was in no ready state for it: he had left his wig and ears and flat-edged teeth with his clothes yesterday, and he would not for a moment pass for human.

Nor would he in his present garments pass for a wall. So he rolled back behind the counter to collapse among the traveling-bags, and mimicked a heap of rumpled clothes instead.

"... that they should have the best of everything – that they will have the life of the Eadan boy and now of his slave too?"

That was Twoblood. Fours closed his eyes and flattened himself further than he had thought possible.

"Take care that you aren't hearing things unsaid, Second."

That was the Azahi, his voice instantly recognizable by its warm, even tones, and the undiscriminating use of Marín's respectful *you*-form. As the avatar of Island Town and appointed representative of the Kingdom of the Sun, his personal pronouns were almost exclusively *we* and *us* and *our*; you would not hear *I* except in confession of some singularly intimate fact, or else – very rarely – as warning of an offense so dire that it would require him to lay down his marks of office before answering it.

Here, however, his tone was one of grave patience. "Our intent is to learn the truth from the half, and to render our decision accordingly. If he is to be called responsible for his own acts, then his master's death is nothing less than murder, and must be answered accordingly... but then, the same will have to be true of Dulei Marhuk. Or is there some doubt remaining about the author of the crime?"

The Azahi's voice marked him as he paused somewhere near the stove in the far corner. Twoblood was announced by the striking of her boots, each one palpable through the hard clay of the floor as she came closer and closer still, and finally stopped right at the other side of the counter. Fours ceased his breathing.

"... no, First; it was the half." It came from right above him, right on top of him, and Fours with his thundering-loud heartbeat couldn't have been saved by anything except Twoblood's all-consuming distraction. "But it doesn't – it isn't fair! Where is the white boy's family? When do they get to choose between blood and money?"

There was a little silence then, which guaranteed a fair hearing of the question. "That is an unfortunate truth. If he has been unjustly slain, then we will be obliged to decide on their behalf, and to hold the payment in trust for any of his relations who may come after him. It's a sad necessity, but not one we haven't known before."

"But it isn't the same – for that very reason, it can't be the same, and we can't pretend that it is!"

There was another silence then, four heartbeats instead of two. "You are exactly right. It isn't and can't be the same, and we would not abuse the truth by claiming otherwise. Yet we must consider not only this present inequality, but also its parent."

Fours cautiously resumed his slow, silent embezzlement of this private moment's air.

"The Eadan knew or should have known that he took a risk in crossing the border with his two-colored man, and in taking residence here without seeking our guestright, and in doing business outside the boundaries of the day. No such thing is true of Dulei. The Marhuka entrusted him to us with the understanding that he would live as a night-citizen under our law – that he would take the protection of his kin rather than that of our watchmen. And to deny his kin the right to act for him, when his soul is or was in greatest need of their protection, is more than we are prepared to do."

At first, Twoblood's only audible reply was a slow surrender of air through the nose. Fours dared to open one eye. Twoblood loomed like a giant up above, her back turned but her figure defined by her off-white hat and her hair, so much thinner at her right side than her left, and by the white flecks at the shoulders of her dark blue shirt, and by the heart-stopping defeated *thud* of her hand on the counter-top. "So you are decided, then. The half is either a slave or not a slave, and has been made to suffer for nothing, regardless."

The reply was sharp enough to crease paper. "For nothing? Can it be true that we have inflicted needless pain?"

Twoblood had better have an answer for that: there were no slaves in Island Town and no torture either, and this Elim had challenged them on both counts.

"No, never! We did – *I* did no such thing. I will say it again: everything I have done from first to last has been for the good of the town, and for his own safety, and I won't apologize for any of it!"

It had to be tiring, to hear all of Twoblood's lunging and growling, and to answer without any of the same. "Whose voice do you hear calling for one?"

There was a little scraping then, like fingernails curling on wood. "I have ears, Hara. I hear what is said outside my presence. And after last night, after what you ordered me to do, it will soon be said to my face as well."

"You know that we dread more than anything to lack for understanding, Second. What was said, and by whom?"

"THEM, all of them! And you will hear it soon enough: the next time someone dies of a fever, or there is a spread of water-colic, their voices will say plainly enough that I was the cause, that I have been giving evil gifts."

That was an idiotic idea if Fours had ever heard one. Any town-sweeping sickness would almost certainly come from the sexual stew that Miss Addie kept simmering at La Saciadería, and it would strike first at the night-people, with whom Twoblood had little contact.

But in the depths of his infinite patience, the Azahi said no such thing. "So it might be. And if it passed to you from your close quartering with the half, should we expect it to continue in the same way, and seep first into those who share nearness with you?"

Twoblood did not seem to grasp the idea. "... yes, First; it would have to. Everyone knows that."

"Certainly they do. Our watchmen, then: have they shown any hesitation in standing with you, or in handling him on your behalf?"

The pause was telling, and the strain in Twoblood's voice still more so. "They – there was Wi-Chuck, she said... no, that was about the crows. Barking-Deer and Feeds-the-Fire, they were with me last night, and I practically had to –"

There was a sudden flash of shadow from up above. Fours startled and looked up as Twoblood whipped off her hat to scratch with savage ferocity at the left side of her scalp, and then suddenly it was right there in plain view: there on the right, that great big kidney-shaped patch of exposed yellowish skull.

In Island Town, the fact that Twoblood had been scalped in her youth was superseded only by the legend that she had afterwards hunted down and retrieved her missing piece from its taker. It was whispered among children that she kept it in her desk drawer.

"– they wouldn't, though, they wouldn't tell me any such truth, nor let me suspect for a second that they were even thinking it – they don't have the stones! You wait, though; give it time, and you'll hear it too; I promise you will."

"Well, the truth is in the teeth."

This was a common expression, an everyday way of saying *we'll find out soon enough*. But suddenly it was as if Fours were hearing it for the time.

Because although it probably had its origins somewhere in the nameless depths of history, when the first human-seeming mereau had been exposed by its smile, it applied equally to a great number of human beings. The double-wide shearing teeth of the Washchaw, for example, and the fangs that Twoblood had inherited from the Lovoka – and the extra incisors of the Ara-Naure.

So if Fours could just get that Elim fellow to open his mouth...

"And while we wait, what else does diligence require of us?"

Twoblood answered with a deep, soul-emptying sigh, and replaced her hat. "... I'll have Fours do what he can for the half."

"Very thoughtful. And what else?"

"And I'll fetch – I'll find Día, and have a word sent to Huitsak. Did you want anyone else?"

"Not unless he wishes to have company of his own choosing. And was there anything else that should be said between us, before we see him?"

The implications were obvious even to Fours: any complaint Twoblood still harbored had better be aired now or not at all.

"No, First. Your will is mine."

Twoblood disappeared from Fours' view as her footsteps retreated towards the door.

"Then it is our will that you should execute your promises and then have some rest – an honest sleep, not a tip in that damned chair."

Twoblood snorted. "You slander my furniture – but I'll do it. It's good that you're home again, Hara."

"I am welcomed by your service, best. Please go and begin as we have agreed, and we will meet you there shortly."

There was one more space of silence then, but Fours

could not have said what it contained. It was ended by the opening and closing of the door.

Then came a sigh – a signed confession of weariness – and a few almost-inaudible footsteps, and a sound like beads spilling onto the low-set table.

The Azahi had taken off his headdress. Fours felt suddenly desperate to remove himself before he could overhear anything else, before the First Man of Island Town said or did something that would humiliate him within earshot of the lowest and least-deserving of his servants.

So Fours turned to crawl, noiselessly except for the little shiftings of his garments, back towards the steam-room door. It was going swimmingly, perfectly – until the first far bend of his foot overtaxed his toe-hold on the sole of the sandal with one fatal, heart-stopping *thap*.

"Damía, are you coming to see me?"

The cat didn't have a name. Or if she did, she hadn't told it to the Azahi, and he would not presume more familiarity than *Milady* in the meantime.

Fours would happily allow Milady to take the blame for his misstep, but even she wasn't likely to own up to opening the door. What the devil had made him push it hard shut in the first place?

... and why had he come here again?

In that moment, Fours couldn't muster the energy for even one more self-saving scheme. He returned to his natural coloring, crawled over to the counter's end to stand up, and with his hands balled into a covered fist at his stomach, bowed from the waist, awaiting the axe's fall. "No, First. It was only me."

The man seated at the table turned to regard him with

an expression that did not belong nearly as much to the Azahi, the supreme authority of Island Town, as it did to Sut Hara, a man too damned tired to bother getting up for familiar visitors.

"Oh – Fours. Whatever were you doing there?"

He didn't have much of his characteristic splendor just then. His marks of office were presently a pile of brightly-colored beads and feathers and linked golden scales on the table, leaving him dressed in just his customary denim pants and white cotton shirt, with his thin black hair tied, folded and pinned behind his head. His soft-touched features and amber eyes revealed nothing more than sober attention and the beginnings of middle age. Even his gold-flecked skin looked a bit faded.

Fours bowed again, a breaking of eye contact which made it infinitely easier to bury the truth. "Please forgive my intrusion, First. I had only meant to sit in a moment and rest. The sound of the door just now startled me."

He was never good at brazen lies, but Fours could craft an admirable mosaic from broken pieces of the truth.

And from outward appearances at least, it worked. "Well, you are very welcome in any case. Please, be comfortable."

Fours looked up in surprise, but if the Azahi had indicated any place in particular, Fours had missed it. He dropped down to a bandy-legged squat and laced his fingers together, steeling himself for the inevitable reckoning.

But the Azahi only turned on his mat and rubbed his forehead. "We are glad you stayed, and would dearly wish to remember our purpose in speaking with you…"

...which would almost certainly have something to do with why Fours had given shelter to smugglers, or what he had been doing tearing naked through the Burnt Quarter last night, or why he had not entrusted Twoblood with the truth when he had the chance, when things might have been somewhat salvageable...

"... but the only item that consents to be remembered is a bottle of mackerel sauce, which we will have in hand for you..." The gesture at the counter encompassed all the piled luggage behind it, and was accompanied by a vaguely despairing look. "... presently."

Fours was ashamed at his instant, stomach-awakening zeal at the mention of *peisalat*. He might well be condemned to eat like an earth-person for the rest of his life, but by the Artisan's broken blisters, he was going to season like a mereau.

He swallowed down his appetite. "You are very kind to think of my comforts, First, and I am sorry to have interrupted yours. Would it be better for us to forego our discussion until you don't have so many others waiting for you?"

There must have been a spark of inspiration somewhere in there, as the reply was quick in coming. "No, no; we are well-remembered now." The fresh focus of his golden eyes was piercing even from this distance. "Tell us about your mother."

Fours blinked, and sat up straighter. "Sir?" He could not imagine what the Azahi could want to know about Mother Melisant, and hurried to think of how much he could permissibly tell.

"Your queen, Opéra – is she not your Mother?"

"Oh." Fours let out his breath. "Yes. What would you like to know?"

The Azahi's features hardened ever-so-slightly. "Only the truth, and we will make ourselves plain: tell us what you can, and we will do without the rest, but we will not be lied to. Are these words clear to you?"

The words weren't needed: the look alone was enough to make Fours wish the ground could turn to water under his feet. He swallowed, and his skin browned to copy the Azahi's in a fervent pledge of loyalty. "Yes, sir."

Some of the lines smoothed out from the Azahi's face, and he replied in softer tones. "Excellent. Then tell us, if you can, why she would suddenly wish to forge friendlier bonds, after so many years of silence."

Fours' eyes widened. So that was why she had come. She couldn't have known about Faro's dealings – she'd never have taken aim at Elim if she had – but it would have to be a momentous occasion for her to personally visit this far upstream.

His feet shifted as his mind raced, mindful not to lie. "I couldn't – I'm sorry to say that I don't know," he said. "But if I were to guess... I think it will have something to do with horses."

The Azahi considered this with interest. "Horses."

"Yes, First. They've become quite valuable to us, and you will know better than anyone how difficult it's been to find good ones. We've been able to trade for a few at a time with some certain citizens," which rendered the word *a'Krah* almost wholly unnecessary, "but as more traders bring theirs across the border to sell, I would imagine that we'd have all the more reason to watch the rivers closely, and make the necessary arrangements with people who could help us drag a wider net, as it were."

"That is a considerable suggestion. And would that go some way to explaining the way we met yesterday?"

Fours looked down at the ground. "It would, First. Further than I could go myself."

Because as much and as often as he had wished to simply throw himself at the Azahi's feet and say *help, please help, we are spies and hostages to be killed on her whim*, and as gratifying as it would be to hear the Azahi's shock and disgust, the sad fact was that the master of Island Town was master of the island only. The river still belonged to her – to them – and the one ruled only by the passive and continuing consent of the other. The Azahi might well defy her, throw Faro out on his false ear and proclaim a haven for freshwater exiles within his walls, but it would be his last act.

And so long as Fours let that go unsaid, he was free to fantasize that the Azahi would do exactly that – would forsake a thousand for the sake of three.

"We understand. And why are you in so much need of horses?"

Fours could not raise his eyes then either. "I couldn't say, sir." But surely he did not need Fours to tell him of the drought. The provinces of the Emboucheaux were shrinking, their freshwater roads drying up, their vast network of tributaries and channels choked to strangling by the barren sky. What didn't they need horses for? What else were they going to use to hold the world together?

But the Azahi kept to his promise, and showed no sign of anger. "Very well. Then perhaps you can tell us whether we may reasonably trust Mother Opéra at her word – whether she will be faithful in her pledge to repay our trade with information and security, and to defend us from enemies on either side of the river." The Azahi glanced up at the ceiling, and at the unimaginable weight of all those goods housed above it. "You know there are those who still remember what happened to the people who lived here before us, and we will have to answer their questions."

Fours crouched lower, shielding himself between the high peaks of his knees, and wrapped his arms across his stomach. "I remember, sir," he said to the dirt between his sandals.

He would always remember what had happened on the last night of the siege, when the mereaux came crawling up one by one out of the church well, and ran with silent, dripping footsteps to open the gate.

"... and I wouldn't – I wouldn't count on any of us dying for the cause, exactly, but it's good for us that we have you here, and we certainly don't need to go breeding enemies out of friends, and, and if you can convince her that you won't go feeding her business to rival interests, then I'd think, I'd certainly think that we would do everything possible to earn your trade and keep you safely, just where you are."

It was a wretched thing, to have to speak as a part of that *we*, and hold himself always apart from this one.

"We would ask for nothing more," the Azahi said. "And you, Fours? If we commit ourselves in this way, can we trust you to go faithfully between us?"

Fours' insides curled in on themselves, and his colors faded to match the floor. "No, First," he said. "Not with them."

It would have to remain as it had been from the beginning: Fours was for the Azahi an inherited thing, as much a requirement for keeping the town as he had been for taking it. To pretend that that could be changed, to have a golden disc tied around his neck, would have been a lie more monstrous than words.

"We understand." The Azahi's tone could have been weariness or disappointment. "Well, do for us all that you can, and we can expect nothing more. Thank you for your time, Fours."

Fours looked up at the sound of his dismissal, irrationally gutted at having arrived so quickly at such a failure of an ending.

He wanted what Twoblood had gotten – wanted desperately to be a pillar of support, a welcome servant, a unique and faithful help to the great man sitting before him. But Twoblood had earned hers with grit and guts and the bullet-biting force of will needed to make hard decisions and stick by them, even when they turned out a bit wrong in the end, and Fours had only cowered and stumbled his way through a lifetime of inaction. The hero's welcome was not for him.

Only he was a mereau, albeit not an especially good one, and they were gifted at the art of seeming. So if he didn't have it in him to actually *be* a blessing and a brave man, at least it couldn't hurt anything to *seem* like one – just once.

Fours crawled over to the sitting-table, not bothering to hide the noise of his sandals. The Azahi watched with interest and perhaps some concern, and Fours forced himself to keep going until he was right next to the great man himself, so close that it would not matter if Faro was listening outside the door. He splayed out his toes to balance on his haunches, and spoke in a soft, reedy whisper.

"There is... just one thing more valuable to us than horses, sir."

The Azahi sat at rapt attention, attuned to Fours exclusively. "What is that?"

And for once in his life, Fours managed to meet his golden-eyed gaze without flinching.

"Horsemen. Any brutal fool can beat them into compliance, and ruin them for reliable service. But there are those, a certain particular few, who have the *savoir-faire* – the, the talent, the art – to teach the animal to trust its master's mind." Fours stole a furtive glance over at the doorway. "And we will kill to get them."

THE CALENDAR OF Atali'Krah, which was without equal, divided the year into four seasons, and each season into five months, and each month into eighteen days. To this understanding was added the custom of the fishmen, which divided each day into day-time and night-time, and each of those into twelve parts, called hours.

Vuchak had no timepiece ready to hand, but he didn't need one. It was the day of the Needle, in the month of the Hare, and the only hour that mattered was the one in which Huitsak would fetch him for the inevitable reckoning.

So he lay there in the dim and slowly-warming interior of Pipat's home, feeling her soft breath at the back of his neck, and watched the sun lay siege to the door-curtain.

Huitsak would not defend them. Or if he did, it wouldn't be for their sake. Dulei's murderer had lived, and the wrong man had died, and caught as if in the very act were Vuchak and his senseless *marka*. It was that part, not the doing but the failure-in-doing, which would condemn them both.

But then again, that rope-strangled corpse did not

belong to any citizen of Island Town. The price for Halfwick's death was payable to no-one but his kin, who weren't here, meaning he had no advocate at all, except –

Shit. Would the half count? He couldn't count – he was a slave – but what if the Azahi allowed him a place of kinship? What would he choose for the life of his master: blood or money?

No, no – it wasn't as bad as that. The a'Krah had been owed a life for Dulei, and surely something could be arranged. They could take Halfwick instead of the half. He'd surrender any grudge in exchange for his freedom; what slave wouldn't?

So that was why Huitsak hadn't come. He was arranging things with the Azahi. Vuchak could be castigated after the fact, and Dulei's soul would do without its vengeance, because after the way in which it had slipped from its body, it had very little right of complaint.

Everything would be fine.

The calendar of Atali'Krah, which was without equal, also provided for five uncounted days, which were made six during every fourth year. These days, which were collected into no month and fell under the providence of no star, were the *Pue'Va*, and those born into them were *a'Pue*: people of bad omen, whose luck was as an incorrigible slave, and would desert them at every opportunity.

Vuchak had always hated his mother for her inability to hold her labor.

So he got up, poured his jewelry out of his boots, and was no sooner shod than departed. It was no good hour for hunting down slaves, but at least one of them would be easily found.

* * *

IT TOOK FOURS considerably longer than usual to craft his face afterwards. The shakiness in his hands kept spoiling the work of the knitting-needle as he sculpted the sides of his nostrils, and the paint for his lips kept giving them too much color or not enough, and for his heart he couldn't get symmetry in his eyebrows.

And that Halfwick had had the nerve to curse him for failing to answer his door at the pit of midnight – as if he had nothing to do but climb out of his bath, bless himself and instantly be made presentable!

When Fours finally finished with mirror and opened the drawer with the little bowl that held his veneers, his eye caught the jar of coldwater pupfish packed in yellowing vinegar. It was easily a quart large, but he could devour it all inside of a minute...

... but no, if you ate like a 'fish-man' then you were going to sweat like one too, and although the smell could be masked with a little perfume or toilet-water, there was no such preventative for that one-in-a-hundred earth-person who would break out in a blistering rash at the slightest contact with your skin secretions. And from the sound of things, that Elim fellow didn't need any more help in coloring his hide.

So Fours smothered his appetite with a few dried currants and some stale corn-bread, set the two half-rings of hollowed human teeth over his own, and ventured downstairs to at least make a pretense of being open for business.

It was best to keep busy today. There would be time enough for other things after dark.

Right now, his only task was not to succumb to wretchedness, but to mash the thistle-poppy to a fine pulp, heat and stir it to a syrup, and then take it to Twoblood's.

And when he did, he was going to have a look in that caged man's mouth, and find out exactly how much he had to be wretched about.

BUT WHEN THE door opened again, it *still* wasn't Sil – just Día, thankfully not looking any worse for wear, and three Sundowners.

One was the speckled mule, whose grizzled visage was enough to make Elim sit up straighter in his cell. One was a great dark fat man with oily braids and a ruff of black feathers laid over his shoulders.

And one couldn't be anything but a chief. He wasn't big or tough-looking – in fact, his plain cotton-jeaning pants and white shirt with the half-rolled sleeves reminded Elim of nobody more important than a printer's clerk working after-hours in a hot office. But modern and ordinary as he was otherwise, this fellow clearly wielded some more ancient authority, and wore it in a leather head-band that began with a jewel-colored rainbow of beads hanging in neat shoulder-length strings from ear to ear - red to yellow to green to blue - and ended with a hammered gold disc at his forehead. And even without that, even without the telling details of his sandals and earrings and the little tattoo on his foot, his goldenish skin and especially his amber eyes said plainly that this man here was *different*.

It was to this dazzling pagan authority that the deputy hopped up and submitted himself, and to him that Día stepped forward and directed Elim's attention.

"Elim – oh, but I'm sorry to see you this way. This is Sut Hara, the First Man of Island Town, whom we call the Azahi. He has come to see to your case in person, and to guarantee that you are fairly treated under the law." The frown in her brows and the concern in her eyes was powerfully affecting.

"I sure do appreciate it," he said with a nod to the chief, "but really I ought rather to have Sil here before we get into any of that." And he'd apparently had his manners baked out of his brains, or else meant to say that she wasn't a lady. Elim eased forward and made a start on getting to his feet. "Thanks awfully for saving his bacon, by the way. We both owe you a heap, and I'll make sure you hear that from him too, just as soon as he sees fit to roust himself out of bed and get over h –"

But although he was careful to keep his tone light and easy, she seemed to grow more upset with every word, and finally cut him off. "Elim, I can't – I thought you already knew. He isn't coming. He died last night."

Elim staggered a step on his way up from kneeling, and the words gave him an awful scare even though he knew they weren't true – even though he knew that Día was just a bit addlepated and had gotten things mixed up somehow. "No," he said, "that ain't right. I heard him holler at me after you cut him down. He's coming for me directly – just wait right here and you'll see."

But Día looked just devastatingly sensible. "I am terribly sorry. I hurried after the fall – I thought there was still time – but he was already gone."

And suddenly the look on her face, the sound of her voice, was more than Elim could bear: he lost it, hurling himself forward to hit the bars. "Don't LIE to me!"

In the time it took Día to flinch back, the speckled mule and her deputy had twin pistols leveled on him from opposite corners of the room.

But Día only stopped still, and declined to be intimidated again. "You will find no such thing laid out on my altar's slab," she replied with hot lucid eyes. "What is there is cold and heavy and beginning to stiffen. It has no pulse. Its face is white, its eyes are fixed, and soon it will begin to bloat and to smell. I am telling you what I know, Appaloosa Elim, because I was there and you were not — so you can either accept my word as the truth, or sit in that cell and wait until the reek of his corpse reaches you even here, and tell me then which of us was mistaken."

Elim felt the floor sliding away. He clutched at the bars and dimly reckoned that he ought maybe to sit down, and had made it most of the way to kneeling before he slipped and toppled heavily to a seat.

Día knew, because she was there.

And Sil was dead, because they'd come too late.

So Elim didn't have anything left to be afraid of, because the worst of all things had already come true.

CHAPTER FOURTEEN
TEETH

A LESS HURRIED man would have tied a *yuye* over his eyes to shield them from the sun. But Vuchak's was back in that over-hot common bed-room with the rest of his things, which meant going the wrong way and stepping over all those sleeping bodies even if he didn't wake any of them, and all at the risk of being too late to learn anything, if he weren't already.

As the saying went, sometimes there was nothing to do but to guard your fruits with one hand and your eyes with the other.

Vuchak followed that only half-literally, and threaded a path out of the Moon Quarter, skirting just enough of the Burnt Quarter to let him head south without ever being visible from Twoblood's window.

The forge was not abandoned, as some visitors first thought. It was operated now by Walla-Dee, though there was not so much need for it now as there must have been when the Eaten first built it. So if your animal needed shoes or you had some tool or ornament that wanted fixing, then you could go down south and ask his daughter, and she would arrange for him to come and do your work.

In the meantime, Vuchak would take advantage of the dearth of business to go around back, to the three-walled sheltered part, which was left open on one side for animals, and which at its northern wall was so near Twoblood's jail that a man could scarcely lie lengthwise between them. If Twoblood's door was opened, as it would be if they were going to free the half, then Vuchak would hear it. And when orders were given, Vuchak would hear those too. All he had to do was exercise a crow's patience, sit down, and wait.

And wait.

And wait.

And at some point, his free-soul must have left his body to do the waiting by itself, because his next awareness was the sound of voices from the opposite side of the forge.

"... not for a minute, First, it's no trouble at all. I'm honored to see you at any hour, and there have been far too many since you were last with us."

Vuchak jerked his head up from stiff-necked sleep. That was Huitsak, and by inference the Azahi too. Nevermind what they were doing on the wrong side of the building – Vuchak rocked forward onto the balls of his feet, readying himself to move in a moment if they made sounds to walk around back and discover him.

"We would wholeheartedly agree, Maga-Kin," the Azahi said, using Huitsak's formal title, 'Group-Master', as if he had known him for eight hours instead of eight years. *"Would you prefer us to converse apart? We two have already enjoyed the substance of our discussion, and would be glad to offer you the same courtesy."*

"I wouldn't hear of it, First: how should I welcome the right hand of our fair city and not the left? Twoblood

has been more than generous with us in our time of grief, and we are endlessly grateful for her company – stay, Second, do stay."

And in spite of everything, in spite of every hateful happening, Vuchak's heart soared with pride to hear his *maga*'s honeyed voice. He had all but formally recognized Twoblood as the Wiping Hand of Island Town – to the Azahi's very face! – and polished the title to such a complimentary luster that any objection from its recipient would appear vulgar and paranoid. He'd even managed to work in a dog's command.

"... your pardon, First. I will go and see that Day is not long in coming."

"Certainly; we will await her here."

Twoblood's boots ground a hard track through the dirt until Vuchak couldn't hear them anymore.

"She is diligence in the flesh," Huitsak said, *"and we are both eager to help you put this present sadness to rest. Tell me your will, First, and I will make it mine."*

"You are invaluable in equal measure, Maga-Kin. We would ask that you join us in learning from the half how he is to be treated. Twoblood says the Eadan called him a slave who acted faithfully on bad direction, and asked to be made responsible in his place. If the half agrees that this is so, then we are prepared to honor the eastern custom and his master's last wish, and consider Dulei's blood debt paid. Will this agree with your wisdom as well?"

"Perfectly, First." All smiling luster was gone from Huitsak's voice. *"We would ask only to retain the boy's body, and to lay it to rest beside our own stilled son."*

Vuchak sat further forward, hardly daring to believe this great turn of luck.

"*We will see it done. But consider now the other side of the coin: if the half is not a slave, then we must understand that the act was his, that his life is yours – and that the Eadan's was wrongly taken. You will have no difficulty in seeing this view as well.*"

Huitsak didn't miss a beat. "*None at all, First. The lives of the Eadan's assassins are at your disposal. Or will that also be decided by the half?*"

To date, Vuchak had never taken a knife to the gut.

And yet here he was, listening to his *maga* offer easily, breezily, to end Vuchak's life at the Azahi's call, or even at that of some monstrous misbegotten two-blood, and asking about the particulars with as much passing disinterest as if wondering whether the tea was of sunflower or rose.

"*We had thought to reserve it for our own judgment. We would prefer to leave ourselves with honorable recourse if the Eadan is ever sought-for by his family.*"

"*That is very far-sighted of you, First.*"

Vuchak's ears, which still attended the conversation with the smallest remainder of his mind, registered some passing shift in Huitsak's voice – a return to cleverness of one kind or another.

"*I must say, though, it is a rare man of any color who would stand up and mortgage his own flesh to clear the name of his dead fellow. If I were a betting man, I would lay odds against it.*"

"*We haven't been clear,*" the Azahi replied. "*The half is to identify himself first, honestly and without any knowledge of the consequences. We are interested in the truth above everything, Maga-Kin, and you know how rarely it blooms once profit and expectation take root.*"

"*Certainly I do, First; it is the rarest treasure of our*

times. Ah, and here she comes to answer her name, truth
escorted by diligence. You are a marvelous cultivator of
talent; I have always said so."

"We do seem to find it growing in the unlikeliest of
places..."

There was more after that, pleasantness and
supplication and what promised to be a fresh iteration
of this damnable pact for the grave-woman's benefit,
but Vuchak had no stomach for any of it. His numb and
tingling haunches tipped him back, obliging the dirt to
receive the graceless impact of his buttocks and leaving
him free to sit there, staring stupidly out at the clash
of sunlight and shadow on the ground, struggling to
discern some reason, some pattern to their intersection.

It was easily found. The irregularity in the half-
shadowed yard was caused by the lone *ihi'ghiva*
standing there, instantly recognizable by his plain and
undyed garments, and by the hair tied in slave-fashion
at the base of his neck, and by the black *yuye* which
he wore tied around his eyes, not just in daylight but
always.

Well, at least someone had thought to bring one.

SIL WAS DEAD. Hanged, murdered, and really, actually
dead.

Elim sat stupidly beside the bars, dumbstruck. It
couldn't be true, not after how he'd burned his brains
worrying about it. That was the whole point of worrying,
to keep your eye leveled on the worst so that it couldn't
spring out and come true while you weren't looking.
And yet it *had*. All the promise of Sil's short life was over
before it started, plunging Elim's red-hot *what-if* into

cold reality until there was nothing to haul out again but a heavy and irreversible *what-now*.

"... Elim. Elim, look at me, now."

After a time, someone began prodding his ears with the sound of his name. It was still Día, now dropped to a squat to look him in the eye, the thick human-smelling ropes of her hair falling over her shoulders. "Listen, Elim – I know, I do, but you must listen closely now. They are here to decide what is to be done with you."

He looked further out past the bars at the four strange and heathen-looking Sundowners, and Día here at the fore was right at home among them.

There was not a pale face to be seen anywhere, not a blue eye for a hundred miles, and the last white man to set foot in this godforsaken place had taken pains to display Elim as a slave before he died.

He was done for.

Well, let them decide, then, and let them do it on the quick side. Elim dropped his gaze and waited for it to be over.

"You assume too much, Elim Horseman."

Elim glanced up again at the strange adulteration of his name, as the speaker – the Azahi, by their custom – maneuvered forward to stand before the bars. He folded his arms and looked down at Elim with keen bright eyes.

"You came here with the boy Halfwick, is it true?"

And now they'd have him accuse himself. "Yes," Elim said.

"You knew that you came outside our law, is it true?"

"Yes," Elim said, "and I told him not to, for all the good it did."

That didn't seem to impress. "You shot Dulei Marhuk to his death, is it true?"

"It was an accident!" Elim cried, and it came out louder than he meant.

But it garnered him no reaction at all. The Sundowner just stood there, cool and calm, looking down at Elim and apparently still waiting.

"Yes," Elim said at last.

"And you are his half, is it true?"

Elim blinked. "What?"

That provoked a nerve in the Sundowner's forehead, as if Elim had offended by failing to take his meaning. He looked aside as if he'd have notes ready to hand, but there to his right was only Día.

"*Kirase,*" the Azahi said to her, his beads clicking as he tipped his head towards Elim.

She fixed Elim with a level gaze, but it didn't belong to the Día who had come to him yesterday. "We are in two minds about your you," she said. "We know that Halfwick showed you to be a slave, and can plainly see the proof." She did not point at the brand on Elim's arm, but he still wished he could have put it out of sight. "He said that you could not be considered responsible, and asked that we hold him accountable in your place."

The heat in Elim's back suddenly burned hotter. Surely not. Surely Sil had not willfully walked off a balcony. He was powerfully partial to his own life, and besides which he was clever, much too clever for that. And yet somehow his cleverness included ordering Elim to strip down and bare the brand...

"And yet," Día echoed, "your every mention to me was of your friend, your associate; you professed no master but Him who made you, and took pains to ask His forgiveness. If you are a slave, you are not of a kind that we have known before."

By the end of it she was looking at him with a special-particular kind of intensity, her voice lightening up on her last few words as if she meant to leave a question, as if she meant for him to follow up on the invitation and agree with all of what she had said just there.

But Elim's ears were filled with her twisting his every word and confession to suit her purpose, of her having hoarded up everything he'd said and fed it right back to that council of part-timers behind her, of her all but whipping off her robe to reveal a deerskin dress underneath.

They were the Sibyl's children, all of them, but she had to be one of Her firstborn favorites.

Elim stared right back at her, and by bullet-biting willpower kept his mouth clean in answering. "So which is it?"

But the Azahi must have picked up on his hate, and replied with a severe quickness. "You say it to us, Elim Horseman, fast and sure: are you a slave or no?"

Elim looked up at him, with his exotic jewelry and foreign accent and hard-eyed stare, and beyond, to where the speckled mule and the fat man stood apart, and wondered what they were hoping to hear.

If he hid behind the brand, then maybe they'd reckon that justice was already done, that Sil had paid for the dead boy's life with his own, and that Elim was property no different from Sil's hat and saddle, unclaimed and marketable. Or more probably, being as they didn't have a taste for mules out here, they'd figure he was trying to weasel his way out from under the corpse and plug him for a gutless lying coward.

But if he did as he'd been taught, and owned himself and all his deeds... there wasn't room for much 'maybe' there at all.

So maybe he was fooling himself to think that his life was even still on the table. Maybe the only dickering-point to be decided on was whether he took the bullet to the head or the gut. And if that was so, if the only difference he could guarantee was the one it made to his own self...

Elim looked back at the ground, and had to work some before he could get the words out. "I ain't a slave," he said at last. "Please just get it over with quick."

"We will see," the Azahi said, and turned away.

Elim waited on tenterhooks while they made their powwow, and agonized over his answer. He hadn't thought it through right. It wasn't really to himself that he was answerable, but to Boss and Lady Jane. He was theirs; they'd bought him and raised him and taken every pain and care with him, and the only thing worse than thinking of how they were fixing to lose him was how long they'd spend not even knowing that they had.

It was the fat man doing most of the talking, him and the Azahi. The speckled mule seemed to wind herself tighter with every word that went between them, and the silent, blazing anger in her eyes was Elim's only hope. She wanted him dead, sure as Sunday, and her smothered outrage had to mean that it was going the other way – that she wouldn't get to air her holster on Elim after all.

Then Día volunteered something, just once, and the sound of her familiar voice speaking foreign words poisoned his heart.

If he lived to be a hundred, it wouldn't be long enough for him to mistake her again.

The Azahi turned back to him, and Elim's breathing stopped by itself. "We see that you made the death of

Dulei Marhuk, and must answer for your making. You will take his body to his home, and tell his families the way that it happened, and make any payment that they ask from you. When this will be done, and if you still live, then you will have no more crime here."

Elim let out his breath, and didn't know which way to think. It was not death, it was not slavery... not yet, anyway. He swallowed. "Where do I go?"

The fat man's voice was calm and fluent. "To the place where our people were born, which we call *Atali'Krah*, the Crow Home."

Of course: Elim fixed on his black-feathered mantle as he said it, and should have guessed it before. They were crows – diviners, necromancers, eaters of the dead – whose idea of a good end was living long enough to thank the birds as they pecked out your eyes.

None of which the fat man bothered to deny. "To reach the mountains is perhaps five days; another two or three finishes it. Dulei's uncle and his manservant will go with you, and they know the way."

It didn't take Elim long to figure the math. That was at least two weeks, there and back again. Assuming he ever *got* back again. "But Sil – I got to take him home – and I... there's people waiting for us..."

The Azahi folded his arms. "We will bury him here, and give the truth and his life-price to any person who may come saying your names."

Which would have been considerably more comfort if there was even a single living soul who would think to look for them out here, God *damn* that Sil Halfwick.

The Azahi lifted his brows, as if stumped by whatever he found on Elim's face. "Or will it like you better if we burn him?"

"No – I mean, no, thank you; I don't reckon he would want that." Elim could imagine what Sil might want, but he wouldn't bet on Will and Nillie having the means to take him back east and lay him in next to their parents. It was a hell of a thought, that the little town that Sil had tried so hard to escape might keep him forever.

But anything was better than here.

So Elim would do what he could to make sure they both got back, later in preference to not-at-all, and racked his sun-burnt skull for anything else he should find out while he had the chance. "And the horses? Our gear?"

The Azahi nodded once. "Everything you have, you will use them for this work. Any that is left after is yours."

Well, that was about as good as could be expected. And although Elim was reasonably sure on the answer: "And if I won't go?"

The Azahi stared hard down at him, and his keen amber-eyed gaze held Elim fixed in place. "Then we will be your only judge... and we do not like men who refuse the law of the gods."

That was not a promise, but Elim understood it perfectly: this was his one chance to do right by the same rule that Sundowners shared alike with civilized men, and he had no business expecting any more mercy than that.

His hand went to his heart all on its own, to the place where the dead boy had touched him. "I'll go," Elim said, as much to get himself firm on that as any of them. "Just tell me what to do, and I'll go."

The Azahi nodded again, and his solemn approval

was clear to see. Then he glanced back at his council. *"Sansores, par favor exkusados'ean."*

They filed out of the room – the fat man first, the speckled mule with a keen eye on him afterwards, and the deputy closing the door quietly behind them.

The Azahi returned his attention to Elim. "The family-men will come for you soon. My Día will be your help before then."

"Thank you," Elim said. "It's real – it's mighty fine of you."

The Azahi tipped his head. "It is good that you will do this, Elim Horseman. From you I expect more good still."

Then he went, and the last of Elim's resolve went with him.

What the hell had he just signed up for?

The all-powerful hope of living drained right out of him, leaving no feeling but the one still making him sick to his stomach.

Then something black stepped in to block his view of the door.

"Elim? I'm sorry to have said it that way. You know that I'm here to help."

He wanted it to be black outside too, to be night so that he could sleep and sleep and not wake up until the dream was over and he was home again.

"Is there anything that I can get for you?"

But he was already so tired that maybe he could get an early start on it.

"Elim, please – won't you even answer me?"

Elim lay gingerly back down, taking pains to keep his crispier parts off the dirt-packed planks of the floor, and rolled over to face the wall.

After awhile, the last of the sounds emptied out of the room, and it was finally quiet enough to rest.

THEY WERE A class of slaves above all others, the *ihi'ghiva'a*. In many ways, they ranked even above free men. Schooled and trained by Aso'ta Marhuk himself, given the *yuye* to show that they could not see or be tempted by the wealth and corruption of the world, they acted as the far-reaching, all-doing hands of the a'Krah. One was a necessity for any group-master, whether he employed him as a scribe or a spy or even a poisoner of cups. For his exceptional service in Island Town, Huitsak had been honored with a second.

There was no telling which of the two Vuchak was staring at now, but he did not press the matter until the conclave of voices had removed itself into Twoblood's house.

"What are you doing here?" he demanded in the loudest of whispers. "Who sent you?"

The *ihi'ghiva* maintained the same perfect detachment as he dipped his head in deference to Vuchak's lesser-superior status, and answered in a suitably soft undertone. "My master called me to attend him at the Second Man's summons, and resolved to wait in this more shaded place. When he saw you here indisposed, he ordered me to keep watch for spies and hidden listeners, and declared to the Second Man his wish to take fresher air at the south wall instead."

In other words, Huitsak had walked right around to find Vuchak asleep, and had crafted a lightning-quick pretense to keep Twoblood from discovering the very same rat in the grain as had already been caught fouling the nest last night.

On reflection, maybe Vuchak really should let the half end him and be done with it.

"... *nodat hafwik choudju tibi a-zlev, end-ken plenly si ti-bruf...*"

Of course, the conversation that would decide his fate was all in Ardish.

But as his ears dredged the voices for any translatable thought, his eyes had nothing to study but the slave – average in height, soft in the stomach, graying at the temples – and no lack of opportunity to notice the way he kept his hands clasped behind his back and his head tilted just-so.

Vuchak watched him with suspicion. "You understand them?" he whispered.

The slave held perfectly still, and left a pause. "The Azahi names the man, demanding the truth."

Vuchak's stomach clenched tighter. "And?"

Another pause. "The man says he is not a slave."

What? "Your ears fail you," Vuchak snapped, not as quietly as he should have.

The *ihi'ghiva* made no reply, and Vuchak was just on the verge of demanding a more exact translation when he was halted by softer, harder-to-hear but altogether more sensible words.

"... *that he is yours, Maga-Kin. What shall we say to him?*"

"*I have considered it carefully, First, and I ...*"

Damn it, they must have moved away from the window. Vuchak lunged back up to one knee and pressed himself closer to the wall.

"... *home alive. It would raise both of us in... ...to offer him to the Marhuka.*"

"*A very noble thought. Do you... escort?*"

"*Not at all, First.*" Huitsak pitched his voice a little stronger than before. "*I have them already fixed in one mind: the one is bound by blood to the task, and the other I must urgently put out of my reach or strangle. Are you sure you won't have his life?*"

A tempest of oil and water was brewing in Vuchak's gut. The thought of receiving leave to go home again was too good to believe, just as the idea of going anywhere near their murderous plaguey half-man was too terrible to contemplate.

"*You are kind to... be content with the twenty scruples.*"

Vuchak sucked his teeth in almost-physical pain at the number: he and Weisei hadn't brought in that much since... not since they were first sent here. That the Azahi was commanding money instead of blood for Halfwick's life was scant consolation: Huitsak would have to pay it, regardless of whether Vuchak lived or died, and therefore had no reason not to empty Vuchak's veins right along with his pockets.

Well, except for this misbegotten errand here.

"*... believe he will do it?*"

"*I think so, First.*" That must have been the grave-woman. "*... seemed to me to have a faithful heart, and a great desire to... in the eyes of our god.*"

There was more after that, returning again to Ardish, but it hardly mattered. The truth, the only truth that mattered, was that Vuchak's *maga-kin* had sold him like so much cheap wine.

"The Azahi is giving the agreement to the man. He asks questions."

Vuchak stared up at the slave in uncomprehending disgust. "Who cares? Who asked you to speak?"

The *ihi'ghiva* made no reply, but that was fine. He would say plenty later on. He would be all too pleased to tell Huitsak, or Aibak, or some wall-dwelling fellow slaves somewhere, of how he had seen Vuchak huddled up like a frightened child listening to the squabbling of its parents, and of how cleverly Huitsak had humiliated him within his own hearing, exactly as he had done for Twoblood just before, and of how good and impotently Vuchak had sat there and taken it like the quivering sheep-hearted milk-drinker that he was.

It was a thought that seeped into his mind slowly, as rain into over-saturated earth.

Of course, it was not as if Vuchak warranted any special leniency in the first place. It was not as if his fourteen years spent serving Marhuk's least-capable son, up to and including prying him out from Wi-Chuck's clenched fist, merited any consideration against his heinous two-seconds' lapse in judgment yesterday. To imagine that he was somehow deserving of the same regard that one would afford to an average common servant, or even a reasonably-good hunting dog, was a laughable overstatement of his worth.

There was more foreign speech, and the door's opening, and something in all of that which inspired the *ihi'ghiva* to express a second unwanted thought.

"Of all my life's errors, the ones I have most regretted were those made in innocence."

This was said in the same soft under-voice as before, the blindfolded slave looking down at him with no discernible expression, least of all one which would suggest sympathy.

Looking *down* at him.

Vuchak lunged up and forward and slammed into him, hard enough to send him sprawling to the ground except for the intervening hand with which Vuchak seized his shirt-front and dragged him around the corner of the forge and out to the road, where Huitsak and Twoblood and Barking-Deer were plain to be seen even in the blinding daylight. Vuchak thrust the *ihi'ghiva* contemptibly to one side and offered his silver-shackled wrists out to Huitsak in a deep and respectful *asshet*.

"*Maga, forgive my disgraceful interruption,*" he said, straightening without being invited to speak, "*but I have only just now caught this faithless servant plastering his ear to the wall to learn things not fit for his knowing. Please, what would you have me do with him?*"

Huitsak pulled himself up to his full height and stared, squint-eyed, his face slowly warming with rage.

And for long and telling moments, there was no cleverness to be heard from him, nor anything to suggest an explanation for his very-public failure to control even the most menial of his underlings.

Twoblood remained silent, as did *her* menial, and as Vuchak dared to look up at her – just to guarantee that she would notice and remember the sight of his face – he felt a powerful and traitorous affinity with the Left Hand of Island Town.

"*Get out of my sight,*" Huitsak snarled. "*Both of you.*"

"*Yes, maga.*" Vuchak's moment was ruined, or perhaps made even better, by the perfect timing of the slave's words with his own, and the unison with which they made their *asheta* and departed.

His heart drummed loud and fast in his ears, as if he had run four times around the walls, and his mind was reeling, racing, as loose and wild as if he'd drunk four flasks of juniper wine between laps, and he felt alive, as proud and brave and utterly fearless as a well-chosen *atodak* ought to be.

When he finally tired of noticing the soft footsteps behind him, Vuchak whirled around, forcing the slave to stop in an instant. "And?" he demanded. "What do you think of that?"

The *ihi'ghiva* raised his brows behind the blindfold. "I think I would not trade places with you for all the wealth of the world."

That was brazen, and surprising enough to pause Vuchak's thrillsome thoughts. Who was this with nerve to speak to him so plainly? "What name are you given?"

The slave bowed again. "Only Hakai, sir."

Vuchak looked him up and down, the heat and brightness of the day already promising a headache. He was too pale to be a'Krah, though he spoke like one competently enough, and with half his face hidden, the only certainty about his parentage was that it had been accomplished at least forty years ago.

That was fine.

"Well then, Hakai," Vuchak said as he turned to resume their northward course, "it is past time you learned how to make more deliberate errors. They are the only kind with any savor to them."

And the beauty of this particular error was that regret had no place in it: if Vuchak was already sentenced to march off and die at either the hands or the plague of that misborn half-man, then all that remained between now and then was to deserve it.

* * *

DURING THE PACKING of his case and the walk to Twoblood's and right up through the tapping at her door, the majority of Fours' mind was occupied with setting aside what he'd overhead this morning, preparing himself to ask the correct questions, and in short, making sure he got clean away with his eavesdropping.

"Be here!"

That ended with his first glimpse of the patient.

He was lying with his face three inches from the wall, and from this distance his scarlet flesh looked wet. Fours knew better: he recognized those hundred innocent-looking droplets of water for fresh blisters even before he'd gone to kneel at the bars.

Twoblood must have heard his first little hiss of air at the sight, or else had been stewing in guilt. "It wasn't for cruelty," she said from her desk. "There wasn't any other way."

"Yes," Fours heard himself say. "If only this could have been prevented somehow." And then, to forestall any furtherance of that thought: "*Elim, do you hear me?*"

Fours fancied that he did, as his breathing was exceptionally silent for sleep, but Halfwick's mule gave him nothing else to go on.

Fours opened his suitcase, and rubbed his hands first with brandy from the one flask, and then with boiled water from the second. The alcoholic tingle was inappropriately refreshing. "*I've brought some medicine for your back. Why don't you sit up so we can put it on?*"

Except for his breathing, he might as well have been dead. "He's done that since they told him about his master," Twoblood volunteered from behind. "Do you want me to get him up?"

So he'd believed it, when Shea called out to him in Halfwick's voice. Poor fool. "*I won't force it, if you don't want any,*" Fours said, "*but I'd appreciate the courtesy of an answer.*"

That didn't yield anything at first, and Fours was just on the verge of clapping his hands to his knees to rise in exasperation when:

"*I wouldn't be holden to your mistress,*" Elim said, low and slow, "*but thank you kindly for your interest.*"

It was a strange thing to say, and Fours' understanding ultimately had to be fetched from the far-back dusty recesses of his mind. It had been a long time since Peter Fournier had last taken a seat in the pews, though the verse was a common one.

Refuse to your last breath the Sibyl's gifts, or be beholden to her forever afterwards.

Of course. To this farm-raised fellow here, Sibyl wasn't an allegory for the presence of evil in the world, but a creature as real as any he had ever met – and to assure himself of that, he had only to point at any living mereau, or probably any native human being for that matter, and call them all the bastard half-demon offspring of the First Temptation.

Well, let him. Certainly there was nothing Fours could say to convince him otherwise... especially not after the spectacle Elim had seen last night. "*Then I won't offer it again.*" Setting aside his indignation at having wasted so much time and effort, Fours steeled his nerve and plowed on forward. "*But I was hoping you could do me a considerable favor, and... and allow me to inspect your teeth.*"

This time the answer was as quick as a snakebite. Elim rolled – hurled – himself at him, the *thud* of his shoulder hitting the bars smothered by the *bang* of Twoblood's chair from behind, and topped off with the *click* of a cocked pistol. "Fours, move!"

Fours had frozen, his skin perfectly floor-colored, but no matter: he hardly had anything to hide from either of the two earth-persons. Instead, he worked at loosening his locked jaw, and before Elim's livid, staring features had firmly decided on whether it was worth his life to reach out and smash his skull against the bars, Fours finished his thought with a steel-forged, day-old sense of conviction. "*... and not for me, you understand, but for my sister, whom you owed – owe – a very considerable debt.*"

Some of the leaking outrage on Elim's face was absorbed by the confused knot between his brows. He scrutinized Fours' features, as if in search of some resemblance.

"... what are you saying to him?"

But when he was done, he had no anger left in him. Elim let his head down, his forehead resting against the cold iron bars. His eyes closed as his mouth opened.

"*Thank you,*" Fours said. "*I won't take much time.*" And then, mindful to keep a low, calm voice: "If he bites off my fingers, feel free to shoot him."

But Elim was the soul of compliance as Fours put one damp and gentle hand to his feverish forehead and the other to his jaw, tilted his head back just enough to get the advantage from the lone window's light, and had a first look in his mouth.

His canines weren't worthy of the name – nothing more than ordinary human eyeteeth – but Fours hadn't expected anything there. Fangs like Twoblood's were more common to the Lovoka than the Ara-Naure, and would have been noticeable at first glance two days ago. More disappointing were his incisors. The people descended from Grandfather Coyote – the Lovoka, the Ara-Naure, the Ohoti nations, and the fox-marked Wibei – almost universally retained the same small, uniformly-sized fore-teeth of their common ancestor. But the top middle two of this fellow here were as distinct from their neighbors as a pair of prairie barns in a street of sod houses.

Well, but U'ru's boy was only half native, after all. He might have his father's mouth.

Fours took a deeper look towards the back. The light and the angle weren't good enough to confirm much more than the obvious: he was still young, with nothing much worn or broken or missing. He'd do well to savor that while it lasted.

Fours slipped an exploratory finger behind Elim's cheek and began feeling out the contours of each tooth in turn. He stopped before the end, having surely missed a crevice somewhere. But no, there it was again: where he ought to have had three or possibly four proper molars, each one roughly square in proportion, the whole space was taken up with just two, each one half again as long as it should have been.

Fours' brow creased; he pushed up his glasses and tilted Elim's head slightly more in hopes of a better glimpse, catching an open eye and a look of some concern as he did.

"*Just a moment more, please,*" he said, and squinted to confirm what touch had already told him. He felt carefully along the tops and sides of both teeth, and then verified the same thing behind the opposite cheek as well: the man's molars were too wide by half, their little cusps and valleys considerably shallower than should be expected, their tongueward sides peculiarly ridged.

Washchaw, then, the sharper surfaces having been filed off by some enterprising barber long ago. Or an abnormally-formed Set-Seti, or even some perfectly well-formed example of a tribe whose dental particulars Fours had never studied. The only guarantee was that this Elim did indeed wear his heritage in his mouth, and that neither it nor he had ever belonged to the Dog Lady.

Fours sat back on his heels and sighed, years of his life escaping in a single breath. He wiped his hands on the towel in his case.

She might still be alive. She might even still be saved, if he could retrieve the bullet without bleeding her to death. But the thought of doing all that, and of telling her the truth of what he'd seen here, and then leaving her to take up her post and wait for the next poor eye-spotted fool to start the whole thing over again... by every god, where was he meant to get the strength?

Something of that must have shown in his face. When Fours looked up again, it was to a stare of the most perturbed intensity. Perhaps Elim had begun to suspect that this had nothing to do with appraising his fitness for sale.

Fours took Twoblood's jar of globemallow hair-wash from his case and closed the clasps. "*That's very fine,*" he said, taking liberties to pat the unburnt side of Elim's shoulder on his way up to his feet. "*Thank you for your kindness. I'll leave ours here, in case you change your mind. We won't ask for anything more.*"

Elim nodded once, plainly mistrustful. Well, let him

be: Fours had no comfort to offer anyway. Elim's hopes of going free were almost as dead as his foolish partner.

Fours could have commiserated. The last of his confessors was dead or dying, and the thought of rescuing her and resuming their hellish status quo was suddenly infinitely less unbearable than going on alone.

"What's wrong with you? You look like a man with seven daughters."

Fours blinked, surprised to find himself still standing there. Twoblood sat there at her desk, the hat on her head an easy excuse for her to deny sympathy to anyone, the gun on her desk a nasty reminder of every one of her barking, bullying threats, the look on her face suddenly intolerable – as if she of all people had any right to feign ignorance of misery! – and Fours hurled the jar straight at her.

In a just world, there would have been a great cathartic shattering of glass. But in this one, there was only a modest *thap* where its pristine surface met the meat of Twoblood's palm, and nothing for a consolation prize but the scraping of the chair as its occupant bolted to her feet. "Fours, what the fuck are you doing?"

"Go to hell," Fours cried, "and take him with you!" He stormed out, the bang of his case against the doorframe much improved by the one that punctuated his slamming of the door. But the part of him that craved to hear it flung open again, to feel himself knocked to the ground and savagely beaten, went begging as he was left to stalk off unapproached and unmolested, walking fast, going nowhere.

CHAPTER FIFTEEN
THE INDIGENT AND THE DEAD

"VICHI! VICHI, WAKE up!"

Even through the haze of sleep, Vuchak recognized Weisei frantically patting at his shoulder – but it was much harder to find the will to do anything about it.

"Oh, Vichi, wake up, you must – they've unrecognized me!"

The word, *savash*, then yanked him straight into wakefulness. Even though it was an absurd idea, even though Weisei had to be talking utter nonsense, Vuchak yielded to the phantom crisis and sat up.

And after he pinched the sleep out of his eyes, he recognized Otli folding his garments, Tadai at the far wall plaiting his hair, and Dakat still endeavoring to sleep.

The bed-room. Yes. No going back to Pipat's, not after his performance in the street. Vuchak sighed. "Otli, what's the hour?"

But Otli went right on brushing stray hairs from his leggings, as if he had gone stone deaf.

Vuchak's stomach twinged. "Otli? Tadai, in seriousness: what's the joke?"

Tadai ignored him too, but he had to stare at the doorknob to do it. Vuchak felt a sudden, powerful urge to walk into his line of sight and shake him until his eyes rolled up in his head.

But that feeling reminded him of yesterday, and what he had done with that eyeless slave, and suddenly the idea of *savash* didn't sound so implausible after all.

"You see?" Weisei exclaimed. "You see, they've unrecognized us!"

Vuchak poured the jewelry from his boots. He took his time in putting it on, staring at Tadai all the while, and tasted bile-tinged satisfaction as the other man faltered in his plaiting. All at once, Tadai stood and left, his sloppy braids fluttering behind him.

"Well?" Weisei said, kneeling even closer to Vuchak's side, as if he would crawl into his skin. "Say something, Vichi – say it isn't you too!"

Vuchak combed out and re-plaited his own hair, right side first, nurturing his anger. "Oh, be sensible, Weisei. Look there – you could learn something from Otli. It is a brave man who will hold *savash* on his own friends, much less on a son of Marhuk himself. You wouldn't see such a man flinch at a knife put to his very eye, nevermind go tripping down stairs bleating for his *maga* the moment the she-dog of the Azahi barked in his direction..."

Otli slammed the door behind him. Dakat swore under his breath and rolled over, and then everything was quiet again.

But truth lived in the silence. Now unrecognized as fellow a'Krah, Vuchak and Weisei were to be treated as strangers, no better than foreigners, who might be safely ignored, cheated, disrespected, or – in Vuchak's case – even killed, freely and without fear of reprisal. To be the object of *savash* was to endure a living death, and those who suffered it would not be recognized again until they had atoned for their behavior.

And Vuchak would put down money that the shape of their penance was already known to him.

He pulled on his boots and stood up, but Weisei failed to follow him. He just knelt there, hands laced behind his head, elbows tucked under his chin, and stared at his blanket. The wounds he'd taken from Vuchak yesterday had already faded to a faint discoloration under his eye.

"Well?" Vuchak's voice made an indifferent, impatient tone, under which his guilt-fed fear could not be heard. "Come on, idiot; it's not going to get any better for wishing it."

"It isn't fair," Weisei said to the rumpled red triangle-patterns in the wool. "We didn't do anything wrong."

Not true: *Weisei* hadn't done anything wrong, or at least not any more than was generally expected of him. Vuchak opened his mouth to say as much, but all that came out was, "Well, let's go and see Huitsak."

Weisei himself might have been holding *savash* for all the answer he gave.

"Please?" Vuchak tried again. "I can't do it by myself." More to the point, there was no telling what Weisei might get into, or what the others might do to him, if he were left alone now.

But thankfully he accepted the sweetened lie, took hold of Vuchak's silvered wrists and allowed himself to be pulled to his feet – though not without a certain glint in his eye. "Really, Vichi, you must learn to do without me sometimes. I can't always be minding you like this."

Vuchak made the sign of a merciful god, and let him

walk ahead. But as Weisei opened the door, Vuchak pulled the knife from his boot, making its wrapped handle warm and familiar to his hand as they ventured out into the halls of the vast night-house, and prepared to serve his *marka* with greater diligence than he had in a long time.

THERE WAS SOME discord among Penitent scholars about the interpretation of the Twenty-Fifth Verse, and specifically its ninth line: *animus apud secunda nocte egrediet.* Which was popularly translated as *the soul will depart by the second night,* except that the word *apud* might mean either *before* or *by,* and had occasioned considerable controversy about whether a wake could be held on the second night following a death. That did not even begin to touch on the age-old disagreement about what should be counted as the first night, when someone passed between the hours of sunset and sunrise.

In short, it was very possible that Halfwick had no soul remaining to want comfort.

But while there was still any chance that he might, Día would not begrudge him the effort. As the light faded from the gaps in the roof and the buckled wall, she untied the linen cord from her waist, unhooked the clasps from the neck and side of her cassock, and slipped it down from her shoulders. Finally, she stood before the body on the altar dressed only in her white chemise, and the small golden sun-wheel on the chain around her neck.

It was difficult to look at him without thinking of how stridently his living mind would have refused this arrangement. "I'm sorry it's come to this," she said. "I know you must be sorely wanting for more familiar company. I thought that you might find mine preferable to having none at all, but I'd... I hope you will let me know if you would rather we lie apart."

Día stood still, hands clasped before her, and opened her senses. But there was no telling chill in the air, no warning tingle in the soles of her feet, and no sign of Halfwick's presence, much less his will.

So she stepped forward to the altar, pulled back the shroud, and climbed up to lie with him on the cloth-draped stone slab – not intimately, not presumptuously, but in compassion and modesty, with her body lying at his left arm and her head on his cold shoulder.

It was an act she had never performed without at least a little lingering trepidation, and tonight was no exception. He was young and worldly and had died a sudden and brutal death. In venturing to lie beside men like him, Día had on more than one occasion woken from horrific bloody nightmares, or found herself thrown violently to the floor.

But he'd had goodness in him, even if she hadn't seen much of it herself. So she closed her eyes in faith that whatever remained of Halfwick's soul would do her no violence, and went to sleep with a mind still listening for any last thoughts he might wish the living world to know.

IF THERE WAS any doubt remaining about their status as outcasts, the walk through the house ended it. Vuchak expended no energy on politeness as he cleaved a path through harlots, guests and fools, Weisei trailing unhappily behind him. He indulged his anger just once, lunging at Otli as they passed each other in the hallway, and felt a rush of obscene gratification as the other man flinched back, nearly knocking over one of the painted women in the process. But the pig-eyed fool could not retaliate, not without breaking *savash*, and Vuchak was free to continue on his way, reveling in this new and filthy kind of freedom. What couldn't he do now?

"Vichi..." Weisei waited until they were clear of the kitchen door. "Please, don't let's be angry. Let's just try to fix things, and make it like it was before."

"A wonderful idea," Vuchak replied, much too quickly. "Would you like to prop Dulei up at his usual place, or will I?"

There was no answer but the sound of their footsteps in the long, dry grass. Vuchak knew he was drinking dirty water again, that he should have been using his voice to tell Weisei what he'd done with the *ihi'ghiva* and make apologies for it, but what was the point? They'd only have another fight, and Vuchak meant to save all of his for Huitsak.

A dull reddish light flickered in the cellar's lone window. Vuchak tipped his knife to the eye of Marhuk above, then stowed it and applied his shoulder to the door, which always wanted to stick in the summertime. The light inside was dim and spotty, and his ears reported the dripping of water from the back of the chamber.

As they took the last steps down, Vuchak saw that it was not water, but the faint *tap-tap-tap* of a hammer-wielding *ihi'ghiva*, who might or might not have been Hakai, delicately driving a nail into the half-built wooden planks around Dulei's body.

His clothes had already been burned, save for the

yuye that served less to blindfold his eyes than to hold his broken skull together. Now he sat wrapped in his black-feather cloak, his forehead bowed to rest on his updrawn knees, his wrists tied together to encircle his shins, and his ankles bound likewise. The a'Krah did not practice the burying of men in boxes, but when such a box was temporarily unavoidable, it would be built to accommodate its occupant, and not the other way around.

Vuchak and Weisei offered their wrists first to Dulei, and then to Huitsak. He was sitting at his little table, massive and shadow-blackened and still, and although his account-books were still spread out in their usual fashion, the ink-bottle in the corner was corked. Huitsak sat leaning forward, elbows at table, fingers to forehead, and stared down at the open pages.

Ages passed this way, measured in *tap-tap-tap*. Finally, Vuchak dropped his *ashet* and straightened, reminding his voice to sound respectful. "You sent for us, *maga*?"

"Ah." Huitsak looked up, and made the sign of a provident god – not at him, of course. "Weisei. Thank you for coming so promptly. Please, be ready."

Weisei dropped his *ashet* and stood at-ease, his gaze flicking from Huitsak to Vuchak and back again. "Yes? Ah, yes, *maga*."

Huitsak nodded, so agreeably. "Very good. Tell me then, Weisei – what do you think of all this business of the last two nights?"

So this would be the game. Vuchak did not interrupt, but held himself still, his arms crossed over his chest, and waited.

"I, ah, I don't – well, it is terrible, *maga*, and I don't understand it. Dulei – Dulei never hurt anyone, and neither did Afvik, and now they are dead, and my – and Vuchak is wounded, and nobody will talk to me, and it is not FAIR! None of it is right anymore!"

Huitsak nodded over his papers. "I could not agree more. What do you think we ought to do now?"

Weisei looked over his shoulder for help, but Vuchak would be damned if he was going to offend Huitsak's ears with the sound of his voice.

"I don't know, *maga*," he said at last. "We have to take Dulei back home – oh, but look, see, you have already thought of that." He pointed with his chin, as if Huitsak could have missed the grim carpentry going on in the back. "And Afvik too, but I don't know where his home is, and... oh *maga*, I don't think anyone here does." Vuchak watched as he tried to think through an entire idea, and was swiftly overwhelmed by the enormity of the task.

Sure enough, it was just a matter of moments before Weisei dropped to a squat, staring at the floor between his knees, and put his fingers through his hair as if he would keep his head from bursting open. "The fire-child said to me that it didn't matter, that he was safe in the house of their god, but I can't remember why and it isn't, it can't be right – it isn't RIGHT to, to just bury him where he dropped as if he were dung in the street, but what can we do? What are we supposed to do?"

The man-mountain looming over one side of the table looked down at the man-child huddled beyond the other, and steepled his hands. "Would you like to know what I think?"

Vuchak's foot took a half-step forward before he could halt it, outrage boiling up inside him. Huitsak had engineered this, had planned this vicious scapegoating from Halfwick's last gasp, and now he would cast himself as the answer to all their problems –

– and Weisei could not buy into it fast enough. He tipped forward onto his knees, his hands clasped anxiously between them, and dignity – as usual – was nowhere in his mind. "Oh, please, *maga* – please tell me, what should we do now?"

Huitsak nodded, just once. "We are shamed, Weisei. *You* are shamed, for reasons which you well understand. Dulei must go home again, and more than that, his death must be answered. Would it please you to know that I have secured for you Halfwick's still-living slave?"

Weisei blinked – revenge and repayment having figured nowhere in his thoughts – and then seized the idea two-handed. "Oh – oh, yes," he said, as if this were a gift of genius. "We can take him back with us, and he can tell Grandfather where Afvik must lie! And he will confess himself, and we will give Dulei to our cousins, and then we will know how to give Afvik back to HIS cousins, and after we do that, we can come back, and everything will be well again! –Won't it, *maga*? Won't it then be well again?"

It was as impressive as it was disgusting to watch how Huitsak so effortlessly teased Weisei's greatest trouble from his heart and then buried its solution under a mountain of gruesome, arduous, humiliating toil, knowing that Weisei would dive cheerfully into that steaming shit-heap just for the promise of his prize.

And he didn't even get that much. "I should certainly think so," Huitsak demurred, his glossy black plaits slithering off his shoulders as he tipped his head forward. "Now what will you need in order to do all that?"

Weisei pressed his hands to either side of his nose, thinking hard with his whole body. "Dulei, of course – but you have seen to that. Afvik's man must come too. A cart and mules to pull it, and food for them, and for us, and water enough for everyone, and our cold-night things, and our weapons, and the correct traveling tools and – oh, and really we should have gifts also, we can't go home without gifts... but what should we give?"

Huitsak folded his hands, and corrected Weisei's course with an effortless nudge. "It is best not to keep the dead waiting, I think. So let us work quickly: I will see to Halfwick's man and to our honored brother here, and Vuchak may be persuaded to help with the mules and wagon while you gather our supplies, and if we are clever and work well, then perhaps you can be on your way tonight. What do you think of that?"

Weisei bounded to his feet with alacrity. "Oh, yes – we will, *maga*, of course we will!" Then he seemed to remember the other half of *we*. "Won't we, Vichi? We will, won't we?"

Vuchak jerked his chin up in silent assent. Anything, really, to get the gullible idiot on his way.

Fortunately, Weisei needed nothing else. "How blessed we are! Thank you, Vichi – thank you, *maga*! I'll go and get the things ready, and you will see how quickly!"

He bounded away and up the stairs, making the sign of a provident god as he went.

Then there was only Huitsak and Vuchak, and the *tap-tap-tap* of the slave's hammer filling the space between them.

Presently, Huitsak flipped a page in his book. It was the sound of Vuchak's patience breaking. "Well?" he demanded.

Huitsak didn't look up. "Was there something you wanted from me?"

And then there was no more of respect. "I want to know why you have done this!"

Huitsak glanced up, and the room seemed to grow just that much darker. "How curious. That same thought has come to me so often lately."

Vuchak shook his head, itching to finish with civility. "It was wrong of me to interfere with the fishman's evil act," he said, "and to allow myself to be caught listening, and most especially to put myself before you in the midst of better company, and I welcome and expect your anger on every front. But to be sent away with a plague-born half and have it pretended that we will return alive –"

"– and who said that you were meant to return at all?"

Vuchak stopped, momentarily speechless. He waited in vain for Huitsak to meet his gaze. "Why – *maga*, what can you mean?"

Huitsak turned another page. "Have I been too hasty? Is there some service which you perform here that I have failed to note?"

Vuchak took a belligerent step forward. "I have served you every day without fail –"

"*Horseshit!*" It was a bark loud enough to stop the slave's tapping hammer, accompanied by the clattering fall of the chair as Huitsak heaved himself up to his feet, his face burning. "You have failed me every day without serving!"

"How?" Vuchak easily matched his fire. "What humiliation have I not endured for your profit? When have I failed to help a drunken idiot waste his money, or to sit like a trained animal at Addie's table and choke down her slop at every wretched one of their feast-days, or to keep this womanhearted fool out of –"

Huitsak spat through his fingers. "I would take a hundred of him before you!"

Vuchak's ire faltered, caught off-guard in spite of himself. "And what does he do for you that I don't?"

"He makes them WELCOME!" The word, *tlihiya*, which had such a fine and inviting sound, emerged from Huitsak's mouth as searing blasphemy. "He is charming, delightful, pleasant-seeming to every eye – he has them kissing glasses and blowing on the dice as surely as the best of Addie's women – and he does it all while YOU sit sulking and brooding like a robbed hen. And since you have refused to make yourself agreeable, or to learn their language, or to craft even the slightest reputation as a profit-maker or a broker of agreements –"

That was insult beyond bearing. As if Vuchak should strive to be anything like Wo-Bat the procurer of worthless animals, or Way-Waiting, who paid to put his name in the mouths of every ferryman and river-rat within three days' ride! "I am an *atodak*, not some two-tongued coyote," Vuchak said, full of righteousness, "and this is how you presume to punish me for –"

He was startled in spite of himself as Huitsak slammed his open palm on the table. "Idiot, this is how I presume to save your worthless hide!"

Vuchak had missed a step somewhere, or else brought a knife to a wrestling-match. "... from what?"

Huitsak's hand rose to wipe an invisible pain from his forehead. "You know very well that Addie's second-mouth is lined with cougar's teeth, and now you two have violently frustrated her favorite servant, who also serves Mother Opéra herself. What do you think is going to happen if I leave you here?"

Addie wouldn't, though – surely not. But the thought trickled into Vuchak's mind like cold water on an empty stomach: he couldn't promise that she wouldn't *allow* it to happen. And he couldn't promise himself anything about Faro's other mistress at all.

So then Faro had to die –

– except that that would only triple the size of the initial offense, not just inviting but *demanding* vengeance from one or both of those sinister women –

– which left no recourse except for... what, exactly?

Vuchak's forehead wrinkled, blazing anger crumbling into charred stupidity. "So we should go away and never come back?"

Huitsak waved the air to one side, as if the sound of Vuchak's voice were a bad smell. "No — be quiet and listen. Dulei's death, and the half's admission of his own guilt, has left us with a white-robed opportunity. I have learned from the Azahi that the half is wanted by the fishmen, who see in him some valuable skill with horses. So he will serve us twice. You will take him first as your excuse for going immediately to Atali'Krah. Once there, you will explain to the Eldest his second-value. If their vision agrees with mine, they may arrange some price for selling him to the fishmen, and your faithful service in delivering him to their grasp – along with your profound apology – must certainly unmake any hostility between you. Is this much clear?"

It was hard to know what to say then. It sounded so well-thought and perfectly arranged – just what any sensible person would expect from Huitsak – and yet failed to account for the fatal hole in his strategy.

"It's most clever," Vuchak said, not insincerely, "but *maga*, we can't – he may be hiding ten thousand diseases!"

Yet he must have said *but he may not wish to go with us,* as Huitsak's expression could only be awarded to an objection of stupendous irrelevance. "So he may!" Huitsak swore. "And the ground may open at any moment and swallow us whole – what of it?"

Vuchak shook his head. "But he could –"

Huitsak put his hands to the table, and leaned forward until he looked like an immense sweat-glazed bear. "Vuchak, where do you think you live? Do you imagine that these strangers we entertain lead wholesome lives? Did you see how that Halfwick coughed and sniffed and scratched his welts to our very faces? Did you fail to notice the closed door last month, to hear the slow death of the woman behind it? We have people of every conceivable kind here, all sharing glasses and beds and breathing-air and the gods only know what else. Do you think that half can possibly gift you with anything that hasn't been traded here before?"

"YES," Vuchak replied, "and if we take it home with us to Atali'Krah –"

"– then won't you already be sick with it before you get there?"

Vuchak stopped, stilled to his core. That wasn't guaranteed. Weisei would very-probably have immunity from his divine blood, but even ordinary people could be spared, randomly and for no reason known to any but the gods themselves...

... except that Vuchak was *a'Pue*, born under no star, possessed of no luck. If there was any illness that could befall him, any misfortune that he could be made to suffer, he would feel it.

His absent gaze returned to Huitsak. "That is all, then. You will wager our lives on your faith that he is clean."

Huitsak folded his arms. "For all that is truly necessary for the a'Krah, I will."

And that was right – that was right and correct and anything less was cowardice of the worst kind – and yet Vuchak felt not at all strengthened by the thought. He rubbed at his forehead. "The Kaia, and the Maia, and the Ara-Naure..."

"... are gone, their gods are dead or broken, and nothing more will be said of them." Huitsak straightened again. "And why do you suppose we are still strong in the world, so long after they have left it?"

"We are better than them!" Vuchak replied with instant passion. "We are nothing like the defenseless child-men of the Corn Woman, or the fanatic fools of the Dog Lady. We do not throw ourselves away for thoughtless reasons – and we do not cry and beg to our god after we have allowed death-breathing half-men to crawl into our beds!"

Huitsak tipped his head in conditional agreement. "We do not hide from the world, but take care to see that we inform ourselves of its every new development. We do not expect to dwell always in perfect safety, but knowingly accept those risks without which we cannot live in the way that our Grandfather has ordained. And we do not throw our people away for the sake of any single one of us, but expect that each single one of us is prepared to give everything of himself for the sake of his people."

This was indisputably so. It was not the only distinction between the a'Krah and the Ara-Naure, but it had been the last one — and it would hold true only so long as each one of Marhuk's people was willing to prove that it did. Vuchak would swear himself to the service of the a'Krah, or deserve *savash* for the rest of his meaningless life.

He put himself down to his knees then, and looked no further than the space between them. "*Maga*, I have been foolish and selfish and am undeserving of your grace. Tell me – assure me that I am called to this not for punishment, but because it is the best and most necessary service I can render, and I will do it for you gladly and – and at any cost." He put his upturned wrists out in the *ashet*, freely offering his life's blood, which no-one would convince him might not be required for the task.

There was a rhythmic heaviness in the air and the ground, which said that Huitsak was coming forward, but Vuchak kept his thoughts fixed until he felt himself taken by the arm – not at the wrist, not where he wore the silver manacle or the mark of the *atodak* underneath, but at the crook of his arm, just below the elbow, where he was nothing but himself – and pulled effortlessly up to standing.

His eye was then at level with Huitsak's shoulder, and read every detail of the thin white cloth and the twinings of the plaited black hair before it. "You will do this because it is important, and because it is necessary, and because it needs the best and most able among us. You are the strong heart which moves his royal blood, Vuchak, and between you is shared a single great purpose."

There was almost certainly some manipulation in that, some of the same sweetened suggestion as had been fed to Weisei before, but Vuchak would swallow it willingly and relish the taste. To be something more than the bitter keeper of an idiot son, to be respected – more than that, to respect himself — and more than that, to respect his *marka*, to not merely act the part but to actually feel for him the unbreakable, unendable pride and loyalty and death-scorning holy passion before which the bodies of thousands had crashed to earth at the hands of great *atodaxa* since time was counted... Vuchak would share cups with every bastard half ever born just to taste it once.

He sighed, letting his last ill-taken breath pass out of him, and drew the next with a clear mind. It filled his lungs with the aroma of hair oil and piñon smoke. "I will prove you right, *maga*. I will make it true. And I will... and I'm sorry for all that I've said and done to vex you."

Huitsak's blunt fingers left Vuchak's arm to knead the sinew of his shoulder. "The things I said about you were lies I told myself." He pushed back to compel them to share eyes again, and when Vuchak looked up, it was to a face full of flesh and wisdom. "Do you understand how to begin?"

Vuchak thoughts rose to see the whole of the task with bird-eyes, absorbing the purpose and order of each part. "I'll take Lavat's wagon; he won't want it much until spring. And to pull –"

Huitsak nodded. "See Fours for that – the half is commanded to use all that he has in our service, and that will include the two horses. Perhaps Fours will trade them for his mules; if not, pay him what he requires."

That was money Vuchak wouldn't see again, but it would buy something much more valuable. "I will. And Twoblood will give up the half at our first asking?"

"Yes, but see that you do it soon; every hour will find her less agreeable to the sound of the stick at her door. What else?"

Vuchak thought further forward, past Lavat and Fours and Twoblood, to Weisei and his list of needful things, and of what he might not have considered.

"*Maga*," Vuchak said then, "without for a moment questioning your vision... do you really think Winshin will be shown the man who took her son and not tear him to shreds?"

"*Shit*." Huitsak cast his gaze down and to one side, as if the answer might have been dropped on the floor. "Hakai!"

Vuchak startled and took two automatic steps backwards. Despite having long since fallen out of Vuchak's awareness, the blindfolded slave was still there by the corpse-box at the back of the room, and straightened to await his master's instruction.

Huitsak pointed up at the stair. "Leave off doing graces for Dulei's murder and fetch me the head of the white man responsible. You should find his body at the church."

In the slave's place, Vuchak would have been terrifically interested to know how he was meant to do that when the grave-woman would almost certainly be guarding the body, if not actually lying with it. But Hakai only set down his hammer and made the *ashet*. "Yes, *maga*." He picked up the saw at the far end of the table and departed up the stairs, silent-footed and unspeaking.

"Winshin might be comforted to know that he was a true-blooded Northman," Huitsak said then. "I understand they are rare now."

As it turned out, Vuchak had not been emptied of surprise after all. "What? That is – yes, *maga*, I will be sure to tell her... but how did you know?"

Huitsak tipped his head, left to right. "I prompted him to give me his hand, and found him as cold as meltwater. You will learn much more about the world's people, *atodak*, when you do not always hold yourself apart from them." His voice grew distant, as if his thoughts had scouted on ahead. "Regardless, see that you go quickly: he will mean more to her if he is still fresh when she receives him, and if I am going to buy the wrath of the Azahi, I want it well paid-for. Perhaps we can claim some misunderstanding..."

Huitsak still fixed his attention on Dulei's box, but Vuchak was occupied with the slave. Hakai had heard everything that had passed between the two of them – had seen Vuchak on his knees confessing himself! –and would keep the memory bright and polished next to the one he already had collected from the morning's shameful spectacle.

"*Maga*, let me take Hakai," Vuchak said, possessed by the idea as soon as it came to him. "Please – we will want a good man, and I see how well he serves you."

Huitsak clicked his teeth in surprise. "Him – an *ihi'ghiva*? Would you not rather have Viket, or one of the other –"

Vuchak had sworn himself to respect and loyalty, but impatience still wormed its way between them. "No, I don't want – it's not a strong back that we need, but a wise mind and a deft hand and – and a mouth that can speak to the half, besides which. Please, *maga* – I promise we will keep him well, and return him safely to you."

Huitsak lifted his head, reducing his two chins to just one, and stared hard down at him. "See that you do, or I will break the other side of your face. And why am I still looking at you, you goat-suckled irritant? Go, do it!"

"Yes, *maga*!" Stung to action, Vuchak made his *ashet*, turned and took the steps two at a time, his plaits flying freely behind him.

AND FOURS HAD so occupied himself with all of that, with cooking the salve and counting the teeth and calculating whether and when to go find whatever was left of Shea, that half the afternoon was gone before the obvious thought finally occurred to him.

Ki-Meh hadn't come – and of course he hadn't; Fours had discussed as much with Ah-Shi-Shah the day before.

So the horses had been standing hungry in their filth since yesterday.

The swearing he'd done at Twoblood's was nothing compared to what he said then, volubly and in three languages, as he ran to the barn.

It was still a shambles: stalls half kicked in, doors and tie-posts all but torn off, the whole thing reeking of stale urine and unskipped manure, the walls echoing with the plaintive hybrid whinnies of two ravenous mules and one left-over black gelding as soon as Fours let himself inside.

They were all right – by the Artisan's grace, none of them seemed to have suffered anything worse than a day's neglect – but the needless, thoughtless suffering of those poor creatures was somehow his worst sin yet. Fours' whole body seeped with remorse as he filled their buckets and doled out their rations, until his face was dripping and his clothes wet through.

He was poorly built for the work, and for too long had relied on human hands to do it for him. By the time he had pumped and hauled forty gallons of water, forked out three piles of hay in the corral and turned them out to it, and then raked out and inspected the battered stalls, afternoon had turned to full night.

But the work made him feel better, used him up for a necessary and appreciated purpose, and by the time he led them back inside, things were almost all right again. The smaller of the two mules – whom in the privacy of his own mind he had taken to calling Bonbon – had pulled one of her shoes loose, but that was all right. He would remember to visit Walla-Dee's daughter tomorrow to see when that could be corrected, and make a note of the date in case the mule sold before her next full shoeing.

It was a pleasant and ordinary thought, one which so preoccupied him that Fours had already picked up his case and let himself back into his shop before he realized that he hadn't needed to unlock the door.

He froze three steps into the dark. He never left it open, not with a roomful of amphibious cosmetics upstairs and a flooded cellar below. His key fell forgotten to the floor.

"Oh, relax, Fours – paranoia doesn't become you."

She had scarcely done with *oh* before Fours' eyes tracked the light from the far window, which filtered the moon's early rising through the dirty curtains, illuminating the drape of violet silk beside his counter.

He clutched his case tighter, blanketed by blind relief, skewered by unshaped fear. "I, I don't – it isn't – you shouldn't be here," he stammered. Literally *should not be here*, not up and about and teasing him as if none of it had ever happened.

"And what kind of a welcome is that?" she demanded – speaking Ardish, which she didn't generally. Something rattled against wood. "Did you think you were rid of me? After all we've done together? Now be sensible and put on a light; I'll have some glue."

Fours didn't use lights after dusk, not in any room with a window. It reminded passers-by that there was someone at home, and that was attention he could live without.

But he set his case down and shuffled obediently through his dusty second-hand labyrinth to his collection of lamps and candles. His head spun, but not from the smell of kerosene.

"You can't," he said, softly, stupidly, and mostly to himself.

"What are you mumbling about?"

"You can't – you can't just carry on acting as if nothing happened," he said, his fingers fumbling for a light. "Say what you want to say and let's be done with it."

"Why Fours," she said in a honeyed, wounded tone, "whatever do you mean?"

His temper ignited as quickly as the wax match in his hands. "I sold you out!" he snapped as the damn thing fizzled. "I went to Opéra the minute I saw her and told her exactly what you were doing, and do you know, I'm not the least bit sorry for it. I'd, I'd do it again, even, and I'd tell Faro, or Twoblood, or the Azahi, or anyone who wants to know exactly what you're after, and I won't care one lick what they do to you when they find out. I – *merde*!" he swore as a second match flared and failed, shaking his burnt fingers and reaching angrily to strike a third. "– I'm done with fronting for you, that's all, so if you're half clever you won't come around here for anything BUT glue, because I... I..."

Fours paused as the little stick he'd thrown into the lamp caught the wick, suffusing the nearer parts of the room with a warm, smoky glow.

That was not Shea.

That was her dress, right enough – dye-streaked and bloodied and lying folded over the crook of Faro's arm.

He smiled, a flash of sharp teeth, and spoke then in his own voice. "Why Fours, I have never been so proud."

Fours' heart went cold like a fizzled match. "Faro, you didn't – where is she? What did you do with her?"

"Oh, but you don't care anything about that Fours, not now. You've made your choice – splendidly, if I may say – and your Mother is my Mother, and your family, shall we say, is mine."

She was dead, then. She was.

Fours bit his tongue until he thought it would bleed, just to keep from saying it aloud: Opéra's soul was as barren as her womb, and she was a mother to nobody – not even Faro.

"It was masterfully done, Fours, really it was: in the morning I gave you the task, and by nightfall you had not only got your kin to do all your dirty work, but even set it up to take the fall for you! But why did you leave out the most important part? Mother wouldn't have fired at him if you'd just told her what he was!"

Because if he'd told Opéra that part, if he'd said that Elim was a horseman, she would have realized that Shea was not merely engaged in garden-variety misbehavior, but treasonously plotting to steal a critically valuable prize. Stupid as it was to think so, Fours in the panic of the moment had thought that if he only said that much, *there is an earth-person who is wanted for murder and Champagne is trying to help him escape*, she would have been let off with a proverbial slap and a lecture.

Needless to say, he had been considerably wrong about that.

He looked down at the lamp in his hands, and twisted his answer to fit the facts. "I wanted her gone," he said. "And – and I couldn't have planned it – I didn't think for a minute that Mother was coming to visit – but when she put me in the honored place at her side, and when I heard Ch – Shea begin to tell those wretched lies about having murdered the man herself – just so that Mother would let her free before she was punished for it! And I knew that she was going to tell about your present and take all the credit for herself, and I..."

It was a two-colored thing to say, only half untrue. Because as he had squatted there on the shore and listened to Shea incriminate herself piece by lying piece, even as Opéra took the gun and aimed it squarely at her, Fours' only thought had tasted of bitter coppery outrage. She had the nerve to drop her life in the dice-cup and toss it out on the table – as if it were her private property, as if it were of no consequence or value to anyone but herself! – and for no possible gain but the truth about a boy, a man, who didn't need or want it in the first place, and whose sole overwhelming desire could not have been more ambitious than to be let free to glean whatever scant joys he could from his paltry lot in life: an honest want that Champagne understood or respected no more in him than she ever had in Fours.

"... I wished that she were dead."

The floorboards squeaked, accompanied by the rustling of the dress. Fours did not resist when the lamp was taken from his hands and set on a shelf, nor when he felt the arm slipped around his shoulders, pressing his body sideways against its new perfume-smelling neighbor.

"Oh, Fours, I am sorry – it's always hard when someone close to us outlives themselves." This, as if the dispatch of one's own siblings were as common as the death of a pet. Maybe for Faro it was. "But be cheerful, old boy! You see here how I've brought you a keepsake to remember it – her, I mean. And look just there: do you know what that is?"

Fours did not look at the bloodied dress, but had to follow Faro's point. In the poor single light, a half-full cloth sack and some sort of tool was just visible at the counter's foot.

It took him longer than it should have to recognize Elim's bag and the rifle leaned up behind it, and longer than that to guess at their purpose. "For me?"

Fours felt the abrupt half-laugh in Faro's frame, stifled before it could be given voice. "Why, after a fashion, it is! Because I so appreciate all your good work, you see, I've decided: you simply must have the honor of putting the finishing touches on our dear Mother's gift."

Fours' mind lurched like a machine without oil. "Gift? But I thought – weren't they going to give him to the a'Krah?"

"Well spotted!" Faro replied. "And what do you think the a'Krah will do with him?"

There was something big here, but Fours could not grasp it. He stared blankly at the rifle. "They'll take him back to their homeland, and give him to – to whoever Dulei belonged to, and then they'll kill him."

"And that would be a great waste, wouldn't it? If only it could be prevented somehow..."

He was driving at something, but Fours was busy holding deathly still, avoiding even the slightest touch from the dress on Faro's arm. "You can't, though. The Azahi has already made his decision, and anything you do to them here will only –"

Faro pivoted to the side. Fours automatically flinched, and looked up at his falsely-incredulous face. "Why, Fours, what can you be saying? Had we better do it somewhere else, then?"

So that was it: Faro would see the funeral party out of Island Town and then have them slaughtered somewhere along the way. And Fours' first wild, dreadful thought was that Faro meant to frame him, be rid of him somehow, and had set someone to listening outside for just this moment, when he would be caught conceiving the unborn murder of the a'Krah. "I won't – I won't do it," he stammered.

Faro burst out laughing – horrible, gale-force peals of mirth that would surely wake the whole town. Fours cringed at the sound.

"*Bless you, Fours,*" he said in Marín, wiping a false tear from his eye. "I wouldn't trust you to kill a trapped rat. You just sell trinkets to the damned, just like you always have, and leave the rest to me."

Fours had never had so much empathy for the rat.

And he had never liked that use of his nickname. In Ardish, it happened to sound like the plural of the number four, which he had always translated literally, so that in Marín he was *Cuatros*. But there, just there when Faro spoke the Ardish sounds with the Marín accent, it became *Forza*, which meant *it forces*.

He hardly needed the reminder.

But Faro gave him no time to dwell on it: he clapped him once on the shoulder and strolled back to toss the dress on the counter. Then he stood there, hands at his hips, and looked around the shadowed recesses of the shop for inspiration. "Now then! What can we provide to speed them on their way?"

Fours tried to follow his thinking. The bag and the gun had to figure into it, but that couldn't be the right answer. "The mules," he said, after a moment's mud-mired thought. "And their grain, tack... I've only got the one collar, though..."

Faro's tone sharpened as suddenly as a papercut. "Do you have what they need or don't you?"

Fours glanced up at the warning in Faro's finely-crafted face. "I'd – I should – I mean, yes, as long as their cart's meant for single-harness, and I don't – I can't imagine why they'd have anything else..."

The stiffness in Faro's jaw thawed in an instant; he smiled, his natural teeth a jagged contrast to the splendor of his human costume, and thrust his hands into his pockets. "Excellent! So you'll give them everything they require, expeditiously and without any dickering, and do you know what I have for you then?"

Fours tried to look interested, though his heart surely couldn't take even one more surprise today. "What?"

One of Faro's hands emerged and tossed a something small and bright at him. It hit Fours' chest as he missed the catch, and fell into his hand thereafter. A tobacco tin, battered, unremarkable, and half full of –

Fours opened it, and stopped at his first whiff. "Blacktail." He stared at the cigarettes, waiting for an understanding that didn't come. The blacktail trade was controlled by the island-dwelling Castamarín, whose vast saltwater trade network could scarcely wait to devour the crumbling provinces of the Emboucheaux. "You've been double-dealing."

"Nonsense!" Faro scoffed, but his heels rapped sharply on the floorboards as he returned to Fours' side. "Just a lucky find, that's all. Now you keep that safe – you can get a nice price for those, you know." He plucked the tin from Fours' unresisting fingers and deposited it into the pocket of his worn buckskin vest. "And see what you can do to get our little pilgrimage safely on its way, and – oh, but I hardly need to remind you of the value of discretion in this business, do I?" Faro let his hand travel languidly up Fours' chest and throat and to his chin, which Fours was compelled to raise until he was staring straight into Faro's vitreous inkwell eyes. "You always have had a marvelous talent for fostering innocence."

She was not really his daughter, of course. For reasons best known to Herself, the Artisan had not granted the gifts of sex to lesser-born mereaux.

And Fours was content with that, would never have sought more than that... except that when he had followed the little stifled whimpers coming from behind the scorched sacristy door and found her there, huddled and staring up at him with her vast white-edged eyes so sharply distinct from the rest of her solemn soot-dark features, it seemed not just natural but inevitable that he should pick her up, and wipe her nose, and see what could be done to find a place for the two of them somewhere in the still-smoking afterbirth of the new world's first day.

Small wonder that Faro, who sensed love as so much blood in the water, had so quickly taken her hostage.

But that was all right – by Fours' own doing it was still all right, because she'd grown up strong and good and so unaccountably splendid, without ever once feeling the knife at her neck. To her, Faro was just another passingly-familiar face, and as long he got what he wanted, he would never be more than that.

So Día would go on sharing her virtue with the indigent and the dead, and Fours would go on mutilating his soul. And when at last it left him, he did not believe for a second that it would be spared any of whatever torment might be waiting... but as long as she lived, she would remember him as a good man and a loving father – as the person he had meant to be – and that was a better and surer reward than any that had ever been promised by one wishful thinker to another.

"I understand," Fours said. "It won't be a problem."

After all, he'd abetted the deaths of so many already... another three or four would hardly make a difference.

"Splendid!" Faro clapped him heartily on the shoulder, and from his pocket produced one final curiosity: a pair of broken human veneers. "Now how about that glue?"

CHAPTER SIXTEEN
DEPARTING, UNRECOGNIZED

IT WAS THE right thing to do.

Twoblood hunched forward in her chair, her gaze still fixed on the half-man's blistered back, and chewed her thumbnail with vicious frustration.

It was the right thing to do, and the others' disapproval only confirmed that she had been right in doing it. For one thing, the very fact that Fours had dared to take such a tone with her earlier, even as he so clearly suffered in the grip of some unfathomable madness, said plainly that his opinion was a disordered one, that his persistent refusal to pass even a word of the truth was now poisoning him as surely as a blockage of the bowels.

Nor was the cold silence of his cowbird to be counted for anything. What right did Día have to speak about sense or mercy for anyone else when she had none for herself? Fair enough while she had still been a fosterling child, but even a cowbird had to know when to leave the finches' nest and seek out its own kind. The fact that she still sat and served and stayed *here* of all places – she, who was pure-bred, who was one of tens of thousands exactly like her! – was proof enough that she didn't know what was best for herself, nevermind anyone else.

And as for the Azahi, and his most obnoxious brand of indirect questioning un-criticism...

... well, if he didn't like what Twoblood did in his absence, then maybe next time he would do the sensible thing and allow for the closure of the western gate as well – as Twoblood had wanted, as common sense dictated. Either that, or he could try his hand at finding himself a new Second, one from some undiscovered tribe with the gift of all-ordering perfection.

No-one could say that Twoblood didn't care for her fellow one-of-a-kinds – not with any measure of truth. But she would not be seen to lose even an hour's sleep for their opinions.

Instead, she heaved herself out of her chair, walked to the cage in the corner, and pulled out the plate of food that had sat untouched for hours now.

"You're an ungrateful son of a bitch," Twoblood said to the back of the man inside, who might or might not have been asleep. Nobody could eat after him, so now it would go to waste.

But he looked like he could be trusted to stay still for the time it would take to toss it out at the garbage-heap and clean the dish. Twoblood went to do just that –

– and opened her door to a plain brown dog, sitting there as politely as if it hadn't yet had time to knock. She – it – broke into a panting grin.

"Uh, uh, uh..."

Twoblood dropped the plate.

She would have been glad to live her life without seeing another dog ever again. And this one had the nerve to sit there, attentive, wagging, as if it would have the whole town understand that she, Tu Voh, loved her as dearly as if they shared blood.

Nothing could be further from the truth. Twoblood lunged forward to kick it.

But the dog declined to cringe or even to blink, as if it were too stupid to understand what she intended... or as if it understood perfectly what Twoblood herself had failed to put across today, and knew better than to shrink from her irascible posturing. "Uh, uh, uh..."

She stared down at the dog. It lifted its head, and then broke eye contact to sniff at the spilled mess between her feet.

Twoblood looked out again at the town beyond her door – at the little pinpoints of light and the trails of smoke rising from La Soleada's proud silhouette, and the roof-fires of the Moon Quarter licking brightly at the emerging stars, and La Saciadería's red-lit windows, signaling the beginning of another night of sordid and pleasurable entertainments – and all of it carrying contentedly on without her.

Twoblood ran her tongue over her teeth, considering.

"Well, come on," she said, and stepped aside to shoo the dog in. It – she – lunged forward, and as she set to wolfing down cold squash-bake and beans, Twoblood closed the door on everything else.

THERE WAS EVERYTHING still left to do, and the night's first quarter was already gone. Its loss would have to be made up by exceptional efficiency, and Vuchak wasted neither a step nor a thought as he ordered his mind. Lavat first, who could be made or paid to pull the wagon to the cellar for loading, then south to Fours to start him on the harnessing and animal provisions, and then – only after everything else was done – to Twoblood's.

And before that, before Halfwick's slave could contaminate even so much as Vuchak's thoughts, he would take care of the first and most needful of tasks.

"Pipat," he called on his way up the road, "where do I find you?"

He could already see the firelight spilling from her open window into the street, and the telltale interruptions in its glow.

But it had made a great noise as it ate the wood, or else her lack of hearing was explained by some other part of her work. Vuchak halted before her door-curtain, the aroma of her buckwheat stew seducing his nose, and spoke clearly this time. "Pipat, where do I find you?"

But there was no answer, nor any reason for its absence. When he broke etiquette to look through the window, she was on her knees before the mealing-stone, her back turned as she rolled the hand-stone back and forth over something – sunflower seeds, maybe – and ignored Vuchak as if he were as silent and unseeable as her husband's ghost.

Vuchak stared, appalled past breathing, at the supple motions of her back and shoulders, which spoke to him on behalf of her indisposed front.

The first forward-leaning movement said that she had already heard all of what he had done, and accepted whatever stories she had been told as the truth.

The second one then added that she had her own place to consider, and could not be seen with a man who had fallen outside the bounds of public esteem.

And the third, deeper and more pronounced than the rest, which caused some of her long silver-streaked hair to fall before her shoulder, said that his truth or feelings had no part to play in her decision. There was to be no word, no sign, not so much as a bag of corn-cakes left by the door to acknowledge that he had ever entered her home or might be wanted there again. He was dismissed.

Vuchak held still, the surrounding neighborhood house-noises as good as a thousand watching eyes, and felt himself bitten again by that same caustic, venomous anger that had taken him outside Twoblood's house.

Savash did not apply to a man's wife or still-growing children, who were as living extensions of himself... but there lay all the error in his thinking. This was not his house, and that was not his wife, and if she had been content enough to serve him in the manner of a wife – to cook his meat and spend his money and take his seed – that only showed his mistake in thinking of her as anything but a finer kind of whore.

But he would be perfectly glad to correct his error, to behave as a whore-user did when his woman displeased him. Vuchak started forward to rip the door-curtain down and throw it on the fire, to pick up the stew-pot and hurl its boiling contents over her proud body, to seize her husband's knife from the wall and drive it into the earth between her legs so that the first people to answer her screams would find her pinned to the ground by the crotch of her dress and know her for what she was –

– to prove in the space of ten unreasoning seconds that Huitsak was wrong to have ever trusted him.

Vuchak took a step backwards, blood pounding behind his eyes, and stood fast to weather the evil assault of his other self – the one that betrayed his *maga* and derided his *marka* and failed every day without serving, the one that now clenched his heart in a merciless grip and needed only to crush it past beating to have him in there ravaging his woman like the worst and filthiest kind of Eaten. She had made him into a whore-user, but she wouldn't make him into that.

He seized that idea, picked up that nobler second-anger like a fresh weapon – she wanted to make him into the man she thought he was, but he was *better* than that, and her – except that his worldly hands desperately needed a purpose before they seized that curtain and every damnation behind it.

So he put them to the braid at his left ear and pulled out the feathered tie, unraveling the plaited twists with hard yanks and shaking fingers. He had no sooner seized the woven leather thong she had made for him than ripped it free and hurled it through the window into the fire. His hands were matched in their faithful service by his feet, which did not allow him to stand there inviting the abyss, but turned to walk and then run away from the house and all temptation, back towards his newer, better purpose.

THE ONLY CERTAINTY about the fire was that it had started in the church.

But it seemed likely that the wooden pews, pushed and stacked so high against the single great southern door, had ultimately served too well as a barricade, holding fast to their purpose even as the inferno consumed them, refusing to yield to ash until long after those inside had surrendered their lives.

It was through the resulting empty doorway that the man, Hakai, walked with silent feet, shuddering just briefly as he crossed the threshold. He passed by the stone well and continued forward until he stood in the center of the crossing.

Its northern wing ended with a small, closed door, which would open to a storing-room called the sacristy. To the west lay three shallow steps up to the scorched stone floor, and the altar which crowned it. Starlight beamed in through the broken wall to the east.

The man, Hakai, stood still and listened – to the far-distant sound of voices coming from the Moon Quarter, and beneath that, to the night breeze whispering across the ragged edges of the church's eastern gap, and beneath that, to the sound of a single human being, breathing evenly in sleep.

He turned towards the altar, the saw ready in his hand.

And stopped.

And turned more, and then returned, not to the doorway but to the well, and put his hand down to touch its broad stone lip. There was a drip of water from far down inside.

The man, Hakai, thereafter sat at its rounded edge, and tapped on the dry stone interior with the saw's jagged tip – one-two-three, one-two-three.

A ragged whisper echoed up the chamber: "Día?"

He set down the saw. "Only Hakai."

A pained sigh rippled up the well-pipe. "Oh, Mister Hakai, whatever can you want from me now?" The voice was weak and wet and profoundly weary. "I am hardly in a position to do you any services now."

The man, Hakai, folded his hands. "I am sorry to hear you feeling so poorly, Miss Shea. I would not trouble you now, except for your advice."

This did not impress. "And why should I give you anything? Why should I give anyone anything now?"

The man, Hakai, tipped his head. "I could not say, Miss Shea... though it seems to me that that lead in your lung must pain you terribly. I think you would need someone with a gift for earthworks to remove it for you." His brows lifted behind his blindfold. "It is a great shame that there are so few left in the world."

There was a long silence from the well. "... and what is it you want?"

The man, Hakai, looked out past the crossing of the church, to the closed sacristy door. "The head of the white man responsible for the murder of Dulei Marhuk. My master said that I might find him here."

"Your master is mistaken."

The man, Hakai, tipped his head. "Would you have it done now, Miss Shea? You know I am no doctor."

There was then a second silence, impeded only by the sound of low, labored breathing. "Well," the voice said, its whispers growing increasingly hoarse with effort. "I know that you are an honest man, Mister Hakai. Give me your word, and I'll give you my help."

"My service to you will be second only to that which I am bound to provide for my master," he said.

"... good enough," the voice agreed. "But pay attention; I won't repeat myself."

The man, Hakai, then listened intently to the dictates of the voice in the water.

IT WAS DARK when Elim woke, roused by the rapping at the door. *"Kien me kiere?"* the speckled mule snapped.

"Vuchak dela'Krah," came a man's reply.

"Espera." There was that squeak again – the speckled mule getting out of her chair – and her heavy-booted

footsteps, which ended not with the opening of the door, but with a sharp kick at Elim's cell.

He startled, staring up at the hostile shadow above. "*Te-levanta,*" she said, and by the window's faint light, he could just about make out the upward-summoning motion of her hand.

So maybe it was time to go, then. Elim gathered his aching limbs, and rose stiffly to his feet.

But the speckled mule made no move to open his door. She stood there and beckoned him forward.

Elim squinted, but could not tell whether she had her gun. He shuffled nervously up to the bars.

She raised her hand, and for a flinching instant, he thought she would reach through and strike him. But no – she only put one finger to her own face, tapping under her left eye. And then at her ear. And finally, when he was too thoroughly confused to see it coming, she reached in and clasped his wrist – not hard, not to pull at him, but the way you would hold onto somebody who was venturing out over thin ice... just in case.

Then it got easier to translate.

Watch.

Listen.

Stay alive.

Elim stared at her, wishing hard for better light. He couldn't make her out as anything but the vaguest black-on-black silhouette: the hybrid curl of her hair above her shoulders, the rumpled collar of her work-shirt, the strange bald patch on the left side of her scalp. But apparently it was only here in the unrelieved dark that he could finally, properly see her... and only now, at the last possible minute, that he began to wish he'd understood things much, much sooner.

He clasped her wrist, a pledge given in silence between iron bars. She held onto him, one two-colored body joined with another.

I will.

Then the speckled mule – the lady – no, the sheriff – let go and went to answer her visitor, pausing just long enough to retrieve her hat from the desk. Elim steadied his mind and rubbed his wrist, readying himself for whatever was about to come through that door, and whatever else might be waiting for him outside it.

WHAT HAD STARTED badly, with Vuchak's visit to Pipat's house, continued in the same way thereafter. Lavat was nowhere to be found, and his wife wouldn't hear of having the wagon taken without his approval – as if he were going to have something to say to Huitsak about it! – and then, once Vuchak had invited her to console herself in its absence by riding her husband for a change, and had personally taken up the twin lances and pulled it all the sweating miserable way to the cellar for loading, it was down to Fours' house to be regaled with the great story of the mule with the loose shoe, and how it couldn't be given at Huitsak's command or anyone else's until it had had its foot fixed, and how there was no substitute for it but Halfwick's horse, as if anyone would want a flighty delicate thin-skinned tenderfoot *horse* for the work ahead.

But nevermind: it was a single-pull wagon anyway, so they could harness the horse and pack up the mule and be reasonably sure of getting to Atali'Krah with at least one of the two.

Vuchak contented himself with that, and used the inconvenience to strongarm Fours into delivering both of them up to the cellar for hitching and loading. Which left Vuchak free in the meantime to do the worst of jobs, and fetch that one remaining animal.

He was not expecting the dog, though. Medium-sized, with stand-up ears and thick hair, it lay asleep in front of Twoblood's door, and woke at the sound of Vuchak's footsteps. It did not snarl or bark, but only sat up and watched him, tail wagging once or twice as he reached over its head and tapped at the door.

"*Who wants me?*" came Twoblood's voice from inside.

"*Vuchak of the a'Krah.*" He folded his silvered arms to make an appropriate impression. What he had done here in daylight hours had been an act of lunacy, and he would make sure Twoblood understood that there was nothing of solidarity between them.

"*Wait,*" she said.

From inside, wood squeaked and boot-heels clopped down hard on the floor. Then there was a silence, which stretched out longer and longer, until Vuchak's fist itched to take to the door again. Finally he could hear movement again, and this time it ended correctly.

Twoblood stood there, her clothes and freckle-spattered face still rumpled with sleep, and eyed him up and down. "*You have a turkey's nerve,*" she grunted, and stalked back inside, her furry sister following.

"*And you have a lousy guard dog,*" Vuchak replied, and went in after her.

And for a moment, he wished that Faro had blinded him outright, so that he would have been excused from seeing the great misshapen giant in the cell. It loomed huge and horrible – a monstrous, massive wreck of a man, Wi-Chuck's bastard brother – with matted hair and rough, ugly features and not the slightest trace of reasoning sensibility in its eyes.

And it hardly reacted as Twoblood unlocked its door.

"*Well?*" Twoblood said. "*Are you going to tie him, or do you have a slave coming to do that for you?*"

Shit. Vuchak cursed the thoughtlessness that had kept him from shaking a rope out of Fours on his way over.

"*I am no mother-clutching Ikwei,*" he answered, "*and I can handle him very well without one. You!*" he barked in Ardish, with an attention-getting snap of his fingers. "*Go here!*"

The blistered creature stared at him, stupid, unblinking, but finally understood him well enough to trudge forward. "*So did you come for cruelty, or only for sport?*" Twoblood asked from behind.

"*Neither,*" Vuchak answered, never taking his eyes off the half. The blisters would have come from the sun, not the pox.

"*Then why take him tonight? You see his condition –*"

"*I do see,*" Vuchak said, "*and thank you for it, and will keep him exactly as you have made him: burnt and spent and too miserable to think of bashing my head in the first time my back is turned. – Go out,*" he commanded.

The beast scrutinized the open doorway, and then looked at Twoblood, who assented with a jerk of her head. The half shuffled obediently out.

The dog turned to follow, but Twoblood moved first, and held it fast by the neck. "*Mind him well, crow-man,*" she said, with a tone that hoped the half would find the chance to crack his skull open anyway.

"*I will do as I like, mule-blood,*" Vuchak replied, and did not wait to be escorted to the door.

The door, in turn, did not wait to slam shut behind him.

But that left the matter of tying the half, and Vuchak had no tools and nothing to do it with. The two of them stood there in the street as Vuchak considered waiting there, or going around to the forge to see if Walla-Dee might have left some rope, and finally decided on walking his odious charge up the road towards the whorehouse cellar, where at least he could be tethered to the back of the wagon.

Vuchak pulled out his knife, and pointed with his chin. "*Go out,*" he said again.

Yet although he looked at the knife and its direction, the half only continued staring at the red-lit windows.

That couldn't be for any lack of understanding: he had just obeyed the same words without difficulty. "You bastard, I said *go out!*" And he jabbed the half's arm hard with the tip of his knife.

That got better results.

"*Ga-damyu!*" the half swore, stepping sharply back to slap a hand over his wounded part. Vuchak took an identical backwards step, promising with the knife in his right hand what would happen if the half did not follow the obscene pointing of his left.

Gradually, the half seemed to understand the new order of things, and began walking.

Which left Vuchak free to drop to a squat and hurriedly rub his knife and hands over with fresh dirt. He kept his eye on the half as he said a quick prayer, tossed a bit of earth over both his shoulders, and then sprang back up to his feet, lengthening his stride to catch up with the prisoner.

It was going to be a long trip.

And it promised to be made longer still. They had not consumed even a quarter of the road before someone came hurrying out from the Moon Quarter, stooped with sacks and bags. "Vichi! Vichi, don't go without me!"

This, loud enough to secure the attention of anyone on the roof who hadn't already stopped his meal to watch the shameful proceedings below.

Vuchak held fast to his promise to Huitsak, and did not say even one of the nine things that leapt to mind. "Weisei, why are you" – nevermind; it was just as well – "did you bring any rope?"

"Of course!" Weisei replied, dumping the whole load with a relieved gasp. "You think I wouldn't – oh."

He had no sooner straightened than stared up at the half with wide, solemn eyes.

Vuchak took a perverse pleasure in that. "And this is to be our fine and loyal traveling-friend," he said. "What do you think of that?"

Weisei's brow furrowed, his attention still fixed on the half's empty features. "I think I shared drinks with him, a night or two ago. He didn't seem very happy then – I don't know why – but he looked a deal better than he does now." Weisei glanced over. "Vichi, doesn't he have any proper clothes? Or shoes?"

"How should I know?" Vuchak snapped, falling fast into a world where Weisei had willingly contaminated himself and only just now bothered to mention it. "Am I his mother? Am I to chew his food as well?"

Irritation creased Weisei's face. "Well, I will do it, then: he can't go to Grandfather looking like that!" And without waiting for an answer, he turned and ran off back down the road, shouting up at the fires as he went. "Hey, Oyachen! Is Deidalei there? I will buy from him, if he can find me quickly!"

Which left Vuchak keeping guard over a pile of baggage and a murderous slave.

They stood there awhile, Vuchak watching the half, and the half watching the ground between his two-colored feet. Presently, he ventured to speak. "*Huerz-zil?*"

"Be quiet," Vuchak said.

Nothing more was said for a long time. The silence left Vuchak's thoughts to ripen like so much unattended fruit, which was soon crawled over by worries and second-thoughts of every kind.

What if Huitsak had meant what he said to the Azahi? In a way, the journey to Atali'Krah was the least-worrying part of it. There was this hulking swine here, who might have diseases and who certainly did have murder on his mind, and there would be thieves and broken men and twisted *marrouak* prowling out from the ruins of Merin-Ka... but those were known things, understandable things. Which kind of Huitsak would be waiting for them when they returned to Island Town, and what further bargains would he have made in their absence?

And who said you were meant to return at all?

At long last, Vuchak heard the sound of hooves and wheels, and moved so that he could see without taking his eyes off of Halfwick's slave.

And was most gratified to see his own slave, Hakai, coming down the road with their caravan. The horse had been hitched to the wagon, as Vuchak had wanted, and the mule dressed and burdened, leaving empty space in the wagon-bed next to Dulei's coffin. Huitsak's blindfolded *ihi'ghiva* walked with the horse's reins given to his right hand, leading the mule and carrying a small cloth sack with his left. Something was dripping from the bottom of the bag.

Vuchak made the sign of a provident god at the sight. How splendid it was to receive more than expected, having been so long accustomed to less! "Well served," he said, and meant it. "Watch him while I –"

"*Huerz-zil?*" the half said again. His eyes, fixed on the coffin, looked livelier and more dangerous than before. "*Huerz-zil? Ah'ont go-til azíem, ah'ont –*"

Before Vuchak could ask what he meant, Hakai opened the sack and held it out to the half – who took one look at its contents and jerked away as violently as if he'd been struck.

So Hakai had gotten past the grave-woman after all.

"Tie him," Vuchak snapped. "There, use that rope there and tie his wrists, before he thinks better of it."

"Yes, sir." Hakai did as he was asked, as quickly and as efficiently as anyone could have wanted.

Vuchak was sorry about Halfwick, and yet he felt an irrational satisfaction at having afflicted his slave. He would keep the bag well at hand, he decided, and display its contents as necessary.

In the meantime, the half stood there as his rope-scorched wrists were tied once more. His staring at the wet-bottomed sack was interrupted by a nicker from the horse, who pulled the cart three steps forward to thrust his nose under the half's arm.

The half's surprise fast melted into something else: he nudged the horse's shoulder with his side, and spoke soft-edged words.

"… *Ax? Hei, budí – joudchú gidal mixtúp innis? Yarekin yumait com-wit?*"

This was strange, but well enough: if the half was thinking of the horse, then he wasn't thinking of violence or slaughter.

So Vuchak let him alone and reached up to the wagon's raised seat to retrieve his marks. His hand delighted at the feel of his great leather-wrapped spear, its long bone head ground to deadly sharpness, its four-clawed neck crafted from his first slain cougar, and its every part made by his hand exclusively. His arm welcomed the weight of his round rawhide shield, strung at the sides and bottom with the same royal crows' feathers used to make his *marka*'s cloak. It was painted in the interior with the single eye and the yellow silhouette of the water-dancer underneath, which said to every beholder that the shield and its bearer belonged to Weisei Marhuk, and could not be destroyed except in his service.

They were satisfying, solid-feeling reminders of Vuchak's best purpose, the one larger than his own life, and he resolved to keep a strong hold on both.

"Look, look!" Weisei called, rabbiting back out of the Moon Quarter with prizes in hand. "See, I found a hat for him, and a *serape* that will almost do." He set both into the wagon before allowing Hakai's waiting hands to help him on with his cloak. "And Deidalei sold me leather as easily as that, and cheaply besides, and I already have needles and a thong and can make new shoes for him while we are on our way –"

And for once Vuchak let him go right on talking as Hakai finished loading the bags and tethered the half to the back of the wagon. At last they began to move, down the deserted street and out through the western gate, and thereafter took the first steps out of Island Town, towards home, with only a dog's echoing barks to mark their passing.

INTERIM

BUT ALTHOUGH ITS limbs had long since stiffened, and its lower portions purpled with settled blood, the body on the slab persisted in its chill, and declined in spite of every present circumstance to warm to room temperature.

Glossary

A – Ardish, the primary language of Eadan settlers

AB – Ardish slang used mostly or exclusively on the Bravery

AN – Ardish slang used primarily by Northerners

F – Fraichais, a language spoken by freshwater mereaux

M – Marín, a trade language, the international standard for business

K – ei'Krah, the language of the a'Krah people

a'Pue (K) – literally "people of no star"; children born during the Pue'Va. Since they were not born under the auspices of any constellation, they are considered highly unlucky.

absquatulate (AB) – to leave in a hurry, to flee

addlepated (AB) – confused, muddled

ashet (K) – a gesture of deep respect, performed by lowering the gaze and extending the arms, wrists upturned.

atodak (K) – partnered with a marka

bangtail (AB) – an exceptionally fast horse; one fit for racing beefed (AB) – killed, murdered

betty lamp (A) – a simple grease-burning lamp, shaped like a gravy boat and often hung.

bit – a unit of currency, based on the international pearl standard. It is worth about 1/12 of an Eadan dollar, or roughly eight cents.

blacktail – a tropical pepper and a mild stimulant, frequently dried and smoked to relieve respiratory congestion and inflammation. Also used for seasoning.

bollocking (AN) – a blistering reprimand

braces (AN) – suspenders

broken – in reference to money, a coin that has been literally cut to pieces to make change.

bushwhacked (AB) – caught by surprise, ambushed

bust-head (AB) – homebrewed liquor, or strong alcohol generally

calf slobbers (AB) – meringue, a sweet topping of beaten egg whites and sugar

case counter – an abacus-like frame of beaded strings, used to count playing cards

catawamping (AB) – blundering

chew finer (AB) – to repeat oneself, or explain what was just said

concho (M) – derived from the word for "shell", a concho is a disk of metal hammered into a decorative seashell-like shape. They are often used to adorn leatherwork, such as belts, boots, and saddles.

corn maze (AB) – much like a hedge maze, with multiple twisting paths cut into a field of mature corn plants. A popular rural entertainment at harvest time

country-pay (A) – payment in goods, usually local crops

cowbird – a brood parasite: the female cowbird lays her eggs in the nests of other birds, leaving her young to be raised by unwitting or unwilling foster-parents.

crinoline – a rigid skirt-shaped frame, worn under eastern ladies' dresses to make a distinctive silhouette

cul brulée (F) – literally "scorched ass" – a slang term for a mereau whose tail has been cut off, and the resulting wound cauterized to prevent regrowth.

culo (M) – ass, buttocks

day-people (M) – in Island Town, citizens who have elected to live under the Azahi's protection. Most live on the south side of the island, and work during the day.

dimeto/a (M) – refers to a disordered, mentally unstable person

dram – a unit of weight in the apothecary system, 1/8th of an ounce

earth-person – among mereaux, the polite term for human beings

eho (M) – boy

faro – a gambling game played on a pasteboard marked with thirteen cards, from ace to king. Players bet by laying chips or money on cards of their choice; they win or lose according to the cards the dealer draws from the deck.

frail (A) – to beat someone/thing, often by whipping

front-fall (A) – also known as fall-fronts or drop-fronts. A type of men's trousers which open with a horizontal flap, rather than a vertical fly.

gift (M) – an ability shared by a certain nation or group of people. Similar to Ardish 'talent', but with the added connotation of something generously given, indebting the recipient.

grave bride (A) – in the Penitent faith, a celibate woman of the church. Her duties include tending and burying the newly deceased.

half – a common term for people of mixed race; see also 'mule'

hang-fire (A) – a firearm malfunction, in which there is a delay between the triggering of a weapon and its firing.

hellbender (A) – a kind of salamander

ihi'ghiva (K) – a special kind of slave, who wears the ritual blindfold (see 'yuye') and has received years of exacting training as a scribe, go-between, and sometimes assassin. He is considered incorruptible, and may not be bought or sold.

ima (K) – a term of respect for an older woman

jimmy (AB) – to nudge or jiggle something (for example, a key in a lock)

kindlic (AN) – "singed", a pejorative term for people with Afriti ancestry.

knack (A) – a natural, sometimes borderline supernatural aptitude for a certain skill or craft.

maga (K) – literally "master," but essentially "boss"

maga-kin (K) – "group-master," the designated title for the leader of an a'Krah outpost or gathering

maître d'hôtel (F) – "master of the hotel"; a manager who oversees guest service.

man-price – a form of wrongful-death settlement, paid by the family of the perpetrator to the family of the victim. Goods or money are most common; less frequently, the bereaved are compensated by indentured servitude or the gift of a "replacement" person.

marka (K) – partnered with an atodak

marrouak – a monstrous, infected creature, no longer human

medicine-hat – a horse with a hat-like coloring of the ears and top of its head; one or both eyes may be pale blue.

mereau – plural 'mereaux'. The amphibious people colloquially called 'fishmen'.

mestizo (M) – a person of mixed race. See also 'mule'

mule (A) – a slang term for a person of mixed race; see also 'half', 'mestizo', and 'two-blood'. Mules may be referred to by the mixing of their colors ('piebald', 'skewbald', 'oddbald' or 'tried'.) They are also sometimes identified by their patterns – a 'marbled' mule's colors are divided into large, distinct patches, for example, while a 'speckled' mule might have only a smattering of spots or freckles.

mutilé (F) – mutilated

narthex – the entryway of a church, also known as a vestibule. Non-worshippers may be restricted to the narthex until they have been formally initiated or reconciled into the faith.
nave – the body of the church, where worshippers sit or stand during services.

necktie sociable (AB) – a hanging

niveles (M) – the distinctions between groups of people, especially those artificially imposed, like caste or social rank.

nostrum (A) – a patent-medicine, usually fraudulent.

night-people (M) – in Island Town, citizens who have forfeited the Azahi's protection in exchange for the right to settle their own grievances. Most live in the Moon Quarter, and work at night.

paregoric – an opium-based medicine, useful as an expectorant, cough suppressant, and pain reliever. A weaker relative of laudanum.

part-timer (AB) – a highly pejorative term for a native person, so called for the belief that they spend only part of their time in human form.

partial (AB) – affectionate, kindly inclined

peisalat (F) – literally "salt fish", a sauce made by fermenting small fish

placket – an opening at the waist or neck of a garment, often closable with buttons or string

pony (A) – as a verb, to lead one horse while riding another
Pue'Va (K) – the five "monthless" days of the a'Krah calendar. They are considered highly unlucky: no business is conducted, visiting is discouraged, and children born during this time are highly suspect (see a'Pue).

pueblo (M) – a multi-family adobe building

put paid (AB) – ended, finished, in the manner of a completed transaction

rustler (AB) – a livestock thief

sacristy – a separate room for storage of holy objects, usually behind the altar of a church

satlaka (K) – people of deviant sexual appetite or identity; considered a natural defect.

savash (K) – literally "unrecognition"; the symbolic expulsion of an a'Krah who has committed a serious offense. Such a person is considered invisible, or at worst a hostile foreign presence.

savoir-faire (F) – skillfulness or adeptness; see 'knack'

scruple – a unit of weight in the apothecary system, 1/24th of an ounce.

serape (M) – a blanket-like outerwear garment. Also called a poncho.

shaved – in reference to money, a coin whose edges have been illegally shaved off and melted down for scrap value.

skault (AN) – "burnt", a pejorative term for Afriti

sobracho/a (M) – a "leftover person". Refers to Eadan settlers who continue to live in territory that has been formally returned to indigenous control.

sod-buster (AB) – a pejorative term for a farmer

soleado/a (M) – sunny

Sundowner (A) – a common term for a native person of any nation

taillé (F) – "clipped" or "trimmed"; a mereau who has had its tail and toes amputated in order to pass for human.

talent (A) – a supernatural ability believed to be exclusive to pure-bred people.

thunder-jug (A) – a chamber pot, so called for the way it amplifies sound during use.

tlimit (K) – a highly toxic poison

truck (AB) – as a verb, to barter or do business

two-blood (M) –a common term for people of mixed race. See also 'mule'

unshuck (AB) – literally, to strip the leaves from an ear of corn; figuratively, to undress.

vakat (K) – a game of exchanges, often played with a deck of cards and improvised tokens. It bears a passing resemblance to faro.

virgin – in reference to money, a pristine new coin, not broken or shaved.

voix-douce (F) – "sweet voice". It has an agreeable, mollifying effect on human beings. Mereaux are not affected.

yuye (K) – a blindfold made of coarse linen. a'Krah have superior night vision, but are exceptionally sensitive to sunlight. The yuye may be worn ritually (as by ihi'ghiva), or by a'Krah who work during daylight hours.

PEOPLE & PLACES

a'Krah – a native tribe, sometimes called the People of the Crow. Children of Marhuk, they tend towards dark skin and a sensitivity to sunlight. They are gifted with exceptional night vision.

Actor – Sil's horse, a six-year-old black gelding. "Ax" for short.

Addie – the fearsome madam of La Saciadería, sometimes called its queen.

Afriti – a race of dark-skinned people, originally imported for use as slaves. Their innate talent for fire-starting has been considered dangerous.

Ah-Shi-Shah – an older Washchaw woman; mother to Wi-Chuck and Ki-Meh. A member of the Ant-Watching Clan.

Aibak – a grim a'Krah, and Huitsak's right-hand man.

Alto – one of Opéra's two voices. She speaks in Ardish.

Ant-Watching Clan – the largest Washchaw clan in Island Town. Their sacred duty is the protection of the small, the weak, and the needy, and they are prohibited from having any voluntary contact with the dead.

Appaloosa Elim – a marbled mule who belongs to the Calvert family. He is remarkable for his size, his knack with horses, and the palm-sized brown patch over his left eye.

Ara-Naure – a dispersed native tribe; children of U'ru, the Dog Lady.

Ardish – the primary language of Eaden.

Artisan (F) – the crafter of the world and all its creatures

Aso'ta Marhuk – one of the a'Krah Eldest, who lives in Atali'Krah.

Atali'Krah – the ceremonial capital of the a'Krah.

Azahi – a native people whose kingdom in the south has risen to considerable power. Sut Hara, the First Man of Island Town, is popularly called "the Azahi."

Barking-Deer – one of Twoblood's four deputies; Set-Seti on his mother's side. He is the soul of diligence, even by Twoblood's standards.

Boss Calvert – a small-time horse rancher in Hell's Acre, and the axis of Elim's world.

Brant – the evening host of La Saciadería. Has some funny ideas about hospitality.

Brave – a person who lives on the Bravery.

Bravery – the great plains at the western edge of Eaden. A tough place to make a living.

Burnt Quarter – the northwest quarter of Island Town,

so called because it burnt to the ground on the night the town was retaken. It is almost entirely deserted.

Dr. Cartwright – a physician who lived in Sixes; Fours (as Peter Fournier) was his apprentice.

Castamarín – a nation of saltwater mereaux. They are the owners of a vast trade empire.

Champagne – Shea's given name.

Clementine "Clem" Calvert – the younger of the Calvert family's two daughters.

Corn Woman – Ten-Maia, holy mother of the Kaia and the Maia.

Dakat – an a'Krah, employed by Huitsak at La Saciadería.

Dayflower – a young woman of the Ikwei.

Deidalei – an a'Krah cloth-dyer; a genial, sloppy fellow.

Día – an Afriti grave bride, and ambassador to the Azahi. Sometimes called a cowbird.

Dog Lady – U'ru, holy mother of the Ara-Naure.

Miss Du Chenne – formerly Sixes' schoolmistress, and later an ambassador to the Azahi.

Dulei – a mildly insouciant, highly unfortunate young man of the a'Krah.

Dos'angres – Twoblood's name, literally rendered in Marín.

Eadan – of or from Eaden. It describes a nationality, not a race, but non-white Eadans are more commonly referenced by color.

Eaden – short for Eaden Federacy; the nation founded by descendants of the Northmen. It includes the Bravery, and its western border is the Rio Etascado.

Easy-Hey – the Ardish name for Izi'hei, an Ikwei man who lives in Hell's Acre. He works at the tannery, and sold Marín language lessons to Sil.

Eaten – a pejorative term for an Eadan.

Echep – Dulei's atodak. He was sent to Atali'Krah on an errand and is long overdue.

Eldest – the most reverend elders of the a'Krah.

Emboucheaux – "mouth-of-the-river people"; a nation of freshwater mereaux.

Etascado – the name of a former Eadan territory, now returned to indigenous control, and the river which seperates it from the Bravery.

Faro – the dandily-dressed clerk at La Saciadería; sometimes called its maître d'hôtel. Will strike you a hell of a bargain.

Feeds-the-Fire – one of Twoblood's four deputies; an Ohoti Woru, with more earnestness than sense.

Federate – of or from the Eaden Federacy. See 'Eaden'.

First Man of Island Town – the title of Island Town's governor. Currently held by Sut Hara, often called 'the Azahi'.

Fours – an unhappy man, currently running a livery and secondhand-goods store in Island Town. One of the Azahi's two remaining ambassadors.

Fraichais – a native language of freshwater mereaux.

Hakai – one of the two ihi'ghiva'a who serves Huitsak. He has a knack for respectful insolence.

Hattie – a 'medicine-hat' filly, and the only horse Sil managed to sell at the fair.

Hell's Acre – a small town in Washburn County, on the Bravery. Elim's hometown, and Sil's long-term residence.

Huitsak – the master of the Island Town a'Krah, formally titled 'maga-kin', and sometimes called the 'king' of La Saciadería. In size, strength, and intellect, he is overwhelming.

Ikwei – a native people renowned for their hardiness. They are children of Kweyaa, the Lady of the House, and are gifted with exceptional stamina and endurance.

Island Town – the modern name for Sixes.

"Lady" Jane Calvert – Boss Calvert's wife, an older woman of considerable education.

Kaia – a native tribe; children of Ten-Maia, the Corn Woman.

Ki-Meh – a Washchaw boy, Ah-Shi-Shah's son and Wi-Chuck's brother. Fours pays him to do stable chores.

Kweyaa, holy mother of the Ikwei – Lady of the House.

Kingdom of the Sun – the realm of the Azahi people.

La Saciadería – the great hotel at the northern end of Island Town. Sells enjoyments of every kind.

La Soleada – the pueblo at the southern end of Island Town. Most of its residents are Ikwei, with some Washchaw and Set-Seti families included.

Lavat – an a'Krah; he runs Moon Quarter's lime kiln.

Lovoka – a native tribe, one of the Great Nations. Sometimes called the People of the Wolf. They originally ranged far across the Bravery, and have been feared and hated by its white settlers.

Maia – a native tribe; children of Ten-Maia, the Corn Woman.

Marhuk – also called Grandfather Crow, holy father of the a'Krah.

Marín – a trade language, and the international standard for business. The native language of the Castamarín.

Melisant – a greater-born mereau, and Mother to the house that bears her name. Fours is one of her children.

Merin-Ka – the great canyon city of the Ohoti Lala. Its fall is spoken of with horror on both sides of the border.

Merrily "Merry" Calvert – the elder of the Calvert family's two daughters.

Molly Boone – Elim's horse, a bay mare of considerable size.

Moon Quarter – the northeastern quarter of Island Town, home to most of the town's night-people and reasonably welcoming to foreign visitors. Most of its residents are a'Krah and Ohoti Woru.

Nillen "Nillie" Halfwick – Sil's sister, and Will's twin. She has an exceptional talent for ice-making.

Northman – the common name for a 'pedigreed' white person from the far east. Some retain a talent for freezing or chilling items, but generations of breeding for talent have left them diminished in size and health.

Ohoti Woru – a native tribe; children of Grandfather Coyote. They are renowned for their craftsmanship. Outsiders sometimes have difficulty distinguishing them by sex.

Opéra – a greater-born mereau, and Mother of the house that bears her name. The Etascado River, and by extension Island Town, is part of her domain.

O-San – the Silver Bear, holy mother of the Washchaw.

Otli – an a'Krah, employed by Huitsak at La Saciadería.

Oyachen – an a'Krah who runs a popular eatery on the rooftops of the Moon Quarter.

Penitence – the majority religion of the Eaden Federacy. It has many denominations, but all are based on belief in one true God. Its adherents are called Penitents.

Peter Fournier – Fours' alias during his time as a resident of Sixes. He was a doctor's apprentice.

Petit-Four – Fours' given name.

Pipat – a older widow of the a'Krah, and Vuchak's companion. She does not suffer fools gladly.

Second Man of Island Town – the title of Island Town's second-in-command; a sheriff of sorts. Currently held by Twoblood.

Set-Seti – a native tribe, renowned for their gift of mind-reading. Children of the Twilight Twins, Dawn and Dusk.

Shea – a hostess at La Saciadería. Her vision is terrible, and so is her mouth.

Sibyl – in the Penitent faith, the Sibyl is the originator of evil, and mother of demons. Her seduction of the First Man introduced suffering to the world.

Silflec "Sil" Halfwick – a sickly young Northman burning with ambition. Long on charm and short on patience.

Sixes – the former (Eadan) name for Island Town.

Soprano – one of Opéra's two voices. She speaks in Marín.

Starving God – a pejorative term for the god of the Penitent faith.

Step-Lightly – a Ikwei woman, Yes-Yes's loving wife. Fierce in her affections.

Sut Hara – commonly called "the Azahi." The current governor of Island Town.

Tadai – an a'Krah, employed by Huitsak at La Saciadería.

Teitak – an a'Krah boy, not suffering from any overabundance of respect.

Twilight Twins – Dawn and Dusk, holy fathers of the Set-Seti.

Twoblood – the curiously-titled Second Man of Island Town. Remarkable for her fangs, freckles, and unshakable dedication to her job. In Eadan parlance, she would be called a 'speckled' mule.

Two-Pie – a yearling horse, and a notorious outlaw.

U'ru – the Dog Lady, holy mother of the Ara-Naure.

Voh'loh – an elder of the Set-Seti; he does not translate his name.

Vuchak – an irascible a'Krah, often seen with Weisei. The one may have something to do with the other.

Walla-Dee – a Washchaw man who runs the Island Town forge.

Washchaw – a native tribe, sometimes called the People of the Silver Bear. They are recognizable by their considerable height and build.

Way-Waiting – an Ohoti Woru, and a businessman of some renown.

Weisei – a cheerful, almost child-minded a'Krah, conspicuous by his unplaited hair. Often seen with Vuchak and a drink in hand.

Western Way – Island Town's main east-west road.

Wi-Chuck – one of Twoblood's four deputies, a Washchaw. Judicious in authority and hugely intimidating in size.

Wilord Watt – a resident of Hell's Acre, and owner of the tannery where Sil took language lessons from Easy-Hey.

Willen "Will" Halfwick – Sil's brother, and Nillie's twin. He runs Halfwick Wholesale, and is much esteemed among Hell's Acre's residents.

Winshin Marhuk – Dulei's mother, regarded among the a'Krah as a fearsome force of nature.

Yellow Bone – an elder of the Ikwei.

Yellow Kelly – a barn cat who belonged to the Calvert family.

Yes-Yes – one of Twoblood's four deputies; an Ikwei, and Step-Lightly's devoted husband.

ACKNOWLEDGMENTS

"You know what's really great about writing novels?" my teenaged self thought so often. "It's not like making a movie or a TV show, where you have all these people changing your stuff around and telling you what to do. I'm totally in charge here. I can do it all by myself."

Ah, youth.

But if there were going to be a bona-fide Hollywood-style credits crawl for this book, it would look like this. (Please imagine the haunting riffs of A Perfect Circle's "The Noose" in glorious ear-blasting surround sound as you read.)

Jon Oliver
Executive Producer and Editor in M.F.C.
Jennie Goloboy
*Production Manager, Patient Hand-Holder,
and Agent Supreme*
Mike Yates
Associate Producer, Life Coach, Crymaster

Tomasz "Tomek" Jedruszek
Cover Artist; Senior Paintomancer
Gillis Bjork
Lingonberry Map Wizard

Jason Wells-Jensen
Constructed Language Architect (Conlanger-in-Chief)
Gabriel Guerrero
Wood
Arch-Translators

Ro Freeman
*Equestrian Fact-Checker, Fictive Horse-Gelder,
and Tireless Cheerleader*

Jonathan Rafferty
Alpha Reader, Philosopher, and Fanboy Prime
Kristen Coster
*Staunch Latinist, Benevolent Grammarian,
Friend of Friends*

Kerri Linn
Kim Moravec
Daniel Bensen
Sarah Carless
Matt Borgard
Beta Readers, Gamma Editors, and Delta Force Five

DFW Writers Workshop
All-Purpose Pancake Posse

And that's just the people who pruned and shaped and dressed this modest final product. It says nothing at all about my own executive producers (hi Mom and Dad!), my fantastic family, or the many, many splendid Earth-persons whose company has loved, enriched, and irradiated me into the person I am today.

No, teenaged self, you really can't do it all on your own. But I've never been happier to be so wrong.